The Flame-Haired Woman

By

Mhari Matheson

To Selena,

With my very best wishes,

Mhari Matheson

LLYFRAU CAMBRIA

Published in the United Kingdom in 2015 by
Cambria Books; Carmarthenshire, Wales, United Kingdom

ACKNOWLEDGEMENTS

My thanks to my readers who enjoyed 'The Tinker Girl' and have continually urged me on to write the sequel.

To my U3A Writing Group, who also gave me unconditional support and never failed to enquire how the early drafts were proceeding, but never once reminded me that my attention was not all it should have been throughout the year.

To Peter for guiding me through the complexities of the making of gun powder, the need for acetone during the First World War and the resulting government closing of smaller distilleries.

Once again I am indebted to Christine, Elsie, Iau, Mari, Maureen, and Pat for reading my drafts, sharing their thoughts and giving me continual support during the final stages of this writing journey.

Craig also came on board towards the end and had the insight, and the courage, to tell me I could do better. The book has benefitted from his suggestions and I shall always be in his debt.

I continue to be amazed at the artistic skill exercised by Kevin in developing my rough ideas and designing the cover. His enthusiasm and patience, despite my frequent revisions, deserve a medal.

My thanks must also go to Cambria for publishing the book and holding my hand through the procedure.

Finally, to John, whose constant critical eye, support and confidence in me were vital to the completion of the book.

To all of the above I am indeed grateful.

DEDICATION

For Verity May and Romilly Rose

Two special little girls who bring a great deal of joy into my life

Chapters

Prologue 1913

Cate, followed by Rory, waddled to the summerhouse, caught her breath as she leant on the fretwork at the entrance, then swiped away the autumn dust and cobwebs from the cane table and chair before easing her heavily pregnant body into the seat. This was her haven, isolated on the far boundary of the garden. Here she was nearer to her beloved Beinn Nishe, the mountain of her childhood. She sat amid the comforting stillness, watched as the last of the leaves were released from a nearby tree and fluttered to the ground, and spied a blackbird searching the rowans for the remainder of the shiny red berries. Rory, satisfied with his snufflings in the surrounding foliage, bounded into view and brought her back to the problem she was now trying to solve.

Why had she not been aware that her dear friend and neighbour, Dinwoodie, was falling in love with her? His sudden proposal of marriage had confounded her. She'd done nothing but think about it, was no further forward, but knew she must give him an answer soon. Deep in the muddle of her thoughts she became aware that her fingers were beating out a nervous tattoo on the arm of the chair. She leant forward, put her head in her hands as though the now silent fingers could prise a solution from her brain. Rory, head cocked, watched with a puzzled frown. At her deep sigh the dog muzzled her bent head and, though she muttered at him, he persisted till she sat up and patted him.

"There now, settle down. I'm jumpy enough without you joining in." Cate fondled the yellow Labrador's ears. "We've come a distance since you chased into the woods and led me here. Go on, Rory — lie down now." Dog settled she let her mind roam over the past years. She'd bought Craigavon, the house they'd found that day and, established her accumulated 'family' here. It'd once been the home of a Kevinishe Laird's mistress, and Cate couldn't stop the bitter memories that always surfaced at the word. Unbeknownst to her at the time, it mirrored exactly what she'd been to Alashdair, the man she'd fallen in love with and hoped to marry. When she discovered he'd a mentally disturbed wife secreted away in Glasgow, she'd no choice but to send him out of her life. Then she'd found he'd left her pregnant.

That'd been a terrible time but, with the help of her friends, she'd come through it. Dinwoodie had known all of this, and quite understood that to give birth to an illegitimate child in a closed community like Kevinishe would bring shame on her. But would it be fair to marry him, without the passionate love she'd discovered with Alashdair? Oh, there was affection, respect, and she knew she didn't want to lose his friendship, but marriage?

Here in Kevinishe she'd been an orphaned tinker girl, spending her early childhood with the Cailleach and the tinker matriarch. Then there'd been the happy years in the Laird's house looking after his younger grandson, until young Davey's untimely death. These thoughts gave way to black ones of her nemesis, the older grandson, Bruce MacNishe. Rape was never a good basis for mother and child bonding, and at sixteen what had she known about babies anyway? Might it have been different had Rhoddy not been his son?

What a disastrous parent she'd turned out to be! Her circumstances after his birth meant he'd been left with Maggie, her housekeeper now, and her daughter Lizzie for too many years while she'd worked, studied, and clawed her way upwards in the world. Her son's behaviour had always unsettled her. The truth was they simply made what they could of a bad set of circumstances. This was another reason the old house had been so important to her. It seemed that here she'd found the peace and security she'd longed for all her life, despite Rhoddy being difficult. Would it always be like this? Would marriage provide not only respectability but also a father figure for Rhoddy and her unborn child? A sudden sharp pain reminded her of the imminent birth. She ought to return to the house. By the time she'd reached the front door she'd made her decision. When he was next in the glen, she'd repeat all her misgivings to Dinwoodie, and, if he still wanted to marry her, she'd accept.

Part One

1914 Kevinishe

Chapter 1

Maggie watched as an unfamiliar car came to a halt in the Craigavon drive. Opening the door she found a stranger looking for Mrs Dinwoodie. Full of curiosity, she showed the visitor into the drawing room and went to tell Cate, who was working in her study.

"We're not used to uninvited people calling here. Did he give his name? Say what he wanted?"

"That he did not."

"Bother! I'm in no mood to be sociable, Maggie. You'd better get a tray of something from Cook. I'll go down now and get rid of him as soon as possible."

As she confronted the man, his rather forbidding look made her feel a little uneasy. This was no friendly visitor. "Good morning, I believe you wish to see me, Mr…?"

"The McPhail, Mrs Dinwoodie. I'm come on a personal matter."

"I'm sorry, I don't understand."

"It's quite straightforward. I'm related to your son, and that's why I'm here."

Cate looked bewildered. "But I never heard McAlister talk of a relative of that name."

"Come, let's not play games, Madam. You and I both know your husband — your late husband that is — adopted the boy. Whatever you say, I've been informed by a very reliable source that the boy is a MacNishe. "

A stunned Cate could feel her world tilting, but with a great effort she replied in an icy voice, "I'm afraid you've been misinformed then. I'm sorry you've had a wasted journey, but my son is Rhoddy McAlister and is therefore in no way related to you." Reaching for the bell pull, she continued, "My housekeeper will show you out."

"I'll leave, but be quite clear about this: you'll be hearing from me. You see I have positive proof of the boy's parentage, and, as a blood

5

relative, I won't rest until I have gained access to him. I must admit you're an admirable liar. Had I not known the truth, and been forewarned of your duplicity, I might well have been convinced. Good day to you."

A confused Maggie, complete with tea tray, saw the visitor sweep past in the hall as he took his leave. Then, to her consternation, she found a trembling Cate in the drawing room. "What in the name...?"

"He said Rhoddy was a MacNishe!"

"Well, we know that — but no one else is supposed to. Who was he, Cate?"

"McPhail, or so he said."

"Master Rab's wife's kin!"

"That's nonsense, Maggie. Lady Sarah's family came from England somewhere."

"Cate, you're forgetting she wasna Bruce's mother. Margaret McPhail was — Master Rab's first wife. Died in a carriage accident she did. I mind Fisher telling me in a letter all about it. So he has the truth of it!"

"So Bruce knows?"

"Oh lass, I'm afraid he must do."

The stranger's visit had so upset Cate, that with Dinwoodie in London, she decided to go to Glasgow and her good friend and lawyer, Gordon Wiseman. He was mystified when she arrived and explained about the McPhail's visit.

"But I thought he was Mr McAlister's..."

"It wasn't something that I was about to shout to the world was it? I never deceived him though. McAlister was told before we were married, and, before you ask, so was Dinwoodie. Can't you understand the stigma attached to all of this? Now that swine Bruce MacNishe has — Oh, Gordon, what can I do? Rhoddy must never be allowed to go near that evil man or any relatives of his."

"I'll have to do some research on this. What does your husband say about it?"

"Dinwoodie? He doesn't know."

"Cate, you must tell him! If we're to fight this, we need all the help we can get. He's not called the Iron Baron for nothing. Didn't I read somewhere that he was also friendly with Lord Monroe? Now there's a legal man who could make a difference to your case!"

Cate stared at him in horrified silence. To have to share her teenage disgrace to so many was more than she could bear. Once again Bruce MacNishe threatened the secure world she'd fought so hard for and this time he seemed to have garnered a powerful ally.

Although he was always glad to see the entrance to the glen and the blurred blue-grey of Beinn Nishe hovering in the background, Dinwoodie was not looking forward to his arrival at Craigavon. As the sigh slipped from his lips, his eyes caught those of the ever-watchful Morrison in the driving mirror.

"It's yet another problem, and one that will not be easily solved," he explained, and his driver nodded in sympathy. Dinwoodie knew the man had picked up the bones of their wasted journey to Fettes College. As the Daimler glided to a halt at the front of Craigavon he was surprised to see the grooms and Maggie, deep in conversation by the entrance.

"Oh, Mr Dinwoodie, sir, it's right glad I am to see you home!"

"Is everything all right, Maggie?'

"Indeed it's not. An army man from Fort William has taken the horses, and herself is after storming out of the house with no overcoat an rain threatening."

Dinwoodie, having persuaded the others to occupy themselves till Cate returned, left Morrison to see to the luggage and motor in readiness for their southbound return later in the week. Then he made straight for the ever-full decanter of Craeg Dhu on the silver tray in the drawing room. Pouring himself a dram, he swirled the liquid round in the glass, staring into the amber waves, wishing they would engulf him and thus provide an escape from all his problems, which would now include the army requisition of the horses. Before he had time to lift the glass to his lips, the door opened and Lizzie shepherded the twins before her. The arrival last year, of two babies, had been a surprising joy and his role as a father to the pair had been revitalising. David, as ever, toddled as fast as he could across the room, followed by the slower approach of Cameron. Disentangling himself from the blonde bundle now at his legs, Dinwoodie waited for dark-haired Cam, as they called him, and then, seating himself in his chair, hoisted a twin onto each knee, while smiling at Lizzie.

"The boys were so excited about Rhoddy coming home. Where is he, Mr Dinwoodie?"

"Lizzie, leave these two here with me. Tell Maggie we'll have tea in here today. By then I hope Cate will be back and I'll give you all the news." As she left, Dinwoodie turned his attention to the twins and bounced them up and down until Maggie entered with the tea tray.

"Will you be alright with the boys, sir?"

"I'll manage, but if Cate's not back by the time Lizzie's had her tea in the kitchen, send her through to rescue me."

Meanwhile Cate Dinwoodie, Rory at her heels, was stamping ever upwards on Beinn Nishe, but today her love of the mountain was buried beneath her anger at the loss of Lady Jemima's horses. She felt as though she'd been disloyal to the dead woman by letting the animals go, but the army lieutenant had given her no option, and she'd been lucky to save Midnight, Satan, and a couple of the mares for breeding purposes. Although Kevinishe had not been affected by the murmurings of war, today had proved that the army were certainly preparing for one.

Hearing the comforting sound of the running stream, she made her way to the waterfall. Surely she could rest here and leave her problems behind, if only for a few hours. Lying on the ancient heather bed in the cave, she knew there was no evading her worries. Dinwoodie would be home by tonight with her son, and Rhoddy would then begin his ongoing battle of wills with her once again. Her hasty marriage to Dinwoodie, and the birth of her twins, just seemed to have made him more of a trial. It was to be expected of course with new arrivals in the family, though he was better when Dinwoodie was around. Perhaps she'd close her eyes for a few moments, surrounded by the soothing sound of the water as it spilled over the ledge, and made its way down to the pool, where it was captured to make Craeg Dhu, their single malt whisky.

When darkness fell, and Lizzie had sung the twins to sleep, those in the kitchen at Craigavon kept their thoughts to themselves as they refilled their cups from the great china teapot on the table. In the drawing room a tired Dinwoodie, lulled by the dram of single malt, had fallen into a light sleep. Down in the stable bothy, Stevie tried to forget the sight of his beloved steeds being led away.

The slamming of the front door roused the household, and they made for the drawing room, where the first lady of the glen stood waiting for them, knowing she'd overslept in the cave and worried them all.

"I don't know why you all look so cross. I just took my time on the mountain. I'm sorry, Dinwoodie, I meant to be here for your arrival, but no doubt they've filled you in about the horses. Where's Rhoddy? Surely he's not sulking already?" As no answer was forthcoming, Cate now focused her attention on her husband. "Dinwoodie?"

"Cate —" As he hesitated he felt the tension build.

"Dinwoodie! What is it? Tell us, man. Your silence is worse than bad news. Come on. What's Rhoddy done now? What schoolboy scrape has he landed in this time?"

"Cate, he's not at school."

"I know. You brought him home today to save me the journey to Edinburgh — a good job you did, or that army man would have left us with an empty stable!"

"Never mind the damned horses! I'm trying to tell you that Rhoddy's neither at school nor here, because he was picked up by his father, supposedly for a weekend with him."

With blanched face, Cate felt for the arms of the chair behind her, and sank into it. The others waited for the usual storm, but there was no temper this time, just a shocked silence. Dinwoodie knelt before her, unclasped her arms, and taking her hands in his said, "My dear Cate, I warned you it was always a possibility that Bruce MacNishe would discover that Rhoddy was his son, and now he has."

A shake of her head was Cate's only response, so Dinwoodie spoke to the others.

"It's late. We're all worried and tired but we can do nothing for now. Go on, have your supper. Cook, put something cold upstairs for us, and I'll take Cate up later."

When the others had dispersed, Dinwoodie pulled Cate to her feet and enclosed her in his arms. "Cate, look at me! Don't shut yourself away like this. Speak to me." He watched as his wife shook her head as two tears slid onto her cheeks. Wiping them away with his fingers, he held her close, until finally she lifted her head and whispered.

"Oh, Dinwoodie, I didn't want to believe…"

"I know, and how I wish I could have persuaded you to consider it, but all we can do now is search for them. I'm afraid, with all that's gone on of late, we've been too occupied to concern ourselves with Bruce MacNishe. I've contacted Pearson and he'll try all the usual haunts of that blackguard. We'll find Rhoddy and bring him home. This time Bruce has gone too far."

"It's no use. You see he told me…"

"You've been in touch with Bruce MacNishe? How could you after…?"

"No! Not him. The other one."

"Cate, you're speaking in riddles. What other one?"

"The — the McPhail."

"The who?"

"His mother's family and…"

"Suppose you start again. Whose mother? What family? And why do I know nothing about any of this?"

"Well — I meant to tell you, but I thought nothing might come of it."

"And now it has?"

"I think so. He said it would."

"Cate, exactly where did you go to meet this person without bothering to tell me about it?"

"It's not what you're thinking. I didn't go anywhere. He arrived here one day and threatened to take Rhoddy."

"This is beyond belief! Someone threatens my stepson and it never occurred to you to tell me? To involve me?"

"I know. Gordon Wiseman told me to…"

"So, the boy could well be in danger and you go straight to one of your old admirers! Your tame lawyer! Exactly how do you think that makes me, your husband, feel?" Angry now, Dinwoodie turned away until he had control, not only of his rising temper, but also the sudden flare of jealousy at her deception.

"I'm sorry. I just thought nothing might come of it. Then Gordon said McPhail must be in touch with Bruce and we'd have to go to law."

"That, I would have thought, was precisely what we would have to do."

"Surely not. I can't be out there in the public and be disgraced all over again!" "You may not have an option. Since you haven't bothered to discuss it with me, I've no opinion at the moment. Anyway it's late. We must both eat and sleep, even though there'll be little appetite and even less sleep for us. I'm going up." Dinwoodie was too angry with her to soften his tone.

Once in their bedroom Cate huddled close to the dying embers in the fireplace, her arms tight across her body, as if to save it from more blows, while Dinwoodie, still cross, picked at his food and prepared for bed.

Chapter 2

Wullie the Post handed the foreign letter to Angus at the distillery gate, watched as he read the address, and waited for the reaction. Satisfied at the startled look on the other man's face, Wullie nodded his head before speaking. "That's right. It's for Miss Cate. It's from him right enough. Is it to be another summer like the last one? We'd be the better without it, but I canna destroy it, even though he might be after starting it all up again."

"We dinna want the wee paper mannie here again. What would Himself say?"

"Angus, I had it in mind to speak to him first. I mean it wouldna be fair to him would it?"

"Look, here's Mr Solly coming. He's close enough to the pair of them. Here, take it. Wullie. As the Kevinishe Post, how about you give it to him, an he can decide whit to do?"

"Man, that'd be a fine way to be getting us out of the problem, Angus. They'll no take on so much, him being management an all." Wullie wheeled his bath chair towards Solly and explained the predicament.

"I'm afraid, Wullie, whether we like it or not, the letter is addressed to Miss Cate, and so she must have it."

"Aye, but mind the trouble there was…"

"I know, but it's not our decision to make. Give me the rest of the mail and I'll see she gets this." With that, Solly, who was equally troubled, left the two men and made his way to his office. To his consternation, both Cate and Dinwoodie were waiting for him. "I, um, I met—here's the post." Solly dropped the letters on his desk and turned to leave.

"Where are you going, Solly? Is something wrong?" Cate asked.

"Nothing, it's just…"

Sensing the man's discomfort, Dinwoodie turned to him. "What's worrying you?"

Solly retrieved the suspect letter from the desk and passed it to him, glad to have someone else deliver it. Dinwoodie, on seeing the address and postmark, handed it to Cate. "For you, my dear."

As she studied the letter, her hand trembled, but she understood now why Solly was upset. "Fine, I'll take the rest of my mail now. If there's nothing else, I'm in the office all day." With that, she left.

As the men watched her go, the Accountant felt he ought to explain. "Mr Dinwoodie, it's from…"

"I know, but she must deal with it, not us. I'll check up on her, so don't worry, and I've no doubt I'll find Wullie and Angus just happening to be at the gate as I leave!"

"It'll be a wonder if the whole village isn't there by then. They'll all be concerned." Solly gained nothing from the older man's expression, so he opened the door for him, and watched him leave.

Dinwoodie was not as unconcerned as he appeared, but he refused to start worrying before he knew how it would affect Cate. To that end he knocked lightly on her door and entered before she answered. His worst fears were confirmed when he saw her face. "My dear…"

"It's alright, Dinwoodie, it's alright! It's in the wastepaper basket unopened. I sent him away and I meant every word of it. I have no need of letters from him. My life is here, so off you go to Glasgow, and then on to London as planned."

"Are you sure, Cate? I don't feel I ought to leave now. Whatever's in that letter could mean…"

"Dinwoodie, we'll never know, because I'm not opening it!"

Days later, with her immediate work in the distillery completed, and Dinwoodie occupied in London, where he was also intending to purchase a new Daimler, Cate was at home, her mind still unsettled by the arrival, after all this time, of that wretched letter. As she thought about it, she rose, paced the study floor, halted at the window, and drummed her fingers on the sill. Then she moved to the cabinet, poured a dram, and paused by the desk. It was the letter arriving at the distillery that had stirred the once happy dream she'd had of marrying Alashdair. Why had she retrieved it? Brought it home? Returning to her chair, she sipped the fiery liquid, seeking solace in it, as the memories of past years came flooding back.

Alashdair couldn't have found out she was pregnant, could he? Only those close to her knew that he was the boys' father. She'd always assumed he'd never learn of their existence and his connection to them.

How could he? He'd cut his links with Scotland. Said without her love there was no future for him here. Then why send a letter? Oh God, the twins — that could be the reason for it!

Frantic now, she rose, spilled the remnants of the whisky and, ignoring the glass as it fell off the table, bounced on the rug, and bowled across the wooden oak floor, she hurried to the locked drawer in her desk. With trembling hands she ripped open the letter, but before she could read it she was interrupted by a knock, followed by Maggie opening the door. Cate could see by her expression that there was a problem of some kind. She shoved the letter in the drawer, closed it, and gave her full attention to her friend and housekeeper.

"It's Cook, she's missed a step on the stairs. Her knee's swelling up, and she's hobbling round that kitchen determined to carry on. She'll no listen to me, so you'd be the better of seeing to her, before she makes it worse."

"Right Maggie, I'll come with you now."

Like most of the inhabitants of Scotland in May of 1914, Kevinishe seemed either unaware or unheeding of the European jam pan that was bubbling almost to the point of a rolling boil.

Cate was planning ahead for the August shutdown, when the bulk of her distillery workers concentrated on their crofts, bringing in the hay, buying and selling new beasts, and catching the fish that would be dried or salted to see them through the winter months. A skeleton staff, led by Donald Uig the maltman and Murdo the tun man, always saw to the annual distillery maintenance at this time while Solly occupied himself with, the accounts, the stocktaking, and the excise visits. Even the team of sewing girls, the current dress catalogue orders all being complete, laid down their needles, took the scraps home for quilting, helped their menfolk on the crofts, and gutted the fish.

Only in Glasgow, where Dinwoodie was now working in his foundry office, did the finger of European unrest wag it's warning. He'd paid a visit to the Krupps site in Essen the previous year and been amazed at the set-up. It was like no foundry he'd ever known: a vast industrial community, where the workers and their families were not only housed, but also had all their other needs catered for. Though he'd been taken aback by the size and planning that had gone into this 'steel town', it had been the diverse range of metal processing that had left him amazed at the progress the Germans had made. But it was their sheer productivity that had sent him home with a real fear for the future.

When he'd returned to Glasgow, the yards on the Clyde seemed old-fashioned, and production even appeared to be slowing down. He'd shared his fears with other industrialists, minor politicians and a couple of newspaper editors he'd met socially, but they'd mostly shaken their heads, told him he was worrying unduly, and reminded him it had been Britain that launched the industrial world.

At about the same time he'd made enquiries in Glasgow, for personal reasons, about a reporter on the Gazette and had been astounded to hear the young man had been branded a scaremonger, with all his talk of imminent war. However, admiration for this shared viewpoint had been swamped by his own emotions over the relationship the young man had developed with Cate McAlister. As time elapsed and he'd helped her deal with the death of her mentor, Fisher, the distillery owner and stillman felled by a massive stroke, he'd found himself falling in love with her, though with little hope of anything coming of it. However, when the affair with the reporter had ended abruptly, he'd offered marriage, but at first she'd refused. It had taken much persuasion to change her mind, and the low-key registry office service in Glasgow was barely over when Cate produced twin boys, whom they'd named David and Cameron.

Meanwhile the distraught young man, unable to bear being in the same country as his love, had given up his job on the Glasgow Gazette, unaware of either Cate's pregnancy or the birth of his sons, and headed for Europe, hoping to earn his living as an independent correspondent. However it appeared that no newspaper evinced an interest in his current reporting, and at present it was unknown where he was or how he was making a living.

All this would have been, if not forgotten, at least pushed aside, until the arrival at the distillery of the letter for Cate that had set the inhabitants wondering if 'the wee paper mannie', as Fisher had dubbed him, was once more to have an impact on the community. Dinwoodie now faced a major dilemma. On the personal side he worried that the emotional connection between the two had never been truly extinguished, while, as an industrialist, he hungered for the reporter's European information, which he was certain would provide proof that his unpopular predictions were accurate. If they were, the plans he was already working on to meet the demands that hostilities would make of his business would be even more urgent. The letter, now discarded, was

14

lost to him, but somehow he could not rid himself of the notion that it was vitally important. Either way, wife or war, his world was at risk.

On his return from Glasgow, Dinwoodie, tired after his long journey, sent his driver, Morrison, to the kitchen for a meal. But when he went up to Cate's study, he found it empty, so he made his way to his own. Now that he'd time his thoughts turned to the missing Rhoddy. Pearson, his private investigator, could find no trace of him in Edinburgh, and the school had confirmed he was now absent without leave. There was no doubt the boy had had a hard time when very young, but Cate constantly tried to make up for that and, in his opinion, she spoilt him. Though his position as 'The Iron Baron' had made him a rich man, he'd never forgotten his own hard youth,

In those long gone days of the Eighteenth Century, his family from Lanarkshire had become textile workers, but they were made both jobless and homeless when the industry slumped due to the fall in supplies of cotton. They were bad years, and only his father and uncle had survived the hardship. The loss of their family embedded in those two a fierce determination to make certain they would never again be at the mercy of conditions beyond their control. In their youth they'd tackled any job they could and, when they were strong enough, took advantage of new openings for labour in the iron founding and engineering works that had sprung up. In time, with families of their own, the brothers had moved to Glasgow. There the growth in the shipbuilding yards had afforded the opportunity for many more forges and foundries. So it was here that the brothers advanced their careers, though they had also begun to grow apart. His uncle moved into management and his father remained wedded to the production side of the iron industry.

As Maggie arrived with his tray, Dinwoodie poured himself a cup of tea and, when she'd closed the door, continued with his memories. Usually he had neither the time nor the inclination to just sit and ponder personal issues. His father had always made sure that he adhered to the family tradition of never wasting a moment, either at work or study. His uncle had taken the study route, but his father had always been too exhausted at the end of his tough manual working days for reading, and gradually the brothers drifted even further apart.

Then his father's lust for living had been destroyed with the sudden death of his wife and stillborn daughter. Grief had taken him to a dark place where his very surroundings became anathema to him. This lack of concentration in the foundry had led to an accident that was to haunt him for the remainder of his life. Too proud to seek his brother's help, his father took him away from school and they travelled as far away as possible in the hope of building a new life.

A chance meeting with a charcoal burner in the Kentish Weald in England provided work for them both and, following his broken-hearted father's death, Dinwoodie had continued until that came to an end. He then became apprenticed to a blacksmith, who encouraged him to learn all that he could. This led to him turning to wrought-iron work, when that became popular, and he began to take studying seriously.

The sound of the outer oak door slamming shut jolted him from his reverie, and he stood as a flushed Cate entered, clad in the riding breeches that she favoured and he so disliked. He embraced her and then stood her at arm's length.

"You look just as I imagine you did as that wild tinker girl dressed in boy's clothing."

"Nonsense! For a start I was always filthy, usually barefooted and — well nowadays it's still so much more comfortable flying in the breeze without all the long skirts that fashion inflicts on us women. Anyway, I know you don't approve, but we didn't expect you till later, and I'd have been encased in the flouncy folds by then!

More to the point, Dinwoodie, has Pearson any news? Has he found Rhoddy?"

"There appears to be no sign of them in Edinburgh."

"Then where are they?"

"Cate, MacNishe won't walk around in the streets with Rhoddy. He'll be holed up somewhere, perhaps moved to another town. Give Pearson some time. I know it's hard, but we must be patient, let the man do his job. Turning to a brighter subject..."

"Oh, I'm sorry — the car! Did you get it?"

"I did indeed, but it's late now. You can see it tomorrow."

Chapter 3

Meanwhile in Serbia, Alashdair, Cate's erstwhile lover, was crammed into an airless room in the town of Sabac trying to make sense out of the various gabbled conversations going on around him. The lodgings were the home of the railway gang, of whom he was the newest member, servicing the railway line. Tonight there seemed to be some strangers amongst them. In the months he'd been working here he'd not only strained every muscle imaginable in unaccustomed labour, but had also garnered a basic understanding of the language. The current conversations were, as usual, Serbs ranting about Austria-Hungary, Slav territories, old racial conflicts, politics, woman, and sex. He might just as well have been back in the pubs of Glasgow, where men's conversations were sprinkled with rants about the English, lack of work unions, employers, governments, and, of course, sex.

Still he'd learn nothing about the current unrest in Serbia unless he joined these gatherings. Suddenly he realised the atmosphere in the room had changed. One of the strangers was now speaking. There was a guarded quality to the words. Try as he would Alashdair could barely follow it. 'Black' — 'Fist' — 'Hand', perhaps? He couldn't tell. He'd need to look it up after the meeting — but it seemed to connect to the earlier racist conversation. Was something afoot? He'd already discovered that the National Defence, the 'Narodna Odbrama', was still smarting from previous annexation of Slav territories. Was this to do with them or something new?

The strangers left soon after that, and he knew it would be unwise to raise any questions tonight, so he finished his drink and ambled off with the nearest group as he made for the squalid dormitory he shared with five others. Once abed he wondered if tonight had been one of those meetings when yet another splinter resistance group of some kind had been suggested, or was it an indication that arms were floating around, being offered for sale? It was common knowledge that, after the last fighting in the region there had been many who'd held onto their weapons, which, for a price, could be bought. Or had it merely been an invitation to men away from home to spend their wages on a visit to a new brothel. Tired now, his concern turned to the morning and the knowledge that once more his weary body would have to rise to the challenge of wielding heavy tools. His eyes began to close with the thought he would be better off going across the nearby border into Austria-Hungary, where he might pick up, in a bigger town, an easier job than his current one. Then thoughts of Cate and his letter, neither never far from his mind, sent him to sleep.

At the end of the week when Dinwoodie was ready to leave Kevinishe, Cate walked around the new vehicle and was duly impressed. When Morrison, the chauffeur, stowed the bags away in the trunk, she was amazed at it's capacity, joking with Dinwoodie that they could almost carry a person in there. It was as he kissed her goodbye that Cate remembered she still hadn't told him about saving the letter, but as they were all loaded up, with Morrison at the wheel, she felt it could wait. But the thought of its unread contents was still with her as the car drew away. Back in her study once more, she drew the now crumpled missive from her drawer, spread it on the desk, and couldn't stop herself from reading

Şabac, Şerbia. May 1914

My Dear Cate,

Please don't throw this away before you've read it. I have no intention, though every inclination, to disregard your dismissal of me. I have not yet been able to kill my feelings for you, but I continue to try. These long months have been hard but I believe I have found some little respite in my wanderings. I still write, but can find no newspaper interested in my copy. As a reporter this is hard to bear.

In my travels I have gradually begun to understand the bitterness that exists between some of the smaller European countries. You may remember that my editor, Scottie, in 1913 would not print my article on the possibility of war, but I have found much over here that convinces me I was right.

Even if you do read this you'll take me for a scaremongering fool, but perhaps your husband might be more inclined to listen. I now know....

At this point Cate, jumping to conclusions as ever, dropped the letter, rose and put her head against the cool windowpane as if that would ease her troubled fears. It was as if those words threatened her world. Alashdair, Dinwoodie, the twins, how could they all remain untouched by this discovery? It was a moment before she found the strength to return to her desk and read the words that would surely plunge her and those around her into turmoil.

...you married the Iron baron, Dinwoodie, and have young twin sons. He's a good man, and I always believed he was more than fond of you. I also heard of the expected death of Fisher. A blessed relief for him, but I cannot imagine how you coped with the loss. I know you were devoted to him, and I wonder how you are managing without him in the distillery.

When you cast me out of your life, I felt mine wasn't worth living, but perhaps losing you and fleeing abroad forced me to think of what else I could do. This unrest in Europe and where it might lead could be the subject I've searched for, the book I know I can write. I'm a nomad now, so there will be no safe place to hoard my scribblings. Cate, I need a favour. Would you be willing to look after them?

To gain both the necessary insight and knowledge, if War does come, I will have to become immersed in events as they occur. I must know that my notes would be safe

19

with someone I trust. Should anything happen to me; the drafts would be yours to do with as you wish.

You need only answer this letter if you don't want to help. If not, your silence will be my safekeeping.

Alashdair.

Not knowing quite why she was so sad, Cate sat with thoughts racketing through her mind. The relief of her secret being safe was tempered by the emptiness of the life of the man she had once been so in love with. Still disturbed, she returned the letter to the drawer, locked it, and, pulling on an old cloak, headed for the Black House on the moor, Rory at her heels. Why she needed to do this she didn't know, but it seemed that returning to the scene of her youth would somehow erase the intertwining waves of pain, grief, remorse and pity that threatened to overcome her.

Back home once more, Dinwoodie studied his wife as she drew feverishly on the pad balanced on her knees. It was unusual for her to sketch downstairs. She much preferred to work in her study, but he supposed the late sun beaming through the drawing room window had enticed her there. Ever since Rhoddy's disappearance Cate had been distracted. He knew she worried away at her discordant relationship with the boy, just as Donald Uig fretted about his emerging green shoots of barley on the malt floor in the distillery. But he sensed there was something else troubling her. "Cate, I know how much the reappearance of Bruce MacNishe has upset you, and to know that he has Rhoddy, is alarming, but he's the boy's father. I doubt he'll harm him. We know it's you he means to hurt."

"I know that."

"Then is it something else bothering you?" Dinwoodie was dumbfounded when he saw her lips tremble. He leapt to his feet and pulled her into his arms, scattering pad, and pencils around their feet. "What is it, my darling? Won't you confide in me? A troublesome weight invariably feels halved when shared."

"I don't know how to tell you. I've deceived you."

The words knifed through him, but he kept his countenance clear and gently asked. "Is it the letter you threw away?"

"That's just it. I did throw it away, and then I didn't."

"Cate, you're not making a lot of sense…" And then he understood. "You retrieved it?" At Cate's nod, his voice hardened as he persisted. "And you read it?"

"Not for some time. I did try to tell you, but you were away."

"We spoke on the telephone. You had the opportunity to broach the subject. Why didn't you, Cate?" Dinwoodie felt her pull further away from his arms and watched as she left the room. He sank back into his chair, mind whirling. Deep down he'd always feared this situation would arise. She'd been honest with him when he'd proposed. 'A good and true friend' she'd called him, but had not wanted to make use of him to give herself respectability. He'd loved her even more then, admiring her desire to be frank with him. When the door opened again, he corralled his painful thoughts and rose as she entered. He was not surprised to see she was carrying the somewhat crumpled letter. How many times had she read it? The unspoken question hurt unbearably.

Handing the letter to him, Cate tried to still the mixed emotions that threatened to overwhelm her, and sat quietly while her husband read. When he raised his head she was surprised to see a glimmer of damp around his eyes, and it was then that she realised it was going to be all right. "You see, my mind's been assaulted by so many feelings."

She stopped as Dinwoodie rose and walked to the sideboard. There, with his back to her, he asked the question he dreaded. "Are you still in love with him?"

Cate joined him. Poured two glasses from the decanter before answering. "I suppose a part of me always will be, but I have grown to love you too, and somehow I need to make you understand. Do you know what I feared before I read it?" At the shake of his head, she continued. "I thought he might have discovered about the twins. Might want to take yet more of my children from me. Destroy our lives here. Then I felt a deep stab of remorse when I read of his lonely life. I couldn't help but compare mine with his. But I feared what you would say. Oh, I know you gave the letter to me, but I also understood how you would feel. Just look at how all the others acted — as if that terrible summer was about to be repeated, tearing the heart out of us all. No wonder I dreaded the effect on you! That's why I threw it away. But then for some reason, I don't even know why, I brought it home and put it away."

21

She thought for a moment before continuing. "You see I'd no idea if I could cope with reopening a deep wound like that, so I left it in the desk. Then one day I had this sudden fear about the twins and I thought that was perhaps why the letter came. But as you know, he merely assumes they're yours. Then, just as you did, I found I was moved by the words, had conflicting emotions, and didn't know what to do for the best — for me, for us, for the twins, and indeed for him. All that's been pounding away in my head like the hammering of the coopers on their barrels."

Dinwoodie carried the glasses to the window seat to catch the last warmth of the day's sun and patted the cushions. "Cate, come, sit with me. We'll have our dram and toast the Scribbler, while you tell me of your intended response to his cry."

As she sipped her malt, she began. "There is another side to this. You've always believed what he says might well happen. If no one else will listen, you could. You can see from his words he admires you. What if you read his letters when they come? You see I believe him when he says he will not reopen old wounds, and I have no wish to do so either. We cannot deny that there was once great love between us, but circumstances robbed us of our dreams. Dinwoodie, in the deep recesses of my heart I already store McAlister and am thankful for his love, although I regret that I never told him before he died that I was learning to love him. I now hold Alashdair there, in the knowledge that we shared a great passion, but aware it might not have weathered the differences that were bound to appear over the years. And then there's you, looming as large as Beinn Nishe in my life, and every bit as important as the mountain of my youth. My life is here with you and my family."

She ended the speech with an embrace, and Dinwoodie was hard pressed to deny his damp eyes for the second time that afternoon.

The end of June and the sun continued to shine on Kevinishe. In the distillery Cate made her way to the malt floor with a query for Donald Uig.

"Well now, to find an answer to your question I'd need to go around the bodachs, each and every one of them, for you know as well as I do, Miss Cate, that not one old man agrees with the other."

"Donald Uig, I really wasn't serious when I asked if they could tell whether this good weather would last."

"Well, an it must be yourself that's in good fettle, if it's joking you are."

22

"I'm like the rest of you, man, when the sun is on my back. It banishes the dreary days of winter and fills me with hope. Indeed it's a day too good to be working. That's why I enquired about the weather — do you think it will last?"

"I've a feeling you're not after asking the question that's concerning you."

"You're right, Donald Uig." Cate hesitated for a moment. These people that were now hers were steeped in generations of tradition. Would they move with the times, or indeed the weather? "If this good spell is to last, might it not be an idea to start the annual summer closure early?" She saw his shoulders stiffen and a stern expression cross his face.

"Miss Cate…"

"It was just an idea, Donald Uig."

"Well now, don't be racing to change your mind. It'll be a discussion we must be having first. It's no small thing to be changing the habits of old."

She should have known this would be the response, so she resigned herself to a conversation that would be lengthy.

"I was about to say I'd be getting the malt floor ready for the next lot of barley. Would you be after wanting me to leave it be, then? Though it'll still take the same time to be shutting the whole place down, now wouldn't it? And I've no doubt there'd be some worrying, not only at the disturbance to their routine, but also of tempting the fates they're forever considering, if you take my point."

Cate couldn't help smiling at herself as she remembered the occasions that this good man had stood at her back ready to defend her. It was only seemly that she should let him have his way.

"I see with the smiling face of yourself it is your mood that is as bright as the very sun itself, Miss Cate."

"Thank you, Donald Uig. But let's be serious now. Shall we start the holiday early? I would certainly prefer to."

"It's yourself that has the power to decide, nach eil?"

"Tha, Donald Uig, tha."

"Well now, isn't it yourself that's coming on with the Gaelic you never had as a tinker."

"Indeed! So I've made the decision. We begin today. By the time we're ready it'll give us an earlier week, perhaps even two, and if the sun doesn't last you'll no doubt blame me and my modernising ways."

"Indeed, as you would say, Miss Cate."

Decision made according to the customary debate, Donald Uig held the door open for Cate, and then made his way to the mash tun to have a craic with Murdo and pass on the news.

The second letter arrived when the distillery was closed, so Benjamin drove the post bus to Craigavon to deliver it. Maggie opened the door and, after the usual pleasantries, laid it on the silver salver on the hall table and went to find Lizzie. In the nursery, David and Cam were playing with the wooden figures that the coopers had carved for them, and Lizzie, as usual, was busy sewing.

"Lizzie, there's to be trouble. I know there is!" Maggie pulled up another chair before she continued. "A foreign letter for Cate, would you believe, an it can only be from the paper mannie. An that Benjamin from the Post even brought it to the house."

"Why'd he do that? Wullie the Post drops ours with the distillery mail."

"Och, he's no knowledge of how things are going on in Kevinishe. You mind, that him an Rebecca, his wife, were brought here on account of them being Solly's cousins, to be the Post when we knew that Wullie, bless his soul, would never walk again after the accident at the Quarry."

"Aye, Mammy, he was gey lucky that Cate found him when he was near death."

"If it's luck you're on about, it was nothing of the kind. Wasn't it herself with the *Second Sight* that had the saving of him? An Benjamin has no idea that the holiday doesn't mean there's no a body in the distillery. Wully the Post, never mind Angus, Donald Uig an Murdo, will be that put out at not having a wee look as to who's writing to Cate!"

"True indeed. Do you think he's after chasing her again — the reporter?

"Who knows? But it'll be a black day if he shows up here." With her warning delivered, Maggie returned to her laundry and pounded the washing to rid herself of the concern she felt for the woman who meant so much to her.

Returning from her ride on the moors, Cate took the letter to Dinwoodie's study, and, leaving it there, made her way to the kitchen, where the smell of Cook's fresh scones assured her she would be welcome. Greetings exchanged, she was concentrating on guiding the friable scone, now spread with home-made bramble jam and good salt

24

butter, to her mouth without dropping a morsel, when a worried Maggie appeared. With a mouth full, Cate mumbled, "Goodness — mmm — you look as if the sky— mmmn — is about to drop on you! Whatever's the matter?"

Maggie sidled up to Cate and whispered her concern. Cate smiled at her housekeeper before, mouth now empty, she spoke. "It's okay, Maggie. He knows about it. The letters will continue and cause no upheaval, so you can stop worrying."

Not wishing to say more in front of Cook, Maggie left, far from convinced by the cheerful tone. She waited till Cate re-appeared from the kitchen and tackled her again. "Mind it's just me saying, but you've been mistaken more than once as far as men were concerned. What about you no knowing that Mr McAlister had feelings for you? Then falling in love with the wee paper mannie when everyone else knew it would never work out, caused heartache all round didn't it?"

"Dear Maggie, I know it's just you worrying over me like a clucking hen, but believe me, I do know what I'm doing, and yes Dinwoodie agrees with me, so you can stop fretting."

Dinwoodie, home from his business trip, hot and sticky after the journey from Glasgow, was surprised to see Cate weeding in the garden, watched by Rory lying in the shade of the laburnum tree. "You've forgotten your hat again, and that pale skin of yours will burn." He greeted her. "Why are you here anyway? Playing truant from the distillery, are you? Where's the gardener?"

Cate rose from her knees and kissed him. "What a load of questions, Dinwoodie! I forgot the hat, we've closed up early for the holiday period, and that's why he isn't here. And before you ask, I'll give you the reason: I've gambled on the sun maybe lasting long enough for the men to gather the hay, coax additional flies to tempt the herring, and dry the salt from the seawater they've collected, while you and I sit in the sun without you feeling cold, lowlander that you are!" Linking her arm in his they made for the front door before she remembered the other thing he didn't know.

"Oh, there's another letter on your desk." She knew he understood, and arm in arm they continued indoors. Maggie watched them as she served their afternoon tea. When she'd left, Dinwoodie enquired, "It may be I'm imagining things, but did you see Maggie's less- than-covert glances when she thought we weren't looking?"

"Indeed I did. I've had plenty practice in the last week. The letter came here. Benjamin brought it. He's not quite sorted the rhythms of the distillery year. So now Maggie's joined the queue of troubled villagers, waiting and wondering if Alashdair is to appear. I've told her not to worry, but knowing her, worry she will. More tea?"

For a fleeting moment Dinwoodie was at one with the housekeeper, but chided himself for lacking trust in Cate. Yet it was difficult for him. Tea finished, he excused himself, avoiding his study, going first to change and bathe ready for the evening meal, although he couldn't help wondering what news the letter held and whether it would have any more details about the assassination of Franz Ferdinand.

Later, meal over, Dinwoodie opened the letter and began to read it aloud.

Austria-Hungary June 30th[th], 1914

Dearest Girl,

What I've just found out will, I'm sure, mean trouble for us all. Two days ago in Sarajevo, a Serb student and his companions killed the Archduke Franz Ferdinand. The exact details are unclear. A bomb and a pistol were used and now both the heir to the Austria-Hungarian Empire and his wife are dead.

It'll be dressed up as just supporting an ally, but I think perhaps this is what Germany has been preparing for. They already have the biggest standing army in the world. This could mean we may soon be at War.

Alashdair.

"He couldn't make that up, could he?" Cate asked.
"You haven't read the papers, my dear. It is true."
"But kill a Royal...?"

"Royals seemed to be more in danger throughout history than anyone else, Cate. Great power and wealth will always alienate, be they royal or not. In a way this isn't about whom they've shot. It's not the man: it's the country. That lot have been enemies forever, just as we were in the past with England. Land, Cate, that's the prize. Land and racial disputes, borders where they shouldn't be, grudges held for years: pick any of those and you've an excuse for war."

"My, Dinwoodie, that's a heated speech for you!"

"That's because I fear for us all."

"But this Serbia — I don't even know where it is. Why should a wee war in God knows where mean so much to you that…?"

"Because, my dear sweet wife, it won't be in, to quote you, 'God knows where'. Listen, Europe is full of alliances, big and small, so when there's a quarrel…"

"Ah I see, the friendly ones join in. But that's plain daft! Anyway we're not involved. They'll fight it out among themselves won't they?"

"I'm not sure, Cate. Let's do as the man says: wait and see. I only hope to God both he and I are wrong. Because, if we're not, the world is in danger."

Chapter 4

With War declared and the British Expeditionary Force in Belgium, back in Kevinishe, when the news arrived that the first battle of the war had ended in victory at some town called Mons, Cate made a mental note to get Dinwoodie to bring a map back from London. Then she could follow these foreign names and plot the progress of the war. At least Alashdair's next news should be cheerful, however pessimistic his thoughts were. And perhaps the hope that it would all be over by Christmas might still come true. In the meantime the glen was wearing the usual purple heather cloak of autumn, and Cate busied herself with her work, her garden, her home and her toddling children.

Alashdair's next letter arrived weeks later. Cate took it home and, when their meal was over, they sat down and Dinwoodie read it aloud at once.

France August 1914

Cate,

I'm traipsing along a rough road in northern France, with the British Expeditionary Force. I suppose your newspapers were full of a victory for us at Mons in Belgium. Well I can tell you it was short-lived. Our boys had no time to savour it before they were forced to retreat from the advancing Germans, and they are still doing so a fortnight after the battle.

They are very disgruntled —— they want to fight, not run away! I sympathise with them, but for my own part I

---

feel this war is truly underway and I have begun recording it.

Alasdair.

They sat looking at one another for some time, and Dinwoodie had begun to fill his pipe, when Cate jumped to her feet.

"Damn them! Why are the papers here crowing about victories and we're running away?"

"Hardly running away, my dear. I assume that with the enemy pressing the attack those in command decided retreat was the best option. After all, you need to get space between you and your foe before you can regroup, especially if the other side is moving faster than you are."

"Dinwoodie, I have a bad feeling about all this. Consider how many men are rushing to volunteer. There's a whisper that the younger men might sign up here. If we do lose some I may have to scale down production. I could perhaps press the few older ones who'd retired into service again, but after that there are no more men available."

"I do understand. The same thing is happening all over the land. It's not just the desire to fight. There's an element of bravado in it. Patriotism plays its part too. There'll be some who have no jobs, others whose pay and conditions are unpalatable. Finger-pointing, people calling them cowards, will also send some scurrying to the call."

"All this for someone else's wee war."

"I'm afraid, Cate, it's gone beyond that now. Before long other countries will ally themselves on either side and I fear that we will have to call on forces from all over the Empire. Your 'wee war' is fast becoming a world war. And now I must see to some papers in my study."

Cate stayed up late to check the financial statement that her lawyer, Gordon Wiseman, had sent her. Despite the panic in July when thoughts of war had precipitated a rush to exchange bonds for gold and the banks had closed for a day or two, her current balance was not displeasing. Indeed having funds at all still seemed strange for a once penniless tinker. A quick look at the clock on the mantelpiece made her realise just how late she was. Wasting no time, she tidied everything away and, with lights out, went to check the key was turned in the front door.

The sudden hammering on the other side of it made her hesitate until she recognised Stevie's call. Opening the door she could see the man was beside himself.

"What is it? The horses…?

"It's Gregor, Miss Cate, he's — real bad — in awful pain…"

Cate was up and running before the groom finished speaking, her mind filling with memories of Gregor: teaching her to ride; galloping for help when she'd near burned to death; following her to Craigavon, old as he was and near crippled with the rheumatics. Gregor couldn't be going yet. She had to help him. She owed him that and more.

Up in the bothy Gregor writhed on his pallet. Cate ran her hands over the restless body and, feeling heat, sent Stevie to wake Maggie with instructions to come with the herbs and salves. While she waited, Cate reappraised the groom, and it was then she changed her mind. The problem, she decided was in his head. When the others returned, she waved away what they'd brought, and they stood back and watched. Cate now knew that whatever was going on in his skull was fatal, but she could ease his journey. Remembering the Cailleach's instructions, she flexed her fingers and prepared to try to take his suffering away. She began to move her hands over his scalp and then, as the warmth crept up her arm, she knew it was beginning. This was a journey she'd never taken, but for him, and what he meant to her, she would do it, however long it took and, regardless of the risk.

When it was all over, neither Stevie nor Maggie could put words to what they'd seen. The sight of their Mistress drooping beside the dead man left them bewildered. No one moved. It was the appearance of Dinwoodie, a greatcoat over his dressing gown, which startled Maggie into speech.

"Sir, sir, he's deid an she's near to joining him I'm after thinking. Oh! Sir…"

Pushing his way past the other two, Dinwoodie was horrified to see his wife's prone body hanging over the old groom, who, after a quick check, Dinwoodie knew to be dead. But Cate — what the hell had gone on here?

"Maggie, Stevie, come on, tell me what's happened. Why is Cate…?"

"Sir, you'll — I mean — it's as though she took — to herself I mean, she…"

"Maggie, for God sake! Make some sense. Why is Cate…?" He couldn't frame the question. She was — as though she'd fallen asleep. Putting his hands on his wife's shoulders, he made to lift her, when Stevie stopped him. "Get out of my way, man! Can't you see she needs to be indoors, warm, out of here?"

"No sir, ye canna move her. I've heard the old ones speak of this. Maggie, fetch those horse blankets from below. It's got to work its way out, sir. If we're lucky she'll be all right. Hurry, Maggie!"

Maggie disappeared down the ladder. Before long her head reappeared above the stairs, and she all but tumbled into the bothy as the young stable lad pushed her up from behind in his hurry to see what had happened. Dinwoodie stared at them as if they were losing their senses. His wife was — "What do you mean, 'we'll be lucky'? Stevie, there's nothing wrong with my wife — she's just fallen asleep. She should be indoors." Bewildered, he tried to shake the groom's arms free, and it was only when Maggie shook her head at him, that he realised these two good people were sure of what they were doing.

He knelt by his wife, a stricken man. Was this another side of *The Second Sight*? What witchcraft had happened here? He couldn't lose his beloved Cate! God, it was only weeks ago he thought she'd leave him for the reporter, and now it looked as though she'd left him — "There — did she move? Did you see? She moved, didn't she?" No one answered him and so he laid his head on Cate's back, too afraid in this unreal scene to do anything else. He was unaware of the grey dawn when it broke. He only knew he was stiff and cold. Then he did feel her move. "Cate, Cate, are you alright?"

A drained and empty Cate glimpsed the waiting audience, her husband holding her hand and, as she remembered, turned to Gregor and gently closed his eyelids. With a sigh, she struggled to rise, and Dinwoodie guided her to her feet. As she looked around the faces, she saw they all asked the same question, but right now she couldn't explain it herself. "I'll be fine. I just need a drink and some sleep. Thank you for your help. He's at peace now."

Dinwoodie was about to question her when Maggie spoke. "I think we'll be needing the horse shifter, Stevie. Can you and the boys do that? Get her to the house?"

"No need, Maggie." Dinwoodie forestalled the answers. "I'll carry her myself."

"Mr Dinwoodie, you'll no carry her down the ladder for fear you'll drop her."

"Nonsense, Maggie! I'll…"

Stevie interrupted him before he could finish. "It's too dangerous, sir. We'll strap her in the hoist, and then you can carry her on the level ground. Please, Mr Dinwoodie, let us do it for her. Remember she's saved the lot of us in her time, and we'd do anything to see her right."

Cate knew her strength was gone, and pleaded with them. "Don't argue about me, please. If the men can carry a wounded horse they can cope with me. I'll be fine on the shifter. Just let them be, Dinwoodie."

Once the precarious descent was over, he scooped her in his arms and made for the house, grateful, after the first few steps, that though his wife was almost as tall as him she'd always been slender. By the time he'd reached the door, he cursed himself for a fool, and turned into the drawing room rather than going up the stairs, which he now realised he couldn't manage.

Cook soon had hot sweet tea in their hands, and bade the others get themselves to the kitchen, where she'd prepared the daily porridge early. Reluctant to go, they backed out of the room, leaving Maggie and Dinwoodie to sit with an exhausted Cate.

It was nearly evening before she awoke. Realising she was alone, Cate closed her eyes again and thought how she'd miss the grumpy old man. Indeed they were all dying, those milestones of her youth — the Cailleach, old MacNishe, Master Rab, Fisher, McAlister, Lady Jemima, and now Gregor. His name brought back the scene in the stable. From a very young age she'd used her hands for healing injured animals and easing human pain. The warmth as she laid her hands on was always familiar, but it had always been merely a surface massaging action combined with her herbs and salves that brought results.

How had she been so certain Gregor was dying? Indeed how had she known there was only one way of easing his pain? But she had known and, by doing it, using all of her strength and inner energy, she'd taken his pain on herself. She'd also understood there was a risk involved of danger to her. By doing so — then she tried to remember the disjointed instructions the Cailleach had muttered on her deathbed. All that time ago she hadn't wanted to listen to, never mind understand, what her grandmother was handing down to her. Bit by bit she pieced the remembered fragments of conversation together. According to the Cailleach, as a healer, a layer-on of hands, it was possible to do what she'd done during the early hours, but, even if used carefully, there was always danger and it had to be used rarely or — she couldn't quite remember what the 'or' was, but, as she never intended to repeat the night's actions, it didn't matter.

Now she had to convince the others that it was lack of sleep that had produced her collapse. Difficult, but she had to try, to make sure that not a word of this leaked out. It was bad enough the whole glen knowing she had the *Second Sight*. She'd no wish to enlarge on that. Dinwoodie would be the difficult one. She'd never seen him so shaken. He would neither accept the truth, nor believe her story.

Three deaths in a row: first Gregor, then Maggie's older sister Jessie, and now Donald Uig's mother. Cate smiled at the thought that the old ones in the village would perk up now that the Almighty had had his quota of three. She watched the cortège make its way to the church, on the hill outside the village, before she slipped away to her office.

She wasn't in the least bit surprised when an hour later someone knocked at the office door. "Come in, Donald Uig. I was expecting you."

"Now don't be after telling me it's…"

"Nothing to do with the supernatural, Donald Uig. I imagined you'd waste no time in changing the name of the tenancy now your mother's gone."

"Well, and won't they be welcome to her in the hereafter. My only hope is that my poor father will get word of her coming and move himself elsewhere before she starts in on him with that fierce tongue of hers! Indeed it's putting my name to the paper I'm after, Miss Cate. We've waited years for the old woman to go. I believe she'd have been gone long ago if I hadn't had an 'intended'. It was just to thwart us, you see."

Though chuckling with him, Cate was still working out how she could broach what was in her mind. " I have the deed all ready, but…"

"Now then, Miss Cate, it's always been the same. As long as the remaining relative is still in work with the distillery…"

"Man, would you let me finish! Of course the tenancy is yours, but as a wedding present to you both I want to renovate the cottage. Would it be possible for you to share with Murdo for a time? I know Wullie the

Post is there now, but it wouldn't be for long, and would mean the work could be done much quicker at the house without you."

"Well now, that's a very big gift to be giving a workman. It would be too much of your silver — she let it go, you know."

"Donald Uig, I can do what I like with my silver. Remember the numerous occasions you've been there for me when I was in trouble. You know full well you're no ordinary workman, and I'm also indebted to Kirsty. When I came back to the village as a grown-up, she was one of the only Kevinishe women to talk to me. She's been a friend for a long time and, she's one of the founder members of my sewing team. As long as you're willing, let's get on with it. After all, Kirsty has waited years for a home of her own." As the Malt Man tried to thank her, Cate waved him away, knowing it would embarrass them both. "Off back to the wake with you."

When he'd left she took out her village plan and thought about the cottage. By sacrificing the outhouse there she could enlarge the building, make it more suitable for the family man she hoped he would become. A new generation was essential for the distillery to continue, and the thought of a better house might encourage one or two of the younger men to settle down in the glen. Her money might as well be in the village houses rather than be left in the hands of financiers who were again running scared of this war.

Sometime later, Cate was tackling her correspondence in the distillery when there was a knock on the door. She called, "Come in." When the door opened she was surprised when Murdo appeared. This was unheard of. She wondered what had finally made him, after all these years, come up to the office.

Listening to his request as he stood in front of her, what he was saying was so unexpected, she struggled to understand, but, as the meaning became clear, Cate could find no words to express her feelings. It was preposterous! Aghast, she shook her head in bewilderment. This stolid-looking man, twiddling his flat cap in his hands, collarless shirt covered by a waistcoat, a glimpse of braces, a stubborn look on his face, and his feet in their sturdy tackety boots planted like a silent message of defiance, and determination not to be moved, had truly shocked her.

"Am I to have your blessing then, Miss Cate?" He asked to break her silence.

The mere thought of letting him go to join up, never mind blessing the man, was ridiculous! Her anger loosened her tongue. "Murdo, I don't believe I'm hearing all this. It's pure nonsense. Why? Why would you — why in God's name do you, a settled bachelor, a prized craftsman, just, just, why — I — I, I can't find the words! That's how daft this idea of yours is!"

"I'm to be away tomorrow, if you please, Miss Cate, to Fort William to sign up to fight for my home as did my forefathers. I've no relatives, no one but you dependent on me, an there's many a one would take my job. You'll no be left wanting, Miss Cate, an I'll be telling you I'll no be the only one who feels the need to respond to the call."

"There's nothing I can do to change your mind? Persuade you to stay?"

"An be a coward! Indeed there is not. Now I've had my say, and if it's all the same with you Miss Cate, I'll away back to the mash tun."

As the stubborn man closed the door behind him, furious now, Cate picked up her paperweight, a heavy bronze model of the still, and flung it as hard as she could at the innocent door. Her frustration wasn't helped when she saw the dent she'd made, and she was practically bowled over as Solly came rushing in to find her stooping to pick up the hapless paperweight.

"Cate, I'm so sorry. I heard…"

"I know." She held the bronze aloft. "I threw this at the damn door. Why?" she asked the question for him. "It's Murdo. The stupid, stupid man is away to sign up to the army. Going to fight! Oh, don't say anything. There's nothing we can do. I've tried. Now I've lost patience!"

Recognising the still simmering temper, the accountant nodded and sought the refuge of his own quiet office, but the picture of a furious Cate, still waving the bronze, with strands of vibrant red hair escaping their jailer pins, stayed with him for some time.

By the end of the day Cate had sounded out all those who might influence Murdo. Even Donald Uig, distraught as he was, had tried, but to no avail. She'd failed! For her it was never about being short of a skilled workman. It was — she was — it was just — God dammit he might get hurt! Maybe killed! After all, he was one of her villagers. She should have been able to keep him safe. Still in her office, she sat in the glow of the desk lamp with her mounting problems. Children's bedtime story, evening meal, the lateness of the hour, were all forgotten.

She'd tried to ignore the circumstances, but it had happened just as Alashdair and Dinwoodie had said it would. Oh, they'd had all the to-ing and fro-ing of politicians, the posturing, the negotiating, but in the end the Germans had entered Belgium. Then everything moved on, ultimatums were ignored, and now British soldiers were out there fighting. Volunteers were rushing to recruiting offices throughout the land, seeing a soldier's lot as a way out of boring or low-paid jobs, and a chance for adventure. God help some of them who thought it would be fun to go and send the Hun back where he belonged. Britain was now at WAR, and she'd been unable to keep one of her own stalwarts, with a patriotic fervour, from rushing headlong to join up. Right now, or at least by tomorrow, Kevinishe would truly be involved and, she could no longer believe that her beloved glen would remain untouched by the far away hostilities.

Chapter 5

With bleary eyes, Dinwoodie watched as Morrison guided the car into the garage. No doubt his driver was as ready for his bed as his employer. Maggie met him as he entered Craigavon.

"Mr Dinwoodie, sir, your eyes are near stuck together. It's a good dram of Craeg Dhu you'll be needing, with some fresh Highland food and your bed after that."

"Maggie, what would we do without you? But where is everybody? It's too quiet by half."

"Lizzie has the wee ones in bed and, before you ask, I've no idea where she is."

"You mean Cate's let the twins be bedded down without her?"

"It's no like her, sir, no at all, but she rushed in here this afternoon and was away on that black devil of a horse of hers before I could even ask the question."

"If that's the case, let's go back to your original idea. If the boys are asleep I might as well eat."

Cate was always meticulous in her domestic routine — in all her routines. Her conscience seemed to drive her to tackle all her responsibilities as if for some reason she might be found wanting. Her strange childhood, believing no one cared for her, seemed to have left her with the idea she had constantly to prove herself — to herself, as much as to the world. Still, this rushing off on Satan during working hours was unlike her. Dinwoodie silently chided himself as the uncomfortable thought that the boys' father might have returned from Europe, became uppermost in his mind. When would he learn to trust the good fortune that had made Cate his wife?

The thought was banished as the heavy oak door to Craigavon burst open and slammed shut. Cate was home. Why she could never arrive quietly he'd never know, but he smiled with relief as the dining room door opened and his wife, face flushed by the speed of her mount in the windy evening, approached.

"Dinwoodie, I'm so sorry to be late. Did Maggie explain?"

"Explain what, my dear Cate? And doesn't a husband home from his War work deserve a kiss before any explanation?"

Embraces exchanged, Cate was about to speak when Maggie entered.

"Maggie, it's okay, I got there in time."

"Now what sort of time and where would 'there' be? You're speaking in riddles, Cate, an, by the by, yon wee ones were no so very happy with you no being there at bedtime."

"Don't tell me I rushed out without…?"

"Exactly so. You'd better be setting us all right now. Here's Lizzie coming in just in time, so on with your story, Cate."

"Sit down, Lizzie. Thank you for putting the boys to bed. Well, at lunchtime today, Angus happened to mention that some of the village youngsters had gone to Fort William to sign on."

"What foolishness! The glen needs all the manpower it has." Dinwoodie said.

"Boys, Dinwoodie — they were only boys, and most of them under age! Charlie went with them." Cate couldn't disguise the break in her voice. Young Charlie, a mere seventeen, had grown up in the distillery, modelling himself on Fisher, the previous stillman, who'd been Cate's mentor and had given the boy the duty of looking out for Cate, before he died. For that Charlie was very dear to her. Steadying herself, Cate continued. "Benjamin drove me to the recruiting office and I was there before the boys. I spoke to all of them. You wouldn't credit it but two of them, were schoolboys, like Rhoddy, almost twelve. Three of the older ones wouldn't be persuaded, but Charlie and the others came back in the post bus."

"Well done, Cate. There's enough carnage out there already, without youngsters, especially as young as that, going as German cannon fodder. Though I daresay the recruiting sergeant wouldn't have let them go anyway. Right, after all that, I suggest we get to our beds. I, for one, am very tired, and we've all got work to do tomorrow. You know the words, 'there's a war on'!"

With the news of the halt of the German advance and the success of the French on the Marne, Cate felt that Dinwoodie's words of war could be laid aside in the splendour of this late autumn day. Beinn Nishe was once again, clothed in it's purple cloak of heather, and the azaleas in the long borders winked at the sun as it struck their bronze and golden leaves. Harsh thoughts of winter and war could be forgotten in this splendour. Anyway, the news that Paris had been saved by taxis ferrying French reinforcements to the battle was amusing enough to brighten anyone's day. Perhaps this was a turning point. Thoughts of turning made Cate aware that she'd spent too long riding and she'd better get to work, or at least to check on the builders at the Uig cottage.

Checking her plans, she was pleased to see that the old outhouse was already gone and the new wall half up. When it was complete and the roof extended, she could discuss her internal layout plans with Kirsty. The renovation needed to be done as fast as possible so as not to inconvenience Donald Uig.

Returned from a week checking the foundries in Glasgow and London, and with November looming, Dinwoodie knew the scrap of information that Pearson had gathered about MacNishe and Rhoddy would do little to ease the worry in Craigavon.

"Hasn't Pearson any leads or information — suspicions even?" Cate asked as her husband crossed the threshold. "They can't just disappear, Dinwoodie."

"No, nothing. "

"What are we going to do? We must find them!"

"Cate, we've done all we can. Pearson is investigating. I'm confident he'll make progress. Sooner or later someone will remember something. When that happens he will follow it up until he succeeds."

"And if he doesn't?" Cate willed Dinwoodie to say Pearson would succeed, but just looking at him she understood he couldn't. Cate crossed the room and sheltered in his arms. Her voice muffled against his chest, she confessed her pain.

"It's a judgement on me. I know I should have told you about that man, and I'm so sorry. We might have warned the school or something. It's my fault, both as a mother and wife. I failed Rhoddy and you, just as I failed Sarah. It's more than I can bear, Dinwoodie — much, much more."

"Cate, listen to me. That's nonsense. Yes, you were wrong not to alert me, but I can understand your fear. You haven't always dealt the right way with Rhoddy, but your relationship with him was set long ago when you had no control over what happened. You did what you had to do. As for your daughter Sarah, you were beset by grief over the death of your husband, McAlister. Giving birth to her and then losing him within a short time of one another was a huge mental and physical blow.

You can't be blamed for the trickery that his daughter played on you when she took Sarah to America. In both cases you were the victim, not the cause. My dear, Bruce and Caroline are two evil people who follow their own wicked plans, the man out of hatred, and the woman out of jealousy. Nothing you did or did not do could have stopped them."

"Dinwoodie, I so wanted to give my children all the things I never had when young. I set out to — I wanted to have the perfect family."

"My dear Cate, I don't think that exists. You always aim too high. When this awful war is over we'll continue the search overseas for Sarah. In the meantime Pearson is acting on my instructions to find MacNishe and Rhoddy, however long or much it costs, though you must make no more moves without telling me. You will do that, won't you?"

At her nod he comforted her until her shuddering quietened and then led her to the fireside. He'd quiz her on this McPhail character another time, though he'd make his own discreet enquiries anyway. Silently he swore to spend whatever it took to restore his precious young wife to happiness.

As the train sped further from Scotland, Bruce MacNishe savoured his long-planned revenge on the filthy tinker woman. Twice, during the years since he'd raped her, he'd thought he'd destroyed her. She should have died in the fire. Then, after he and that bastard Fisher had fought and the big ox had had a stroke, the distillery ought to have been his. Bloody lawyers had been useless.

Ever since he'd discovered Rhoddy was his son, he'd planned to take him away from the tinker. He smiled as he remembered how he'd cultivated Rhoddy, in secret, during holidays in Kevinishe and lately in Edinburgh, unknown to his mother, whenever he and his school friend could get away from Fettes College. The other boy had easily been persuaded to join in the subterfuge, and gradually he'd been able to influence them both. Liquor and extra spending money had helped to cement the father-son bond. He'd made sure that Rhoddy was more difficult at home in Kevinishe. A few carefully crafted lies and subtle insinuations about the mother, ensured the son's attitude had quickly turned from dislike to something much more destructive. This time Bruce knew he was going to succeed. He'd make that bitch suffer! Oh yes, she'd rue the loss of her oldest son for the rest of her life.

According to the boy, the loving mother was becoming more frustrated and angry with him, and of course those twins were now the centre of her attention. Then there was bound to be trouble at the distillery. How could an ignorant woman like her run a business that had been in the MacNishe family for generations? Work problems, her son estranged, and with any luck the aging Iron Baron, worn out with all the War work he was doing, might even drop dead, and then where would the tinker slut be? The timing was perfect. He'd finally teach her a lesson.

After all, she was nothing but a tinker harlot. She'd schemed her way into two marriages, the last one to the Iron Baron being the worst to stomach. His cousin Lachlan McPhail could burble on about the law, but he had his son now, and lawyers weren't needed. Though the money his cousin had lent him, once he knew about Rhoddy, had been useful. Not that he'd told Lachlan, or indeed anyone else, he'd lost the estate and Dinwoodie was now the owner. Trust the banks to sell Kevinishe to a jumped-up smelter just to satisfy a parcel of creditors. He'd also not bothered to tell his cousin that he no longer owned the distillery and all that belonged to it. He smiled when the thought that the Iron Baron would most likely throw the tinker whore out when he discovered that he, Bruce MacNishe, had had her when he was not much older than the son was now. Nothing could go wrong this time.

In the darkness as the night train rumbled on, Rhoddy thought that it'd seemed such a lark running away from school with his father. Looking sideways, he studied him, wondering what he was thinking. Rhoddy shut his eyes and tried to remember those distant days when this man had come galloping along the shore at Kevinishe, spurs shining, horse sweating, and had halted beside him. He hadn't known who he was then, but he'd been impressed. Now though, as the train rattled through the dark night, Rhoddy felt a little uneasy — not afraid, but not as excited as he'd been in Edinburgh, with his father ordering everyone about. They were going on a great adventure, he'd said. What was this adventure in London, he wondered?

At last the train jerked to a stop with lots of hissing, and his father grunted and shook himself awake. "Right then, my boy, we're here. Get your coat and let's get off. Got to meet old Stuffy at his club. Should get a reasonable meal and a decent bed out of him. Come on then. Don't dawdle." Outside the Army and Navy Club, Bruce presented his card and they were ushered into the lounge, where the heir to the Dalmiddle Estate rose to greet them.

Later in their room at the Club, as they bathed and dressed for dinner, Rhoddy listened to his father chatting away about his schooldays with Stuffy and all the things they'd got up to. Whether it was London, where he'd begun to wonder if this was such a good idea, or whether it was because all of a sudden these stories seemed to have lost — he wasn't really certain what. Before, when his father started his yarns, they'd been exciting, and to him they'd seemed to offer a way into a thrilling world well away from the petty restrictions his mother imposed upon him. Just for a moment, though, he almost felt he'd rather be back in Kevinishe. But that was no longer possible, not after he'd just run away. He could never go back now.

Suddenly, his father grabbed him by the shoulder and shook him hard. "Pay attention when I'm telling you things. You'll need to be smart now we're…" Bruce paused. Better keep quiet about the future plans — didn't want to frighten the boy. Still, he'd have to learn who was in charge here. One thing to play the tinker harlot up, but this was a different game altogether. Better send him off to bed as soon as they'd dined in the club. Then he and Stuffy could enjoy their port, and discuss the travel arrangements.

Damn good job he'd bullied old Stuffy at Fettes. Hadn't peached on him at school either. Old man Poerscot-Hudson would disinherit his son if he knew what had gone on back then. Stuffy was still afraid it might all come out so he'd agreed to get father and son over to France. Smiling to himself, Bruce turned to the boy, who was looking a bit cowed. No bad thing, that. Let him understand his father was not to be meddled with. "Right then, young Rhoddy. Let's have a look at you. Must say we two MacNishe men make a good picture. Let's go down and dine shall we?"

Chapter 6

Today there was another letter and parcel from Alashdair. Holding it made her thoughts turn to France, and Murdo. It was so strange to see Finlay by the mash tun. Where was Murdo now? She'd hoped that perhaps he'd fail the medical, but that was never going to happen. Murdo was one of the fittest men in the distillery, one of the very few belonging to the army auxiliaries. Cate opened the front door as soon as she heard the car return. She knew the news was bad by the look on her husband's face.

"Dinwoodie, what is it?" she implored, clinging to his arm.

"Cate…" He couldn't go on. How could he tell her? Waving Morrison goodnight, he guided his distraught wife into the drawing room, where he reached for the decanter and poured two drams. Straightening his shoulders he crossed to the fireside and handed Cate her glass. "Sit, my dear, and I'll explain."

She grabbed at his sleeve again making him spill drops of the single malt. "Dinwoodie, just tell me." Cate knew it would be bad and, amid her own fears, she felt for this wonderful husband of hers. She knew he was only trying to spare her, but if he didn't tell her soon, she'd end up screaming at him.

"Pearson reported this morning. They were hiding in Glasgow, not Edinburgh. They've now travelled to London. There they went to the Army and Navy Club in Pall Mall, where, according to the doorman, an old school chum met them and they dined before staying overnight. The next morning he drove them to the boat train for France."

"France! Oh, my God! Why? Can we follow them?"

"Cate, there's a war on. We can't possibly go to France. It's out of the question."

In her despair she raged at him. "Well it may be out of the question for you, but not for me. Not long ago you said you'd do anything to get my children back, and now, at the first chance, you deny me! Can't you see? I have to go. Rhoddy's my son and God knows what that evil man will do with him!"

"Cate, do you really believe I would give up so tamely? You do me an injustice. I know you're upset, but taking your anger and sorrow out on those close to you isn't going to help. Instead of shouting at me, why don't you listen to what I'm saying, and let me put the whole picture in front of you first?"

Aware that she'd been unfair, Cate sat and gripped her glass of malt. She craved action. With this new knowledge of the pair's whereabouts, all she wanted to do was go after them. Dinwoodie was right though, as he usually was. How could she get to France? Once again she was failing the boy.

"Listen to me, Cate. Pearson speaks fluent French and will go to France. I'd go myself but I'm needed here, not only for you, but also for the foundries. Once I've checked on Glasgow I've arranged to meet him in London in three days' time. Before you start berating me all over again, that's the soonest I'll be able to see him, I must spend time at the London works first. I've also contacted Fettes and explained the situation. I have another shock for you, I'm afraid. It was Rhoddy who told the College MacNishe was his father."

"Rhoddy? He knew before?"

"Oh yes! They've had weekends away from school on several occasions, spending time together in Edinburgh, so it was not unusual when he was picked up for a long weekend. It would seem that your son appears to have inherited his father's devious ways. Pray God that he never develops his wicked sexual habits. I'm sorry, Cate. I know this is one blow after another and hard for you, but I've had a long trail home today and I'm exhausted. Do you think we might have a simple supper later? In the meantime I'll take a bath, and then we could both do with some sleep. I'm almost at that point where my body is ready to ignore everything but sleep."

Unable even to close her eyes that night, however hard she tried, Cate could not get the idea out of her mind that Rhoddy and Bruce had known one another. Was that why she'd sometimes wondered about her son's actions, his speech, both of which had seemed too mature for a boy? Should she have been more suspicious? How had they met in the first place, and why hadn't she ever suspected it?

Somehow they'd got through the intervening days, and now she watched Dinwoodie get into the car. Morrison would drive him to

Glasgow and then her husband would take the train to London. Would Pearson be any use at finding Rhoddy? What was Bruce MacNishe thinking, absconding with the boy, taking him to a country at war? Cate couldn't make sense of it. She'd known the man since boyhood. He'd been a coward then and he'd be a coward still. Why then go where he'd be in danger? Somehow it didn't seem right. 'Always put one's self in the other person's head when trying to figure out what they would do,' that's what MacNishe, the old Laird, had told her when she was young. Bruce wasn't very intelligent and he was too lazy to work much out for himself. So he must have some help. There was a mite of information, somewhere at the back of her mind, a snatch of conversation from those long-ago days. She knew it was important and would help, but it was out of reach.

If only Fisher had still been alive. He'd have been able to tell them all about the relationship between the MacNishes and the McPhails. She and Fisher had been the only people who really knew Bruce, understood his underhand behaviour. They'd fought him at every turn as he tried to suck all the revenue out of the estate for his own base purposes. Fisher would have known what to do in her present situation — might even have been able to remember what she was desperately racking her mind for now.

Thinking of the man to whom she owed so much, the old anger about his sudden death returned. No one had ever been able to prove that Bruce had had a hand in Fisher's massive stroke, but, deep down, she'd always thought, he had been responsible. If she hadn't hated the MacNishe heir enough for what he'd done to her, that act, robbing the glen of the one man strong enough to guide them and the distillery, would have earned him her everlasting hatred. Perhaps the elusive words would surface when she was thinking of other things.

Well, she'd work to do. With four men gone she'd need to get onto the new scheduling, might have to trim their production level so the remaining staff could handle the work. Thank God the distillery could still run, in the capable hands of Stuart Monteith the stillman, and Donald Uig the Malt Man, but the missing Murdo was never far from her mind. Thoughts of him made her smile wryly. Never mind fighting for his glen — he'd been sent to England to train with the Black Watch! As yet there had been no more word of him, though one of the retailers visiting the distillery had thought that the Black Watch were over there by now. Cate hoped this was not so, but could do nothing but wait for word that he was safe. So, with Solly up to date with the accounts, and no new sales work to do, she could leave the distillery for a day or two. Under Maggie's watchful eye the house and the twins were also well cared for. She dismissed the thought that it was leaving her elder son in the care of others that was partly the source of her ongoing problems with him. She needed something else to occupy her mind. Why hadn't she gone to Glasgow with Dinwoodie? She'd check everything in the office and at Craigavon once again, to ease her conscience, and then take the Post Bus to Fort William and train to Glasgow.

Once in Glasgow, having discovered from Snowy, their Glasgow housekeeper cum cook, that Dinwoodie was in Edinburgh, en route to London, Cate, as a temporary respite from her problems, arranged a meeting with her good friend, Sister Mary Anne. Seated in the Willow Tea Rooms in Sauchiehaul Street, Cate remembered her days as an invalid in the Infirmary: McAlister dead, baby daughter Sarah abducted to America by Caroline Bryant, son Rhoddy in the convent, and Mary Anne the only one to believe her story. Her thoughts were brushed aside as the plump figure of her friend appeared in the doorway.

"There you are, Cate, and would you just look at yourself! Four children to your name and still wand slim! Do you never eat or what?"

"Look at my plate, Mary Anne. The Willow's creamiest cake and four more on the cake stand."

"I swear by the Holy Father, life's not fair, so it's not. If I as much as look at those fancies there, sure and it's an inch on my waist and hips."

"If things keep going as they are in this rotten war, there won't be such things as fancy cakes, Mary Anne. We'll be forced to eat less and there'll be no luxury foods available. Anyway, how are you? How is the convent working out?"

"Oh, Cate, it would break your heart so it would, if you could see some of the poor souls we scoop off the street these days."

"Like you scooped me, eh?"

"If only it was like that. Nowadays it's soldiers we're bringing in. You should see them, Cate. A leg gone, an arm in bits, a face shot away, and that's not the worst…"

"Don't the military look after them? They can't just abandon them once they're no use for fighting."

"I think they try, but there are now so many of them. The Infirmary is overflowing. They've commandeered buildings and, in the name of the Father, you wouldn't believe the state some of those are in. It's pitiful to see, so it is. Mind I think the ones that are —" She hesitated. "There was a man in the ward this morning, rocking back and forth, hands clasping his body so tightly he could barely breathe. At the least sound, he crumpled to the ground whimpering. Thing was he had not one scratch on him, so he hadn't, Cate."

Cate leant across the table and held her friend's hand. "Tell me more. Perhaps I can help."

"There are just so many of them coming back injured, and some of them no more than boys. One or two of them though don't seem right in the head — I suppose it's all those murderous things they've seen. I've neighbours who've men sent home and they're like strangers. Won't talk about the war, and sure they're not even fit to work, so they're not. It's pitiful, and there's just not enough help around. We've men in the convent we can't control. The Infirmary has no room for them, and they put the fear of God into their families, so they do. Sorry, Cate, I've just let it get to me this morning. Come, let's eat our cakes, I'll hear your news and then I must away back, for I'll be needed."

Cate then relayed the awful news re Rhoddy, Bruce MacNishe, and the ever-present threat of McPhail. Mary Anne, much as she appreciated the enormity of what had happened to her friend, could find little to say that would comfort her. Despite the underlying sadness, they ate, and chatted about the times they'd shared at Craigavon, nursing Fisher, before Mary Anne's return to nursing in Glasgow, and even managed a few laughs. Soon it was time to leave. As they parted in Sauchiehaul Street, Cate hugged her friend, "I'll think about your problems, Mary Anne, and perhaps I could at least do something there, for I can't help Rhoddy at present."

"Ah Cate, it's sorry I am about the boy, and the trouble the other two are being to you. We must hope he's soon found, and it all works out for you. As to my problems, aren't you after doing enough with your donations to the convent? I shouldn't have let it out, but somehow these suffering souls are always with me. I feel we ought to be doing more, but sure and I don't know what. I'm working all hours as it is. Anyway, with your own worries, work and family, I can't be seeing you in a hospital." As soon as the words were out, Mary Anne, hand to mouth, looked abject. "How could I ever forget the nursing you did for Fisher…?"

"I know you didn't mean it, Mary Anne, and I'll think about your problem."

Worried now, her friend became concerned. She knew that look. Cate had thought of something and, in her usual impulsive manner, was likely to act. "Now then, there's no more you can be doing, so away back to that Highland fiefdom of yours and your family, and, in the name of the Good God, don't you be doing anything rash!"

"I love you, woman! Back to your convent and leave me to get on. Go on, away with you before I remember how much I miss you in my life. Away, before I embarrass us both!"

"I know what you mean, and may the Good God, that you don't care about, go with you."

Cate watched the dumpy figure till it was out of sight and then made for her lawyer's office, the germ of an idea niggling away all the while.

The receptionist smiled as she saw Cate in front of her. "Good morning, Mrs Dinwoodie. He's with a client at the moment. Can I get you a cup of tea?"

"No thank you, Mary. I've just been to the Willow."

"Aye well, we can't compete with them. Take a seat and I'm sure he'll squeeze you in next."

Cate, over the years, had come to realise it was no secret in the office that Gordon had more than a professional involvement with her. She knew her peculiar history was, or at least had been the talk of the town. Then, with her hasty marriage to the wealthy Dinwoodie, who was seen as a confirmed widower married to his foundries, the gossip had begun again. She couldn't help smiling as she idly leafed through the paper, ever conscious of the curious glances coming her way from the receptionist. As the inner door opened, and Gordon caught sight of her, he gave a broad smile while showing his current client out. Cate noted the inaudible sigh and slump of the receptionist's shoulders and took Gordon Wiseman to task as they entered his office. "Give that poor girl out there a smile now and again. She's fair pining for recognition."

"Jean? She'd wonder what had come over me! She just lives for her work. No time for smiles."

"Ah, men! There are times I wonder why you've eyes in your head. The girl thinks the world of you. You're the one who has no time for anything but work. You need a good wife, Gordon Wiseman." Cate wished she hadn't begun that line of conversation. Shaking her head, she continued. "I'm sorry, but I'd have been no good for you, and you know that as well as I do. Anyway, think about what I said. Now to business! If I needed a largish sum of money quickly, could you get it?"

"Depends how much and how quick, but it's not a good time and wouldn't your husband…"

"No, no. Dinwoodie isn't involved."

"I trust you've told him about the other matter. It was a mistake not to do so immediately."

"Yes I have, and received a thorough telling off. Dinwoodie was very angry about it."

"You always were one for fighting your own battles, Cate, but I'm glad he knows. By the way, I've often wondered why you never use his Christian name?"

Gordon Wiseman, like many others, had assumed the surname meant she'd never cared for the man. He was not the only one in Glasgow to be amazed when she'd upped and married the widower. Of course the newspaper correspondent had also figured in the triangle, and rumours were rife at the time, but Cate Dinwoodie never enlightened anyone. He gave a wry smile as he waited for her answer.

"Now then, Gordon Wiseman, what's the smile for?"

"I remember my father warning me about you, saying you'd devour better men than me!"

"And I thought your father was a dear old man! Still he was probably right and I think sometimes Dinwoodie would agree with him. As to his name, the first grown man I ever really knew was the old Laird MacNishe and he told me to call him MacNishe. Back then, being young and ignorant of the ways of the world, I thought that's how you spoke of all men. Later, with my first husband, being my employer to begin with, it was sort of embarrassing, so again I used his surname and felt at ease with that. Now I suppose it's become a habit — it's what I do."

"If I'd understood that, I'd have realised sooner that 'Gordon' was a hopeless cause!" When their laughter subsided, he asked, "Any particular reason for the financial request? Surely not another enterprise in these worrying times?"

"Not an enterprise as such, more a cry for help."

"Cate, you give enough charitable help as it is."

"It's an idea I've had and it's probably not even very sensible, but that's all I'm saying for the moment. I shall have to work on it, but I take it that I still have funds at my disposal?"

"It may take a little time, but of course you do, though I'll need to know the scale of the project, with specific details, costings, etc. I must

51

look after your interests, guide you to spend the money wisely, otherwise I wouldn't be doing my job. Mind you I've never known anyone spend as little as you do and never on yourself."

"Living in poverty teaches you to be careful, Gordon. One thing I've learned is that you never know what's round the corner in life, and without money you're unable, particularly as a woman, to control what happens to you."

"If you're going to 'beat the suffragette drum', as they say, I've clients waiting. Remember to keep me informed re the other matter."

"I'm sorry, Gordon, and thank you for squeezing me in." She leant across the desk to plant a light kiss on his cheek. "Never forget you're a dear friend, and I value those more highly than most things. Goodbye. I'll dine with you next time I'm in Glasgow, if I may." Leaving the office she wondered if she should have told him about Bruce and Rhoddy, but Dinwoodie had said not to make any more moves on her own, so she hadn't. Turning her mind to Mary Anne's problems set it racing. The skeleton of a big idea was growing, but she'd need to put flesh on it. She now knew funding would be available, but other obstacles might be insurmountable and. of course, the biggest one of all would be Dinwoodie.

Chapter 7

As Morrison pulled into the Craigavon drive Dinwoodie, was not looking forward to telling his wife that Pearson had not been able to give him any further news of Rhoddy, but as the investigator said, 'it was always going to be a matter of patience'. However, patience was not one of Cate's many strengths and right now he was too tired for more emotional scenes.

Going straight to his study when he found his wife was not at home, he began to unpack his papers. Eyeing the foreign letter on his desk, he felt by reading it when Cate came home his lack of news could be postponed. In this he was disappointed.

Cate's arrival was announced by her opening the study door after the briefest of knocks with the question already on her lips. "What news did Pearson send you this time?"

"He's barely had…" Dinwoodie began before she interrupted him.

"Nothing? I thought you said he was a good investigator. If he still doesn't know where Rhoddy is, why doesn't he find someone who does?"

"It's not as simple as that, Cate. We must be patient."

"Patience! I have little enough of that, so where am I going to find more?"

"I understand how worrying this is for you — for us both. But we can do no more. I see we've war news," He picked up the letter. "Come, let's go down for supper and we'll read it afterwards."

Meal finished and the clearing done, Dinwoodie opened the letter.

> The Marne, September 1914.
>
> Dearest Girl,
>
> I feel very guilty as I write this. When I begged you to save my scribblings, it did not cross my mind for a moment that, by doing so, you would possibly be aiding me in a criminal act! It is only now that I have realised all home mail from soldiers and official correspondents is censored.
>
> I have no doubt that some may very well be doing as I am, avoiding the official channels, but I really have no right to ask you to take that risk. I have written quite a lot in these last couple of months, and I have also made friends with a civilian who travels to Paris from time to time and has agreed to post my parcels.
> Cate, I am reluctant to give up the opportunity to have my drafts safe in your hands, yet I see that this now compromises you. I will understand if you decide otherwise. You must let me know. The return address I'm using is inside the parcel. Once again, your silence will be my safekeeping.
> Alashdair.

Cate looked at her husband, and sighed. "I suppose we should have realised about letters and reports being censored, but it never occurred to me."

"I was so keen to hear and read his war news that I just didn't think of it, but I should have done. What will you do, Cate?"

"It's a bit late to back out now, when we've already received letters. We're so out of the way up here, is it really likely that, with all their energies focused on the war, they'd ferret out our part in it? He does say others are doing it. In a way I somehow feel I owe him, and although

54

what he did was wrong, that one mistake shouldn't be allowed to ruin the remainder of his life, should it?"

"So?"

"Let's just say nothing for now. I'm sure if he feels we're in real trouble he'll let us know."

"Agreed, and now I have more unsettling news for you."

"Dinwoodie?"

"I can only stay for a few days as I've several important meetings next week, and I've also had to bring a lot of paperwork home."

"You work so hard, and I shouldn't be shouting at you the minute you come back, but I'm desperate to hear news of Rhoddy. At least we can have our meals together and perhaps snatch a walk or a ride on the moors. You know you never get enough fresh air."

"I promise I'll find time for at least a walk. My bones may not quite be up to what you consider a gentle ride. Meanwhile you must try to carry on, and believe that we're doing everything we can to trace him."

Cate nodded as her husband left the room and didn't move till she heard the study door close. He was right. Life had to go on, and she was needed at the distillery, but it was with great difficulty that she forced a brief smile on her lips when Lizzie came to say goodnight, because her thoughts were still on the missing Rhoddy, evil Bruce MacNishe, and a War that was destroying lives all over Europe.

With the year-end news bleaker than the dank, misty February scene outside the study window, Cate, sketching dresses for the sewing team, could feel her worries nibbling away at the confidence she pretended to have that all was as before. Her mind on the war, she was taken aback to see she'd speckled the dark-panelled ankle-length skirt she was working on, by doodling miniature soldiers across it. Damn! The sketch looked — ripping it from her pad she screwed it up and threw it on the fire. The peat embers licked at a corner, then searched elsewhere until the cream paper began to curl and brown. As she watched the colour spread and darken, it began to change.

Then the mist was upon her. There they were, the panoply of dead and wounded, acrid smoke billowing in the breeze, and men running, staggering like drunks, while cries that were demented screams ripped from their throats as they struggled to escape, and then Murdo's lifeless body lying in a shell hole appeared, others treading on him in their flight. The scene faded, leaving her cold and shaken.

She stretched her trembling fingers towards the warmth of the now flaming parchment in the fire. Stared at the scattered fragments of paper ash fleeing upwards, prisoners of the forceful chimney draught, as surely as the depths of the shell hole had imprisoned Murdo. With a frightened sob, Cate sank to the floor, Rory muzzling up against her in sympathy.

Weeks later, Cate was checking the builders' progress at Donald Uig's cottage when she caught sight of Wullie the Post pulling something behind his bath chair.

"What on earth are you trailing there, Wullie?" she asked when the postman was level with her.

"Just a bittie firewood for the stove." He shrugged his shoulders as if to make light of the fact that he'd been struggling for hours to complete the task.

"Wullie, there are folks galore who would do that for you."

"Aye, but a body canna be dependent for everything. An that's another thing to be said. I need to be leaving the cottage, for I canna be letting Murdo pay the rent for me from his army pay. No with him away and fighting like. It's wrong."

"But, you're looking after it. Murdo wouldn't want it left empty."

"Mebbe not, but since he's no here, I canna be doing the wee jobs for him like I did before. A body has to be doing work so's no to lose respect."

Cate knew this was going to be difficult. She'd learnt, eventually, to have faith in her glimpses of the future, but she could say nothing here and now. It was no use offering to pay towards it for him, and she couldn't think of anything else that would persuade him to change his mind. It would be so simple if he'd just accept things as they were, but the stubborn pride of him would see him leave before he did that.

"I'll away to the east coast an my cousin Fergus as soon as I get the letter from him, Miss Cate."

"Right then, we'll leave things as they are for the moment. Now I'm needed at the distillery, so you go carefully with your load." Both the day's fleeting sun and her mood had disappeared behind clouds. She had to find a way to keep him that would satisfy them both. If he went, she might as well have left him under the shattered van in the rock fall, where he would never have known the pain of losing almost everything.

The dark mood stayed with her on the morning rounds of the distillery, and as she picked up another letter and a parcel from Alashdair. Then she called in on the sewing group, where they were making up the drawings she'd done in Glasgow after having a thorough look round the big stores in Sauchiehaul Street. Though once the dresses were complete whether there would be many women buying, with the war on, remained to be seen. Right now she didn't want to think about that, France, Rhoddy's disappearance, her vision of the dead Murdo or Wullie's rent problem, so she headed for the stables. Stevie saddled Midnight up for her, and she made for the moors. Somehow, whenever she rode out here, her thoughts inevitably turned to Fisher and, their shared love of them. Today, thinking of him and his plight at the end of his life made her remember Mary Anne and their meeting in Glasgow. That's what she'd do! Go up to Kevinishe House and see if her idea for helping Mary Anne would make sense. As ever, doing something positive spurred her on.

When she arrived and rode up the long drive, Rory at her heels, Cate was aghast at the state of the grounds. Dinwoodie was preoccupied with all that had been going on in the last couple of years, and, to be fair, she hadn't thought overmuch about Kevinishe House either. Dismounting at the water trough she fed Midnight some oats from her breeches pocket, and offered Rory a peppermint from the other one. Both horse and dog were used to this and she knew they would be there when she returned.

Sliding the stone thistle on the steps aside she retrieved the large key from its hiding place, unlocked the great oak door and, entered the silent house.

Uncovering the dustsheet over the desk in the library she scrabbled in the drawers for pencil and paper. With these in hand she was ready to begin her inspection, but not without some trepidation. Even as a child she'd never really liked the house, and she'd refused to consider living here after her marriage. It was Dinwoodie's property, and she would have to bear this in mind when making plans. Although they were well suited, they were equally determined, and that could be a problem.

As she left the library, her eye was caught by the many spaces on the shelves. She fingered the dust on the bare wood and sighed for the loss of some of those wonderful leather-bound first editions, sold presumably to fund Bruce MacNishe's wayward lifestyle, that had opened the world of reading to her. Making her way up the grand oak staircase, she was met by similar gaps on the wall. The silent spaces stood as ghostly memorials to the once proud MacNishe ancestors, who'd sat for famous artists of their time. Moving on from room to room on the first floor, the figures of her childhood came flooding back: Old

MacNishe, her first mentor, his son Rab, and Lady Sarah, Rab's wife. Memories of the woman made Cate head for what had been her private sitting room. Though all was carefully covered in dustsheets, she removed the one on the chaise longue and was at once that tinker girl again. Scrubbed red raw, she'd been pushed into this beautiful room and met another world. She sat, even now, on the edge of the seat, remembering how the gracious Lady had offered her breakfast and then given her the first opportunity of her orphan life — as nursery maid to the invalid younger son David. She felt the familiar sadness at the memory of the beautiful blonde boy who'd died so very young. He'd been the first human being she'd ever grown to love and she'd never forget those few short blissful years and what turned out to be the beginning of her education.

Remembering why she was here, Cate rose and began to circle the room. Yes, this one would make a pleasant sitting room for staff and they would appreciate the beauty of it after long hours of hard, seemingly impossible work. Yawning, Cate realized that sleep, elusive since the news about Rhoddy's disappearance, was overwhelming her. She returned to the seat, pulled the dustsheet over herself, and slept.

Much later she awoke to a sense of fear. Not knowing what made her uneasy, she hurriedly replaced the dust covering and made for the stairs. That was when she remembered! She searched in vain, but the portrait was neither where it should have been nor in any of the other gaps. He'd sold it! The fool of a man! Had he no ear for the past, his heritage? Cate sank onto the nearest step. She was shaking. Too much of the feyness of the true Celt dwelt inside her to ignore what that idiot had done! The portrait of the *Red-headed Woman* was gone! The curse, which foretold the failure of the MacNishes, was already at work, and Rhoddy was doubly damned, for his parents were both descended from the ancient lineage.

As though retribution might land on her head this instant, Cate scrambled to her feet, pelted down the stairs and out the door. Not even bothering to secure it, she leapt astride the startled stallion and made for the moors again, the dog doing its best to keep up with them.

Back in the Craigavon kitchen, Cook was bemoaning the fact that another meal was going uneaten. Maggie tried to console her by explaining why Cate was absent yet again.

"I'm sure I don't know where she is, Cook. She was in her breeches, so likely just riding as far and as fast as she can to get ease from her troubles, poor woman,"

"Well then, we'd be the better for eating this saddle of lamb before it's cinders. Not that she'd notice these days, even if you just left the empty plate in front of her. She's done nothing but push whatever I've given her from one side to the other. What's happened to her healthy appetite?"

"You can't blame her, Cook, she's that much to worry her, what with Rhoddy's disappearance, Murdo leaving the distillery and himself away so much. This village is her life."

"Many's the day I've wondered about that. I mean with the stories I've heard of the old days when they'd have nothing to do with her."

"It's in her blood, she's…." Friends though they were, it was not her place to tell Cook that her mistress came from a long line of MacNishe Lairds' by-blows. Some things were better left unsaid. "It's the mountain that draws her. Everything else just seemed to happen, as you might say." At least both those things were true. Maggie was glad to see Lizzie come into the kitchen and put an end to any further questioning.

"Mammy, do you know where Cate is?"

"Riding I would think. Why?"

"She promised those wee bairns she'd be back in time for stories. It's their bedtime. I don't know why, but Cate's changing."

"You're no often disapproving, Lizzie. What is it?"

"It's Cate. She seems too busy for us these days, Mammy."

"And no wonder with the distillery, Rhoddy…"

"If she'd spent more time wi' Rhoddy when he was little mebbe we'd no be in such a pickle now." With that Lizzie left the kitchen.

"Well I never! Fancy young Lizzie going on like that."

"Cook, there's truth in what she says, but I've never heard her speak up that way. If you or me had said anything like that, she'd have the head bitten off us!"

"All I know, Maggie, is this house seems to have lost its heart these last few weeks. I blame the war, I do."

Maggie wasn't sure who or what to blame, but Cook was right about the house.

From her usual stance at her sitting room window, Cate watched as the twins, either side of Lizzie, made their excited way to the stables to see the new Highland ponies she'd bought for them. Lizzie had made it quite clear that she felt they were far too young to be going near stables, with their big horses, and learning to ride. Even so, Cate still felt it didn't explain the undercurrent to their chats these days. From the age of fourteen, Lizzie, two years younger than herself, had been a devoted supporter. As the years passed and their paths separated for a time, it had made no difference to their friendship, so what on earth was wrong with her now? Anyway, with Dinwoodie due home in a few days she'd far too much to do to waste any more time on the problem.

Ever since she'd come back from Kevinishe House, she'd been indecisive. Should she abandon her scheme? Could she even dare to enter the house again? Somehow she'd been waiting for a sign. Would the *Red-headed Woman* appear as she'd done throughout her younger life? Or was the removal of the portrait already working against the MacNishe strain in her? She had to stop the thoughts getting the better of her, and so she ploughed on; poring over her notebook; transferring the main points; backed up by designs, sketches, layouts and likely costings, to her drawing paper, ready to show Dinwoodie the minute he arrived. She found that, when she had something like this project to mull over, she could, for a time, forget her troubles, even this new one of the missing painting. By staying up late into the night working and planning, it removed her worries for a time and, because of the late nights she was grateful that her tinker background meant she could sleep anywhere, although her dreams were always fretful these days.

Today she was frustrated because she simply didn't have enough knowledge to decide all that was required, and she was aware that she dare not make any definite moves until she'd Dinwoodie's approval. It was his house, and he hadn't become the Iron Baron by letting other manufacturers take advantage of him. His workers were devoted to him, but could be firmly reprimanded if he thought it necessary. She'd only once had him lose his temper with her, when she'd pushed him too far, and, though that was before they were married, it'd been a warning. But surely he would understand what she was trying to do?

Maggie interrupted her by knocking, coming in, and standing by the desk. "They've just rung to say Solly's ill. That Rebecca at the exchange says he's been like it for days, but didn't want to tell you."

Solly had a history of illness. He'd a weak chest. Still, since he'd left Glasgow, he'd seemed much better. Now it meant she'd have to go to the distillery and do the daily accounts, when all she really wanted to do was complete her plans to show Dinwoodie. "Fine, Maggie, I'd best get to the distillery, and then I'll ride round and see if he needs anything. If he's really bad, I think we ought to have him here, where we can keep an eye on him. Could you get the blue room ready for him? I know it's little, but it's cosy and not far from the bathroom." As she left the room, Cate called over her shoulder. "Oh, and can you tell Lizzie I may not be back in time for the boys' tea?"

When Maggie arrived in the kitchen to give Cook Cate's message, Lizzie was already there with the boys, having their morning milk and biscuits. "No lunch for Cate — she's away to the distillery, Cook, and, Lizzie, she'll no be back in time for nursery tea, as she'll be away round to see to Solly."

"Why should she be going round to Solly's instead of seeing to her children's teas?" Lizzie queried in an angry voice, before banging her cup on the table and shooing the twins before her out of the kitchen. Both Cook and Maggie stared after her.

"Maggie, what…?"

"I've no idea, Cook. I've never seen her like this."

"Maybe the wee ones are too much for her, Maggie? We forget that that poor leg of hers can be right sore sometimes."

"Even if it was, you'd never hear a word from her. Those bairns are her life. No. No. It's Cate seems to be the problem, and if Lizzie has trouble with Cate, though I canna think she would after all these years, then it'll make things difficult for all of us. How can I take sides either with my daughter or my employer? Friend though she is to the both of us, we must mind Cate's our boss. That's the top and bottom of it."

Later that evening the Carter, the son of the one who'd been killed in the quarry disaster, delivered a shivering Solly to Craigavon, and Stevie, the groom, and Cate helped him upstairs, bundled him into bed and set about filling the room with steaming bowls. Cate sat up all night and Maggie kept the pans boiling on the range. By morning he seemed a bit easier and they left him sleeping.

After a brief breakfast, Cate slipped away to fetch some salves from the Black House. This was where she'd spent her winters as a child, and visits there stirred deep emotions. The Cailleach, the old woman who'd taken care of her then, when the tinkers were not on the road, had lived in this ancient house all her life, and when she died she'd left it to Cate. It was here that she'd learned about natural medicines, the only remedies the poor ever had, and found that she had what was known as 'healing hands'. On the old lady's death, MacNishe had done up the house for her and Rhoddy. Then his grandson, Bruce, had set one of his henchmen to burn it down with her inside. Cate thought how different things would have seemed during her childhood if she'd had some inkling that the old woman was her grandmother. But it had been the Cailleach's way of ensuring that she could look after herself. And it had worked.

Eventually, she'd put a new turf roof on the blackened walls and brought some basic furniture from Craigavon. It was here she practised her healing. The house was set on the moor well away from the village, but closer and more approachable for the villagers than Craigavon. It was also handy for collecting any of the wild flowers and herbs she didn't grow at home. Indeed she regarded the old house as a marker for her life's journey so far. Here she'd begun with nothing, and it served as a reminder of just how hard life could be. The mountain, this house and Craigavon had been major factors in her life — only a few weeks ago she'd been assuring herself that that life was perfect, the one she'd sought, suffered and worked so very hard for.

Today this house reminded her sharply that things could and did change. She'd left it once, only to return penniless and with an illegitimate child. Once again her life was in turmoil, and she could feel the hard-fought-for security slipping. This time though, no amount of work would right things. Once again she was at the mercy of others, not forgetting the ancient curse on the MacNishe line.

Chapter 8

When the telephone rang in Craigavon, Cate answered it. When she heard her husband's voice, she wondered whether the news would be good or bad, as he continued to speak

"It's only a scrap of news but…"

"What is it, Dinwoodie? Does he know where they are?"

"They were in Paris and…"

"My God, the Germans are nearly in Paris! Is he safe?"

"Yes, Cate. Pearson has news that he's alive and with his father."

"And?"

"They've made their way to the country and Pearson is following the trail. I wanted to let you know the minute I heard, but I must go now. Take care and I'll be home in a few days."

She put the phone down and realised her hand was shaking. At least today's news was heartening, but they were still no nearer to bringing Rhoddy home.

The day Dinwoodie was due home, her ride, and the essential work at the distillery were all completed at breakneck speed so that she would be home in time to greet her husband. Would he have any more news? Might he even be bringing Rhoddy home? She paced up and down her study, went to the kitchen to see to the details of the evening's supper, retraced her steps, and then went down again to the drawing room to check the car hadn't arrived.

By the time it did draw up at the front door, Cate had convinced herself they'd never see Rhoddy again, but managed to wait in the hall this time until Dinwoodie came in.

"Have you heard anything more?"

Dinwoodie took her arm and led her to the drawing room.

"Yes, my dear, I have. Pearson has traced them to a country estate. He can't gain entry to it, but he'll do what he does best, watch and wait. They'll reappear eventually and then he'll pounce."

"What if they don't come out? Even if they do he might miss them."

"Cate, there are countless possibilities where things could go wrong, but there are the same number or more that could result in Rhoddy being returned to us.

We'll have to trust the man. It's his job and one he's been doing for years, so for our part we have to carry on with our lives, try to be positive and hope he succeeds."

"I'll try. Oh, there's another letter and a parcel this time. I've left them on your desk."

"Right, I'll get the letter and we'll leave the parcel and its detailed notes for another day."

As they made their way to the drawing room after the evening meal, Dinwoodie drew the letter from his pocket, and once seated began to read.

Western Front, January 1915

My dear Cate,

I wonder if you have any idea how precious your silence has been to me? To thank you seems hardly enough, but I hope you know how much it means to me.

This war has ground to a halt. On the Western Front, as it is beginning to be known, the latter part of 1914 was spent in digging trenches. Whenever I was able to get a chance for a chat with soldiers from the front line, it was all moaning about digging. Aching backs, blisters, sandbags and sniping, duckboards and death, were their daily diet.

There are some strange episodes in this trench warfare. Over Christmas, men on both sides of the front line sang carols in their trenches. Some even walked out in no-man's land, still singing, and exchanged addresses, gave one another keepsakes, and then started a game of football, if you can believe it! Of course as soon as the officers found what was happening the men were all ordered back to their lines and the sniping began again. I get the feeling the ordinary German is much like us. They don't appear to be the monsters we were told to expect.

In this stalemate I have been able to write more, and you'll have it by now. Funny thing is, despite the hardships in the trenches, I've seen comradeship that reminds me of the men in the shipyards on Clydeside. I believe it is the one enduring thing that saves the soldiers from going mad.

I hope you are still able to keep the distillery running and that you have avoided the losses and hardships that others over there appear to be having.

Alashdair.

Dinwoodie put the letter back in the envelope and, as Cate appeared to be deep in thought, he left her and went to his study. Once there he began to dwell on the disturbing closeness to Cate the Scribbler managed to produce in his letters without any definite endearments other than those opening words. It was always an effort for him to fight down the spark of jealousy that reading them produced. There were times when he wondered if they'd been wise to continue, and yet the war content contained in the drafts was riveting.

With winter reluctant to hand over to spring, Cate was chatting with an excited Kirsty outside the cottage as they surveyed the progress in the rain, when Wully the Post trundled his bath chair towards them. One look at the man's face and Cate knew before his hand dipped into his pocket and revealed the crumpled telegram.

"He's gone, Miss Cate. The silly bugger's gone and got himself killed, so he has, an him only new out there in the fighting an… " It was too much for the erstwhile postman and he thrust the dreaded news at Cate, before covering his face till he regained his composure.

"Oh Wullie, I'm so sorry." Pushing the telegram into his pocket, she laid a comforting hand on his shoulder. "We'd better go to the distillery and see Donald Uig. Kirsty, run ahead and get them to fetch him. Come, Wullie, I'll push you." She said no more. What was the use?

For the next few weeks distillery and village were subdued. Cate visited Wullie, did her best to console him, but his loss was too raw to talk about the future. She knew that with Murdo's death it would not be long before the tenancy question arose again, and this time he would want to go immediately. Somehow she must find a way to preserve his pride and keep him in the cottage.

The months dragged on and there was no fresh news of Rhoddy. Dinwoodie was once more in London, Solly had recovered, Lizzie was still not her usual self, and another letter from Alashdair had arrived. War news in the papers and on the wireless was that trench warfare had developed, and the Post Bus had brought the telegram telling them that yet another of the villagers had been killed in no man's land. The death was doubly mourned as the remains could not be retrieved, his grave unknown. So, just like Murdo before him, there would be no funeral, no village grave for loved ones to tend.

These miserable thoughts were occupying Cate at breakfast, when she heard the car. Surely they hadn't driven through the night? Had they brought Rhoddy? She dashed to the front door, but as it opened and a grey-looking Dinwoodie entered, she knew the news was not good. Hugging her tired man, she brought him to the table and plied him with tea with a 'cinder' of Craeg Dhu in it. Maggie rushed in with a plate of steaming porridge and even Cook hovered at the dining room door, with Lizzie behind her.

Between mouthfuls of porridge, and having dispatched Cook to feed Morrison in the kitchen, Dinwoodie began his grim tale. "The news from the front is not good."

"We've never gone and lost, Mr Dinwoodie?"

"We're certainly not doing very well, Maggie, and the real trouble..."

"Dinwoodie…"

"Your news is not good either, Cate."

"Pearson hasn't managed to get Rhoddy?"

"No, Cate, he hasn't, and there is another problem. Because he saw no sign of them, he followed the chap from the cottage and engaged him in conversation. It seems that MacNishe has left Rhoddy there and gone to Paris, he thinks. Pearson tried to persuade him to hand over Rhoddy, but the man refused, afraid of losing his home and job I suppose. But Pearson will get him somehow."

"Do you really believe he will, Dinwoodie? Alive, I mean."

"Don't go imagining the worst, Cate. You know Bruce MacNishe. He's an evil, cunning man, but think about it — he's also vain. Believes the MacNishe line is superior to all others. He's hardly likely to hurt one of his own."

"But supposing…"

Dinwoodie silenced her with a wave of his hand. "Let's not be diverted. Stick to what we know. Two points to remember, my dear, Rhoddy ran away — obviously with the contrivance of his father — and the purpose of that was to hurt you. If anything happens to Rhoddy, it would be dreadful, but it would be finite. My thinking is that MacNishe intends to keep the boy alive, nurturing in him this hateful desire for revenge against you. Now that's not something that would be served by abandoning Rhoddy, if we look at the worst thing that could happen."

"You mean keep him and…"

"It's an awful thought, but that's what villains do. Find their adversary's weakest link and exploit it. Rhoddy, my dear, has always been your 'Achilles Heel'. "

Maggie hadn't understood. "What's one of those, sir?"

"He was a Greek soldier, Maggie," Cate answered, "whose mother didn't want to lose him in their never-ending wars, so she dipped him in a sacred river and the ducking made him invincible."

"So what's his heel…?"

"She'd to hold him in the water by his heel and because it did not touch the water it wasn't protected. That's how they killed him, I think."

"Exactly, Cate. You're the opposite of MacNishe. He appears to have little or no conscience, whereas yours overburdens you, my dear, particularly where Rhoddy is concerned. This may be painful, but the truth usually is. You've never actually liked, or perhaps even loved your son…."

"Those are harsh words, Dinwoodie. I had to work."

"Aye, but Mr Dinwoodie's right, Cate." Lizzie intervened. "You didna have time for him. It was all about you, Cate, no Rhoddy."

"Lizzie, what're you saying?" Maggie demanded.

Lizzie turned to her mother, "I know what I'm saying. It's all about Cate. She aye had time for others — my uncle Fisher was her best friend, an I never even knew him. Then there was Mr McAlister, and the reporter, yon lawyer — oh all of them! And Solly, most of all, He's aye saying, 'Cate this' and 'Cate that.' She didna really like Rhoddy, an that's the truth of it."

As her accent thickened and her words tumbled out, they watched her run from the room in tears, too stunned to continue. How could Lizzie, sweet little Lizzie with the bad leg, say all these things?

Maggie was the first to speak. "I'm right sorry, Cate. I don't know — these last few weeks she's been — well different. Mebbe she's sickening for something."

Dinwoodie felt that young Lizzie had just saved him from a crisis in his marriage. He looked at Cate and Maggie and wondered how they could be so blind. Was it because it had never occurred to either of them to go beyond the 'wee Lizzie' perception they held of her? He remembered a frightened Lizzie, one night, years ago, alone in Craigavon, confessing to him that she liked Solly, but that she was a moth to Cate's butterfly. He'd told her then there were some lovely moths, and she should stretch her wings and make Solly notice her.

Shaking his head at the others, he said "Ladies, your wee Lizzie has grown up and is, and has been for years, 'carrying a candle', as they say, for Solly. But you must admit, Cate, he is, and always has been, your most devoted admirer."

"Don't be ridiculous, Dinwoodie. Solly is a dear and close friend, that's all, and Lizzie has never shown any interest in him anyway."

"Cate, there are times when you are too busy 'doing' to think. Just lately you've been stretched in all directions with your various worries, and what's been pushed to the side are the twins."

Cate made to protest, but Dinwoodie carried on. "I know. I know. You love them dearly, want the best for them, but you don't spend enough time with them. And nor do you spend the time with Lizzie anymore."

"Why am I in the dock now?" Cate demanded. "Lizzie's the one who's been rude, and critical, yet it would appear I'm in the wrong, and you're joining in. How dare you, Dinwoodie, and in front of staff!"

"Well now, Miss Cate, we're your best friends 'as long as we live, Maggie' was what you used to say, but now you're on your high horse we're staff. Well, let me tell you, Lizzie's right both about the twins and young Rhoddy. You never gave him, or them now, enough of you. Your work always comes first. Always has and always will!" With that she too flounced out of the room.

Dinwoodie, with a long look at Cate, left her to her thoughts and made for the study. The foreign letter was the first thing he saw. Picking it up he fingered it for a moment then made his way downstairs again. Cate was fiddling with a flower arrangement in the hall and when she saw him she turned and walked into the drawing room. He followed her and when they were both seated he opened the letter and began to read, though omitting the greeting. Those two words made him uneasy.

Ypres, Spring 1915

Dearest girl,

The War goes on. A continuing pattern of advances and retreats, dead and wounded. I swear the maximum gain by either side can be measured in a few paltry pointless feet. More new recruits appear on the road from time to time, but sometimes it's only a matter of days before they reappear on stretchers, dead or wounded.

Just before I began this letter I was chatting to a group of soldiers, newly out of the line. Cate, you cannot believe what they were telling me. It seems they spend more time keeping their trenches habitable than they do fighting the enemy! Continual shelling blasts their defences, and rain, when it comes, turns the earth to mud that swallows the duckboards. I also saw men take their tunics and trousers off, light cigarettes and run them up and down the seams to kill lice!

Of course it's not just in the trenches the men suffer. Wherever there is food, or casualties lying about, rats appear.

Yesterday I found myself staring at a dead body lying in a shell hole by the side of the road. Rats were gnawing at the ragged flesh. Over here such horrors are commonplace. I never dreamed I would see such things.

Alashdair

"Well that pretty much tells us what we knew," Cate said in a cold voice, and left the room. Dinwoodie was beginning to think the domestic situation in Craigavon was looking as fractured as the Allies' opposition to the Germans. In both cases all he could do was watch and wait, though neither of these were comfortable options.

At last the Craigavon household had settled back into a comfortable routine after the falling-out. Cate had had to admit that she'd been at fault, spending too much time at work and leaving the others to tend to the twins. She'd truly intended to improve in that respect, but continuing news of the horrific casualties the war was producing intensified her determination to turn Kevinishe House into a hospital. Much of her time in the spring months of 1915, when she was not at the distillery, was spent there refining her basic plans. As yet she'd not confided her intention to Dinwoodie, and for good reason: she knew he would not be easily persuaded.

Seated at her desk in Craigavon, Cate studied the ever-growing file. Dinwoodie was due to leave for the foundry in Glasgow in a few days en route to London for a lengthy visit. She couldn't leave it any longer. She'd tackle him after the evening meal.

Later that evening, as they sat sipping an after-dinner malt, Cate rose saying "I've some work I'd like you to take a look at if your not too tired."

"Now then, it's rarely you involve me in that side, but I'll be very happy to do so."

She collected the file from her study and handed it to him. Then picking up her sewing she pretended to concentrate on that.

"My, you've been working hard! This is a fair weight of work, Cate." His admiration was obvious as he smiled at her. With that he proceeded to go through the papers, but before long the smile faded and his face took on a stern expression before he spoke.

"Cate, you know my thoughts on Kevinishe House. We'd agreed that nothing was to be done till peace eventually came. Once again you've ignored my wishes." Dinwoodie closed the file and dropped it at his feet. "Nothing has been either said or done by me to mislead you into thinking I'd changed my mind. It's not long since this household was in an uproar because of your devoting too much time to work. Even though you spend less time at the distillery now that the trade is falling off, you've simply found more work to do instead of concentrating on

70

your family and domestic commitments, which is what you should be doing. Haven't you enough to worry about with all that's going on? So let's have no more of this nonsense."

"Dinwoodie, I do my worrying, but there's a war on."

"Don't state the obvious! Because of the foundries I'm much more aware of what's really happening on the Western Front than you are. This is no time for playing around with hotels, guests, holidays, and profit and loss. There's no profit — just horrendous loss among the brave dead and wounded. I thought you'd appreciate that."

"Damn yourself, Dinwoodie!" Cate sprang to her feet at his words. "You haven't understood anything! Who's talking of hotels here? Who's talking of profit and loss? Not me! Those are plans to turn your big empty house into a hospital for the wounded. They're desperate for beds in Glasgow, and here we are with both the premises and the silver between us to do something for those poor souls!"

Pausing for breath, trying to rein in her temper, knowing how it annoyed him, she walked to the window before turning again to him. "You accuse me of ignorance and not caring! How well do you know the plight of those poor beggars wandering the streets of Glasgow? What about the armless, legless, sightless, ones? What do you know or care of them while you're scheduling armament production to maim more? Tell me that before lecturing me! Anyway, I can see you're set on your decision, but I warn you: so am I. If I can't use Kevinishe House, I'll strip Craigavon, the long barn — even the distillery. I've already spoken to Gordon about finance and…"

"Ah, once again ready to do your bidding is he? I have to say I'm rather tired of playing second fiddle to your tame lawyer!"

"What are you talking about? Surely you're not going back over all that nonsense of Lizzie's? You know as well as I do that it's ridiculous! I'll enlist help from any quarter, Dinwoodie, when I've a problem to solve. I went to him to enquire about my financial position, because this hospital is needed and I intend to help with or without your blasted house or permission."

"When you've calmed down…"

"I don't intend to calm down. Mary Anne is breaking her heart at the lack of hospital beds. I need to do something! I admit that I also need to work, more now than ever with Rhoddy missing, Bruce MacNishe up to no good, and the spectre of the McPhail man always in my thoughts. If I sit idle with all of that going on, I'll go mad. I need action,

Dinwoodie. You've always known that, and it's never been a problem for you before."

"If that's your final say on the matter, there's no need for more discussion, so I believe it would be best for both of us if I left in the morning." Dinwoodie rose as Cate continued.

"Fine! Wait till one of the volunteers from your Glasgow foundry staggers home on one leg, or many more are blown to God knows where and their widows come to you for help to survive this bloody war. How detached will you be then? Oh yes, I know you'll put your hand in the foundries wealth, but that won't mend a broken limb, make a blind man see or quiet a tortured mind. Only time, nursing, and care will do that, and when you're confronted by the need in your own business, you'll see how it hurts. So go, Dinwoodie, and be damned to you! I'll sleep in the blue room tonight!"

Chapter 9

Weeks had gone by, the war dragged on and the Germans had done the unthinkable — on the 7th of May they'd sunk the Lusitania with horrendous loss of life. She'd thought that Dinwoodie might telephone to discuss the tragedy with her, but she'd had neither word nor sight of him since he'd left without even saying goodbye to her. Cate knew she'd over-reacted yet again while discussing her hospital plan, but the missing Rhoddy, the constant niggles at home, the telegrams arriving with news of death or injuries to those Kevinishe men who'd volunteered, all upset her and, she needed to be doing something to ease her troubled mind.

In spite of her brave words to Dinwoodie, the practicalities of using her own home and buildings were difficult. She could move her personal household to Kevinishe House, though she'd hate to do that, and use Craigavon as the hospital, but that would simply enrage him. Since the distillery was a working business, and the one empty warehouse and the old barn were not suitable, that too was useless. The sewing team used the Craigavon barn, and the other outbuildings housed her staff and the remaining horses. No matter how many times she checked the availability of buildings, there was no easy solution other than Kevinishe House.

Bored, angry, and stifled by being indoors, Cate called Rory to heel and headed for the summerhouse. As they drew near, the dog stiffened and then bounded forward. Cate guessed young Charlie was there. On her absences from Craigavon, either Stevie or Charlie saw to the dog. At this time of day Stevie would be at work grooming the horses, so it must be Charlie. Right enough, there he was leaning against the side of the summerhouse.

"Now then, Charlie, I see you're waiting for me. What's wrong?"

"No wrong as such, Miss Cate," Charlie replied while he fondled the dog's ears. "Just a wee thought, you might say, came to mind."

"Come on then, tell me about it." Like all the villagers, the boy would take his time to get to the nub of the matter. It always frustrated her, having to wait till they had described the weather, questioned her on her health and whatever else they could think of, before broaching the important subject.

"Well now — it's like this. You've a shortage of work at the distillery and I'm there just for the learning. Mebbe I could be more useful elsewhere and…"

"What's this all about? I thought you were set on following Fisher into the stillroom."

"Oh aye, I was, but see here, other young ones are away to the war. You stopped me going an I just fancied something else for a change. Speaking of Fisher, Miss Cate. When he was here, rest his soul, he set me to keep an eye on you."

"I know, Charlie, but Bruce MacNishe is nowhere near Kevinishe these days."

"That's as mebbe, but news is that it's him that's away wi' Rhoddy, an yourself will always be in danger from him."

"So, what do you think I should do?"

"How about I could be an assistant to yourself, look after you like, seeing as Mr Dinwoodie is aye away."

"Let me think about it, Charlie."

"Aye well, I'll be waiting to hear from you. I've brought Shona with me. She's in the kitchen wi Cook and Maggie. She's wondering, what with her looking after all our young ones, an Jeannie fit for that now, could she be helping Miss Lizzie in the nursery, and earn some pennies for herself like now she's older?"

Cate was delighted with the suggestion. Extra help for Lizzie would surely go a long way to appease Dinwoodie. "Charlie, that's what I call an excellent idea, so let's get back to the house and talk to her."

As the two of them reached the front of the house, Rory barked at the cart that was drawn up there, with Carter on the ground and Wullie perched on top in his bath chair.

"Now then, what on earth is going on here?"

"I've brought Wullie to see you, Miss Cate, and now young Charlie's here he can give me a lift down with this damty chair." As the three of them manhandled Wullie to the ground, Cate, glanced at the parcel in his hand, and wondered what would be next.

"Would you just look at the state of this!" Wullie waved the dishevelled object at her. "A disgrace it is. Now what would your catalogue customers think of that, Miss Cate?"

74

"Wullie, I know the girls are not expert at their packing, but something tells me this one has had some rough treatment to aid your argument! Come on then, make your point. I presume you haven't gone to all this trouble for nothing."

"You don't need legs to wrap parcels, Miss Cate. Haven't I the two good hands for this kind of work. It's in my blood, just like my father before me. What'd you say to letting me do the wrapping for the sewing girls? I could keep an eye on them for you at the same time. After all yourself is not always here to be doing just that."

Cate realized that here was another problem being solved for her. Wullie had intended to go and live with his cousin, now that Murdo was dead, but working with the sewing girls would not only keep him in the glen but also allow him to pay his rent, so saving his pride. "What a good idea, Wullie!"

"I'll start tomorrow, and you need only see to my bittie baccy for two weeks. After that, if I'm suitable, we can discuss the silver. What do you say?"

"Well, it seems reasonable, but how will you manage it?"

"No bother at all. Carter here will see to it for a share of the baccy, and if it goes well, he'll make a bit to put in his pocket. What do you say to that, Carter?"

"I'll have arms like a caber if it's lifting you and your contraption I'm to be doing. I like a good baccy, mind. I see Himself smoking some choice stuff when he's home, Miss Cate."

"Carter, Dinwoodie has the best there is."

"Fine well me and Wullie know that, Miss Cate, but your parcels will be done right and no mistake."

"Charlie, help these two rogues back into the cart before their price becomes even higher!"

When Cate entered the nursery the boys were playing with Shona, and Lizzie was sewing by the fire. She knelt on the floor and beckoned the boys. "Come on, you two. Over, here."

David, the blonde elder twin needed no encouragement. He ran across the intervening space, collapsing at her feet. Cate picked him up and swung him in the air, much to his gurgling delight. Cam, meanwhile, made his way, standing straight and steady, slowly towards his mother, looking at her all the time. Cate clapped her hands in delight.

"Well done, Cam! No rushing around for you."

His face reddened with pleasure under his shock of blue-black hair, as he raised his arms for his swing around.

"Now then, Shona, how would you like to come and give Lizzie a hand with these two rascals? Will Jeannie cope with your young ones at home?"

"Oh, Miss Cate, I'd like it fine, an they're right bonny bairns, though they're no like our twins — peas in a pod ours are! An Jeannie will do fine."

Cate smiled as the boys returned to their new playmate. "Shona, Mammy," David grabbed his mother's hand for more attention, but, catching sight of Cam playing with a wooden truck, he dropped the hand and rushed to his brother, shouting, "No, Cam. Mine!"

Cam put the truck on the floor and stood watching David pick it up and return to Shona.

Cate was having none of it. "David, give that back to Cam — now!"

David studied his mother's face, shook his head, and smiled.

"I mean it." She watched as he put it behind his back and shook his head again. "Right then, this is what happens." Before he knew it, she'd scooped him up in her arms and, kneeling beside the watchful Cam, removed the truck from his brother and gave it back to him, whereupon David flung himself on the floor and produced a theatrical tantrum which Cate completely ignored. In the meantime, Cam took the toy to Shona and they began playing together, while David, seeing no result from his performance, stayed on the floor and sulked.

Cate took a seat beside Lizzie and the two women murmured quietly about the sewing jobs, Shona, and, uncomfortably for Cate, Dinwoodie's absence. That thought reminded her of another. "Lizzie, do you think your leg could stand a bit of dancing? Everything has been so miserable, with the news from the war, once Dinwoodie's back I thought of inviting everyone to a ceilidh."

"Would they all come? I mean Mr Monteith and Solly, even?"

"It would be important to you if Solly came?" Cate smiled as she answered

"Well, he's almost part of the family isn't he?" Lizzie muttered, head bowed over her sewing, to hide the sudden redness in her cheeks.

"I do believe, Lizzie Balfour, that you've taken a shine to Solly. Now that would be special. Anyone can see the two of you would be good for one another."

"But — but you, you wouldn't mind?"

"Why on earth should I mind, you daft gowk? It's high time you both had partners, and you do like him, don't you?"

"Oh, Cate…"

"Looking at the cheeks of you, I know your answer. Now if he's too shy to get up on the floor, you go and drag him to his feet. There, that's settled then — we might even treat ourselves, and the girls, to new dresses. Oh, and another thing — how about Shona here joining the nursery to help you? Don't think I haven't been aware of how hard you've worked since the boys were born."

"Right enough. She's been real good playing with them since she came today, an mebbe if she had one of the attic rooms…"

"What a good idea, Lizzie. But what about giving her the old linen room next door to the twins' nursery? She can look in on them if there's a night-time problem, and, if needed, she can call for you. Shona, would you like to have a bed here? Lizzie will sort you out time to go home each week?"

"That'd be right fine, Miss Cate. I've niver had a bed to myself."

"Well now, I think that suits all round, Lizzie, don't you?"

"Indeed, an it'll give you time to yourself. You've looked a mite troubled of late."

"You're right there, I have worries at the moment. I thought this new world of ours was won, safe, our struggles over, but I'm afraid…"

"Cate, you were never afraid!"

"Oh, yes I was. I just learned not to show it. Now this war…"

"The war's no that close to us up here, Cate, save for Murdo no coming back."

"You're wrong, Lizzie. I can feel it creeping in, bit by bit and, it's making me quarrelsome. I'm even at odds with Dinwoodie. I must go to him and make up."

"He's a fine man is Mr Dinwoodie, even though he's no the one you wanted back then, but that's no his fault."

"Dear Lizzie, as usual you're right. I'll let you know my plans as soon as they're settled." Both boys now playing quietly with Shona, Cate left the nursery well pleased with the discussion. Why she'd never noticed Lizzie's affection for Solly was strange, 'your mind always on other things' Dinwoodie would have said. Now she must make amends.

At the distillery, taking the mail from Wullie some days later, Cate watched as Angus and the Carter hoisted him aloft on the cart and off they went. Making her way to the office she smiled as she remembered the sewing girls' delight when she'd told them about Wullie. They were never keen on the parcelling and had had no hesitation in accepting him into the sewing team. She still hadn't made up her mind about Charlie, though she'd suggested he'd be welcome to come to the stables from time to time to give Stevie a helping hand. In the meantime, Shona had settled in well at Craigavon. Cate took the account letters to Solly then sat at her own desk to go through the remaining mail. There was another parcel and letter from Alashdair, which she put to one side until she'd cleared her desk. As she left the distillery, having put the parcel in the safe, she realized that with today's letter she now had an excuse to go to Glasgow and pass it on to Dinwoodie.

Cate turned the key in the Hyland house in Glasgow and was glad to hear Snowy, the housekeeper, in the kitchen. With a light knock on the door, she pushed it open.

"Michty me, what a fright you gave me, Mrs Dinwoodie!"

"Snowy, how many times do I have to tell you? I'm just the same now as I was all those years ago when you looked after me when I came out of hospital."

"True, true, lass, but you're his wife now, so it'll be Mrs Dinwoodie in speech, though the girl with the shorn hair will be Miss Cate in my thoughts. Now then, I wasn't expecting you. Not a word has he said about you coming."

"I know. Truth is we had a difference of opinion and we've let it last too long, so I'm here to admit my fault. It's the red hair, I'm told. As Lizzie would say, I have to learn to think before I shout!"

"And how is the wee lass and the twins?"

"The wee lass is all grown up and fallen for Solly, would you believe."

"That's no surprise. I knew that when you were all here together."

"You too! Both Maggie and I have been so blind. Ah! There's the front door. Any chance of tea in the dining room after a discreet period, while I make my peace?"

Smiling, Cate made for the front door, relieved Dinwoodie of his bowler hat and black overcoat and melted into his arms. Her muffled apologies were lost in his fervent kisses and arm in arm they made for the drawing room, just as Snowy appeared with a laden tea tray. Winking at Cate, she smiled and left them to it.

Between mouthfuls, Cate expanded her regrets. "Oh Dinwoodie, I'm truly sorry to have left things this long. Only in the beginning, I was too angry, and then I didn't know where you were. But it's gone on too long, and, as usual, I've had time to see that once again I've been too hasty, though heaven knows I've had worries enough — and you don't know the half of it, I'm afraid."

At this her husband lowered his teacup. "Come now, Cate, you afraid?"

"Oh, not you too! Lizzie doesn't believe me either, though I can't tell her of my fear. I've discovered Bruce MacNishe has sold the portrait of the *Red-headed Woman*!"

"Now you've lost me, Cate."

"The curse, Dinwoodie, I'm sure…"

"Do you truly believe that old tale? Ah, I can see by your expression you do. So now you assume that the fates will deal with the current MacNishes: Bruce, Rhoddy, and you. I can't make you disbelieve anything, but suppose we wait to see what happens. At present you're here and unharmed, even though we don't know exactly where Rhoddy or Bruce are, we do think they are alive. And before you ask, Pearson is still watching the cottage. Come, remember the old maxim: no news is good news."

"Well, I'll try. Oh, I nearly forgot, there's another letter and some more writing from abroad. I've put the parcel in the safe and the letter is in my case. I'll just go and get it."

Letter in his hand, Dinwoodie began to read, again ignoring the greeting.

My dear Cate,

The men are back at Ypres, or 'Wipers' as they call it, for a second battle. This time around it has produced the unthinkable. I had heard a rumour, but it seemed so unlikely that I discounted it. I was in the grounds near a field hospital yesterday when a convoy of ambulances arrived. As staff rushed to unload them I could hardly bear to listen to the screams from the stretchers, never mind look at the poor devils they were transferring to the tents.

I found later the men were all victims of a poison gas the Germans had unleashed. I saw soldiers clutching their throats, eyes streaming, mouths foaming. Somehow then it seemed wrong to be putting all this death and destruction into a manuscript, but I feel that the world has never seen conflict on this scale. It must be told.

When time allows I go to Paris, where I can write up and send mail to you. It is an extraordinary city and such a contrast to life in the forward fighting areas. But I find I need relief from watching, continual moving around and recording such atrocities. There are times when the whole nightmare gets the better of me. God knows how our men stand it.

Alashdair.

Dinwoodie shook his head. "We'll probably never be able to connect to these brave men on their return. I'm sure the people at home here simply don't know or can't imagine the life our troops are leading."

"I know what you mean. How could those in Kevinishe ever believe that their precious soldier relatives would be gassed? Murdo, shredded with bullets and…"

"Come now, Cate. You read the telegram that Wullie got. He was killed outright and didn't suffer. So don't torture yourself."

"Alright, but it does make you wonder about it all." As she watched her husband fold the letter back into the envelope, she tried to erase the picture she'd foreseen. It was no use revealing that she knew exactly how poor Murdo had met his end.

Chapter 10

Seated at his desk in Glasgow with the daily paper, Dinwoodie was appalled. He'd just read the open letter in the Gazette, and the accompanying list was hard to believe. So many of the city's soldiers had died or been injured during the Spring Offensive in the second battle of Ypres. The casualty figures were mounting as each week went past. Cate had been right! Among the dead listed were people he knew and respected. Good friends or merely acquaintances, it mattered not. A swathe of the city's manhood was being destroyed in the continuing fighting. Too old and too necessary to be out there himself, he could barely contain his fury at the utter wastefulness. He'd known this war would happen, had tried to warn others, but they'd scoffed at him. The whole damned thing was ridiculous! Nations in conflict, jealous of others' burgeoning empires, seizing the chance to even old scores, or add new territory.

Later, making his way to yet another memorial service, he wondered just how many more he would have to attend before this dreadful war was over. He was wretched throughout the service and stood in misery while the bugler played the last post and the flag was lowered. As he replaced his bowler, he heard his name. Turning, he saw Lord Monroe detach himself from further up the official party and come towards him.

"Ah, Dinwoodie, this is a bad business indeed."

"It is that, and no end in sight."

"Come, let's sidestep the official lunch, Dinwoodie. I have a nephew, on leave, waiting at home for me. Will you share our lunch with us?"

"I'd be glad to. Anything to get away from the thought of all those now lying God knows where, and for what?"

"My feelings exactly. I take it the faithful Morrison is nearby?"

"Indeed he is, Lord Monroe."

"Come now, Monroe will do. After all, rumour has it that with all your war work you may soon be joining me in the title stakes."

"Away with you! How many erstwhile charcoal burners can you count in your ranks?"

"You never did do yourself justice, Dinwoodie."

Lunch taken, the three men retired to the smoking room and, pipes alight, continued their deliberations on the progress of the war. Introduced to the nephew, Dinwoodie liked him. The man, Ewan, was a military doctor, relieved of front line duties and transferred to a special hospital at Craiglockart in Edinburgh. There he was studying the treatment of shell shock, or neurasthenia as they called it, under the direction of Doctors Rivers, Bryce, and Brock.

For the remainder of the afternoon he held the rapt attention of his elders, with accounts of men returning from the war suffering from this complaint. He also horrified them when he explained that the powers that be on the front line often assumed it was down to cowardice and, some men had even been shot as deserters. When the younger man left to return to his duties, the others smoked in silence for a bit, their minds digesting the earlier conversation. Finally Monroe stood, knocked his pipe out on the fire grate, and turned to Dinwoodie.

"Man. It's barely believable, what the lad was saying. Poor beggars! Fighting for us and being shot for their pains."

"Monroe, I must tell you that Cate and I had a bit of an altercation on this very subject. She has a great friend who nurses at the Infirmary and in the Convent here in Glasgow. They met some time ago, and that's where Cate heard of these particular problems. I have to say that I thought she was overdoing the sympathy when she suggested setting up a hospital to help with the overcrowding here in Glasgow."

"Knowing your wife, I suspect that it might be a case of her heart overruling her head. Nevertheless, it could be worth your while contacting Ewan personally and discussing the matter with him. I'll get his details from my desk. Even if it comes to nothing, your case would be the better for an informed opinion." Monroe left the room, and Dinwoodie had a feeling that Cate might well have been right. He must make amends on his return.

Back in the glen a spot of welcome June sunshine had enticed both Cate and Dinwoodie out for a ride. They headed for the ledge where they'd first met. Hobbling the horses below, they climbed the last few feet and sat in the warmth of the sun. Here, Dinwoodie explained his change of heart about Kevinishe House. Told her all about his lunch in Glasgow and the sobering conversation with the army doctor.

"So Mary Anne had the right of it with all her worries?"

"Sadly, Cate, I now believe she did. When Monroe — he sent you his good wishes by the way — and I were left alone, we discussed your concerns, and he suggested we contact Ewan Brodie, his nephew."

"Will you do it then, Dinwoodie? Contact him with a view to setting up the hospital?"

"I will. Leave it with me. When I go back to Glasgow I'll get in touch with him. Though do remember this would come under the auspices of the army medical people and they may have other ideas."

"You mean, even though they are short of medical facilities, they might not allow it? That seems ridiculous."

"Cate, we've no idea what they'll think. I'm just suggesting caution. I don't want you to even mention it to anyone, until we are certain we would be allowed to do this." Taking her hand in his, he continued. "I've admitted I was wrong and I do understand both your desire to help and your itching to forge ahead with the project, but you must do as I say."

"I will, though …"

Pulling her into his arms, he kissed her before saying, "No, Cate, no 'though'. Now come kiss me again and let's continue our ride before the sun goes."

In France, Rhoddy wondered what they were doing in Kevinishe. Not that he wanted to go back, but he was fed up being stuck here in the French countryside. It'd all been so exciting when they'd arrived in Paris. At first they'd stayed in hotels. Then his father had rented an apartment. That'd been exciting. A real home in a foreign country and his mother knew nothing about it! His father often stayed away for a night or two on business trips and he quite enjoyed that too. Wandered about on his own, then came back when he was ready, just like a grown-up! Later they'd moved to the country. Driven to a sort of castle first, he'd been impressed, but they only stayed a week, and after much jabbering in French, they'd come to this poky little cottage place. It wasn't even as nice as the Black House had been after it was fixed up by the old Laird — he'd never known the man was his great grandfather! He'd been brought up as the lawyer's son and his name was McAlister, though it should by rights be MacNishe — another thing his mother had not allowed him to have! Now, though, he'd got the better of her, because he knew who his real father was, and the best bit was that his mother didn't even know he did!

Once settled in the country, his father only stayed for a couple of months before leaving him holed up with — he eyed the couple across the room — this sullen pair, and that had been ages ago. He'd tried to ask the woman when his father was coming back, but she just shrugged her shoulders. He hadn't dared to question the man, because he frightened him. One day, when he'd pushed his plate of uneaten food away — it was disgusting — he'd thought the man was going to hit him. Thinking about it, Rhoddy remembered he was hungry, so he decided he'd make for the village they'd passed on their way to this awful hole. He opened his drawer where his father had slung some money for him before he left and scooped out several French coins and notes.

He avoided the old woman, her husband had gone out, and made for the village. The few people he saw on the way barely looked at him so he trudged on certain he couldn't be far away from some decent food. A lorry passed him and then stopped. He rushed after it and yanked the passenger door open. To his horror it was the man from the cottage and he made him get into the lorry.

Bruce's 'business' was searching for sex. On his latest visit to a bordello, looking for the particular brand of sex he enjoyed, he soon found himself outside again. How dare that slovenly old Madame throw him out! It was a brothel for God's sake. He'd just begun to slap the frightened girl around and the old bag had come rushing in. Another time he'd remember to lock the door — except, he wouldn't be going back there. In fact he'd been removed from a few of these houses lately, and now the better ones wouldn't even let him in, no matter how much money he offered. Time to seek pastures new. His funds were running a bit low, and he'd have to deliver another payment to the estate workers who were looking after Rhoddy. He couldn't have the boy along with him, as he preferred to move around to avoid trouble. Well he'd go back to the cheap room he was renting and write a telegram to Stuffy. His old chum would soon instruct the chateau people to hand over some more finance.

A week later, flush now with the latest funds arranged by Stuffy, Bruce headed for the cottage, where he doled out just enough francs to keep the old couple quiet, and reassured a sullen Rhoddy that they'd soon find somewhere to live together, before taking off to explore the country nearer the fighting. He'd no desire to get within any danger, but he'd heard the officers had specially selected houses where the women were clean and only too glad to offer themselves to the heroic fighting men. Quite right to! After all, the Allies were saving their country for them!

Left on the ground the bombardment was so loud that Bruce almost turned back, but the wagon that had taken him this far was fast disappearing amid the straggling, bewildered peasants heading in the other direction. His first need was to find a room before he investigated the delights of the bordellos.

By the evening, a disgruntled Bruce was seated in a dingy bar surveying the men in uniform milling around there. Three of the officers' houses had already refused him entry that afternoon. Why hadn't he thought about finding a uniform and some information about regiments and things? Well, he couldn't see himself getting any free drinks or uniforms here, and, as there was nothing else on offer, he might as well have stayed in the cottage with his son. Then his luck changed as a rather drunken soldier reeled towards him.

"Cheer up. You look full of the misheries. Letsh's have 'nother drink." Through his hiccups he leaned against the counter, spread his money on it, and put his head on his folded arms, as he muttered, "Two doublshs barman, vite, vite!" as Bruce drank both doubles, the barman gestured at the snoring soldier and pointed to the door. Only to willing to oblige, Bruce dragged the man upright and staggered out with him.

He chose a dingy cobbled alleyway, before setting to work on the drunk. With much pulling and pushing the job was done. Bruce stood for a moment looking at the near naked soldier and couldn't believe how simple the whole thing had been — with the fellow's uniform under his arm, the two doubles warming his innards, and the meagre amount of cash he'd fished out of the man's pockets, he left him lying in the alleyway, and, well pleased with the night's work, made for his lodgings. First thing tomorrow he'd move back to the cottage and keep out of sight for a bit, however unpleasant the old couple's company might be. Anyway, it wouldn't do any harm to spend some time with Rhoddy. He'd neglected him of late.

As Cate shut the front door at Craigavon, she heard the noise from the kitchen and made her way there. The twins, Shona and Lizzie were seated round the table while Cook and Maggie danced attendance on them.

"Cate, Cate…"

"David, that's no right to call your mother by her name — a wee boy like you."

"Don't worry, Maggie, he only does it to gain attention. Ignore him. I do. Right now I don't much care what he calls me. What I need is a cup of tea. No, don't move, Shona, I'll perch here by the range."

"Mamma, I was on Wizzy." Cam whispered.

"Were you? I bet Gregor was pleased."

"He gave me a sweetie."

"Then you must have been good. Well done, Cam."

Cate enjoyed the rosy cheeks as the boy flushed with pleasure at her comments, but was startled as he suddenly cried out and turned towards his brother, who was twisting his arm.

"David Dinwoodie! I'm beginning to get tired of your constant wish to be the centre of attention. Leave the table, and go up to the nursery at once."

David ignored her and carried on eating. Cate crossed to the table, really angry now, picked him up and, with a shake, sent him scurrying to the door, calling after him, "I will not have you bullying Cam like that!"

"I aright…" the younger twin began, but his mother interrupted.

"Oh Cam, you mustn't let him get away with everything. Next time he nips, kicks or bites, do the same to him. He'll soon stop if you hit back. Now finish your tea and I'll go up and change ready for your story when Lizzie's bathed you."

Cate made her way upstairs, followed David to the nursery, and pushed him through the door when she caught up with him. "Sit here and wait for Lizzie. Tonight and for the rest of the week, Cam will choose the story — no, I don't want to hear another word. One thing I'm quite sure about is that I'll have no bullying in this house." Going to wash and change before her evening meal, Cate's thoughts were of that other bully, Bruce MacNishe, and her son Rhoddy. Where were they now?

Through the fingers of mist on the stillroom window, where she'd been going over the contents of the distillery's bonded warehouses with Stuart Monteith, she saw Wullie manoeuvre his bath chair through the gates. Cate wondered if her erstwhile postman was about to deliver another letter from Alashdair. As she made her way down to greet him she was overcome with a great feeling of affection for the man. To have escaped death in the Post Bus when it was buried by the rock fall from the quarry had been a miracle, but it had cost him his legs and a job. She'd had to get permission from the Post Authorities to install Solly's cousin from Glasgow to drive the new Post Bus and deliver the mail, but she'd kept the distillery mail for him, so he'd still be Wullie the Post. She'd also persuaded him to move in with Murdo, and now with his death another pinion of Wullie's life had crumbled.

"More bad news is it, Wullie?" Cate said, as she glanced at the telegram in the man's hand. "How many more must we get before this wretched war is over?"

"Had the black one this morning. Sent to me seeing as I'm his only kin — it's my cousin from Dundee, Miss Cate. Another one with no even a funeral or a grave to go to for a wee craic! Besides, how can a Highland soul lie in peace in some foreign soil? An there's another letter from foreign parts for yourself."

Cate ignored the question, took the mail and, offered practical sympathy. "Come on in, Wullie. We'll have a dram of Craeg Dhu to send your cousin on his way. They're all special to someone, those friends and relations who've gone, and hard to replace." Cate drained her glass as she watched the man struggle with this new grief, added to the already great loss of his best friend.

"Mind, Miss Cate, I'd rather sleep with the seaweed on the shore and have Murdo back, than be in his empty home."

Drams drunk, she watched Wullie make his way to the cottage that was now his by right. It had been a great relief to her solving the rent problem and, though he missed Murdo, at least he was enjoying his work with the girls. But even a distant cousin would have to be mourned and would remind him of Murdo's death. She couldn't help wondering what would be next, and what Alashdair would have to say. With Dinwoodie away she decided to open the letter and find out

Dearest Girl,

As this year draws to a close and bad weather sets in, the news is as bad if not worse. Our soldiers, when I get near enough, complain that they need more guns, more equipment and, most importantly, more men if they are to have a chance to make any real progress against the Germans.

In this weather, I seem to be wet all the time, so I'm leaving the Front for now. I feel no progress will be made until the New Year, and even that will depend on the weather not deteriorating further!

I have had an offer from an American paper to write a column for them; so will concentrate on that in a comfortable room in Paris for the foreseeable future, now that I will be able to afford it!

Alashdair.

As she folded the letter she was cheered by the fact that Alashdair had managed to get some paid work, but worried at the thought that the soldiers over there were not being provided with the necessary equipment to wage war. When Dinwoodie returned she'd discuss it with him, perhaps he'd have more up to date knowledge than Alashdair had. She hoped so. It was dreadful to think of their soldiers with not enough weapons to fight!

In Glasgow, Ewan Brodie looked out of place amid the female chattering in The Willow Tearoom. As his eyes alighted on Dinwoodie he hesitated, and drew a sharp breath, when he saw there was a woman seated with him. Dinwoodie stood to greet the young doctor and introduce his wife.

Cate had seen him pause when he'd caught sight of her, and now she could feel the man's antipathy as he shook hands. Tea and cakes ordered the men opened the discussion. As the talking continued, during which time they ignored her, she couldn't help thinking it would have been wiser if Dinwoodie had warned the arrogant doctor she'd be there. She'd had enough contact with men who didn't believe women should be in business, but this was her idea and she intended to be part of it.

"I take no credit for the original idea. It was Cate's." Dinwoodie said.

Trying to be polite Cate said, "Well partly, Doctor Brodie, but my attention was drawn to the problem by a friend of mine. She's a nursing sister in the Infirmary here in Glasgow, but would be very willing to come up to Kevinishe to nurse instead."

"I'm afraid you've quite the wrong idea how the army goes on, Mrs Dinwoodie, and the nature of the work I undertake. It is dealing with tortured minds rather than broken bones and I fear your staffing suggestions are unrealistic. If you'll excuse me, I have to return to duty. I'm grateful for your proposal, Mr Dinwoodie, but I must make it quite clear, here and now, that it cannot involve civilians, especially women. I've already had words with my superiors and as soon as I have more information I'll contact you, but I fear we may not be able to take the idea further if the ladies are to be involved. Good day to you, sir."

As they watched the doctor weave his way between the tables, scattering baleful glances at the predominantly female customers, Cate took a deep breath but before she could speak, Dinwoodie leant across the table and took her hand. "I know, you're adding him to all the other men who've underestimated you, and I apologise. It's my fault — I should have warned him that you came with the building, but when I spoke to him on the telephone he was so keen on the idea that he didn't give me time to explain."

With a sweet smile, Cate said, "I shouldn't worry about it. I certainly won't." Dinwoodie groaned inwardly. A ranting and raging Cate, apart from being a magnificent sight, was easier to cope with than this demure façade. He wasn't sure, as they left, whether he should be sorrier for himself or the doctor.

Ewan Brodie drove back to Edinburgh in a foul temper. He neither liked women nor knew how to handle them. He'd lost his mother as a young boy. His soldier father had left him with his ancient nanny until old enough to be carted around army barracks where he was looked after by his father's batman and indulged by the brigade soldiers. Boarding school, university, medical school, all followed the same pattern: men, men, and more men. As a result he'd always been wary of women and now Dinwoodie's offer that had had him imagining all the things he could do in a unit of his own had been dashed when the woman had made it quite clear that she intended, along with some female friend, to be involved in his dream. He'd seen enough of the upper class women with their sparse three months nursing training, when as VADs they were stationed at the field hospital. There they'd been, in his opinion, of little use, and now here were two more getting in the way of this new opportunity. He'd already thought ahead to his staffing, and knew exactly who he would like to join him in the new hospital, but how to get rid of the women?

Part Two

1916 The Hospital

Chapter 11

Cate woke and, finding the house in silence, dressed in her riding breeches, thick chunky roll-neck sweater, and shooting jacket. Her stockinged feet made no sound on the oak staircase as she made her way to the boot room. Glad to be outside in this misty May morning, she was saddling up Midnight as Stevie appeared.

"You're early this morning, Miss Cate. I'd have done that if I'd known."

"I know you would, but I woke and the moors seemed to be calling. What you could do is let them know in the house I'm up and away."

"You take care now. Midnight has been a bit frisky these last couple of days."

"Just like myself then, Stevie! We'll have a good gallop in that case."

Stevie watched as she led the stallion out, muzzled her nose to his, whispered in his ear, and then leapt on his back. The groom shook his head. In all his stable years he'd never seen the like of his current employer.

Later Cate had just eased Midnight down to a walk when an unknown horse came charging past her, loose stirrups flying in the wind. There seemed no point in pursuing the beast, but somewhere ahead there must be a rider who'd been unseated and perhaps injured. Cate squeezed Midnight's flanks and urged him forward. Standing high in the stirrups, she raked the moor from side to side until her eyes caught a movement in a bank of brambles. It might well be a deer caught, but it was worth investigating. As she neared the spot, the faint cries from inside the thicket had her hurriedly dismounting to pick her way to the centre, glad of the stout shooting jacket that withstood the thorns. There, with her rear pinioned firmly in the thicket, was a stout elderly female.

Cate, taken aback by the sight, stood for a moment struggling with a mixture of mirth and astonishment that quickly disappeared at the gruff command from the victim.

"If you've come this way just to stand there, you might as well leave!"

"I'm sorry it's — well I wasn't expecting…"

"I don't give a damn what you were expecting! Just get me out of these infernal thorns!"

After a lengthy struggle, Cate, wishing she'd also worn her sturdy riding gloves, managed to remove the majority of the wicked branches, but the woman had also become wedged in what had once been a rabbit burrow, which her weight in landing had collapsed. However Cate tugged and strained, she was unable to lever the much heavier woman upright. Letting go, Cate turned to leave.

"Don't go. Please don't go."

Responding to the plaintive cry, Cate faced the older woman and patted her shoulder. "Wheesht now, I was never going to leave you. Look, my horse is out there on the moor. I'll walk him as close as I can, and then we'll get you out."

Reassured by the close contact, the victim recovered some of her bite. "You'll not make me into a horse drag!"

"That's better! A bit of your feistiness will be useful in the long run. Be still now till I get back."

With Midnight as near to the victim as possible, Cate slipped the reins over his head and, unclasping one of them, retraced her steps. "See, we'll wrap this round you and I'll hold the other end." When she was ready, Cate called to Midnight. "Back now, b-a-a-ack. Good boy! Slowly now! Back, back…" Then, with a sudden rush, the stallion backed away and the stout body shot out of the hole, taking Cate scrambling after her. They collapsed on the heather as the horse, job done, came to an abrupt halt.

Picking herself up with a hearty laugh, Cate patted the horse, as she said, "Good boy, well done."

"Fine! You see to the animal, while I'm still stretched full length on this wretched Highland soil!"

"Ah, but you're free, and Midnight needs our thanks, especially as he's to carry us home."

"If you think I'm getting up on another horse this day, you're gravely mistaken, young Miss!"

"The name is Cate. And you are?"

"Mrs Campbell-Broughton-Stuart."

"That's quite a mouthful, Mrs Campbell Whatsit. But, back to your predicament, you've had a fall and I'll need to check you over. You're also wet through. The morning mist takes time to dry deep in the bushes, so what you need is my home at Craigavon, hot food, whisky, bath, and dry clothes. No argument now! Come on, give me your hands."

With a good deal of effort, Cate finally had the older woman aboard Midnight. Clipping the rein back on she let it dangle, and with a running bound was on the horse's back, much to the astonishment of the bewildered passenger.

"What are you — some kind of circus performer? One thing's for sure — you're no lady, dressed in men's breeches and leaping about. What extraordinary behaviour!"

Cate's laugh was her only answer as she collected the reins and urged the horse into a walk. Nearing Craigavon she realised that her passenger had gone limp in front of her. Holding the woman firmly on the saddle, she made for the front door. Leaning gingerly, while still holding her burden with one arm, she grabbed the bell pull and was almost unseated as the woman jerked awake at the jangling.

Much later in the kitchen, swathed in Dinwoodie's bath robe, cosseted by Maggie and Cook, Mrs Campbell-Broughton-Stuart clasped her hands round a steaming cup of tea, having first swallowed, somewhat grudgingly, one of Cate's possets of spiced hot milk laced with Craeg Dhu. As a refreshed Cate appeared, it was the visitor's turn to be amazed.

"Why, in the name of all that's wonderful, would anyone choose to run and leap about as a hoyden when you can look like that?"

"It's a long story, but now I hear Stevie at the door, back from Laggan House with your clean garments. Once you've retired to dress, I've another unorthodox surprise for you," said Cate with a mischievous laugh. As Maggie helped the visitor up the stairs, Cook with a severe look on her face, remonstrated with her mistress. "Miss Cate, you're wicked you are. Now what are you about?"

"Cook, I've had Lady Jemima's racing sulky gathering cobwebs in the back of the stables for years, so I've a mind to transport Madame to Laggan House in it."

"You canna do that!"

"Why not? I'll guarantee she'll be dressed in ladylike fashion. Anyway, she's not fit to ride a horse again today. She's taken a real fright though she'd never admit it. Don't worry I'll be 'verra carefull' as Angus would say."

With the entire staff on the doorstep, anxious expressions abounding, Cate kept a straight face as Stevie helped their visitor, looking as if she might prefer to have stayed in the bramble thicket, aboard the slender sulky

A week later a purple Daimler pulled up at Craigavon, and the chauffeur escorted Mrs Campbell-Broughton-Stuart to the door and rang the bell. Maggie opened it and ushered the visitor into the drawing room.

"Please tell that young hoyden I'm here to express my thanks."

As Maggie hesitated the older woman smiled. "Come now, I'm not here to upbraid her. Indeed I realise how lucky I am with all of you for near neighbours."

"It's no good, whatever you've come for. She's no here. She's working." Maggie retorted.

"Working — as in earning her living? Surely not! I mean this house, the…"

"It doesna change the fact that she's working, for all she owns the distillery and a good part of the glen besides."

"I do believe, Maggie isn't?" At the affirmative nod the visitor continued. "As I said, I do believe there's an excellent story lurking here. Shall we forego the splendour of this room and head for the kitchen? I've fond memories of blessed hot tea and scones." Waving Maggie before her, the two women startled Cook, who recovered quickly, filled the giant teapot on the stove and opened the oven door on the day's baking of scones.

For the next couple of hours the visitor was in turn delighted, amazed, and enchanted with the lengthy conversation. She thanked Maggie and Cook with the warmest of praise, and left chuckling as she was escorted to the front door, having left her card, with a handwritten note on it on the silver salver in the hall.

As Cate regaled her husband, newly back from his travels, with the tale of the sulky, she enjoyed his ringing laughter.

"And have you returned the visit?"

"Oh yes, but the bird has flown. Gone back south apparently, which is a pity, as I was quite taken by her. In her own way she reminded me of Lady Jemima — somewhat the same but different if you see what I mean."

"You were fond of her, weren't you?"

"Lady Jemima? Oh yes, she did a great deal for me and at the end we were close. I miss her in my life, Dinwoodie. I should have been there to save her, but…"

"My dear Cate, you can't be the saving of everyone you care for. Fate has to have some part in it. Now we've lost the laughter we began with, and these days it's too precious to waste."

"I'm sorry, but I am a little sad at thinking I may not see Mrs Whatsit again."

"Who on earth is she, Cate?"

"It's her, from Laggan House. A great mouthful of a name she had — I think it was Mrs Campbell-Broughton-Stuart.

"Don't despair. She may well turn up again. I see we've another letter from the Scribbler, so lets find out how accurate the news over here is. I must say, like you, I feel what he sends is very much more authentic" Dinwoodie opened the letter and began to read.

The Western Front, March 1916

My dearest Cate,

The American newspaper work has kept me busy these last few months. While doing some research for that, I was injured. It happened when I was travelling along a road with some troops who were making for a train and home leave, when a lone German plane strafed us. Everyone flung themselves into ditches, behind carts, anywhere that would provide some sort of cover. A good number of us were shot.

French nuns who arrived on the scene were wonderful. They helped us into their nearby convent and dressed our wounds. They took such care of me, considering I was neither French nor a soldier, I felt obliged to stay on and help in any way I could once my wound had healed. For me, the death of my mother and then my father's drunken race to join her, made me feel

that religion had no real place in my young life. Yet in the convent here I saw such goodness, such strength of belief, that I almost felt drawn into it. These women, and other civilians as well, are having a dreadful time, and yet they display such courage in a quiet and determined way, despite being permanently under the threat of their land being over-run by the enemy. This has given me much to write about, and will portray the civilian role in the war.
Alashdair.

"Poor Alashdair, I wondered why we'd not heard from him lately. Do you think he'll be all right? Perhaps he'll come back."

"He seems confident that he's over it, and I doubt he'll return before there is peace. Remember he is writing about the war. He could hardly leave the end, whatever it may be, out of a novel."

"With all this writing, do you think he will get it published?"

"I imagine he'll have no difficulty in doing so, Cate. After all, it'll be topical for a brief period once the war is over and before the world moves on." As he spoke, an uncomfortable thought crossed his mind. To get the book published the Scribbler would have to be reunited with the work held in Kevinishe. Would he come to collect it in person?

"I know we've heard most of this, but somehow reading his letters, knowing he's there, makes it — more real, nearer somehow. I suppose everyone who has family fighting must feel the same."

"You regard him as family, Cate?"

"In a strange sense I suppose I do. We were very close at one time."

Dinwoodie folded the letter and, as he could see she was deep in thought, he made his way to his study, hoping it was the atrocities of war that occupied her mind rather than her erstwhile relationship with the Scribbler.

At long last Kirsty and Donald Uig were being married. As they stood in front of the old barn, where Cate had given them a reception, she manoeuvred Lizzie in front of her and, with a nod to Kirsty, stood back. The wedding bouquet arced in Lizzie's direction, but she made no move to catch it and one of the visiting cousins grabbed it at the last moment. Cate shrugged her shoulders in Kirsty's direction. Well, at least they'd tried. The wedding couple were manhandled onto the Carter's wagon and waved a hasty goodbye to the others, who then returned to the old barn to enjoy the remainder of the spread provided by Cate.

"Miss Cate, you've a grin on you that says you've mischief afoot."

"Indeed I have, Wullie, and thank you for keeping the pair of them away from the cottage these last few days. It gave me time to get everything in, with only Angus, the Carter and you in the secret."

"Well now, we werna exactly into the secret — only keeping them out of the way like. Are we to know now what it was all about?"

"Not for the next five minutes or so, Wullie. By then Kirsty will be hollering at the barn door." She'd barely finished her explanation when the bride returned, and rushed towards Cate.

"What— how — when...?"

"It's my wedding present to you both," she added as Donald Uig joined his wife. "I'll not be denied this pleasure, so it's no use the pair of you saying anything. Come, everybody, a dram in your hand and Kirsty here can lead the women to welcome them to her new home. She's waited long enough!"

"Miss Cate..."

"Shoost now! Look at her face, man. That's all the thanks I need. I just gave what I knew would bring her pleasure."

"I'll say it anyway, Miss Cate. It was a blest wind that blew you back to Kevinishe, and may you never leave!"

"I'll tell you what, Donald Uig. On the day I die, I charge you with seeing the coopers make the box to hold my earthly remains from the broken barrels in the distillery yard and line it with moss and heather from the moor. Then the box can be put in the earth beside Fisher, who was as near as any family, to keep me company, so I'll have Kevinishe and the flavour of Craeg Dhu to comfort me on my final journey. Until that day, I may roam, but I'll never leave, and here's my hand on it." As they spat on their hands before clasping them, Cate sniffed and said, "Now I'm away to see to your bride before you have me weeping." And to the astonishment of the curious onlookers, she gave Donald Uig a quick hug, before she left to join the party of admiring females in the house.

By the end of summer the diversion of the wedding and the newly furnished house had faded into the annals of the glen, and everyday life continued, though Cate was becoming increasingly frustrated at the lack of movement on the hospital project. Either the misogynist army doctor had not contacted Dinwoodie or her husband was keeping quiet. Pacing around her study the walls seem to fold in on her. With a disgruntled snort, she made her way upstairs to change into her riding clothes. She might as well be miserable on the moors.

Bringing Satan to a walk, she realised that Laggan House was nearby. Well, it's not as though her breeches would be anything new to the woman, should she be at home, and the staff were bound to have either noticed her or heard of her unorthodox apparel. Dismounting, she rang the bell, and stepped back to get a good look at the outside of the stern-looking building.

"Do you intend to stay out there all day?"

Cate was delighted to hear her voice, but couldn't help the impulse to tease the owner. "Answering your own door, a great lady like yourself!"

"You, Madame, are impertinent. I caught sight of you from my window and shooed the girl away. Now stop dawdling and get yourself in here — and, by the way, I'm delighted to see you. Even though you're in hoyden mode, you must stay to lunch."

With the meal over, both women confessed to being bored and when, Mrs Campbell-Broughton-Stuart heard of Cate's plan for a hospital, her battle to get her husband's approval for the scheme, and her annoyance with the army doctor, she quizzed her on all the details.

"I'm cross because, now Dinwoodie has agreed I could be doing something to help in this war, but that woman-hating Doctor Ewan Brodie has said he'd never work…"

Her hostess' laughter interrupted Cate's tirade.

"What's so funny? I assure you it's the absolute truth. He's a…"

"Cate, I know who you're talking about. Indeed, I not only know him — he's related to me! And I couldn't agree more with your sentiments."

"Oh, just as well you stopped me before I really got going then!"

"Let me fill you in on young Ewan." With that she proceeded to outline her nephew's history, finishing by saying. "After his father, Cuthbert is the only other person he rates."

"Who's Cuthbert, and what a poor choice of name for a man."

"You've put your foot in your mouth again! Cuthbert is no less a person than my brother, Lord Munroe."

"But he's a wonderful man! I know him."

"There we are then — we're destined to be friends! I too think my brother is a wonderful man."

"I'd like that. I used to know someone like you, and I miss her."

"Gone to the Almighty has she?"

"Yes."

"Right, that should take us neatly through the afternoon. So let's have the tale."

By the time they'd finished afternoon tea and Cate was getting ready to leave, her neighbour surprised her by asking for more details about the proposed hospital.

"There's not much more I can tell you. Oh, I've a whole batch of drawings, costings, some suggested possible changes to the interior of the house, and groundwork stuff, but grounded is what it's likely to be now that that man says no women. What can I do?"

"Since he doesn't want anything to do with you, why don't you do it without him?"

"But the army…"

"My dear girl, by the time this war is over there won't be enough hospital beds for all the casualties. The army will be laying claim to all kinds of buildings to fulfil their needs."

"So I could just set up on my own?"

"Not quite. Come, we'll ring for some more tea and I'll tell you how to get it up and running. You don't need Ewan, but you will need help."

Chapter 12

Cate left the distillery and rode home in time for the twins' tea and her husband's arrival home. Although a week had gone by since her meeting with Mrs Campbell-Broughton-Stuart, she was still brimming with enthusiasm and couldn't wait to tell Dinwoodie about it. She'd once threatened to do it on her own, but that had never been an option since Kevinishe House belonged to him. She knew he was not always sure she divided her energies in the right way, but when Ewan Brodie backed it, he'd agreed the scheme was a good idea. Now, with her neighbour's ideas, he'd surely continue to support her, wouldn't he?

Bounding up the stairs, Cate found her husband already in his study arranging papers from his case onto the desk. After a brief hug, she launched into the Laggan House discussion, emphasising points, barely stopping to take a breath, eyes fixed on his face, desperate to gauge his reaction. When he made no comment, Cate couldn't contain herself.

"Well, Dinwoodie, what do you think?"

"I think it would be a good idea if you let me get in the door before you…"

"But Maggie said you've been back for ages."

"Oh yes, at least half an hour!"

"Well?"

"I won't be hurried. Let me think about it. Patience was never one of your virtues, I'm afraid."

With a heavy sigh she made for the door. The visit to Laggan House had so lifted her sagging spirits that for once her troubles hadn't been at the forefront of her mind. She should have waited until after the evening meal. Then, with his pipe alight, he might have been more amenable. In her disappointment she almost missed the chuckle behind her.

"Oh, all right. If you've Lord Munroe's sister, no less, for a patron, I suspect the pair of you will do it anyway. So, my dear, you have my blessing."

Cate turned and ran towards him. "You! I thought you — " she beat her hands on his chest as he continued to smile while grappling with her arms.

"Enough woman! I've agreed — there's no need to beat the life out of me!"

"Thank you, Dinwoodie. Oh, thank you! It's so good not to be at odds with you."

"Now then, away and see to your duties. It's rare that we don't agree, but you must admit there are times you have to be reined in!" Dinwoodie thanked the heavens for Mrs Whatsit. With all the twists and turns of ill fortune swirling around Cate of late, it was wonderful to see, as she left to feed the boys, her face once more illuminated by her special smile. With a smile of his own, Dinwoodie returned to his unpacking, while sparing a thought for the unfortunate Ewan Brodie, whose hospital plans were about to be torpedoed by two of the ladies he so despised!

On watch for yet another weary day Pearson recognised the lorry trundling towards him and raised his hand to stop it. Were MacNishe and the boy inside? He'd soon find out. As it drew to a halt a few yards in front of him, he could see the back was empty. Opening the passenger door Pearson found the man from the cottage was alone, so he asked for a lift to the village. With a reluctant nod of the head the Frenchman agreed.

As they drove on, the man admitted he'd made a mistake in not accepting the offer of cash for Rhoddy when it was offered. Pearson was about to renew the offer to him, when the man shook his head, saying the butler from the chateau had appeared the night before with an envelope for the boy's father, and sometime in the night the pair had left the cottage. The Frenchman told Pearson he knew the letter contained money, for it'd happened before when the man had paid him for the lodgings from it. Not this time though. They'd run out on him, and his guess was that they'd head for Paris.

Later, clutching the loaf and bottle of wine he'd bought in the local boulangerie, a disgruntled Pearson made for the bus stop, where he hoped to get transport to a mainline station. As he waited for what looked like a non-existent bus, he was furious. Once again the quarry had evaded him, and now he'd have to let his employer know he'd let MacNishe get the better of him again. At least he had some information for Mr Dinwoodie — whoever owned the chateau was helping MacNishe with funds. And it seemed likely that they were heading for

Paris or perhaps the ferry for England. That would give him time to find out where they actually were. Drops of rain that rapidly turned into a heavy shower had him soaked in minutes. It was all he needed to complete his miserable day.

Dinwoodie tapped his pen on his chin as he studied the rows of figures his accountant had sent him. The amounts were embarrassingly healthy. He knew he'd only produced what he'd been asked to do, but as thousands were dying in this damned awful war with the products he was providing, his profit made him feel uncomfortable.

A knock on the door was a welcome distraction from his uneasy thoughts. Maggie bustled in with his tea tray and laid it on the table by the fire. "I've put it there for you, so's you'll have to get up for it — you've been sitting that long, your limbs will be stiff."

"Thank you, Maggie. Have all the dress decisions been made, or is it too soon to come out?" he asked with a smile.

"As far as I can tell, every gown she has isn't suitable and she's no in a very good mood, so I would stay quiet in here until all the rummaging around is over, if I were you." Maggie answered as she made for the door.

Thinking of the benefit ball that all the fuss was about, he decided he'd up his contribution by some margin and that would help to ease his conscience. He rose to get his tea, but the door burst open and a red-faced Cate entered.

"I'm not going, Dinwoodie! I don't know anything about eating and dancing for folks to give money. Think of all those high-born ladies and their men, all speaking as though they've pebbles in their mouths, and me none the wiser about all the goings on." Cate reached the tray, leant past her husband, and began to butter a scone.

"That, Cate Dinwoodie, is my tea you're launching into."

"Truth is, I'm not one for all this wining and dining, and I've no idea what to wear, what to say — and I've to be up on a platform at the end!"

"May I remind you that you once stood in the distillery grounds and held a very large audience spellbound while you laid Fisher to rest."

"That was different — they were my people. I belonged both with them and to them. What do I know of these strangers down south?"

With that, Cate proceeded to eat the scone and pour herself a cup of tea.

"Why don't you have Mrs Campbell-Broughton-Stuart over for dinner and ask her advice. She'll soon put you right."

"Oh, do you think so? What if she thinks I'm being foolish, Dinwoodie?"

"She probably will, because my dear wife, you're making too much of it. If you want this hospital, you need to engage the great and the good — get their backing, winkle the necessary funds and goodwill out of them, and move this project forward."

Taking the second scone with her, as she refilled her cup, Cate nodded and left. Dinwoodie gave a rueful glance at the now empty tray and rang for Maggie. He was smiling as she came in.

"Are you finished then? That didn't take long! You usually leave it till its gone stone cold."

"I'm afraid Cate's consumed the lot. Never heard a word I said, just paced round the study as she told me why she couldn't possibly go to Glasgow!"

"We're all near moithered, the state she's got us in. Will she go, do you think, sir?"

"Oh yes, she'll go, and I've no doubt I'll be standing at the back of the room amazed by her performance. Now more tea, if you please, Maggie, and let's hope the days romp past."

"Indeed, and amen to that! I never thought I'd say I'd be glad to see her leave for Glasgow, but it's fair tiring just watching her, and now I'll refresh your tray."

Next morning, Maggie called Dinwoodie to the phone and as she handed it to him said, "It's your secretary Sheena, sir."

When the call ended he replaced the receiver, and with a worried frown went to Cate's study.

"I thought you were supposed to be working hard this morning/"

"I was but that phone call was for me. Pearson's…"

"With news? Oh at last, Dinwoodie!"

"My dear Cate, it's neither the good news you hanker for nor is it entirely bad."

"What then?"

"He's been unable to get Rhoddy away from the cottage."

"That's not good news. Why doesn't he do something?"

"Because, my dear, they're no longer there."

"You mean he's missed them again?"

"I'm afraid so, but we do know not only that the cottage they've been staying in is part of a large estate, but whoever owns it has apparently been financing MacNishe."

"McPhail?"

"It might be, but at least it does give us something to investigate. The other crumb of information is that this has been going on ever since MacNishe arrived in France. Oh, and by the way, they left without paying for their lodgings. Crept out in the night as soon as he got the money."

"That doesn't surprise me! But where are they now?"

"Sheena says Pearson will get in touch as soon as he knows for definite. He thought they might be heading for Paris again. Who knows — perhaps MacNishe has had enough of France? He might even be making for the ferry and then London."

"But he might not, and even then we've still got to find him."

"Come on, Cate, try to be positive. If he reappears in this country I'll make sure the law gets to know about it. They'll soon deal with MacNishe. I'm tired of existing on diverse scraps of information. The worry is too much for both of us, and thinking of that swine MacNishe in the hands of the law is a comforting thought."

As the door closed behind him, Cate could find no comfort in his words. Listening to his reasoning she could feel the fear creeping over her. The mere mention of the law made her think of the menacing figure of McPhail. Where did he fit into all of this? Was he involved in Bruce's dash to France? For some reason she didn't think so. That had all the marks both of Bruce's arrogance and his stupidity. After all, taking the boy away could be a criminal offence, or maybe it wasn't, since he was indeed Rhoddy's father. Fettes had told Dinwoodie that Bruce had simply said he was removing the boy. Perhaps he'd also misled McPhail. The whole idea of pursuit, law courts, witness statements, just to have her son home where he belonged seemed incongruous. Though she was desperate to have Rhoddy home, she was equally desperate to avoid the ignominy of having to have her earlier life subject to public scrutiny.

In the last two weeks the Mistress of Craigavon had driven those around her half mad with all her shenanigans about the ball. Now, with only a few days to go, she couldn't be found.

"You've looked everywhere, Maggie? You're quite certain she's not skulking in the house somewhere?"

"That she's not. I've even sent young Charlie up to the old Black House on the moor, and she's no there. Surely she's no feart and has run away?"

"Kevinishe House? Has anyone been there?"

"Stevie rode up and there's no sign of her. Surely yon MacNishe has no come back for her as well as Rhoddy. Next thing he'll be back for me to look after them all!"

Maggie saw the worried frown on his face and wondered if more trouble was to befall the glen. Two whole days Cate had been gone! Well, she'd work to do, and it wouldn't get done standing still. "I'm sure she'll be back, Mr Dinwoodie. Now I come to think of it, mebbe she's gone to the mountain, but none of us knows where the old cave is." Leaving her employer to his worries, Maggie went to open the shutters in the drawing room, and as she did so the Laggan House Daimler pulled up in the front drive. The chauffeur held the door, while Cate Dinwoodie stepped out, and then handed her a large package. Waving to him, she skipped up the steps and through the front door.

In the drawing room she gazed at the assembled members of her household, while David pulled at the package.

"Mama for me?"

Cate pulled his hands away. "No, it's mine, David, and do stop pulling my skirts. I'm sorry everyone. I was just so cross and — oh, Dinwoodie, then I remembered your advice and left."

"My dear Cate, there is no way I can be held responsible for your…"

"But you were! You told me to see Mrs Campbell-Broughton-Stuart — and by the way we're to call her Cecily, or at least I'm to do so, and her husband, the Brigadier, is to help at the auction — I 'm sorry. I went to Laggan House for advice and I'm to go to the ball after all."

"So I suppose we're all to say, 'fine and dandy', now, Miss Cate, when we've all been worried sick. Employer you may be, but you know right fine you're in the wrong. You should have let us know where you were. Now I've work to be doing!" With that Maggie strode out of the room followed by the others, leaving Dinwoodie alone with his erring wife.

"I would say Maggie summed that up very well indeed. You, Cate Dinwoodie, had better get yourself upstairs and keep out of sight, or have you any other ideas as to how you can make up for the worry you've caused us?"

Cate shot her husband a subdued look and left.

Later, as Lizzie was bringing the twins down for their lunch, Cam pulled at her skirts and pointed upwards. "Mama!"

Lizzie looked up and gasped. "Oh Cate, it's beautiful. Where — how?"

"That's what I've been doing, Lizzie. Do you like it?"

All her friend could do was nod in amazement. The dress was a green satin with gold flowers edging it. The neckline a deep slash back and front, slipping off the shoulder to cape sleeves. The long skirt fell in leaf shaped folds to her ankles with a fishtail at the back dropping to the ground. Her hair, piled high on her head, was entwined with leafy fronds of green, and in her hand she held a gold jewelled fan. On her feet were gold pointed heeled shoes with buckled straps that made her tall figure seem even taller.

"I've borrowed the fan and shoes from Cecily." Putting her fingers to her lips, Cate motioned the boys and Lizzie downstairs and pointed to the drawing room, while she retreated to the landing. Once Lizzie had assembled everyone, Cate made her entrance. After another thorough apology and a mannequin parade, the admiring audience watched the lady of the house mount the stairs and then returned to work. Only Dinwoodie still seemed perturbed. It was not her absence that bothered him any more, but the sheer magnificence of both his wife's apparel and the change from the everyday Cate he knew, that made him uneasy. He couldn't help imagining the great and the good in Glasgow all vying for her attention, and was unable to rid himself of the thought that perhaps there might come a day when she was no longer his.

On the outskirts of Glasgow, the ancestral home of one of the Brigadier's cousins, played host to the moneyed ranks of Scots who flocked to the 'Hospital Ball' organized by his wife, the patron, Cecily Campbell-Broughton-Stuart. The ballroom was filled with tables laid for the dinner and each had a pledge card in a gold stand for the guests to fill in as they listened to the speeches during the meal.

The Brigadier spoke of the plight of his wounded soldiers, Lord Monroe told of the roll call of the dead and missing. His sister spoke of the need for more hospital beds and then called her special guests, Sister Assumpta and Mary-Anne, who recounted the sad stories of the Glasgow Convent and the Infirmary. Then Dinwoodie led his wife, in all her magnificence, to the stage, where, with no notes, she began her speech.

"My husband has kindly allowed me the use of Kevinishe House on his estate to set up and run the hospital you've been hearing about all evening. I'm certain that the pledge card on his table will have his name at the top. So I would like you to join me in thanking him for both these gifts, for without them we could do nothing." Having led the clapping, she waited till it had faded and then continued.

"All of us here, I'm sure, must have suffered personal loss of some kind in this dreadful war. For the dead we can do no more than mourn, but, for those maimed in any way, we cannot allow them to return to find we have no room for them. Remember when there was no room at the inn? Well, I'm not suggesting we put them in a stable, but we do have a large old house, plenty of labour, and, with your contributions, good people, we could provide help for those who have been dealt with by the surgeons and are waiting for artificial limbs, and any others who need help, whether it is in body or mind.

I thank all of you for coming tonight; to Brigadier Campbell-Broughton-Stuart and his wife, our patron, I give my particular heartfelt thanks. It has meant so much to me, and my hopes for this hospital, to have not only this wonderful evening, but also the help, strength, and advice given in support of the project, so let's hear it for them both!" Once more Cate led the applause, and when it faded, she began to talk again. "Please, on their behalf and their belief in the need for this project, give generously. As to your donations, they will be ably processed by our Lord Chief Justice, who has agreed to take on that responsibility, so please show your appreciation for the wonderful man."

When the round of clapping died away, Cate continued. "Ladies and Gentlemen, for those of you who do not know me, let me tell you I have determined to help and heal those brave men of ours who have suffered so that we may keep our lands and our freedom from the Kaiser, his Allies and their armies. So, if you feel the same, please, please sign your pledge cards. When you've thought of a sum, think a little more; perhaps another wounded soldier could be tended if you just increase your bid. Will you join me in this venture?" To the rousing cries of 'yes', she nodded, then turned to the back of the stage, clapped her hands, and watched as two footmen appeared and rolled a barrel of whisky to the front. Lifting a dainty gold-slippered-foot onto the side of the cask, she produced an impudent smile.

"Right gentleman, I hope you've all heard of Kevinishe's single malt, my Craeg Dhu. Well, here it is: my contribution to tonight. The highest bidder has not only the cask, but…" She lifted her gown a fraction, and with a provocative toss of her head said, "And the first dance with me. Brigadier, will you be the auctioneer?"

"Dear lady, I'll get their money for you and I've a mind to beggar myself for the first dance too!"

Chapter 13

Angus opened the distillery gates and stood well back as Cate trotted through and hitched Satan to the railings, pulling a bag of fodder within reach for him. "Angus, he won't harm you," she said as she blew into the horse's nostrils.

"Aye well, Miss Cate, that's mebbe so with you, but the great beast bares his teeth at me, and indeed are the villagers not putting their spare silver on…"

"Are they betting on me or the horse, Angus?" Cate asked with a glimpse of a smile.

"Well now I wouldn't like to be saying, but I'll mind you yon beast's named for the devil."

"You'll have to try and make friends with him then, just in case…"

"Away with you, Miss Cate. You know fine well, I leave as much room as possible between that beast and me. Mebbe I'll just bare my teeth back at him though!"

"Mind you, Angus, you've no so many left now!"

"Aye, true enough, Miss Cate, but I could be borrowing the old woman's false teeth for the job!"

Cate laughed and made for the malt floor. Donald Uig had been in charge there for years and his father and grandfather before that. He knew everyone in the distillery and it was his influence that had made the men go back to work after they'd gone on strike, when she'd first wanted to work there. A quiet chat with him was always useful when she'd been away.

"Now then, Donald Uig, how're things here?"

"Miss Cate, it's glad that I am you're back from Glasgow. It seems there's to be trouble with the barley."

"Surely not! We've never had a bad lot. Can we save none of it?"

"Well now that's just it. We've no over much to save. Barley Jo will be bringing no more they say and me nearly out."

"Right, I'll get onto the supplier as soon as possible. There'll probably be a simple reason for them not delivering, so don't worry. I'll

115

get your next lot here soon." As she climbed the stairs to Solly's office, Cate could feel her shoulders tensing, and it was with a worried frown she spoke to the accountant. "Have you had any notification about the barley, Solly?"

"None. And we've no invoices outstanding. I know that for I was looking for one yesterday. Deliveries have never been late before."

"Right, I'll have to get onto them. Have a word with Donald Uig if you have a minute. He seems to think the supply will stop."

"Cate, they can't. The distillery…"

She cut him off with a wave of her hand. "Exactly! No barley — no whisky."

Back in her own office, Cate stared at the telephone she'd just put down. So Donald Uig's source was right — damn the government, the war, the Germans! Of course people had to be fed, but there were other grain crops.

To give herself time to consider her next move Cate tackled the outstanding mail that had accrued during her absence in Glasgow. Putting one from Alashdair aside she deposited his latest package in the safe. She'd need to find a new home for the packages. There were quite a number now, taking up too much room. Remaining mail dealt with, she reached for the telephone again. Cate spent the next two hours looking for a new barley source, but with negligible results, before leaving, frustrated and bad tempered, for home.

Dinwoodie paid scant attention to the countryside as Morrison drove him back to Craigavon. Ever since he'd heard the rumour he'd been afraid for Cate. Now he'd given himself a headache worrying about her reaction to him. When Maggie met him at the door he was almost glad that Cate was not yet home.

"I'll have tea in the study then, Maggie, and get on with some work."

"By the looks of you, sir, it's too much work that's got you all pale and puckered."

"Just a headache. Tea will set me right I'm sure."

Making an effort to finish his tasty afternoon tea, Dinwoodie, still fretting about delivering his news, even though it was only club gossip, was glad to find another letter from the Scribbler on his desk. He'd made use of them on previous occasions to divert Cate's attention from bad news, and he might have to do so again. By the end of the afternoon, with little or no work completed in his study, he remembered he had a query for Solly. Put through to the distillery he chatted with the

116

accountant, whom he'd not seen for some time, and then invited him to dine that evening. He'd just put the phone down when to his surprise Cate appeared, dressed in her breeches.

"Hello, I didn't expect you back today. Don't tell me I've forgotten you were coming."

"No. I just decided to come because I missed you and home. You're back earlier than usual."

"I'd some bad news at the distillery, felt miserable, and thought I might as well come home to have an evening to consider it."

"I wonder sometimes if the bad news will ever end. We've enough of that already, and, Cate, I'm afraid Pearson is tramping the Paris streets to no avail at the moment."

"There're moments when I feel I'll never see Rhoddy again, after all this time."

"I know, my dear, but there is one thing that interests Pearson. He is more or less certain that someone is following him."

"Why would anyone be doing that, Dinwoodie? Unless — do you think it might be that man again — McPhail?"

"It could very well be, but once again I'm afraid it's a waiting game, and one I'm sure we're both exasperated with. By the way, anything I can do to help re your news?"

"Thank you, but I don't think so."

"I'm afraid I may well have spoilt your work evening though. I had a query for Solly and while we chatted, I do hope you don't mind, but I've invited him for supper."

"In that case let's have Maggie and Lizzie dine with us tonight as well. Let me know when Solly comes, I've neglected him of late. He and Stuart Monteith must get very bored with one another's company. I'll tell the kitchen and then go up and change."

Dinwoodie watched her go and couldn't help thinking that the meal having turned into a social evening might make things worse. There was a slight chance though, with others around she might just listen quietly to him, but he doubted it. Cate would always 'blame the messenger.'

As they dined, the conversation at the table ebbed and flowed while they concentrated on dissecting the trout, until Solly looked across at Cate and asked, "Did you have any luck with the barley suppliers?"

Cate used the fact that her mouth was full to avoid the question, and Maggie, sensing an unwelcome silence, turned to Dinwoodie.

" Any good news from the war, sir? "

"Maggie, that news is almost always bad." And instead of leaving the subject alone, he continued. "I do have some other unsettling news, but it's only indirectly about the war — more of a concern for you, Cate."

"For me?"

"I happened to run into 'Whisky Tom', at my club in London — you know, one of the Dewar distillery family."

"I know who you mean. They sat with us at the Distillers Association ball. Anyway, what's that got to do with your unwelcome news?"

"He fears that the government intend to get out of their lack of men and supplies, by using distillery labour next."

"But that's ridiculous. I don't know about other distilleries, but we can't afford to lose men."

"I'm afraid, Cate, we need even more able-bodied men freed up from non-essential work to go to the Front. According to Tom Dewar, the country also needs all the grain we can grow to feed the nation."

"God dammit, haven't I heard enough about barley today!" She thumped the table, and in the silence the glasses rattled.

"What's the problem with the barley? "

"It appears we can't get any and you know damn well we can't make whisky without grain, Dinwoodie."

"I am sorry, you never said…"

"Well, now you know."

"That may not be your only problem."

"Why? What else is there? You might as well tell us everything. It can't make the situation any worse."

"Cate, I'm sorry but it can. You see we need more chemicals for our armament industry as well."

"Surely that's got nothing to do with us?"

"My dear Cate, I'm afraid it does. It may only be a whispered rumour at the moment, but Dewar fears that in time Lloyd George will call for everything and anything that will spur on his munitions programme. He realises that the Allies are woefully short of armaments and everything must be done to provide them or we'll lose this war."

"Surely we can't do that?" Maggie asked. "Not after the killing that's gone on. That'd mean Murdo's died for nothing!"

"We may well do, Maggie, if we fail to give the soldiers what they need, and better and sufficient weapons are just that."

"I suppose I can see the need for food now that the damn Germans are blowing our ships out of the water with their wretched submarines, but what is the connection between chemicals and the distilleries?" Cate asked

"I believe it's all to do with the fermenting process. Only those distilleries that can switch to providing acetone, necessary for the production of gunpowder, will be allowed to continue their business. The others will be mothballed till the war is over, and I fear small distilleries like Kevinishe will be the ones closing."

"No!" Cate sprang to her feet. "How can they close something that doesn't belong to them?" She glowered at Dinwoodie as she dared him to confirm what he'd just said.

"My dear…."

"Don't you 'dear' me. Nobody is going to dictate to me about my business: not you, nor the blasted government."

"Cate!" Maggie took a deep breath, almost afraid to go on, but trying to calm the atmosphere, she continued. "Shouldn't we just find out why it's going to happen?"

"No, Maggie, because I'll never let it happen. And you, Dinwoodie, can take that answer back to the clubs in London. No one but me can close Kevinishe and I'll tell that to the bloody government if they approach me. They should be concentrating on winning this dammed war, not on disrupting domestic industries. They must be made to understand that if the distillery goes the village will follow." Her spoken thoughts and the enormity of the resulting consequences were almost too much for Cate, and robbed her of both rage and speech. She knew the others were waiting for her to continue, but her mind was clouded with despair and she needed time to think. Pushing back her chair she made for the door. Before continuing. "I'm sorry, please finish your meal. I need…" Lost for words she left.

Later, alone in her study behind the locked door, she ignored various knocks and voices as she dwelt on the early days when she'd pleaded with the stillman, Fisher, her friend and confidante, to let her join the distillery to try to save the village from the evil plans of their new laird, Bruce MacNishe. Her mind roamed over all her work since 1912, and now it looked as though sometime in the near future she might have to put the Kevinishe distillery to sleep. What would happen to the workers, the village, and her?

Breakfast the following morning was a subdued affair. Cate and Dinwoodie studied one another, trying to gauge the impact of the previous evening. Unwilling to bear the heavy silence any longer, Dinwoodie produced the letter from abroad and began to read.

The Western Front, May 1916

Dearest Girl,

The war of attrition continues, with the fighting once more centred on Verdun. The Germans appear to be making a determined onslaught, while French soldiers speak of a tremendous struggle in pursuit of victory on their part. The conflict has been going on for months, and both sides, apparently, are pouring men and supplies in, but neither is making much ground, no matter what the loss of life.

Alashdair.

"May! We're nearly into July now."

"I imagine with all the fighting going on it's getting more difficult for mail to come through, his contact might have been killed, and anyway I don't suppose he was up to writing much when he was wounded."

"I never thought he'd be hurt."

"Be realistic, Cate. He's a war correspondent, even if he's not one for us, he is now writing for the American paper. Think about it: to obtain his information he has to get as near as possible to the fighting to gather facts. There was always a possibility of him being injured; he might even be killed."

"Dinwoodie! What an awful thing to say! Bad enough he's been shot, but suppose he was anywhere near the poison gas of his last letter!"

"I imagine he would have told us if he had been, but I agree the use of it is just one more appalling weapon in this war. By the way, I'm sorry about the barley and the distillery. I do understand what it means, not only for you individually, but for the village you've worked so hard to put new life into."

"I know you understand, and that's why you rushed home to warn me. I'm grateful for that but when I heard last night I just — I had to be

120

by myself. I was up all night worrying — I think I'll try to sleep once the boys have breakfasted, for I've still no firm ideas as to what I can do for the distillery or the village."

Two weeks on and the meagre remains of barley were all but finished. She'd already sent out several more calls for grain, and right now she'd no idea whether they would be successful. Pacing up and down in her study, she knew it was not only the lack of barley that caused concern. There was no fresh news of Rhoddy. Alashdair's war news was awful, and with all that fighting going on, he could well be injured again. Then the rumoured threat that the Government might close the distillery clouded her waking hours and disturbed her nights.

The house seemed to stifle her, so she changed quickly and headed for the stables. Midnight seemed to understand her mood and took off at a tremendous pace, so Cate let him have the rein.

Cheeks burning from the speed and the wind, Cate found herself at the gates of Kevinishe House. Leaning forward, she hugged the horse's neck, her head between his ears, seeking the comfort she needed. "Aye, if he was here he'd know how to ease the pain in my heart, Midnight." Today more than any other she'd a physical need of the stalwart Fisher. Urging the stallion forward with her knees, she groped for the clasp on the gates of the big house and trotted up the drive. She hadn't set out to come here, but perhaps the memories of Fisher and old MacNishe that lay entwined in the fabric of the bleak grey walls would comfort her. With nothing more enticing for him than a handful of oats from her breeches, she led the animal to the horse trough full of rain-water and hitched him to the post there.

Once inside the house, Cate wandered from room to room until at last she climbed to the old tower and stared out of the window at the glen spread below, just as old MacNishe must have done over the years. The mere thought of generations of lairds doing the same wrapped her in a historical web that began to ease her fretting mind. Inside, the room was cobwebbed and dusty, the books damp to the touch. By the bedside was an ancient oak chest, still with the pewter candlestick he'd used before they'd had electric lighting, though it was paler now with it's grey film of dust. Her fingers strayed to the elaborate pewter handles of the top drawer and, on an impulse, opened it. With a stifled sob she picked out the daguerreotype of a young kilted MacNishe in all his glory, with a beautiful bride on his arm. Underneath was a journal of sorts and then

121

the back of another small frame. Turning this over, there in full Highland dress was Fisher. She held it to her face as one would a lover, and she couldn't hold back the tears for the two men who'd done so much for her.

Still sniffing she searched the lower drawers, only to find they'd already been ransacked. Tobacco spilt, kilt socks, ties and kerchiefs in a muddle, this was typical of Bruce, for it could have been no one else, showing no respect for his elders. Not knowing why, she sorted, folded, and tidied the contents before closing the drawers. Something in that simple act lifted her mood, and brought the dead men alive for her. It was then she knew what she would do. The answer to the barley and the distillery was obvious. She'd take the decisions herself before having them forced on her, be it this year or next. Carrying the two frames and the journal, she looked in the wardrobe, and, from the shelf above the hanging rail, pulled a worn MacNishe plaid. Wrapping her treasures for safety, she made her way down to collect the stallion and begin her fight back.

Chapter 14

In the lengthy summer evening the villagers, wondering why they'd been summoned, crowded into the old barn to find it bedecked with heather posies. Trestle tables were weighed down with bannocks, girdle scones, oatcakes, pancakes, shortbread, black-bun and clootie dumplings. Bowls of fresh salt butter, crowdie, and jams, made from moorland berries, were snug between the plates of food, and the big old tea urn was bubbling away. On the platform at the back of the barn musicians tuned fiddles, combs, chanters, harps and accordions ready for an evening's entertainment. The old ones of the glen found nooks and crannies with chairs to ease their limbs, while the young jostled in eager groups, all waiting for the appearance of the Craigavon party, who'd bid them come to the barn.

As the newcomers crowded in, an uneasy murmur filtered round those assembled there. There was no sign of Miss Cate. Dinwoodie, who was as puzzled as the rest of them, did his best to meet and greet as many of the gathering as he knew personally. The eerie sound of the pibroch starting up outside had all eyes turned towards the door. Donald Uig, in an obviously borrowed Highland dress, marched in holding a large object draped in the MacNishe clan tartan. Behind him, in a stark white gown, with the MacNishe sash a savage splash of colour to match the curtain of red hair that fell to her waist, marched Cate Dinwoodie, head erect, carrying a tray covered by an old cloth. The pair made their way, keeping in step with the pipes, up onto the platform, where the musicians stood to the side to make room for them.

Placing her tray on the floor, Cate looked round the barn, took a deep breath, and began to speak. "Caid Mille Failte, a hundred thousand welcomes. I know this is a time of sadness and sorrow throughout the land as well as in our small community. This glen has always marked big decisions with an event such as this, but before we talk of those, and the evening begins, I wish to make an apology. When Fisher died I did what I thought he would have liked, and, as you all know, he was buried next to the distillery he helped to save from ruin all those years ago. I had no wish to let his memory fade, and I can see, by the scowls on several faces, you well remember my graveside tribute. But it served its purpose. Fisher will never be forgotten in the stories told to future generations."

An old man staggered to his feet and clenched a fist towards her. Cate waited, knowing what was coming.

"Aye mho ghoile, an now we're paying for your foolishness. No barley for the still, an yon flask watched over us with care before your troublesome tinker clan ever brought you forth."

"Not so, Tam Shanks. Oh, it would be if, as you all believe, I'd smashed the distllery's precious talisman that day. But, true Celt that I am, I could never have done that, so step you over here, Bodach, for I've something for you." With that, Cate whipped the cloth off her tray and, with both hands clasping the flask, came down and handed it to the old man. As his frail hands took it from her, he removed the stopper, sniffed it, turned to the company, and let out a stream of Gaelic before hoisting it in the air, tears streaking his face. The awed silence was broken first by a few quiet murmurs, that rolled around the room gaining in intensity as they travelled, while one and all crowded round Tam Shanks, hands outstretched to touch the precious object. The band now struck up the old Gaelic tune, Eilean Mo Chridhe, and Cate waited for the furore to pass before holding out her hands for the precious flask.

Once more on the platform, she held it in the air and the crowd quietened. "Tonight when we have feasted, there will be a midnight procession to the distillery, and Donald Uig will replace the flask. To answer your unspoken questions, I took it back to its birthplace in Beinn Nishe, and replaced it for the funeral with another old one I found in the distillery. I filled that from the decanter in the office that MacNishe and Fisher used to toast the mountain on occasion." Finishing her speech, she exchanged the flask for the object Donald Uig had been holding, and turning to the crowd, removed the plaid to reveal a large painted portrait of Fisher. This was greeted by gasps of amazement, followed by cheering and clapping, as they understood what it was. When they quietened, Cate motioned Angus to the platform and handed him the portrait, which she'd had done from the miniature.

Speaking again, Cate began, "Now to the serious matter. I have this day taken the decision to shut down the distillery until the war is over." She waited till the expected angry murmurs subsided before continuing. "We are almost out of barley, and I have heard that the government will mothball small stills in the future. I thought you would all prefer us to make the move, not some government minister down in England. This way, we control what goes on in Kevinishe, and, by the way, none of you will be out of pocket."

One of the coopers stepped to the front. "Aye, we dinna want interference from the Sassenachs, right enough, but how will you fill our pockets, Miss Cate? We're no for charity, mind!"

"There'll be no charity, Robbie. I'm to open a hospital in Kevinishe House for the war wounded. It would be the sort of thing that Murdo would have wanted, and I know he'll be nodding his head up there, even as I speak. I'll see each one of you and we'll work out who can do what. Mark this now — you must all turn your hands to whatever we need to make this hospital a success as well as earn your wage. I need your help. Do I have it?"

Wullie the Post trundled his bath chair in front of the platform, and faced the villagers. "Well, let's hear you then!" The cheering took a long time to die down, but when it did, Cate raised her hand, nodded to Wullie, and waited for silence. Then she gestured to Donald Uig and Angus as she began to speak. "From now on Flask and Fisher will watch over the distillery, and when this war is over our Craeg Dhu will once more gurgle in the stills. Until then we will survive, I promise you."

As she stepped down from the platform, amid the cheers, an admiring Dinwoodie was there, hand outstretched to take her into the first jig of the evening and begin the ceilidh.

The following morning all at Craigavon, and throughout the glen, were bleary-eyed. Cate rode out as usual, but she was far from fresh. Stopping briefly at the distillery she picked up the mail from the previous day and returned home.

Unsaddling and walking Midnight her thoughts strayed to the ceilidh. It had been the right decision with barley supplies running out to mothball the distillery instead of hanging around waiting for the Government edict, especially as she now had alternative employment for the workers. Midnight stabled, she took the mail to her study, and finding a letter from Alashdair decided to take it to the breakfast table. Dinwoodie was already there, and after a brief discussion about the ceilidh over breakfast, he opened the letter and read it out.

The Somme, Summer 1916.

Cate,

The papers must be awash with casualty numbers from the disaster that began on the 1st of July in Picardy. Even now, as summer draws to a close, and the battle on the Somme continues, I cannot clear my mind of what I was told about that first terrible day. The huge barrage that lasted a week was supposed to have demolished the enemy wire and critically weakened their trench network and defences. It didn't! It's almost too awful to put down on paper. Cate, as they went over the top, line after line of our men were felled by German machine guns that were supposed to have been knocked out!

With the pressure on the French at Verdun lessening in August, I suppose the British offensive did fulfil that aim, but at what a price! Cate, I have tried, and probably failed, to capture the horror of the last two months in my writing. The scale of the losses, the continual arrival of new troops to fuel the conflict, and the never-ending stream of casualties that arrive here at the field stations and hospitals is beyond description. This is war on an unprecedented scale. It is too great a task for me at present — words are never going to be able to express this slaughter!

Alashdair.

Both were silent, each with a graphic picture of those dying men. Cate was the first to speak, "It's too awful. Our men going forward in a line like beaters on the moor, only to be shot like the pheasants. Men can't do that to one another!"

"It would appear they just have, Cate."

126

"Dinwoodie, will it never end? It seems like this could go on and on, getting worse and worse."

"There seems to be no move for peace. Trouble is that all sides have invested too much in this war to stop now. I'm afraid there'll be no halting the carnage till one side or the other makes significant gains and then that might allow a peace to be brokered."

"Well, if we carry on with more of these 'offensives', Dinwoodie, there'll be no fighting men left to wage war! Is that what they'll do — just keep on till this generation of men are all dead?"

"No. There will be a decisive strike, hopefully by our troops and then perhaps the politicians will say, 'enough is enough', but I can't see it being any time soon. Now I must get back to Glasgow, and you have a hospital to get ready."

As the weeks went by, with the distillery being readied for mothballing, Cate employed the Carter to bring the available men and women to and from the village to work. With money from the pledges coming in, and the army co-operating with supplies, Kevinishe House was being readied for occupation. The first big job had been to scour the place throughout and rid it of the detritus of the unoccupied years.

At the end of this particular day, Cate brushed a loose strand of hair from her face with a weary hand and leaned on the bucket of dirty water to push herself upright. It had been a long time since she'd scrubbed those tenement stairs in Glasgow! She was getting soft! Still she'd kept up with the other women and, thank God, the house was clean at last.

"We're done, Cate!" An equally exhausted Kirsty joined her with a matching bucket.

"Kitchen and tea, my friend, before we drop." Cate led the way and she had to smile as she saw the others there, all but draped across the big table, too tired to speak. Morag was the last one to appear and she was still holding her mop as she flopped down on the bench.

"Mrs Dinwoodie…"

"I thought we'd decided that you would join all the others and call me Miss Cate, Snowy, though I would prefer just plain Cate."

"Alright, Miss Cate." Snowy shook her head at the girl she'd known so long. "Here, get this tea and bannock down you. What would Mr Dinwoodie say if he saw what you were doing?"

"You tell him, Snowy, and I'll send you straight back to Glasgow!"

"Oh, your secret's safe with me. I haven't enjoyed myself so much since you and Lizzie came to stay all those years ago. Thank you for thinking of me to cook up here. It's good to be part of a family again. Not that I didn't like housekeeping for him in Glasgow, but he was so seldom there and what's the point of dusting rooms just for the sake of it."

"Good. Now, more to the point, have we enough hot water finally coming through those wretched shower things, Snowy?"

"The man from Fort William has not long left and he says they work this time."

"Right! Towels, ladies, wash, change, and home for the day!"

One morning, after weeks in which much progress had been made, found Cate on her knees showing two of the distillery men how to incorporate the seaweed into a planting hole with the compost she'd been making over the years in the Craigavon garden. A cry from the lawn stopped her. "Right, Robbie, carry on until all the holes in this area have been dug and made ready. That'll keep you going for the day."

"Right y'are, Miss Cate, though what seaweed has to be doing with them bushes we're to plant tomorrow I'm no so sure. Mind it's better in the soil than it ever was in my old mother's cooking pot, for I never took to the soup she made with it!"

Still smiling, Cate walked across the lawn to meet Maggie. "Now what? If it's the damn plumbing again, I really don't want to know."

"The water's fine. It's a Major McAlpin here for you. From the army he is, and it's to be hoped he's no going to be a scunner like the one you met in Glasgow!"

"We'll soon see, Maggie. In the drawing room is he?"

"Aye, and Cook's feeding him fresh scones and wondering if he'll be the new doctor on account of her having trouble with her megrims. And the Carter's been with great bales of blankets from the Army. When we've put them out in the wards, he'll take me back to Craigavon, as I'm needed there. The spiders'll be thinking life's right fine, the lack of dusting that's been done there in this past weeks."

Cate followed Maggie back to the house, mentally ticking off the things that had been done and those still to do before the hospital was up and running. This mammoth organising of each and everything that was required was exactly what she liked to be doing. She'd the grace to grimace as she reminded herself that, as of old, she still didn't give enough time to her family, but so far she'd avoided any domestic clashes.

Indeed the entire village had done what she'd hoped. The sewing group, now that the latest catalogue was out and there were far fewer requests for dresses, were gradually packing away the fancy curtains and covers from Kevinishe House and replacing them with more basic items The coopers were beavering away at wooden lockers for patients' belongings. Mary Anne was due within days with three trained staff, and Kirsty and Morag, now the cleaning was done, would be on hand as ward maids. By the time Cate reached the house her mental inventory had been completed to her total satisfaction.

Snowy met her at the front door and showed her into the drawing room. As the door closed behind her old friend, Cate scrutinised the waiting army officer.

"Have I passed, do you think?" the Major asked.

"I'm sorry, was it that obvious?"

"Fraid so, but let's reserve judgement, on both sides." He held out his hand. "Major Hamish McAlpin, MD. I've been assigned to Kevinishe House, to look after your first batch of patients."

Taking the proffered hand, Cate began. "I'm sure you've heard, Major, I'm the woman the other doctor didn't want to work with."

"All I heard was that you've provided these premises, and funded a great deal of the preparation work required, both in financial terms and labour. I also heard about a golden slipper and a barrel of single malt. For that alone you would have my co-operation!"

"In that case, Major, will you join me in a dram?"

"I'll not only join you — I'll make the toast."

Drams in hand, Cate watched him as he crossed to a chair. "I see you have a limp. A war wound?

"One of several over the last two years. Field hospitals may be there to heal the sick, but they're still in the line of fire. Gerry doesn't much mind who he blasts, so along with the poor civilians and soldiers, the medical staff cop it from time to time."

"Are you...?" Cate hesitated.

"Am I fit enough to take charge here? Indeed I am, otherwise the army would not have sent me. Now let's knock the barriers aside and begin as friends. I have no intention of simply taking all this away from you. As far as I'm concerned you come with the premises."

"Then I'll stop twittering and show you your office. I've written out the things I'm unsure of, plus those I'm prepared to undertake. The papers are on your desk. The ancillary staff are all glen folk and they're used to working for me, so that's the obvious thing for me to see to."

Dram and small talk finished, Cate showed him round all the completed alterations, and, as she did so, she began to worry. Would he approve of the accommodation? Had they set everything up correctly? Could she work with this man? To fill the silence as they walked, Cate began to babble. "There's a nursing sister and a couple of orderlies arriving shortly from Glasgow and the local women are willing to be ward maids, and…"

Recognising the nerves, Hamish McAlpin took her hand as he spoke. "I think everything is coming together here just fine. The army could do no better. I'm well aware that this has been an almost one-woman crusade. So far in this damnable war I've lived with the most awful conditions and having this —," he waved his arms around, "— is wonderful. Now did you have an idea as to where I'm to be billeted?"

"Yes, of course, only…" Cate cast a brief glance at the leg.

"Only there's a problem? I see — my leg. Well, let's have a look at the room, and I'll tell you if I can stagger there!"

"I'm sorry, I didn't mean to be rude. It's just that I've given you the tower room. It has the most wonderful view of the glen and the mountain. Although we call it the tower room, it is in fact a bedroom with its own bathroom and a sitting room. I thought it would give you a little distance from the patients, a place to relax when you're off duty, but it is at the top of the house."

"That's wonderful. I believe you do not live on the premises?"

"No, you won't have to put up with me all of the time!" Cate smiled and found she'd relaxed. "I just want to be useful in whatever way I can. At the moment I'm helping to redesign the grounds. They've been as neglected as the house."

"Now that explains your dirty hands."

Cate looked in horror at the hands she'd forgotten to wash after her gardening, but then couldn't help but see the amusing side of it. "Lack of hygiene paraded in front of the new doctor and me assuming I could help in the hospital! That's a good start, wouldn't you say?" Still chuckling they made their way to his office and the notes.

Chapter 15

In the Paris apartment Bruce was not a happy man. What the hell was the point of stealing an army uniform if it didn't fit? In his rage he threw the clothes across the room to Rhoddy, shouting, "Well don't just stand there — pick them up! You might as well have them. The stuff you've got barely fits anymore. You've shot up since we arrived here, almost the same height as me now, though skinny with it. Must be the climate! Go on then — try them on. They'll do till we can buy some decent clothes for you."

While the boy was changing, it suddenly occurred to Bruce that the uniform could well be a clever disguise for Rhoddy, should anyone be looking for him, and it would put off the time when he'd need to spend money on clothes. Thinking of spending, he might well send a note to cousin Lachlan. Bruce knew that having lost his only son; McPhail was keen to use the old tradition of sending a male heir to spend time with a sept of the clan to ensure strong bonding. He himself had spent time with his mother's family in the past for just that reason. Bruce also knew that his cousin was, and always had been, envious of the MacNishe wealth. Any money borrowed would expect to be returned with maximum interest! He might have been better teaming up with him though, because the whole kidnap scheme hadn't quite worked out the way he'd planned. His bright idea of hiding out in France, with Stuffy's help, would certainly have worried the tinker — by now she'd be in despair! Thing was, he wasn't there to see it, and there was no one to tell him how she was suffering, so he was missing the best bit of his revenge!

The boy was now becoming a nuisance, and made it near impossible for him to follow his own desires. If only he'd left him with that miserable couple in the estate cottage, but then he wouldn't have been able to sneak away with all the money. Still, he'd be a free agent in Paris now if he'd left him there. Another thing — his son had become sullen of late, barely speaking. Pity he couldn't send him somewhere else, but where?

Rhoddy, now clad in the uniform, came back into the room, to find his father frowning, deep in though.

The boy spoke first, "Now that you've got money — how did you get it, Father?"

"From the estate, of course."

"But I thought Dinwoodie had bought it."

"Don't be ridiculous! That's just one more of the tinker's lies. That is MacNishe property and will be yours one day."

"She's …"

"You don't need to tell me what she is! I've always known. Don't say you want to go back there?"

"No — no, but…"

"Right, I'm off out to meet a friend. Here," Bruce delved in his pocket and flung some paper notes at the boy. "Get yourself something to eat, and don't wander too far. It'll soon be dark."

As he heard the door slam behind his father, Rhoddy slumped into the chair in front of the miserable little heater and wondered what they were doing back in Kevinishe. He'd never thought about it being his one day. His mother must have known that, so there was another thing she'd not told him. He tried imagining being The MacNishe, owning the distillery, having plenty of money, just sending for it when he wanted, never having to work. And yet Dinwoodie always seemed to be working, although he knew for certain the man owned houses all over the place, as well as foundries. And he'd bet none of those houses looked like this rotten room. His father may well have had more money sent, but he didn't seem to spend it on clothes for him, nice places to live, or pay the rent to people. He'd not enjoyed creeping out of the cottage — he'd been scared the man might catch them. Then they'd had to walk forever. He'd had enough of walking from place to place with his mother, after the death of his father, the McAlister father, not the MacNishe one!

Well, if his father wouldn't spend money, he'd take some more now, and tomorrow when the shops opened he'd try to get some new clothes; at least he knew what size he'd need now to get out of this ridiculous itchy uniform. Crossing to their shared bedroom, he had a search through the forbidden drawers, helped himself to more paper money, just in case his father didn't return for a bit. As he did so, he uncovered a train ticket. For no real reason, he pocketed it as well and let himself out, nodding to the concierge as he left.

The old man tottered after him, crossed the street, and made his way to a dingy café, where Pearson was absorbed in a newspaper. His tailing had finally paid off, and the old concierge had been in his pay ever since MacNishe had returned to Paris with the boy. After a brief conversation and much gesturing by the concierge, he thrust some francs at the old man and hurried away.

Pearson followed the boy, who looked thoroughly miserable as he stared into windows, shuffled from quarter to quarter, and finally entered a café. Letting Rhoddy settle, Pearson waited till he'd been served, and then, pulling a paper from his pocket, he entered the café, looked around, then veered towards Rhoddy. He pulled out a chair, sat, placed the paper on the table, and began browsing through it.

Glad that the stranger seemed absorbed in his reading, Rhoddy sipped his beer and finished his omelette. He'd never been over keen on omelettes, but it was the only recognisable thing on the menu. When the waiter appeared to take the man's order, he was astonished to hear him struggling with the French and finally lapsing into English. It was only then that Rhoddy realised the paper was also in English.

Having set the scene, Pearson shrugged his shoulders and muttered, "Damn Frenchies!"

"You're English. Aren't you?" Rhoddy asked.

"No me. I'm from Glasgow. Do you know it?"

"I've had holidays there, but I know Edinburgh better. I'm at…" He stopped himself just in time. Right now he was at nothing. Not that this man would know anything of Fettes, Kevinishe, or his mother, but he'd better be careful. Still it was good to speak without having to struggle with the language, and he was lonely.

What puzzled Pearson most was why the boy was in an army uniform. Somehow he had to get Rhoddy to trust him enough to get him to the station. Once there, it'd be no problem because he'd a guard with tickets at the ready. Of course, his own French was near perfect, his halting order in the café being for the boy's benefit. Once they'd both finished eating, he needed an excuse to board the Paris Metro that would get them to the Gare du Nord.

"Right, nice meeting you, but I fancy a ride on the Metro. Been on it, have you, or do you like walking?"

"Not really, but my French isn't good enough to do anything but point at things."

"Then you ought to have a ride on the Paris Metro. How about I treat you? It's one of my favourite ways to get about. I'll show you how it's done and then next time you can do it yourself. What do you say? Oh, perhaps you've got to get back. Someone waiting for you is there?"

"No—o-oo."

"Right then, off we go. I'm sure you'll enjoy it" As they boarded the Metro, he couldn't believe how easy it had been. All he needed now was for the guard to be on the lookout and they'd get the boy aboard the train and back to his mother. Rhoddy seemed at ease, but, the nearer they got to the Gare Du Nord, the more the detective fretted inwardly. The Iron Baron was a good employer, paid handsomely, but expected results. Pearson knew he'd slipped up by not collaring the boy in the French countryside, and he couldn't afford mistakes this time. As they reached the terminus, he forced an easy smile as he turned to the boy.

"This is the end of the line. Have you enjoyed it? I can see by your face you have. By the way, have you ever seen the railway station, the Gare Du Nord? It's worth a look. What about a café noir in there to end the evening? It's an experience you mustn't miss."

Rhoddy couldn't believe how much he'd enjoyed this stranger's company. Why, the man treated him like a grown up! So much more pleasant than his father had been of late, and this man was even paying!

"I'd like that. Is it very big?"

"It's the main Paris station. Busy old place, so stay close, we don't want to lose you."

"Who's 'we'? You never said we were meeting anyone else."

"To tell you the truth, I kind of hoped I might see a friend of mine. He's a guard here and there's just a chance that he could arrange for you to get into one of the engines to have a look around. Would you like that?"

"Right in? Where they shovel the coal?"

"Oh yes, if we ask nicely. Look, I think that's him over there. Wait here and I'll go and ask."

Rhoddy watched as the two men spoke, and then he noticed something. His friend was waving his arms about just like the other man. Very slowly, Rhoddy inched forward, till he could just hear the sounds of their voices. They were both speaking French really fast. The man had lied to him! Something was going on here and he had to get away before he found out what it was. His father had warned him not to speak to other people. He'd really wanted this man as a friend. Then he saw them coming towards him and somehow he just knew he was in trouble. He stuck his hands in his pockets to stop them from shaking, and then he felt the railway ticket. He didn't stop to think, but turned and ran in the opposite direction, hearing the shouts of the other two as they chased him. Desperate to escape, he wasn't looking where he was going and collided with a man in uniform.

"'Ere you! Look where you're bloody going! Should've got 'ere quicker!" The man righted himself, pulled Rhoddy into the group ahead of him, and shoved him into the carriage. "Cor, we nearly missed that!" he said to a dumbfounded Rhoddy, as the train began to move.

Rhoddy wasn't listening, because he was watching his two pursuers, waving their arms, and chasing the train as it pulled away, in a cloud of smoke. Soon they were so small he could hardly see them, and he sank back in his seat, glad to have escaped. It was only then that he realised there were no ordinary people in the carriage. Nothing but soldiers! His stupid father had made him dress up in the uniform and now he was — he couldn't be! Surely they could see he wasn't a soldier? He'd better say something. No, they might not believe him. He'd wait. Yes, that's what he'd do. Wait and get out at the next stop. He'd close his eyes — that way they'd think he was asleep and he needn't talk. When the train stopped at the next station he'd just get out. As the wheels clickety-clacked along the rail, Rhoddy felt he'd been rather clever getting away from those two in the station. That would be a story to tell in the dorm, if he ever got back to Fettes. With that in mind, he drifted off to sleep. Several stations passed without either the train stopping or him waking.

At last the army train stopped and Rhoddy was shaken awake. "Come on, you lazy blighter, we're here and you'd better get your arse out there quick or you'll get left behind."

A horrified Rhoddy stumbled upright. He'd meant to get out long before this. Why hadn't the train stopped? Why hadn't he woken up? Why had he gone to sleep? Now what could he do? Mind in a whirl, he dragged his feet after the soldier and wondered if he could just slip away, but now they were all in a siding — it wasn't even a proper station — and there were a large number of soldiers. He lingered behind the other men and, once there was some distance between him and them, he slid behind some scrubby bushes. As he did so he was interrupted by a rough voice shouting at him. "Who the 'ell are you interrupting a man's piss?"

Rhoddy tried to hide, but tripped over, and fell to the ground. All he could do was look up at the uniform the man was rearranging and tried to make sense of the question. "I'm lost and…" he faltered.

"Bloody War! Fuck me if they're not sending bloody kids out now." With that the soldier hauled Rhoddy to his feet. "Come along with me. I've no idea whose lot you should be with, but you might as well stay with us. We're all bloody lost. Bits of several units here, mates all dead, strewn across the bloody foreign fields. Gave us some leave, and now they've landed loads of us back here. God knows where we are. Truth is no bugger knows who belongs anywhere these days! So stop the caterwauling. Save your energy for the march ahead."

"But, but I'm not a soldier. I'm staying in Paris and my father's a Clan Chieftain."

"Yeah, and I'm fucking General Haig! Get yourself over there and get some sleep. None of us are soldiers — butchers, bakers, candlestick makers us. Bloody fools who were looking for a bit of an adventure, same as you — a bit of our own personal glory. Patriots, my arse! More like a load of disillusioned, 'omesick, tired, scared bastards now. So let's have no more of your bellyaching. Only way you get out now soldier boy is feet first. We're marching out again as soon as some ranking fool comes along and gives us an order, so get yourself over there, before I drag you across. Food, what there is of it should turn up soon. Now then, name? Number? Regiment? Who the hell are you?"

At his feeble shake of the head, the soldier searched him for the dog tag and finding none looked at the boy with disgust. "So you're a deserter are you? Well matey, you're going no bloody further! You're in it up to your neck, same as us. Go on over there!" With rough handling the soldier flung him towards the siding, where the petrified boy staggered into the group, his mind now blank with shock.

"Hey, Grabber, where'd he come from? What's his name?"

"'Ow the 'ell do I know? Who knows or cares where the poor bugger came from. Now he's here he might as well come along with us.

"But if he ain't got no name…"

"So, call him 'Boy' for now. 'E'll either come clean, remember who he is, or he may even be loco. Who knows, or cares? Anyway 'e'll be dead soon, thanks to our bloody generals! Now get some shut-eye, the lot of you, before we're on the road again. You'd have thought the bloody train could have taken us nearer the village. Right, packs for pillows, and cuddle up close m' lads, and no funny business either. Should've got rid of all that on leave!"

136

Cate looked up from her desk in the hospital and smiled as Mary Anne appeared. "Well, are you settled in?"

"Indeed I am, and not a moment too soon. Major McAlpin says we're to have our first patients arriving this week."

"So, we're finally going to be a proper hospital!"

"We are that, and I might have known you'd not rest till you'd found a way to help. I should never have let on to you about our troubles and the poor soldiers."

"Nonsense, Mary Anne, it wasn't only you that saw the need. Dinwoodie, Lord Munro, and his dreadful nephew all realised the time had come for extra hospital accommodation. So here we are, with our work about to start in earnest. Was that what you came to see me about?"

"No, the Major wants everyone to meet in the morning room before lunch, so's he can go over some final details. I like him, you know, Cate. He's a good man, and, from what I've seen, a knowledgeable doctor."

"Yes, I'm inclined to agree with you. He's been very appreciative of what we've done here, and he's a kindly soul. Right, we'd better get down there and round the others up."

By the end of the week, the rotas were all in place, Kirsty and Morag were to be ward maids, under instructions from Mary Anne and she and Major McAlpin would combine on the medical side, and the army were sending orderlies to train two of the distillery workers in the skills required for the heavy lifting of patients.

Alerted by the noise of the vehicles, the staff all trooped out to greet the arriving ambulances. Cate did not accompany them. She stood at her office window, and watched as several soldiers, some on crutches, most with bandages somewhere on their body, and three on stretchers, were helped down from the ambulances and guided indoors. She waited as the accompanying boxes were unloaded and watched until the vehicles left and disappeared down the drive. Her hospital was real! Cate stayed in the emotional moment for some time before she returned to her desk, tidied her papers, and, using the staff staircase, made her way down to the kitchen to see if all was in order for the patients' lunch.

By the end of that first day, everyone was exhausted and, with an orderly in both the drawing room, now Ward One, and the dining room, now Ward Two, all medicines given and wounds dressed, the village staff boarded the Carter's wagon, while the Major, Mary Anne and Cate sat on in the morning room, which was now the staff dining room, and discussed their new charges. Cate said little, leaving the other two to go through all the medical details, but listened attentively, knowing she was privileged to be included.

There were ten soldiers altogether. Ward One held the three stretcher cases and two on crutches. Ward two was home to the remaining less injured men, though two of them had not only physical wounds, but also seemed unable to speak.

"Right, Sister, if you could write up their charts ready for the morning inspection, I'll check the drugs inventory and Mrs Dinwoodie…"

"Major, would it be too much of an infringement of army protocol just to call me Cate?"

"I believe it would, but since all the ancillary staff address you as 'Miss Cate', I think we'll settle for that. I know you're doing your best not to tread on our medical toes, so to speak, but apart from your organisational role, I do believe you will play some part in the patients' lives. Indeed many of your staff will be in contact with the soldiers, and I thoroughly approve of that. The walking wounded will need fresh air, outside activity, recreational interests, and those who are bedridden will also require non-medical care, reading to them, helping them write letters, giving them news of the outside world, that sort of thing." He rose, yawned, and stretched, before continuing. "As of tomorrow, we begin the healing process and it's one all of us must and should be a part of, though Sister Mary Anne and the orderlies will work alongside myself on the medical side. Now it's time we were all abed. How that horse of yours will find its way in the dark is a mystery, so be off with you, Miss Cate, and be safe. Goodnight to you both."

Next morning, Dinwoodie eyed the sleeping Cate with pleasure. Just what Madam had been up to the previous evening, however, did give him some concern, if for no other reason than the knowledge that the reckless woman that was his beloved wife was riding around, not only on the horse appropriately called Midnight, but also at that same late hour.

Bathed, dressed, and shaved, he returned to the bedroom to find a drowsy Cate stretching like a cat after it had a good sleep.

"Good morning, Dinwoodie, I see you're up and ready to go. I'm sorry. I seem to have overslept. If you're worried about leaving late, go on down to breakfast and I'll…"

"Right now I'm more concerned about my wife creeping into bed at midnight."

"I thought you were asleep!"

"I wasn't. What kept you?"

"Dear Dinwoodie —" her drowsiness disappeared and her excitement and pleasure in what she had to tell him had her sitting upright and dragging him down onto the bed."

"Stop pulling me about like an old dishcloth and answer my question!"

"They've come! At last they're here!"

"Please calm down and make some sense woman."

"Oh, Dinwoodie, your big old barrack of a house has its war-wounded! Kevinishe hospital is now part of the army's care for its wounded — and you made that possible!" She hugged him till he could hardly breathe."

"Before I pass out for want of air, will you give me room, woman! And remember it was only because my nagging wife berated me that I came on board."

"I don't care how we did it! I'm just so grateful to you, Cecily, the Brigadier, Lord Monroe, and all the donors. First thing today I shall write to them all and keep them informed as to our progress. Oh, Dinwoodie, how can you just sit there? I could dance — I'm fair fizzing, so I am!" And she proceeded to get up and waltz round the floor.

"Ridiculous female! Get some clothes on. Have breakfast and go write your letters. Then get yourself off to your hospital. Work off some of that fizz and let me get on with my work! Remember, if you come creeping in at that late hour again, I'll forbid you the hospital! So you keep regular hours while I'm gone — and don't forget you've others here at home who need your love and attention!"

Chapter 16

The early morning sun cast a beam across the bed and Cate stretched, rose, and donned her riding breeches. If she skipped breakfast, she would have time for a canter on the moors before going to the hospital. Passing through the kitchen she grabbed a couple of bannocks, took a slug of milk, and went to the boot room, where she ate while pulling on her boots.

As she rounded the front of the house she was astonished to see Morrison parked there, so she made her way to the car. "Don't tell me you've driven through the night!"

"That we have, Miss Cate, and bone weary we both are."

"Dinwoodie, all this travelling is getting too much for you," Cate said as her husband got out of the car.

"I know, but as the saying goes 'there's a war on', and, like most people, I have to do what I can. Now, Morrison my bags and then breakfast."

Cate and Dinwoodie chatted while he went to the trunk. They were alarmed by a cry from him. Then, as he staggered towards them, they were shocked to see him holding the side of the car as if he couldn't support himself.

"Morrison?" Dinwoodie and Cate ran to him, fearing he'd had a heart attack. "What is it?"

"Oh sir, back there, sir, it's — I don't — how — it's him!"

Pushing past the chauffeur they in turn were horrified at the sight of the bruised and bloodied man squeezed in and hanging over the bags. Cate was the first to speak. "Good God! We must get him out of there, Morrison —".

"No, we canna do that!" He protested.

"Nonsense man! Here, out of the way, Cate, we'll…"

But Morrison stood between them and the boot, trying to explain. "He's not supposed to be there — and —." He turned to Dinwoodie, and in a shocked whisper said, 'It's Hansi. He's from the works an—."

"I don't care who he is or where he's from. That injured soul needs help. Let's get him out of there and into the…"

Morrison interrupted him once more. "He'll bleed all over us, sir, and — it's my fault for no locking it — and…"

Losing patience, Dinwoodie pushed the chauffeur aside. "You can tell us all about it later. Right now we must get him to hospital!"

Cate saw the fear in Morrison's eyes, and in a quiet voice asked, "Why can't we move him? Take him to the hospital?"

"Oh, Miss Cate, he's — he's a Conchie — won't fight you know — and the word was that he might even be a spy! "

"He's what? Are you telling me, Morrison, that we have a man who is refusing to fight — perhaps betraying us? And he's one of my foundry workers! No wonder he's been beaten up by the other men!"

"Dinwoodie!" Cate couldn't believe what she was hearing. "He needs help right now, not judgement."

"Get him to the hospital and out of my sight then, woman."

"Sir, we can't take him to the army — he's a German!"

"He's what?"

"He's from Germany, though he doesn't speak foreign. The lads used to like him but — see in Glasgow just now folks are throwing stones at Germans' shops and homes — an they're saying he's for the jail anyway."

"Then get him back there! Hand him over to the Major in Kevinishe. I won't be associated with harbouring an alien. One thing I will not have is my reputation ruined, and most certainly not for a cowardly German who should be in prison where he can do no harm! I thought the two of you would be the first to understand that. He's not coming near my house!"

"Dinwoodie!" Cate shot him an angry glance and, knowing he'd said the one thing that would rile her, he strode inside.

Charlie had seen Cate in her breeches, and he now appeared with Midnight, saddled and ready to go.

"I'm not riding, I've changed my mind. So put him back."

After a moment's hesitation, the lad turned the horse and headed for the stables with a puzzled expression. His employer had never spoken to him in that sharp tone of voice before.

With Charlie out of earshot, Cate took charge of the situation. "Right, Morrison, we'll take the car into the garage. Come on now. We must get help." There was a faint sound from the man's swollen lips, and she gave a sigh of relief. "At least he's not dead."

Much later in the day, having revived him, bound his wounds, and listened to his tale, Cate left the man with the chauffeur and returned to the house. As yet she could see no way out of the current problem. But Morrison was right: the man could not go near the army hospital, for he might well be put in jail. To think that people had stood by and watched him being beaten by others was unbelievable, but that's what he'd said. Knowing she was probably going to bring down a heap of trouble on her head, she was still determined to help the young man, whose situation was not so hard to understand when he explained about his family still living in Germany and some of his cousins already fighting in France. Her immediate worry though was Dinwoodie. It was so unlike him to be judgemental.

Hurrying up to his study, Cate could see, as soon as she entered, his temper had not subsided. She waited till he lifted his gaze from his papers, but before she could speak he launched into her.

"I trust you've removed that man. He may or may not be a spy, but we know he is both a coward and a German. Don't you think we've enough trouble with them in France? Where's your common sense? The right thing to do is hand him to the authorities, and that's all there is to it."

"How can you be so, so…?"

"Because you're being foolish. Have you considered for a moment how it would look if it became known I had aided and abetted a fugitive?"

"He's hardly that — simply a man in an impossible situation. And for that he's been beaten up by some of your lads, no doubt with drink in them, and might well have to go to prison because he doesn't want to shoot his cousins!"

"How like a woman! He gives you a sob story and you fall for it! I told you he's not welcome here and I expect you, as my wife, to hand him over to the Major. I'll deal with Morrison once I know how that man got into a locked car."

"Morrison told me he was packing the car and forgot his own bag. He fetched it and his hat and put them in the front. Because he didn't go into the trunk then, he forgot to lock it. By all means deal with Morrison, but if it's welcome we're talking about, Dinwoodie, you know full well I have never knowingly turned anyone away from my house. And may I remind you that I said I would marry you only on condition that Craigavon and the distillery were mine and you'd have no part in them. Likewise, I would have nothing to do with the foundries. That was the promise we made to one another. As I remember, you were only too happy to agree."

"And you promised to obey, or have you conveniently forgotten that fact?"

"I forget very little."

"Good. Then I expect you to obey me in this. Do as you are told! I'll not have my wife being…"

"That's enough, Dinwoodie. I'll not be spoken to like this. I never thought you would be an unreasonable…"

"Damn you, Cate! You're the one who's unreasonable. Do as I say and hand him over."

With her temper rising, she made for the door. Arguing like this would get them nowhere. As she left, she flung her words over her shoulder. "I'll do as I think best."

With this final provocation Dinwoodie strode after her, shook her roughly by the shoulders, and pinned her against the wall. "You'll not disgrace us, woman! I'll see to that!"

"Take your hands off me, Dinwoodie! And don't ever dare to lay a finger on me in anger again. Now get out of my way!" As he released his hold, Cate pushed past him and left.

In the evening Cate, still angry, was struggling with the sulkie bridal and bit, when she sensed someone behind her. Assuming it was Dinwoodie, she turned ready to give her anger free rein, but to her surprise it was Charlie, and she wanted no witnesses to what she was about to do.

"It's late, shouldn't you be on your way home?"

Charlie slowly crossed to the mare, took the reins from her hands, and began unravelling them before he spoke. "Things are not right with you, Miss Cate. I gave my word to the big man I'd always look out for you."

"That was all a long time ago and I don't need your help in any way."

"As I see it, Miss Cate, you're angry, and up to something."

"Mind your own business, Charlie!"

"Aye, that's what I'm doing. You'll always be my business. Now then, the reins are sorted, so whatever it was in the back of the motor you need to move, let's get it done. All this speechifying is just a waste of time."

Somehow the boy — no, no longer a boy, she realised — but a young man now, and a determined one at that! Cate looked at him as he stood waiting for her to speak, and all at once she knew he was right. She would always be able to trust him because of their shared memories of Fisher. Indeed, it was as if the young man standing before her was nothing less than a re-embodiment of the big man.

"Right, Charlie, but I'm doing this knowing it'll bring trouble. If you're with me, that trouble could well be on your head too, so be sure that this is what you want, because, once started, there'll be no going back."

"That's fine. Now, I think we're ready to get going, Miss Cate."

She felt the tension slip from her shoulders at his reply, while making a silent pledge that she would protect him, no matter what. "We need to get the sulkie away without anyone seeing it. Pity it is summer and light till near dawn."

"There's a path hidden in the woods behind here. It's no good ground for the wheels, but it'll get us away. To the Black House is it?"

Cate chuckled, "It is that, Charlie. You've a nose like a bloodhound. Take the mare and I'll follow, then you can wait till I go back…"

"To Morrison to get what he's hiding?"

"How do you know that, Charlie?"

"I know most things, and those I don't I find out by waiting and watching. That Morrison aye goes to the kitchen for his bite when he and the master are home, and there's been never a sight of him this evening, and him liking his food too!"

Later, Morrison watched till she was out of sight, Hansi leaning on her as he struggled to walk. As they disappeared he went inside the garage and cleaned up the mess in the trunk, but as he worked he worried. She'd given no word as to what she was doing, when he asked her. 'It's better you don't know, Morrison', she'd said, and he had to be content with that.

Tonight, Cate sat at the door of the Black House and wondered if she'd ever feel more like her normal self. She knew in the past weeks she's tried to accomplish too much. What with her work at the hospital, the sleeping distillery, and now with her nights here way out on the moor, she was always tired. After her pretence each evening, of going to bed and waiting till they were all asleep, before creeping out here, sleep was becoming more difficult. She was worried too. Dinwoodie had left the morning after their row and she'd not seen him since, nor had she tried to contact him. She'd just have to hope that somehow they'd make up. They'd disagreed before and his way of dealing with it was to get back to the foundries and bury himself in work until one or the other of them apologised. She could only suppose that the whole business of war, all the travelling up and down, and his weariness had made him so unlike his normal self, and yet she could not forget his rough handling of her.

She rose, stretched, and went in to check Hansi was still asleep. Tonight had been a good one for him, as there'd been no nightmares. His face, gradually losing the multi-coloured bruises, was almost peaceful, and she was thankful for that. It had been hard to watch the terror on his face as he relived his ordeal. It was perhaps as well that his parents weren't alive, but what of those relatives in Germany? Did the cousins firing from their German trenches ever think of him? Wonder if he was firing back from the Allies' dugouts. She had to admit that it was not long ago that she'd been cursing the Germans, but then they were merely unknown bogeymen. Now Hansi was here, a gentle soul who'd been misused, and she could not find it in herself to do anything but care for him, whatever his nationality. Once she too had been an outsider, known what it was to be different, suffered the scorn of others. It was never an easy path. "And you, Cate Dinwoodie, have once again chosen the rough road." Saying it out loud somehow made her feel better. She began to prepare Hansi's food, in readiness for Charlie's arrival.

As she worked, her mind roamed over the weeks that had passed. She'd brought Charlie to work with her, and his brother, young Lachy, came into the stables with Stevie. It was pure luck that Stevie had gone south to see his sick mother, the day they'd discovered Hansi, leaving her and Charlie to see to the horses. Had he been there, Charlie would have gone home, as normal, and she'd have had to manage on her own. Now, how long the two of them could keep this double life up, she'd no way of knowing, but keep it up they must. If only the wretched war would finish! Though with the Allies still battling with the Germans on the Somme it was unlikely, so there was no alternative but to struggle on as the year-end approached. She gave a last quick look around before locking the door, and making for the rear of the Black House and Midnight. She rode to Craigavon, as if returning from an early morning ride, had breakfast, and then began the working day!

Once at her desk in the hospital, Cate sorted the mail, and went round the wards distributing the letters, spending time chatting to each patient, especially those who had nothing in the post, before she returned to deal with her own. She'd just begun to do so when Angus, now the odd job man at the hospital, knocked and came in, bearing one of the foreign parcels for her. Cate always enjoyed this little pantomime. He would hum and haw, shuffle his feet, discuss the weather and anything else he could think of, in the hope, by some chance, she might be forthcoming about the contents, or perhaps even open it. Understanding his curiosity she often teased him by looking carefully at the parcel, one eye on him, fiddling with the string, before putting it aside for later. Then thwarted once again, he'd take his leave.

Putting the letter to one side made her think of Dinwoodie. When would he come home to read it? She still felt he'd been in the wrong and perhaps it was that feeling that made her open the letter and read it for herself.

Picardy, Autumn 1916

My dear Girl,

It had been hoped, so I've been told, that a combined offensive on the Somme would knock the Germans out of the War on the Western Front this year. So much was hoped for from the big push, but this has now been dashed. Too little has been gained at too great a price.

It would seem many of the replacement troops lacked experience, enthusiastic though they were. Then the rain set in and has once again become the enemy. Men, vehicles, horses, mules, all struggle through mud that's like treacle.

Another year's fighting coming to an end, and still no sign of a breakthrough!

Alashdair.

Folding the letter away, her mind still full of armies and fighting, she became aware of voices drifting through the open window. To her horror she recognised the Brigadier's. Cate knew, no matter how devious she could be when required, that face to face with the dear man, her guilt would show. She mustn't be in the office when he came up, nor could she use either stair. Then she remembered the other door. Yanking the desk drawer open she clutched the big bunch of housekeeping keys and, with fumbling fingers, she at last found the right one. Once on the other side, in what was in reality a corridor, she checked the far door and was grateful it too was locked. They'd piled all the good items from the drawing room up here for safety, and she knew she had the only keys. Safe now, she allowed herself a smile: here she could curl up and have some blessed sleep! As she drifted off, she heard the voices in her office and then the door being shut.

It was almost the end of November and still the body count rose in Europe and beyond. When would this wretched war end? Cate knew she was overtired, working too hard, her personal life a mess: so long without Rhoddy, even longer without Sarah, Dinwoodie estranged, hiding Hansi, deceiving everyone, and, overshadowing it, the threat of the MacNishe curse — the burden of it all was a heavy one to bear, and God knows how much longer she could cope. The sound of the ambulances arriving outside made her straighten her shoulders, force a smile on her lips, and banish the problems to the back of her mind. As she went down the stairs to give a hand with the new patients arriving, she'd no inkling of just how problematical the future months were going to be. Busy with the patients' personal belongings, and guiding the men to the wards, she paid no attention to the uniformed figure in the hallway. However, as he was still there when she'd settled the patients, she was about to ask if she could help, when the man turned around. To her horror she realised it was none other than Ewan Brodie, the misogynist army doctor who'd vowed never to work with her. What was he doing here in her hospital?

Chapter 17

The Christmas of 1916 had come and gone, and Cate knew she should have made the effort to patch up her breach with Dinwoodie, but, as she was still hiding Hansi, she could see no way of doing so. The trouble was they were each convinced that their reaction to the situation was the correct one, and Dinwoodie's prolonged absence had done nothing to help, indeed had merely alerted the staff that something was amiss. Although he'd returned for the festivities, subdued by the news of the horrifying casualties at the Somme, no one felt in the least like celebrating. Dinwoodie had been distant, staying only as long as he deemed necessary, and then returning to his foundries. It had therefore been difficult to admit that she'd opened Alashdair's last letter. It would only have caused more upset and, since he'd shown he really didn't want to be there, it seemed pointless anyway.

These days her early morning rides included taking supplies to Hansi. He was now installed in the cave behind the waterfall, as he was completely recovered from his beating, and the move allowed him more freedom and lessened the prospect of discovery. It also meant that they no longer needed to watch over him at night, so Charlie returned to the stables and she was able to sleep in her own bed at Craigavon. On reaching the arranged spot she dismounted, unslung the panniers from the saddle, and left them in the usual place for him to collect. Though Hansi was less likely to be discovered on the mountain she knew she couldn't expect him to stay there much longer, and, right now, she still had no idea what to do with him.

To give her more time to mull over her problems she kept Midnight to a walk on the way back to Craigavon, but as she rode up the drive she was no nearer finding any answers. Deep in thought she was unaware of the Laggan car parked at the entrance to the house, and Maggie and Mrs Campbell-Broughton-Stewart in conversation at the front door, until she was almost on them. She knew she owed much to the elder women but her decision to aid Hansi had meant that she'd had to distant herself from all except Charlie. She'd managed to evade the Brigadier on his visit to the hospital, and she'd hoped that his wife would prolong her stay in London, but here she was and Cate knew this meeting would be tricky.

With Midnight now in the stables she would rather have gone upstairs to wash and change, but was aware she couldn't keep her visitor waiting any longer. By the time she arrived in the dining room, Maggie had breakfast laid and was pouring the coffee.

"Aha, the invisible woman is with us at last!" With a deliberate sharpness to her tone, Cecily Campbell-Broughton-Stuart searched Cate's face, looking for answers. "You've been avoiding me, now I wonder why? You've a closed look about your drawn face that tells me you've troubles. I thought we were friends?"

Cate forced a smile as she came to the table, before she spoke. "I don't know where these last months have gone. I kept meaning to see if you'd come back to Laggan, but there always seemed to be something to be done elsewhere, and what with the snow — work and…" Cate could think of no more excuses.

"I've heard that you've been keeping some peculiar hours of late."

"As I said, things have been pretty busy at the hospital…"

"Were you annoyed I didn't warn you of Ewan's arrival?"

Cate was not prepared for such a frontal approach, and considered her words carefully before replying. "It would have been good to be forewarned."

"Surely we know one another well enough by now, Cate, for you to have checked if I was aware of his visit?"

"Well I'm certain he wouldn't have come all this way and not been to see you."

"Now then, young lady, no more of this verbal fencing. You know damn well that I have no more liking for my nephew than you do. I was unaware of his visit till after it had happened, and I sat in that big old house waiting for the Cate I know to come charging up on one of those mad beasts you ride, fling yourself at my doorbell and assault my ears with your opinions and feelings re the wretched doctor."

Cate pushed her unfinished plate away and stared at the older woman, wishing for a moment that she could do just that — let all her worries tumble out in her old impulsive manner. She'd known that her decision to help Hansi, a German, would prove to be difficult, and so it was turning out. If only Cecily wasn't an army wife, then perhaps she could have confided in her, but as she was, nothing must be said.

Aware of the considered silence, Cecily Campbell-Broughton-Stuart, continued her probing. "You, young woman, look weighed down by troubles. Why are you so determined to keep them to yourself? They tell me Dinwoodie is also very busy. So busy that he hardly ever gets home. Now that makes me think that there's trouble between you…"

"I'm sorry, but I think that's my…"

"My dear girl, of course it's your business, but I'm worried about you. I'm not here to pry. It's just that when one telephones here, to the distillery, or even to the hospital, you're simply never there. Now, that I find unlikely. Cuthbert told me that Ewan was delivering patients here and that's the first I heard of it. I did ring and leave messages, but you never answered."

"I'm sorry. I thought that you might have seen him. He delivered his patients, spent time with the Major before he left, and was barely civil to me. I was so relieved to see him go, but — well I have this awful feeling that he'll be back."

"Perhaps he'll deliver more patients from Craiglockart. They are, after all, being treated by him, but that shouldn't worry you unduly."

Cate rose from the table and poured herself a cup of tea. On top of the row with Dinwoodie over Hansi, this was something else eating away at her. She'd studied Ewan Brodie as he'd moved around the hospital looking for faults. He barely registered the wounded soldiers, but spent a long time with the three new ones he'd brought. She'd seen the envious glances he cast around when he thought he was unobserved. Some instinct told her that he would return.

"I know it shouldn't, but it does, Cecily," she answered.

"That's better, you sound more like yourself now."

"Alright, I am having problems at home. My husband and I are at odds with one another because we each think we're right, and there seems no way to end a difference that big. I can't and won't say more, as it wouldn't be fair to Dinwoodie, or anyone else." Crossing to the window seat she continued. "But, I am glad to see you. I'm miserable company for myself these days."

"You'll have to be miserable a little longer then, as I'm on my way South. Too damn cold up here in the winter. Now why don't you consider having a break in London? A change of scenery…"

Cate stopped her with, "I love living here. Why would I…?"

"Because, dear girl, your present world is on the tilt. Oh, no doubt you'd miss your pagan landscape, but away from here, you might just see everything more clearly. Anyway think about it. You have my card with all the details, one phone call, my dear, and the car could be round here,

151

pick you up, and get you on the train heading for the high life in London."
She rose, crossed to the window seat, put her hand under Cate's chin,
and tilted her face so their eyes met.

"I believe that whatever you're doing that's put your world askew is
right for you, but have a care that you don't lose too much by holding to
it. And now I must away. You know where to find me. No, don't come
out, I hate goodbyes."

Maggie, coming in to clear the breakfast plates, joined Cate by the
window, and watched the Daimler pull away.

"I hope the good lady has managed to get to the bottom of that
worry worm that's eating away at you, and don't try to tell me it's no
concern of mine, for what worries and puts you or Lizzie out of sorts is,
and always will be, troubling for me."

"I know that full well, but Maggie…" Cate took her hand, forced a
smile, then went to the sideboard and poured another cup of tea. "Let's
just hope it all works out, shall we?"

"I see. Well you were ever stubborn and aye thought you knew best,
but if whatever's ailing you is no sorted, not only this house and family,
but also your precious distillery, hospital and glen will all suffer. Them
what builds a world aye has to have a care they dinna collapse it."
Knowing she'd failed, Maggie began to clear the remnants of the meal
with drooping shoulders.

When his secretary announced that Pearson was in the outer office
and wished to see him, Dinwoodie assumed the detective had brought
Rhoddy back to them. This news would mean the world to Cate, and
perhaps by reuniting her with her son, they might mend the rift in their
marriage. "Send them in, and bring some refreshments, Sheena please."
Dinwoodie rose to greet them, but Pearson came in alone.

"Where's the boy?"

"I'm sorry sir, I haven't got him."

"I thought for a moment there you had brought him back. Oh,
Sheena, thank you, leave it on my desk. Tea Pearson?"

"No thank you, sir."

"Right, why are you here? What's happened?"

"The news is all bad, sir. I did have the boy. Tailed him to a café,
chatted for a bit and then persuaded him to try the Metro. We travelled
on it to the Gare Du Nord, but something spooked him when we got
there. However many times I go over it, sir, I still don't understand.

152

Anyway he ran away and boarded a train. Unfortunately it turned out to be…" Pearson swallowed hard before continuing, "and it…"

"And it — come on, man, what?"

"It appears it was a troop train."

"Don't be ridiculous, Pearson, they'd never let a boy board one of those, besides which one assumes he had no ticket. You're mistaken. It makes no sense!"

"That's just it, sir. I was puzzled when I first made contact with him because he was wearing army clothing. He ran towards a group of soldiers and just disappeared. We searched everywhere else and there was no sign of him. The troop train was the only place he could have gone, sir."

Dinwoodie slumped to his seat, and tried to come to terms with the inevitable route this conversation was taking.

"Are you saying that my stepson was on a train possibly heading towards the Front?"

"I can't be certain of that. I just know he left Paris on a troop train. There is something else." He waited until he felt his employer had absorbed the shock before continuing.

"At about the same time MacNishe also disappeared. The concierge saw him leave his rooms and followed him. He visited several bars and in one of them he picked up a woman and has not been seen in his lodgings since."

"There's no chance, Pearson, that he's been reunited with his son?"

"I couldn't be definite, as I don't know, but it seems highly unlikely. Look, sir, I wanted to tell you in person. I know I haven't been successful, but I would like to return to France, find the father, and then we would be certain the boy's not with him. And I don't need paying for that. I let you down and I want to make amends. I know how difficult it will be for you to give this news to Mrs Dinwoodie, so it's the least I can do."

For a moment Dinwoodie spared a thought for the man he'd employed all those years ago to try to trace his uncle. Although then the news of the search had also been unwelcome — the family had perished in a house fire, Pearson had never let him down. "All right, go back. We must find the boy. Do what you can. We'll worry about the payment question later. In the meantime, give Sheena your invoices for services to date."

"I can't tell you how upset I am with losing him."

153

"No, I don't suppose you can. Leave me now."

Dinwoodie sat staring at the closed door. How could he return to Craigavon with this news? He'd assured her so many times that he'd bring Rhoddy back. Told her not to worry, that it would all work out. God, as if they weren't estranged enough!

At last a knock on the door roused him, and for one moment he wondered if Pearson had returned and it had all been a mistake, but it was Sheena who entered as he held his head in his hands.

"Sir, are you…?"

"No, Sheena I'm not. Pearson has…"

"Not found the boy?"

Dinwoodie could only shake his head before he spoke. "Cancel anything else for today. I'll take no calls and will be away from the office for an indefinite period"

"Mrs Dinwoodie, she'll be…?"

"This'll be…?" Not trusting himself to say more, he waved Sheena away. He knew he'd have to go to Craigavon. This was one piece of news that could not be dealt with on the telephone. It took him several more hours before he felt able to contact Morrison and, as Cate was not there when he was put through to Craigavon, he told Maggie he was coming home for a short break and would she let Cate know. He knew he should eat, get some sleep, but how could he? He was once more going to Craigavon to greet his wife with the very worst of news and right now he didn't know how he would find the strength to do so.

As she rode out the next morning, engrossed as usual with her burden of worries, Cate was surprised when she saw both Charlie and Hansi waiting for her. It was the German who spoke.

"Miss Cate, it is time to say good-bye."

Cate stared at the young man she'd nurtured. "Hansi, what are you saying? You can't go back! You can't go anywhere! The war continues and those who attacked you won't have changed their minds! You won't be safe."

"I will never forget what you both have done for me, but Charlie has a plan and I'm going to take the chance."

"Charlie, what have you got to do with this? Hansi's in my care! Plan! What plan?"

Charlie moved forward and lifted the saddlebags from the horse, before speaking. "With these bags and what I've brought we've plenty for a few days. Time enough to make our way out of here. He canna

154

spend the rest of the winter in yon cave. You know that, Miss Cate. Now he's mended, it's time."

Cate slid down from her horse and faced Hansi. "I wish I could do more. Perhaps keep you safe for longer."

"No one, dear lady, could have done more. One day, perhaps when the fighting stops, I may meet you again, but I will never forget you."

"Oh Hansi," before the tears overtook her she hugged him. "Are you sure you have to go?"

"Come now, no distress for me. Thanks to you I'm fit and well. Charlie is right. It is time to go. Do not worry, Miss Cate. He is clever, my new friend Charlie. I will be safe with him."

"Miss Cate," Charlie interrupted, "I need you to say you've sent me somewhere on an errand. Can you do that, so I'll no be missed."

"I can see your absence will be noticed, Charlie, but why would I send you and how long will it take?"

"Well now, I was hoping you could think of something, for it could be a while."

"Look, go back up to the waterfall and leave me here to think. As soon as I can, I'll come for you." Walking Midnight down to a nearby pool, she let him drink, and left him to wander while, mind whirling, she struggled to come to terms with this new development. After a time the horse, finding nothing to its taste nearby, returned. When his owner paid no heed, he began to nudge her head for attention.

"Now stop that. Ouch! Stand, Midnight! Daft animal! My hair net's caught in the bridle. Wait!" Untangling herself, she reached into her pocket and fed him some oats.

"That's it! Go on, off you go." Cate began to remove the net and unpin her hair, but remembered the horse had slavered all over her hands. As she reached over to wash them, she was taken aback by the reflection in the pool. With her hair loose over her shoulders she looked nothing like her normal self. It took her a few moments to understand why. There was no wind, but the hair in the placid pool reflection was moving. She grasped a handful of her own hair and pulled it over her face. The reflection never altered. Leaning forward, she felt a strong urge to put her face in the water. The reflection backed away and she followed it. There was no sense of overbalancing, but the cold mountain water seemed to envelope her in its icy bath. She was unable to draw back. The laugh, when it came, was evil and it seemed to break the spell.

Cate reached out a hand to push the reflection away. All she could see was the dark depth of the pool, where she could well have drowned. There was no reflection! Her body trembled with fear. Why had the comforting spectre of her childhood turned into this evil apparition? She moved even further back from the edge, curled up in a ball, and held onto bits of the scrub as though to prevent herself from falling in again.

Midnight pricked his ears up as he heard the voices and trotted towards them. Charlie caught his reins and looked round for Cate, but there was no sign of her. He knew she often left the horse loose as it rarely moved far from her side.

"She's around here somewhere, Hansi. The horse'll find her. Come on then, Midnight, where's Cate?" Both men began to call, and the horse veered left and trotted through the scrub and on to the pool, where Cate appeared to be sleeping on the bank. It nudged her prone body until she sat up.

"You were going to come up for us, Miss Cate. It's time. We want to get on the road." Charlie said.

Cate stared at them. For a moment she didn't even recognise them. And then the dream returned. Had it been a dream? She felt her clothes. Must have been — she wasn't wet, but… Trying to make sense of her thoughts, she began to wind her hair back into the hairnet and faced the others.

"You two get started. Charlie, see if you can make it to the shepherd's hut on the downside of the Quarry. It's about seven, eight miles across the moor. You know the one?"

"I do that, Miss Cate, but have you thought why I'm to be away from the glen?"

"Charlie, I just might have an idea, but I need to fetch something from the Black House first. Anything else you need for your travels?"

"Well, we've little silver between us, but we'll look for work as we go, and some bottled Craeg Dhu could find us a favour when we need it."

"I'll bring both." As Hansi opened his mouth to protest, Cate, with a wave of her hand said, "One day, Hansi, you can repay me, but for now take what I give you this evening as a good luck present to you both. Guard him well, Charlie, and you be safe. I'll not know piece of mind till you're back. Now, on your way, and I must be on mine."

As she rode, Cate relived her experience by the pool. Common sense suggested she'd fallen asleep and been dreaming, but Cate knew it wasn't as simple as that. Though no one would believe her, she understood *the Red-headed Woman* was seeking redress, and, as a MacNishe, she was now in danger. Cate understood then there was only one way to protect both Rhoddy and herself. And that was where Charlie could help.

With Gordon handling her money, paying a quarterly allowance to her, she'd no reason to believe she'd ever be penniless again. Nevertheless she'd been secreting money and one or two other things in the stout walls of the Black House away from prying eyes. Retrieving what she needed from there, she set off along the old drovers road in the dusk, and then went cross-country to the shepherd's hut. There she gave the money, the whisky, and a drawing to Charlie with her instructions, and left them to sleep while she galloped back to Craigavon and the message that her husband was returning the next day.

Maggie opened the door when she heard the car arrive. She was not looking forward to having both man and wife together in the house again. Not after the trouble he'd brought home last time. The atmosphere then had been colder than the February wind howling round the house today. Still, as she watched him come up the steps, she couldn't help feeling sorry for him. There was very little of The Iron Baron about him. He did look old.

"Welcoming committee as usual, Maggie! Did you give her my message?"

"That I did, sir, an she'll be home for tea."

"Good. I'll be in my study till then."

As he passed her in the hall, she had a sudden urge to put her arms round him and give him a comforting hug. How could two decent people get themselves into such a scrambled mess? More's to the point, how were they going to sort it?

Cate came through the door as McAlister's grandfather clock was striking the hour for tea. The events of the day before had left her feeling exhausted and all she wanted to do was go to bed, but tea, and probably dinner, would have to be negotiated first. Quite why he was here she'd no idea and did not look forward to it, though with Hansi gone their quarrel no longer had any substance. With that thought she went into tea.

Dinwoodie watched her as she fiddled about with a scone on her plate, refilled her cup, and sat back in her chair. He thought she looked as bad as he felt. How had it all come to this?

Aware of his scrutiny, and anything to break the blanket of silence, she began to speak. "Dinwoodie, more tea?" At the shake of his head, she felt she might as well finish and go upstairs to get some rest. She rose, put her things on the tray, and made to leave the room.

"Don't go, Cate. Please come and sit down. I've been silent because what I have to say is so…"

"Dinwoodie, you're shaking. Are you ill? Here, let me feel your forehead."

She stood in front of him, hand outstretched and he grasped it, held it tight for a moment, then let it go, before shaking his head.

Puzzled, she returned to her chair across from him.

"Cate, please let me say what I must before you interrupt." He forced himself to look into her eyes and continued.

"Pearson came to my office in Glasgow yesterday. There's no easy way to say this, but he's lost contact with both MacNishe and Rhoddy. They now appear to be separated. MacNishe is probably with some woman somewhere, at least that's Pearson's guess, but Rhoddy…?"

"Dinwoodie. He — he's dead?"

"Pearson says not, but, Cate, he's, well, I mean, he's somehow got in with some soldiers — Pearson saw him get on a troop train. He — he, could be near the Front."

Wide-eyed, she stared at him, unable to make sense of what he was saying. "That's — that's not possible. Boys don't — Rhoddy — how could he, Dinwoodie? It makes no sense. The army? Fighting? It can't be, Dinwoodie! It can't!" Silent then, Cate sat immobile, her ordered life unravelling in her mind: the mothballing of the distillery, her quarrel with Dinwoodie, Rhoddy possibly on the Western Front, killed perhaps! Even Bruce MacNishe had gone missing. She saw her then the evil apparition of *The Red-Headed-Woman* in the pool, heard the bitter laugh, and now knew for certain — it was all a foretaste of the Tinker's curse at work. It was happening as Old MacNishe had said it would. For generations each new laird had kept the painting of *The Red-Headed-Woman* in Kevinishe House, hating its presence, but mindful of why it was there. Now, with it gone, she felt the weight of generations of fear about to crush her — the sound she uttered began as a baby's mewling, and slowly built into the full-blown keening of an ancient tribe as it echoed round the walls of Craigavon, bringing all who heard it rushing to the room.

It was Dinwoodie who got to her first. Kneeling in front of her, calling her name, trying to stop the rocking to and fro. The others, wide-eyed, halted in the doorway, waited and watched until exhaustion ceased the movement and reduced the sound. Then, unsure what to do, they melted away, leaving her in the arms of her husband.

Part Three

1917 Unexpected Events

Chapter 18

Major McAlpin smiled at his unlikely patient as a pale January sun lit the bed.

"You, Miss Cate, have been overdoing things in a big way. However, I think you're on the mend, but no frantic riding across the moor, no return to the hospital as yet, and don't even try to argue or I'll get Maggie to prescribe complete bed rest for weeks!"

"I feel such a fraud. I don't know — the winter — work — things. I think I just had one bit of bad news too many, though I was overtired, so I suppose that didn't help."

"It certainly didn't, and don't think we haven't all noticed how worried you've been of late. Sister Mary Anne is coming for a visit today, so I'd better get back to duty. And by the way, I'll be in Fort William for a couple of days. Don't forget I expect you to behave until I return. Do as your told, and we'll be delighted to have you back. You've been sorely missed."

When the door closed behind him, Cate lay and thought about how well she got on with the Major: he was such a good man. And she had to admit she did feel better for the rest and sedatives he'd prescribed. Her worries, however, were still with her. She needed to know what was happening to Charlie and Hansi. Where were they? They'd been gone for weeks. What was Charlie's plan? He'd mentioned working, but doing what? If only he would come home. Apart from Hansi's future, she fretted over Charlie's errand. Should it be successful then perhaps her worry over Rhoddy would be lessened slightly, and her hidden fear of catastrophe might be stilled. It was all right for Dinwoodie to mock the old ways, but she could still feel that sense of evil as she thought she was being pulled into a watery grave.

Poor Dinwoodie, being the bearer of even more dreadful news this time had not been easy for him. How kind and gentle he'd been with her. The strain of all that had happened to them during this wretched war had affected them both. Nothing was said, either about the coldness between them, or its cause. They'd simply put it behind them after the shock of Pearson's news and her own collapse. Dinwoodie would be home at the weekend, and how good it was to be looking forward to seeing him again. In future she would try to hold her tongue, rein in her temper, and that would surely please him. She knew, while she was recovering from the shock of Pearson's findings, she'd neglected both home and children, so she'd need to make up for that. On her way downstairs to the kitchen she couldn't help a wry smile, knowing full well that keeping all these good intentions would remove the essence of herself, but she'd give it a try!

By the end of the week Cate was more or less her old self. She played with the twins, chatted to the others in the kitchen, greeted the horses, who snorted in response, and walked the grounds of Craigavon with an over-excited Rory, who'd missed her most of all. She'd ridden to the distillery a couple of times, ignoring the Major's orders, checked with Donald Uig that the machinery servicing was going ahead, looked over the accounts with Solly, and picked up her personal mail. Sorting through them she found there was another letter from Alashdair, so they'd have that to read at the weekend, and this one she'd leave for Dinwoodie!

She was on the doorstep with the twins when Morrison pulled up in front of them. The boys raced round to greet Dinwoodie, a leg being hugged by each twin.

"Alright you two, let me get inside first!" he said with a laugh, before taking their hands and climbing the steps to a smiling Cate who embraced him. Then the family went to the drawing room, where Maggie, busy laying out tea, was thanking the fates that had returned the laughter to the house.

With tea over, the twins, well wrapped up against the cold, went for their walk with Lizzie, while their parents sat back in the drawing room and Cate presented Dinwoodie with the letter.

The Western Front January 1917

Dearest Girl,

Yet another year of war! Remember when it was all going to be over by Christmas 1914? Let's hope that 1917 will be the last one. We have seen the most appalling weather here. Deep snow covers everything. The guns still fire, and I suppose the exercise might warm the men up a bit, but with no identifiable landmarks I can't see the shells being effective. At least this white blanket does mask the ruined landscape.

I know you used not to mind the cold in that Highland glen of yours, but the men, in or out of, the line, can't do anything here. No matter what they do, they can't get warm! Any stray bits of wood are so frozen it is near impossible to make a fire. Soldiers' clothes get so stiff they dare not undress. They say they sleep with their boots on, or put them under their pillows so they don't freeze! Their feet and hands are always numb with cold.

Vehicles slip and slide drunkenly over the frozen surface. Engines freeze. Horses' hooves fare no better. There is no grip to be had on the ice. Hot food doesn't stay that way, even if they can get it, and the bread is so frozen it has to be sawn. I don't believe anyone in the trenches, or even behind the lines, manages to have more than a quick wipe of face and hands. It's too damn cold to attempt anything else!

An almost permanently frozen,
Alashdair.

"Not a lot of news there. Understandable if they're snowed in. It was bad enough coming up from Glasgow and more on the way they say."

"I hope not, Dinwoodie, though it would delay your return and that would be good, but I was thinking of Major McAlpin — he's in Fort William for a few days. He doesn't like to be away from the hospital for too long."

"Did he say why he was going? "

"Routine supplies I suppose. Why?"

"No reason, just curious, Cate."

"He may be back, but I'd have heard, I think?"

"Speaking of people returning, when do you expect Charlie home? He's been gone some time now. I'm sure you've told me, but I've no idea why he went away?"

"We haven't spoken of it, Dinwoodie, because I didn't want to fall out with you, but Hansi —." She shot a worried look at her husband as she saw him flinch at the name. "I nursed him, you know, in the Black House, and Charlie agreed to get him back to Glasgow once his wounds were healed. I think that's where they were heading, but he was deliberately vague when I questioned him."

"I've said it before, but it bears repeating, Charlie has turned into a special young man, and all credit to both him and you, Cate, for that. So the German is mended then?"

"Yes, but I never really saw him as a German, the enemy — just a young man who'd been badly treated and hurt. I'm sorry, Dinwoodie, I didn't mean to thwart you. I just felt it to be right."

"With hindsight I believe you were. We civilians may not be fighting, but this war makes us at odds with our lives. Anyway, I'm more than glad that that particular bit of bother is behind us and I have my loving wife in tune with me once more. You gave us an awful fright, you know." He rose and pulled her into his arms, then twined the escaping tendrils of hair round his fingers before murmuring, "I can't do without your love, and these last bleak months have been tortuous for me, not knowing how to bridge the gap and doing nothing but bringing you bad news that would be difficult for you to bear. Don't let's do this again, Cate. Being here, with you and the family, the boys, the glen, it's all — oh Cate —," with a strangled sob he laid his head on hers and held her tightly.

"Shsst, Dinwoodie, all is well now." She caressed the nape of his neck, and they stood like this for some time till they'd recovered, and then hand in hand they went upstairs.

With the snow lessening by the end of March, Kevinishe was a hotchpotch of white, brown, and slush. The current patients in the hospital, bar the two ex-Craiglockart ones, were ready to leave and return to active service. Cate, helping them pack their belongings, wondered if they'd survive their next stint at the front, and for a mad moment thought she might keep them in the glen. It was ridiculous, but she understood their reluctance as they shook hands, and with muttered thanks boarded the army truck that signalled they were no longer patients. She stood in the doorway and waved until they were out of sight.

By tomorrow or the next day there'd no doubt be ambulances with a new intake and the pattern would begin all over again. She turned to find Mary Anne at her elbow. "Right, we'd better get beds changed and everything else sorted ready for the next lot. When does the Major think they'll be here?"

"I don't know, Cate. He wants to see you in the office when you've a moment, by the way."

"I might as well go now before we get started in the wards." With her thoughts still on the departed patients, Cate paid little attention to Mary Anne's rather sombre tones, and made her way to the office. When she entered Major McAlpin had his back to her as he looked out on the Kevinishe lawn that was gradually losing its white covering, with patches of green showing through. He turned as he sensed her presence.

One look at his face and Cate knew that there was a problem. "What is it Major? Not more bad news of the friends you've left at the front?"

"Take a seat, Cate. Notice, I've dropped the 'Miss'. That's because as the truck left Kevinishe my command in this hospital was rescinded." He watched as she sank onto the chair in front of his desk and tried to mouth the multitude of questions he was expecting.

"But why? Your work here has been exemplary. What are the army thinking of?" Cate could only look pleadingly at him, willing him to say it was all a mistake, though somehow she knew it wasn't.

"They require me to return to my old post again. They need senior medics with all the carnage that's going on in the front line. I'm afraid I've had my allotted recovery time, so off I must go."

"But it's not fair!" Cate knew she sounded like a petulant child, but he'd been so right for the hospital here. Everyone liked him, admired the way he got the patients to co-operate, work on their fitness, and enjoy the pleasant hospital atmosphere. It was only then the significance of the two remaining patients became obvious. She looked in horror at the Major as she mouthed the dreaded question.

"It's him isn't it? That's why those two down there haven't gone."

"I can't confirm or refute that, but, like you, I believe that leaving the two traumatised patients here means that Captain Brodie may very well have engineered this hospital to take the overflow from Craiglockart."

"I loathe the man. Have I no rights? No say in the matter?"

"No, Cate. Having gone into partnership with the army, you, like the rest of us, must abide by their wishes. Believe me, if I thought it would have changed anything I would've queried their orders, but I knew it would do no good. I'm as sad at leaving here as you are to see me go."

"But for you to have to go back to this awful war, be injured again, perhaps be killed. I can't bear that for you, Major."

"Oh, Cate, that sentence almost makes it worth my going. I've so enjoyed working with you, and will most certainly miss you and your hospital. So we'll just have to wait for notification of my replacement, and then I'll be on my way. And you should join the others and make everything ready and waiting for its new intake."

He was almost glad of her sad expression as she left to do his bidding. It had been a long time since someone had shown any care for him, and the woman he'd just dismissed had left a warm feeling in his heart that he'd treasure in the difficult times ahead.

168

Chapter 19

The 1917 Easter Season opened with the joyful news on the 6th of April that America had declared war on Germany. At last the submarine hunting and destroying of the American convoys had forced President Woodrow Wilson to defer to the pro-war faction led by Theodore Roosevelt. The announcement was valued more for the hope it brought the allies, rather than soldier numbers in Europe. The American army was still embroiled on the Mexican border, and even if it hadn't been, it was too small as the numbers stood, to be any significant use on the front line.

On Easter Sunday in Kevinishe hard-boiled eggs were stained in tea, faces painted on them, and those at Craigavon were rolled down the slope of the south lawn showing as much joy as they could muster for the children's sake. Cate's moods were brittle since the Major left and Captain Ewan Brodie had taken command of the hospital. They all sympathised with her having to work with him, and though they had no real knowledge of the man, the effect he had on Cate was making everyone else miserable. Any one of them would willingly have gone to the front and brought Major McAlpin back, had it been possible.

With the Easter festivities over and the shock of the Major's departure lessening, a semblance of hope and peace pervaded the Craigavon household. At the hospital, Cate kept strictly to her office, the kitchen, and the grounds. The nine new patients in the wards never even knew of her existence. Rarely did she encounter the Captain, and when she did so they exchanged icy greetings and went their separate ways. Mary Anne did her best to bring a feeling of warmth both to the patients and the other staff, but it was as if the heart of the place had been ripped out. How long this state of affairs would have continued no one knew, but everything changed with the disappearance of Private Laing.

Mary Anne burst into Cate's office with the news.

"Gone missing he has. Of all the current patients he's the most unpredictable. Like most of them, sudden noises frighten him, but he's different. There's an aggression there that's set off by various sets of circumstances. He's likely to be a real danger to someone out there, I'm sure of that."

"How long's he been gone, Mary Anne?"

"Sometime in the night, we think."

"Surely to God whoever was on duty should have noticed his absence. From what you've been telling me about him, I should've thought he'd be the one patient under constant scrutiny."

"Aye, Cate, he should have been, but the Captain upset Kirsty and then we had Donald Uig here having words with him. He took Kirsty home even though she was supposed to be covering for the orderly who was away to a funeral in Strathmore."

"So the man's been gone — it's eleven o' clock now, and say he left just before dawn, that's about five-thirty to six these fine May mornings, then he's been out there for at least five hours. What's been done about it?"

"That's why I'm here. The Captain's ordering everyone in different directions and the distillery men and ground staff are fair scunnered with him. Cate, there's chaos out there. You must take charge of the search. The Captain, God forgive me for saying so, is worse than useless in this emergency, and we'll end up with more lost than found!"

Mary Anne could see Cate was fighting herself, and once again she cursed the army authorities that'd ruined a perfectly good hospital.

"Cate, you have to help. This is your place and you can't take your anger out on the patients, the other staff or some poor deranged fool, who right now is probably floating in the River Nishe."

"Alright! But he'll never listen to me. You know damn well he won't."

"I don't care. Just you get out there and sort this mess. If he won't listen, do it anyway. You've let the man get the better of the Cate I know. Hunkering up here with your hurt feelings. You wanted this damn hospital. You worked so hard to get it, so now go out and save it!" With the end of her tirade Mary Anne left slamming the door behind her.

Knowing her friend was right; Cate took off her skirt and in her breeches made for the kitchen where she knew the staff would have gathered. When she entered she was surprised to see the Captain there as well. She'd barely crossed to the table before he rounded on her.

"Get these men out searching for my patient immediately, Mrs Dinwoodie."

"I take it, Captain, you've already asked them?"

"They won't go. I've ordered them time and time again and they just sit round the table like dumb oxen."

"Perhaps it's the word ordered, that's the problem, Captain." Turning to the others, Cate singled out Robbie. "What's the problem here? I've never once heard any of you refuse help to a missing man."

"Trouble is, Miss Cate, that one's", he nodded in the Captain's direction, "1s sending us off every which way. He doesna know the lie of the land, and we'd soon be as lost as the poor loony devil that is."

"Right. Is anyone out there now, Robbie?"

"Only one of they orderlies in the gardens. Mind, he canna even find his way roond there!"

Unrolling a map she'd brought with her, Cate swept her hand across portion after portion of the estate allotting each sweep to a man. Within the half-hour they'd all upped and left, leaving Snowy standing between her mistress and the Captain. Without a word to him, Cate made to leave, only to come to a halt when he stepped forward and barred her way.

"You're not going to just leave them all wandering out there without anyone commanding them?"

His tone made Cate bridle, and her reply was sharper than it would have been, had he appreciated what they were all doing.

"I've given my instructions, Captain, and right now I know within a few yards as to where each one of them is going. They'll meet me at given points to report as I ride round. Had you come to me in the beginning I would have told you that there is a definite procedure to follow in these circumstances. Knowing the area well, I was the obvious one to direct it. Now, if you'll excuse me, I'll get on. I suggest you send Mary Anne, who knows this garden, to round up your orderly. If he hasn't found the missing patient as yet, he's not in the immediate grounds. Then you can get on with your duties and leave the search to us. We'll do our utmost to find your patient, Captain Brodie, now if you'll let me pass, I'll join the search."

By nightfall all the men were back at the hospital and Snowy was in her element dispensing hot soup and doorstep sandwiches. Then Stevie and Lachy appeared, having brought the spare horses from Craigavon that Cate had requested. Hospital dinner over, the Captain and Mary Anne also joined the crowd in the kitchen. No one dared ask the question as to why Cate had not returned. All, save the Captain, knew of the dangers of being out in the dark and though they knew Miss Cate

171

was daft enough to ride in these unfriendly hours, nevertheless they worried in silence. The thought that the missing man was mentally unhinged made them all uneasy.

Circling the moor one more time, Cate made a detour to the Black House, to collect a lantern, as night fell. It would give her one more chance to continue to search, before returning to the hospital. She didn't bother unsaddling Midnight, but left him in the barn she'd had built some years before, with a handful of oats and a bucket of water. She made for the door, let herself in, felt for the matches on the table, and in the wavering light searched for the lantern and paraffin. While doing so she became aware of a draught at her neck and cursed herself for not making sure the latch was down. Since she would be leaving almost immediately, she didn't bother to stop and drop it, but continued with her work till she had the lantern alight, and then swung round with it ready to leave, lighting up the half-open doorway as she did so.

He was supporting himself by leaning on the doorjamb, and the steel of the kitchen knife in his hand glinted in the light. Cate's first thought was what a pity she'd had nothing to do with the current lot of patients. Had she known the man beforehand, she might have had an idea how to handle him. Her one certainty, though, was that she was in great danger in this enclosed space, with him barring the only exit.

Letting go of the lantern, she pulled out a chair and sat on it, then pulled another one out and gestured to the man. What had Mary Anne called him? His only response was to make a forward stabbing motion with the knife and then lean back against the doorjamb. It was as if they were frozen in time — she in her seat and the man in the doorway. At last, Cate forced herself to move. Very slowly she rose, turned away from him, trying to hide her fear, took the lantern to the kitchen range, and, with a spill from the jar on the mantelpiece lit the ready-laid fire. She filled the pot-bellied kettle from the pail under the sink and then hung it on the hook above the flames. Busying herself with putting larger bits of wood onto the new flames, she stole a sideways glance at the doorway, but the man neither moved nor spoke.

She still collected most of her firewood for the Black House from the seashore and as one particularly salty piece spat and hissed she sensed the startled movement of the man at the door. She turned towards him and with some effort, managed a smile. "I like the sound of a fire spitting and hissing at me, it reminds me of my childhood when I lived here.

There's no need to be afraid, it's just the salt in the sticks that makes the noise."

Getting no response, Cate continued, forcing herself to speak in a light and cheerful voice, though her mind rang with the warning, 'he's a knife and is unstable'. "I'm tired and hungry. You must be too, so why don't you come in and sit down? The kettle will soon boil now the fire's going." With yet still no response from him, she moved very deliberately to the small pantry, to see if there was anything left of her emergency supplies from Hansi's stay. With a couple of eggs, some questionable looking salt bacon, and two hard bannocks on the slate slab beneath the net, she set to on the range and soon had some eggy bannocks and crisp bacon ready to serve.

Returning to the table she split the food between two plates and with a tremulous smile said. "Come, I don't know about you, but I'm hungry." As he made no move, she tried again. "Why don't you sit at the far end of the table? You can keep a good eye on me from there." She repositioned his plate, then sat down at the other end, and began to eat her makeshift breakfast.

She'd learnt early on in her life, while dealing with wild animals, to keep a sidelong watch on their movements so she would be quick to react to any danger either to them or herself. She saw him move gingerly towards the smell of the food, pick up the fork, ignore the table knife. He used his weapon to stab at the food instead, while his eyes remained glued on her.

Cate thought she'd be safe for the moment, but was aware that she was still in great danger, and as yet had no idea how she was going to get out of it. Her other discomforting thought was that, with her absence in the dark, the men would want to start searching for her, and their sudden appearance could be disastrous. She'd told the workers to break off at nightfall, have their meal at the hospital before returning to their homes and then meet her at dawn, to continue the search if they'd not found him, so hopefully they'd do just that.

Her thoughts were broken by a sudden cry from the man as he dropped the fork and clutched at his head, the knife still in his other hand. She let him be for a moment, but as he was more concerned with his head than her, she moved with great care towards him, flexing her fingers as she went. Very deliberately, she put her hands on top of his. When she met no resistance she raised her hands to his head and was just about to lay them on when he turned the knife on her. With both hands still in the space where his head had been, she dared not move. Instead she looked hard into his eyes, forcing every frightened muscle to be still and not betray her fear. When the point of the knife nicked her throat she swallowed hard as she felt the blood trickle. For what seemed forever they were yet again frozen in their stance. Then, as before, the cry came and he cradled his head, so she repeated her tactic of trying to massage it, only for the whole episode to be repeated, though it felt as though the knife contact was more painful this time.

The pattern continued four, perhaps five — she'd lost count — times and her nerves were jangling, never mind the pain and the sticky feeling of her collar below the wounds. She knew she was almost at the point when she could stand no more, when all at once the knife clattered to the floor. In his anguish the man upended the table, threw back his chair, screamed like a banshee, and began banging his head on the edge of the upturned table. Cate moved sideways, snatched a tea towel from the dresser top, wiped her neck, and waited till he raised his head for yet another wallop on the table, then laid the bloody towel on the edge in front of the howling man. For a moment all was silent, so Cate turned his head and looking deep into his eyes, removed his hands once more. With the remnants of her courage, she set about her task of reducing his pain. She wanted no recurrence of the Gregor situation, but proceeded to give his head the most powerful massage that she was capable of and, when she felt he was responding, bent to straighten his chair and ease him into it. She continued the deep massage, then lightened the movement and began humming in an unsteady voice one of the old Gaelic lullabies. Her hands stroked to the soothing rhythm, and finally his head drooped on his chest. Cate struggled to her fallen chair, settled the table once more on its four legs, and then, completely spent, laid her head on it and wept.

Later, staggering to her feet, she was unaware, that she too had slept. Now she had to decide what her next move would be. Quite why the knife still lay on the floor where he'd dropped it, she'd no idea. Why hadn't she picked it up, thrown it away, or indeed left the house herself? She was still considering this when, with a startled grunt, the man raised his head and, with a quick look at the floor his gaze found the knife. The puzzled look he turned on Cate made her shake her head before she spoke.

"I know. It would have been sensible to get rid of it. I — I don't know — it was all too much." As he continued to stare, Cate tried to gather her wits. She was still in danger, the knife closer to him than her.

174

Rushing him would be madness even if she'd felt her limbs would hold her. Gathering her remaining strength she tried conciliation.

"Now that you're fed and no longer exhausted, let me explain. I mean you no harm." Her voice shook as she spoke, but she pressed on. "You were lucky to find this house and me. People have perished on the mountain, you know." His sudden movement all but undid her — "I mean...?"

"You have mountains?" the man queried.

It was such a ridiculous question, amidst all the danger that had preceded it, that Cate wondered if she too was verging on madness.

"Tell me!" the man urged. "There are mountains, here?"

This was all too much for her and she laughed nervously while trying to answer his ludicrous question. "Scotland — at least the Highlands — they're made of mountains." Bewildered she moved to the still open door, only to find the outside world clothed in the proverbial mist and murk that was one of the persistent coats of the Highlands.

The fact that her legs did indeed work, and the knowledge that she'd made it to an uncertain dawn, bleeding, but alive, seemed to return her to some kind of normality. Turning to him, she said, "Look, we can see nothing in this, but if it's mountains you're after, I have one very special one. Up there lies my Beinn Nishe. Now if you come back to the hospital with me, I'll continue to try to ease the pains in your head, and one day very soon, you and I will climb the mountain. I don't think you really want to harm anyone. It's the pain and what went on in the war." At the mention of the word she saw him flinch, turn and stare at the knife.

With great care, Cate closed the door and tried to retrieve the knife, but he eased her aside, bent down, grasped it, then stood and pointed it at her throat. Somehow she knew it was the ultimate test, so stayed very still as the knife came nearer and nearer, and his eyes locked with hers. All she wanted to do was close her lids, remove the night's horror, and escape, yet she understood it would be fatal.

When, at long last he handed her his weapon, she gulped, nodded and taking it from him put it in a drawer. Then she went into the bedroom, removed her top, took one of her salves from a cupboard, smeared the wounds, wrapped a riding stock round her neck, and pulled on a polo-necked jumper, to cover her camisole.

He watched from the doorway with a puzzled frown, before he spoke. "Why?"

175

"Because only you and I know what happened here tonight. It's our business and no one else's. No word of it will come from me, and I suggest you too keep quiet. It would do no good to involve others. You were a man with pain. You lost trust in those around you. From now it will be better. I cannot cure your pain, but I can ease it. Although you don't know me, I work in the hospital and when you need help all you have to do is ask for me. I promise things will get better, however long it takes. Now, as I was saying, will you do that? Come back to the hospital? Here's my hand, see. Here in the Highlands, when we give our word, we spit on our hand and offer it to the person we're giving our bond to." She waited while he considered her long speech and then copied her actions.

"Do you ride as well as liking mountains?"

"Yes. Who are you?" He asked in a bewildered voice.

"Just call me Miss Cate — everyone does." Though as she said it, she remembered the Captain who would have none of it: just an icy, 'Mrs Dinwoodie', as if to demean her, strip her of any authority and, reduce her to a mere wife. It was at that moment she realised she had to change, stop — what was it Mary Anne had called it? Skulking? No — hunkering, that was it! She'd handled the situation in the wrong way. Allowed him to keep her hospital to himself. Well, the man was in for a shock. There'd be no more of that. The Miss Cate who returned the missing patient would once more be fully involved with the Kevinishe hospital, and he'd just have to put up with it!

Out in the barn, with Midnight ready to go, Cate turned to her night's companion, "After all we've been through, I don't even know your name?"

"Private Laing, Miss Cate."

"No, I mean your Christian name. I don't think we need to be too formal after last night, do you?" She surprised herself by being able to smile!

Returning the smile he jumped up behind her and said, "Duncan."

"Right then, Duncan, I found you on the slopes of the mountain, and we spent the night for safety in the Black House. Agreed?"

"Of course. I can do no less. Though I think you ought to know before you take me back, I have not spoken for many months now."

"Then, Duncan my friend, I'm honoured. Do we tell them, or do you want to retreat behind your silence again?"

"But no, everyone must know it was you that freed my tongue. It was a brave thing to do."

176

"I don't think that's such a good idea. How about you go back, tired and hungry, go to sleep and when you wake up perhaps a little talking, and then each day a little more."

"You don't want their praise for what you did here tonight?"

"Oh, let's just say I like a secret now and again. What do you say, Duncan?"

"I still say you are a strange woman. The strangest I've ever met."

"Oh, I'll settle for that! Walk on, Midnight. Home we go."

Chapter 20

Home once again by the end of May, Dinwoodie picked up the Scribbler's letter in the hall, wondering what news this one held, and then became aware of the change in the atmosphere. He was equally surprised to find that Cate had not yet returned from the hospital. Since Brodie had arrived she'd been working there for shorter hours, and he was intrigued. Maggie was the obvious one to question.

"Aye well, sir, she's been her old self and more since all the kerfuffle at the hospital. Out all night she was then, mind. Found the missing patient, she did — loony they say he was — an brought him back safe and sound, though it seems that the Captain didna do so well over the whole thing. All the crowd, staff, patients, even them who've nothing to do with it have the story, so, Mr Dinwoodie, our Miss Cate is once again the 'hero of the hour', as they say."

"Heroine, Maggie, heroine, for she's definitely not a man."

"But that's where you're wrong, sir. Not one of those men, and there's plenty of them, could do what she did, whatever it was. No one knows how she got him to come back, but back she brought him, so 'hero' she is, as she's worth more than many a man!"

Firmly rebuked, Dinwoodie chuckled as he made his way to the study to await the arrival of this newly minted 'hero'!

Later, with the habitual slam of the front door resounding up the stairs, he picked up the letter from his desk and went to meet his wife. Embraces exchanged, they made for the drawing room, where he opened the letter, and read it aloud.

"I don't know whether to salute our allies or weep for the French."

"Will they really give up, Dinwoodie, the French I mean? Surely that would end the war?"

"Indeed it would. The Germans would get a massive boost of confidence and, might even go on to win."

Cate stared at him horror-struck. "They can't, Dinwoodie! We mustn't let them!"

"Let's hope the French generals can somehow restore the morale of the poor wretches of soldiers who've suffered so abominably in this goddam awful war, otherwise the outlook is indeed bleak."

The dinner gong provided a welcome relief from their pessimistic thoughts though the meal was taken almost in silence.

It was not until they retired for the night, that Dinwoodie noticed the riding stock. "That's not exactly alluring bed wear, my dear!"

She hesitated for a moment before speaking. "Well, I suppose you'll have to know, since we want no more secrets between us, but I've given my word, so only if I can have yours, will I explain."

Dinwoodie looked at this woman he loved, as he'd never loved before. She was like the mountain she identified with, layered with depths that seemed full of endless surprises, not all of them good, of course, but he was never quite sure of what she would do next, or what he would discover about her multi-faceted personality.

"I'm waiting, Dinwoodie. I'll not say a word till I have your promise, for I must not break mine."

"I presume this is to do with the missing patient Maggie was telling me about. I have to say I have an uneasy feeling about this, Cate."

"Well then, put up with my less than glamorous night attire. The choice is yours. Surely you can trust me to act on my own?"

"That, my dear wife, is what troubles me, but since you are so determined, what you tell me stays in this room. However, I refuse to engage in your heathen tradition of spitting on my hand before I get into my bed! You'll just have to trust me to keep my word."

"Alright, here we go." As Cate outlined the bones of that extraordinary night, replaying it in her mind as she spoke, she was unaware of Dinwoodie's anguished expression, or his utter shock. "So there we go, that's it. In a way, another lost soul, a bit like Hansi, though his was never a mental problem."

"My God, Cate. You could have been killed! How could you put yourself in such danger?"

"Dinwoodie, I didn't go looking for danger, nor did I put myself deliberately in it. I've told you, I went to the Black House to get a lantern to light my search. I didn't know he was there. I opened the door, went in, and then he appeared. He must have been hiding outside somewhere. I just tried to play as well as I could with the few cards I'd got."

"I don't understand. Why didn't you run away?"

"I couldn't! He was at the door blocking my way, and don't forget he had the knife in his hand. He'd have stabbed me if I'd done that."

"I can't bear the thought of you in that situation. Take that thing off your neck and let me see the damage."

Cate removed the stock, then the moss patch she was using to help heal the injuries, revealing the almost sealed cuts on her neck. To her surprise, Dinwoodie let out a startled cry, and then, folding her in his arms, kissed the scars as his tears fell on them.

"Oh, Cate, the very thought of you in such danger unmans me. My darling, have you no idea how precious you are to me? I love you more than I thought I could ever love. Oh God, just thinking of the risks you took makes me shake with fear even now!"

"Dinwoodie, I'm so sorry to have given you this pain. One more week and the moss would have done its job and you need never have known. I knew you'd be this upset and I wanted to spare you that. Come, let's away to bed in the knowledge that I had a lucky escape, and there's no lasting damage."

Much later, after a loving reunion, Cate stared at the ceiling as she listened to Dinwoodie's breathing, her thoughts turning to the Cailleach, and beyond to *The Red-headed Woman* of the Forty-Five-rebellion. She'd felt, back at the Black House, like two people. The fear that had had her shaking was one, but alongside that was an instinct that had guided her through the night. She always felt at ease in the Cailleach's house. Was it from her ghost that she'd drawn the strength she needed? Or had the danger merely been yet another warning that *the Red-Headed Woman* was carrying out her vendetta on all MacNishes. With drooping eyelids, she cuddled into Dinwoodie's warmth, grateful to have his love and her own safety, and tried to forget about the curse.

Ewan Brodie realised he had mishandled the missing patient incident and that it had weakened his authority in the hospital. Though glad to have private Laing back, two things bothered him: the man was improving daily, with his speech returning, bit by bit, though sudden noise or movement still had him cowering in a corner and behaving unpredictably. And Mrs Dinwoodie now took a great deal of interest in the patients she'd previously ignored. Take Laing for instance, it was to her he complained of the splitting headaches he continued to have, and she spent time massaging his skull. Of course it was all rubbish that, but for some reason he felt unable to protest. What had happened out there that night to change both of them so radically? He'd feel much better if he could find out. As if that wasn't enough to worry him, the army were sending him a patient that had baffled them. Though they believed him to be a spy, they couldn't be certain that he wasn't just another traumatised patient, and they wanted him to do the requisite tests to clarify the situation. What did the powers that be think he was — some kind of amateur detective?

Two days later as he drove through a downpour on his return from Fort William, his mind still occupied with the Laing incident and the new patient arriving, it was only at the last minute he saw the pedestrians struggling through the mist and rain in front of him. Slamming on the brakes, he skidded to a halt into the nearside hedge. As he tried to open the truck's door a slight figure appeared. Another bloody woman!

"Are you alright? Good job the hedge was there. There's a nasty drop below you. Can you get out?"

Typical female — chatter, chatter! What the hell were they doing out in this weather anyway? His temper lessened when he registered the concerned expression on what he could see of her face. He was man enough to admit that he'd not been concentrating, and somehow, as she stood waiting for a reply, he felt rather ashamed of himself. Ignoring his silence, the woman called to her companion and began to pull on the door handle as he pushed from the inside. Of course the wretched door gave suddenly sending her sprawling into the hedge amidst worried cries from her companion, and leaving him hanging onto the handle, feet in mid-air.

"Lizzie, be careful! Don't move! Here, give's your hand." Maggie turned to the man, "Come on then grab her other hand an see if we can hoik her out of there before she falls through."

Within a few minutes the younger woman was wrested out of the clinging bramble hedge, though all three carried its thorns that would remind them later of the incident. Ewan Brodie set about the damaged door, having ushered the two pedestrians into the truck out of the rain while he did so. As he worked, he could almost feel the angry glare he glimpsed on the older woman's face. Knowing it was fully justified didn't make him feel any better. Her scorn he could deal with, but he was discomforted to see the young one, such a slight figure, limping as she walked round to the other side of the vehicle. Both man and doctor in him were concerned. At last, with the battered door held by some rope, he climbed in through the passenger side before he spoke to them in the back. "I'm sorry, ladies, to have put you in this position. Allow me to drive you to your destination."

"Aye well, it's the least you can do. I've no way of knowing who you are, though this here vehicle's from the army, but even a stranger should've taken more care in this weather." Maggie answered.

"I agree with you, Madame. So be so good as to tell me where I may take you." Even as he spoke he was cursing himself for being a pompous idiot, particularly as he saw the embarrassed look on the younger woman's face. Strange that — the only one to have sustained an injury seemed to have no thought for herself, but was sorry for him being the object of the older woman's biting reply.

"Are we to be sitting here all day?" Maggie asked in an irritable voice "We've been up all night with a difficult first birth an could do with our beds, though we've jobs to be doing first."

"If you could tell me where you're going, I'll get started right away. Though I'm not familiar with the area."

"Just you keep on the road ahead an I'll tell you when to stop. You can leave us where the road forks, as it's less than a mile after that."

Ewan Brodie wondered if he could feel any more churlish as these two women, the one silent, shocked no doubt as well as being injured, the other indignant, but quite willing to walk a mile to save him trouble. This was an example of womanhood he'd never encountered. "It's no trouble — after all it was entirely my fault. Now where did you say you were going?"

"Keep going an I'll tell you when to turn. I have to say it would be right kind of you to take us to the door."

Drawing up in front of the pleasant looking house, with it's wreath of early rambling roses drooping in the wet, he rather hoped their employer would be kind enough to let them at least have a rest before they returned to work. Jumping out, he opened the door for his passengers and, as the older woman, with a nod of thanks, made for the house, he handed the younger one down, before he spoke.

"You really ought to have that leg seen to. I'm so dreadfully sorry about the incident. I feel ashamed of myself, and you —" embarrassed, the words dried in his mouth. He tried again. "I mean — I'm a doctor. I could have a look at the leg." It was as he struggled for words that she threw back the copious shawl that had all but eclipsed her face till now, and, for once in his life, Ewan Brodie saw nothing but goodness and concern in a feminine face, not for herself but for him! Bereft of speech and action the moment was shattered by a well-known voice — of all the people, it had to be her here!

Back in the hospital once more, he paced up and down in his office silently castigating himself for a fool. Why had he left like that? The Dinwoodie woman being their employer had been a shock. He'd leapt in the truck and hared down the drive. No explanation to the young woman — just left her gaping after him. It had been such a disturbing moment prior to that. She'd seemed so — he couldn't put words to it, this unaccustomed feeling for a woman. What had the older one called her? Rack his brain though he did, the memory eluded him. It would have been good to know her name. Changing into his whites, he tried to forget the incident and made for the wards. As he descended the stairs he was taken aback to see that woman arrive for the day.

"Good-morning, Captain. You left in such a hurry I had no time to thank you for bringing Maggie and Lizzie home, and I do hope you sustained no injury earlier this morning."

"Thank you for your concern, Mrs Dinwoodie. I am unharmed. Good-morning to you." And with that he continued on his way to the wards.

Cate shook her head at his retreating figure, before heading to her office. Lizzie's words, 'Cate, he was so concerned for us. I think he's a nice man', had her wondering if they were talking about the same person. 'Nice' was the last thing she would have called Captain Ewan Brodie.

Chapter 21

Bruce peered through his bleary eyes and tried to make sense of his surroundings. Where was he? What day was it? Was he still in France? He couldn't tell. The room was in darkness, his head ached, his body was only partly clothed, and an unsavoury odour assailed his nostrils. Struggling to his feet he felt for a wall and then followed it till he found a door. Pulling it open he was immediately blinded by the daylight, and the axe that was splitting his head in two became even more ferocious. His tongue, devoid of moisture, had slunk to the roof of his mouth. Befuddled, he slid to the ground.

Sometime later, having sluiced his head under the pump of an ancient well, he'd found outside, he began to piece the fragments of information that cascaded through his head. Rhoddy — now where had he left him? Try as he might, he couldn't quite remember. The smell? He fought his way through a maze of uncertainty, as dedicated as the finest perfumier. The drink and the hangover he knew of old. The body odour was his, but tainted with cheap perfume and the cloying remnants of coitus. Bit by bit his past movements slotted into his memory like one of the wooden puzzles his mother had given him long ago in the nursery. Rhoddy, the cheap room, came first; the bistros; the bawdy shows; the wine bars; the brothels followed. Then, like a blow from a heavyweight, he discovered his empty pockets!

He'd stayed with that woman, the one with her husband at war, a decent wine cellar, and money from her nightlife. How long ago was that?

Although the water from the well was sour it slaked his thirst. Next, he returned to the room and found the remainder of his clothing. After a desultory wash and a further douching of his head under the pump, Bruce left the deserted shed he'd woken up in and made for the nearest signs of life, though without funds how could he get to London? No! Not London — Paris. He was in France. That's where he had to go. Paris and Rhoddy. Then contact either Lachlan McPhail or Stuffy perhaps, both even, for funds. First he'd have to get back to his son.

Meanwhile, only a matter of miles behind the front lines, Boy, under Grabber's instructions, had just squeezed through a broken grating in an outhouse and was trying to catch a squawking hen, which he did finally manage to do.

"Jesus bleedin' Christ! Why don't you go bang on their bloody front door?" Grabber stuck his hand through the grating and said. "Boy, you're going to be some trial before I make you into a good little tealeaf. Now give's the bloody thing 'ere."

Boy, glad to be rid of the hen, stared as Grabber pulled its neck and then motioned him to climb out again.

They made their way in the dark back to the barn where they'd been stood down to rest, Grabber keeping up a good pace, whistling as he walked. Boy silent as he'd been ever since he'd left the train, still in shock, terrified by the speed that had catapulted him into this motely band of soldiers, and yet grateful to the man who'd kept an eye on him ever since. So he hurried to stay close to the only thing that made any sense in this nightmare that had enveloped him.

By the end of the evening the enticing smell of cooked chicken still wafted around the small group of soldiers by the makeshift incinerator. For this one night at least, the eight had eaten well, thanks to the unlikely pairing of Grabber and his 'Boy'. Along with the chicken, stolen potatoes, cheese and wine had all added to the army biscuits, making something of a feast before they had to return to the fighting.

Back in the line it was another day of sniping back and forth. Grabber was about to crouch down in the trench for a fag when the familiar whine warned him a shell was close. He checked either side of him only to see the latest arrival in this section raise his head — silly bastard! He lunged, but too late — the soldier spun and, as the blood spurted from his forehead, he slumped over the top of the trench. It was only then that Grabber realised Boy was standing upright, hand to mouth, trying to wipe away the splattered blood of the victim that was covering his face. Muttering under his breath, Grabber reached out and pulled the shocked young figure to the ground. "Ow many times do I have to tell yer? Keep your bloody 'ead below the fucking parapet, you gormless bugger." With that he continued his sniping until the firing from both sides petered out. Grabber then turned his attention to the silent figure on the ground.

"Come on now. Let's 'ave you up." Righting the shocked Boy he pulled out a flask from his tunic, unscrewed the top, and passed it to him. Somewhat to his surprise the youngster latched onto it. Fearing there would be none left, Grabber took it away none too gently. "You done this before then?"

Rhoddy, eyes riveted on the dead body, gave no response, but reached out and touched Grabber's tunic.

"Poor little bastard! 'Ow can we do anything to get you out of 'ere if you won't speak? Lou, over 'ere!" He called one of the group, "Get this body moved. The sight of it is fretting Boy."

"Can't he do it? Not a holiday camp 'ere, is it?"

"You want to keep in with us, do as you're bloody well told! The young un is more use than you at shimmying up drainpipes or squeezing into tight spaces, so you do your trench work and leave 'im to do what he does best, or no more sharing perks for you."

"Okay! Okay! No need to get shirty, Grabber, I'm coming. 'Ere, suppose 'e could do with a fag?" he asked pointing at the youngster. "I can spare 'im one."

"Nah, 'e don't need one, but I do. Lost me last one diving for the corpse there."

"Ere then. Now give us an 'and up with 'im".

Grabber loaded, and Lou hauled until the body was firmly on his back.

"Thanks, mate, I'll manage on me own now — another poor mother weeping back 'ome though." So saying, Lou staggered along the trench with the lifeless soldier flopping over his shoulder.

Grabber patted Boy on the back and then eased himself down on the shelf beside him, saying, "Get some rest before they start popping at us again." As he smoked, he studied him. The kid blundering into them on the train had been a lucky throw of the dice for himself. He'd enlisted to avoid being caught for a thieving job, and there seemed no reason for him to stop his old habits once in the army. He'd made a few, not too forceful, enquiries in the beginning to have Boy sent home. But since no one knew anything about him, and the lad still hadn't uttered a word, it all came to nothing. Anyway, they made a good pair for foraging. He'd squared what little remained of his better self by vowing to keep him out of danger whenever he could, and he'd carry on both thieving with Boy and protecting him, till either they copped it or the bloody war was over, and they could return to thieving in Blighty. The shelling began again, so, fag in mouth, Grabber took up his position, checking as he did so that the frightened lad was well below the parapet.

When she returned from the hospital, Cate was glad to see another foreign letter. Each time there was a gap in them she worried Alashdair might be wounded again. She took it upstairs to Dinwoodie's study before she went to the nursery.

Shona and the boys were immersed in a game with the round wooden balls the coopers made for them. Lizzie as usual was stitching. Cate collapsed into the rocking chair rather wishing she'd called into the kitchen first for some tea.

"You look tired out, Cate. Trouble at the hospital, is it?"

"No just the usual, but I have to admit I do feel weary for some reason."

"We'll be going down for nursery tea in a minute, so why don't you stay quiet here and I'll bring something up for you while Shona baths the boys."

"That's just what I feel like doing, Lizzie, though you work hard enough too. There's no need to pamper me."

"I know, but you look as though you could do with it today. Right, Shona, you go on down to the kitchen to help Cook get the tea ready, and we'll have a wee game here before I bring them down."

On his arrival home Dinwoodie, after playing with the boys in the bath and listening to their goodnight story, eventually tracked down a sleeping Cate. Pulling the nursing chair up beside the rocker, he enjoyed a quiet period simply watching his wife as she slumbered. Lizzie's arrival, with a tea tray and a glance towards the still somnolent Cate, gave Dinwoodie the opportunity for some good-natured teasing. "Just what I need after my journey, Lizzie!"

"But I brought it up for Cate! She was weary after her day's work."

"That was good of you, and I shall certainly see she has some when she wakes, but I think I'll make inroads on this one first. After all, it's usually Cate who appears and consumes my tea!" A smiling Dinwoodie did just that as Lizzie took up her sewing again and they chatted quietly together.

Lizzie had always felt a connection to him ever since he'd arrived on the doorstep in Dunoon the day after the police had come to tell them Bert, her stepfather, had been drowned at sea. He'd scooped her and Maggie up and whisked them off to Edinburgh to be with Cate. Now she wondered if she could speak of her current disturbing thoughts.

Dinwoodie finished his scone and spoke. "You're frowning Lizzie. Where's that sweet smile of yours?"

A blushing Lizzie took time to compose herself, checked that Cate was still asleep, and began. "Can two people see a person in different ways —? I mean is only one bound to be right, Mr Dinwoodie?"

"Are we talking about Solly?"

"No, no, just a person."

"Now then, Lizzie, just who is this mysterious person?" an intrigued Dinwoodie asked.

"A certain Captain horrid Ewan Brodie!" Cate announced forcibly from the depths of the rocking chair.

"I thought you were asleep. He's eaten your tea an…" A mortified Lizzie, unable to continue, hung her head in embarrassment.

"I know you did. I'm sorry to eavesdrop, and the answer to your question is no, I'm not bound to be right. It's just the way I feel. He was rude to me the first time I met him, and he continues to view and speak to me as though I'd just rolled in a dung heap! But he was obviously pleasant to you, or you'd never have thought kindly about him — though please don't go liking him too much, putting him on a pedestal or something silly like that!" Cate was too busy laughing at her ridiculous suggestion to note either Lizzie's or Dinwoodie's expressions. Had she done so, she might have paid more attention to them.

Leaving Cate with the remnants of the tea tray, a thoughtful Dinwoodie made for his study and a couple of hours on his correspondence, though he couldn't dismiss the thought that Ewan Brodie was lurking beneath the emotional layers in Craigavon as surely as there was molten lava at the centre of the earth, and he fervently hoped they'd both remain that way. There was quite enough trouble in the wider world without anything else going awry at home. The papers and wireless were full of troop ships going down, they'd had the first night raid on London, the daylight aeroplane raid on the Medway, and the news in May and now the beginning of June, was alarming the home front, and holding out little hope of the war ending.

The evening meal saw man and wife engaged in their own thoughts, and appetites seemed to have deserted them. Pushing her plate to the side, Cate said, "It seems a shame to waste good food when others are having to make do, but — let's leave it. In the drawing room with his pipe alight, Dinwoodie began to read his paper and Cate picked up her sewing. When he'd read enough, he knocked his pipe out on the grate, and waving the paper at Cate, said, "Not a lot to crow about there, I'm afraid, my dear."

"No good news of any kind?"

"No, and you can't help feeling as though this wretched war is never going to end."

"I wonder when we'll get another letter from Alashdair? It seems a while since he wrote. You don't think anything has happened to him, do you?"

"Who knows, Cate? These days anything is possible, but let's wait and see. Now I'm off to bed. Don't be too late with your sewing. You'll strain your eyes if you're not careful."

Cecily Campbell-Broughton-Stewart viewed her nephew with distaste as she poured his tea in Laggan House. "I do hope you're not here to rant about how awful Mrs Dinwoodie is. I might tell you she has no high opinion of you either."

"I don't care, as long as my hospital…"

"Hers actually!"

"Don't be ridiculous, Aunt Cecily! It's the army's."

"You either don't know all the facts, or have decided they're irrelevant."

"Of course I know the facts. Dinwoodie paid for the setting up of the hospital, and that woman tagged along when he leased the building to the army. She's simply lucky to be married to a rich man."

"Ewan, how you ever qualified to be a medic is one of the world's wonders. Your father is a good army man, but not the brightest. You appear to be either completely unintelligent or lacking common sense! Were you so immersed in your own ambitions that you didn't bother to enquire as to how Kevinishe House became the hospital you wrongly claim as yours?"

"I know the form. Presented with the building, the army will have taken it over and set it up as per every other medical unit."

"And you wonder why she dislikes you?"

"I barely give it a thought. I'm polite to the woman. What else should I be? Though we're dammed lucky to have Dinwoodie on board!"

"Oh, finish your tea and get back to work! Next time you see either your uncle Cuthbert or my husband, speak to them about the hospital.

You might just get the shock of your life! Now go before I become even angrier!"

Driving back, he knew he'd been less than honest about the Dinwoodie woman. And he had to admit that he'd been so focused on obtaining medical control of the place, he hadn't bothered to find out how it had been set up. His Aunt obviously knew something he didn't, and that made the second time Mrs Dinwoodie had got the better of him lately. His Aunt Cecily had always had a sharp tongue and never ceased to tell him how much he exasperated her. It was the old thing again: he was hopeless with women, even his own relatives, and they in turn disliked him from the outset. Parking in front of the hospital he sat for a moment, remembering the last time he'd driven the truck. At least there was one woman who'd looked kindly on him, though by now she'd have been instructed by her employer to have nothing to do with him! He'd never be able to venture to the Dinwoodie woman's house, so he'd have no chance of seeing the slight figure again!

He met his nursing sister at the door, to be greeted with the news that the problem patient had arrived. He washed and changed into uniform before going to his office, where the man awaited him.

On first sight the man differed little from the other traumatised patients. The same jerky movements, lack of speech, eyes darting everywhere looking for non-existent shells exploding. Reading the accompanying notes, that told him little more than he already knew, he decided he'd let the fellow join the other patients as though he was just another neurasthenia case. If he wasn't, he'd make a slip-up somewhere in the interrogative tests, and then he'd ship him back to the intelligence service.

"Right then, what do we call you?"

The whimpering cry and the shaking in the chair were real enough when asked to face up to something, so he'd get Sister to bed him down and leave him be for a day or to.

Mary Anne was curious about the new man and the Captain's attitude. The doctor may well be missing any number of social graces, but he was a fanatic as far as his patients were concerned — you had to give him that. But he seemed to be leaving this fellow to his own devices. Strange. Usually he was almost as determined as Cate was to get things started, problems solved. Now there was another thing she could do without at present! Her friend had certainly changed her attitude since the overnight incident with Laing, but with both her and the doctor in the wards she felt it was only a matter of time before there was another explosion, especially as they were now one short with Kirsty gone. She must remind Cate to find out if the girl was going to come back. A sudden screaming interrupted her thoughts and she ran to the other ward only to find the new man under his bed, rolling around on the floor.

With the help of the orderly, Mary Anne quietened him and gently returned him to his bed. She was still soothing him when Cate walked into the ward. Going first to Laing and chatting to him, she made her way across to the new man.

"Who's this then, Mary Anne?" She queried.

"Well, sure and if I knew I could be telling you I would, but this one's a mystery. No papers, the Captain doesn't even seem to know. Have you a minute to sit with him. It's time I was doing my rounds or I'll never be finishing before lunch."

"I'll do that, Mary Anne. Was that him screaming just now?"

"It was that. See he's his face stuffed in the pillow because he's feart to look. I think he can still see all the horrors of war and believes they're here and now, poor devil."

"I'll sit with him till he stops fretting. You get on now, and I'll see you later."

Taking up her position on the bed, Cate felt for his hand and set about smoothing her thumbs across it, humming quietly to herself, her thoughts on the missing Rhoddy as well as all the other poor devils in the trenches, or risking the perils of no-man's land. When she felt the hand relaxing, she rose, and, going behind him, moved his head to the side to let him breathe more easily, then quietly tiptoed away.

Chapter 22

The following day, Cate was delighted to see Kirsty in the kitchen with Snowy. "I'm glad you've come. I meant to check up on you long ago, but you know how it is — there's always more to do than time to do it in."

"I'm fine, Cate. More than fine!" Kirsty looked at her friend with a broad grin on her face.

"Well that's unexpected. Don't tell me you've forgiven our Captain?"

"Not likely. You see I was sick that night and Donald Uig didn't want me to do the extra. Anyway, I did, and with all the hoo-haw about the man, the Captain blamed me, so I went home, and then Donald Uig came up to say I was never coming back. That was because, Cate, I'm pregnant! We'll have a Christmas baby in the glen!"

Hearing the rumpus in the kitchen, Mary Anne came to check it out, and on hearing the news, work forgotten, they sat down over a pot of tea and baby talk. Subject exhausted, it was only as Kirsty was leaving she remembered the other piece of news.

"Cate, Mary Anne, how about Bella replacing me? I've seen her, an she's willing, now that the sewing has dried up."

"I can't see any reason why not. Can you, Mary Anne?" Cate asked.

"Never a one. It would suit all round and surely even the Captain could find no fault with sweet Bella. We'd hardly know she was here, she's that quiet, so she is."

"Unlike me then, Mary Anne?"

"You'll no get me started or I'll never stop, 'Miss Cate', so I'm off, an, for the love of the good Lord, try and keep the peace with the Captain." With a tinkling Irish chuckle, Mary Anne went back to her ward sister duties.

It was several days before Cate cane into contact with the latest patient again. She was busy chatting to Duncan Laing when he pointed to the empty bed and said.

"He's not one of us, you know — the new chap."

"What do you mean, Duncan?"

"Last night he'd some sort of nightmare and I heard him mutter some words."

"Have you told the Captain? Like you, it could be a good sign if he recovers his speech. He's probably up there with him now."

"No, you see, he's foreign — American perhaps. It was difficult to make out the accent clearly, and he said very little."

"I see. Still I think I'll tell Mary Anne. Then it's up to her to let him know. The Captain and I are not exactly on the best of terms shall we say. And your little escapade didn't exactly help!" With a wide grin, Cate gave him a friendly tap on the shoulder and moved on to one of the other patients.

It was as she was going back to her office that she met the Captain and his latest patient. The Captain gave her a brief nod of acknowledgement and the other man simply stared at her as they passed. As he did so, Cate grasped the bannister to steady herself, while her mind raced. That face she'd come to know so well. How could it be on someone else — a much younger man? Who was he? How could he be so like — Malcolm McAlister her deceased husband, and yet not him? Cate carried on up the stairs to her office. She must have been mistaken. Perhaps it was Kirsty's news of the new baby that had sent her thoughts spinning back to Glasgow and McAlister's total joy at becoming a father in his advancing years.

Sitting at her desk, she waited till she had control of herself again, and then determined to return to the ward. She needed to convince herself she was mistaken, and yet he was so like McAlister. Of course Duncan! He'd said the new man might be American. She hadn't known McAlister's son, Ian, well, but she did remember he had two sons of his own, though she'd never met them. How old had they been in Glasgow before they went to America? Even if she'd ever known their ages, she couldn't remember it.

The mere suspicion that the man could be a McAlister pierced the wound she carried in her innermost thoughts. Sarah, her daughter, would be eight this year. Her little girl! What was she like? Had Caroline Bradley, been kind to her after she'd kidnapped her and taken her to America? The thoughts, the fears all came tumbling out, followed by the bottled rage, and the hopelessness of her situation all those years ago: homeless, penniless, beaten, thrown in jail, she'd been unable to find help in searching for her baby daughter. What if this man was one of them? She could feel an instant hatred boil up inside her — and then a spark of hope obliterated it. If the man was a McAlister, and if he could be brought back to his senses, she would have the missing link to Sarah! Frightened now of letting the bud of hope expand and blossom, she concentrated on ways to prove the man's identity.

No matter how she went over the facts, it was still only her belief that she could identify him, and the Captain would never let her interfere with another case. Pity Mary Anne hadn't met Malcolm — Lizzie had though! Oh, she was being stupid — Solly! Of course he'd been McAlister's clerk. He would be able to prove she was not imagining things, and being a man, the wretched Captain would take his word for it! As ever, the thought of action steadied Cate, and she set to, clearing the pending work on her desk, so she could leave early for the distillery, or Fisher's house if Solly was working from home.

With Solly, when he'd returned from holiday, due to make an appearance in the hospital, ostensibly to bring her some documents, Cate had to school herself to carry on as normal and keep her thoughts to herself. Today she made her way downstairs to the wards, where she chatted with several of the patients, some of whom responded, some didn't. This was like any other day. Passing Duncan's bed, she was glad he was asleep. She moved to the foot of the next bed and found herself looking at what could have well been her late husband's face. She stood still as they stared at one another and then she spoke in a quiet tone.

"Hello." There was no response, and so she walked on, but turned suddenly to see his puzzled gaze following her. Cate stayed in the ward, reading to a man, who, most of the time, refused to open his eyes, hoping to block out the hideous things he saw in his mind. The reading was one of the few things that made him relax a little, so she continued till the lunch was served at the big table by the window. Once the patients were all seated, she watched the American, whose movements were so uncoordinated that half his soup splashed on the table. As Morag went to help him, Cate fetched a cloth and began to wipe the mess up. She was about to leave, when he put out a quivering hand and touched hers. Nothing more, but it was enough to send her in search of Mary Anne.

"I know it's far-fetched, but the likeness is so extraordinary, I'm sure he's a McAlister." Cate finished her explanation.

"Well now, am I not just after hearing the Captain's story about the man?"

"And?"

"It seems as though your man there is unknown. No papers, just a report from Edinburgh. Mind the Captain's not over free with all his information, but this patient has not been subject to all the normal tests. It's on my mind that there's a bit of a question mark over the man. Now wouldn't it be fine if you could solve the puzzle? That would surely upset our Captain!"

"Mary Anne, you're wicked!"

"So be it, but it might be an idea to share your thoughts with him, lest it were to come out later. Then you'd be needing all the saints to be on your side to evade his wrath at you keeping secrets from him."

In fact Cate did not go to the Captain, for she was still waiting for Solly to appear, but she did continue to study the man at every opportunity. In the last week she'd been in and out of the ward watching him at different times, and from different angles, but nothing changed the fact that she thought he was the living image of her late husband. She'd even been on hand once when the man had a seizure in the garden, and had helped Mary Anne and the orderly get him inside and calmed down.

At work in the hospital a week later, a knock at her door interrupted her work and she was relieved to see Solly walk in.

"I thought you might be the Captain!"

"Would it have been so bad if I was? Lizzie tells me he's ever so nice."

"Not to me he isn't! Anyway I've asked you here to look over a new patient."

"Cate, what would I be doing with a patient? You wanted me to bring you over the accounts, though they're not all finished yet."

"I know Solly, they were just an excuse. I really wanted to see you."

The accountant blushed at his employer's words, but Cate was oblivious to it.

"You see this new man is an American, we think, but, well I want you to have a look at him for me. We'll just say you're interested in having a look around if we meet anyone."

"It all sounds very mysterious, Cate, but I'll do anything to help you."

Trying to act normally, Cate pointed out various things to her accountant as they made their way through the wards, and she went to several other beds with Solly before stopping in front of the American, who was sitting up staring into space. She dared not look at Solly or give any indication of her suspicions to him, but she was relieved when she heard his sudden intake of breath.

"Cate, he's — I mean it's uncanny! Who is he?"

"We don't know. What's uncanny?"

"I think you know. That's why you wanted me here, isn't it? Is he related to Mr McAlister? Is that what you think?"

"You tell me."

"He's the spitting image of him, but much younger of course."

"Thank you, Solly. Now I'll take you to see the dreaded Captain. Oh, don't worry; he'll be perfectly civil to you. It's only me who makes him mad!"

Cate knocked on the Captain's office door, entered, and waited for him to look up from his desk.

"I wonder if we could have a word with you, Captain Brodie." Cate watched his expression change from astonishment to puzzlement as he noticed Solly, and then back to her with a careful wariness, before he answered.

"Take a seat, both of you. Now how can I help?"

"In fact I may be of a little help to you, Captain Brodie." Cate tried to keep her voice as pleasant as possible.

"Oh!"

"Your latest patient…"

"I'm not at liberty to discuss my patients with non-medical staff, Mrs Dinwoodie. You know that. Your remit is to see to the domestics, I believe," the doctor interrupted her with an icy voice.

She might have known! "Fine! You stay on your high horse. I'll away back to my domestic fiefdom, and leave you to your rarified calling. But don't come running to me when you can't solve the problem, for there'll be no answer then. Come on, Solly — the man is impossible!" Cate barely left the door on its hinges as she stormed out, almost knocking Mary Anne back down the stairs as she collided with her.

When the Sister entered his office with her files, the Captain was pacing up and down, red in the face, and snapped at her. "What do you want?"

"Now then, Captain, there's no need to be taking your rage out on me! I've brought up the files you wanted. See, I'll leave them on your desk since you're in no mood to be discussing them." With that she dropped them on his desk, turned on her heels to leave, and bumped into Solly, who was still making up his mind what to do.

199

"Hello Solly, what are you doing here?"

"He came with Mrs Dinwoodie. I'm not sure why, Sister. I apologise. As you no doubt see, it would seem that Mrs Dinwoodie and myself seem unable to remain unheated if we utter more than a brief greeting."

"An isn't the whole place, patients, staff and probably half the glen aware of that? For two people to be so obstinate as the two of you, when the place means so much to you both, is right nonsensical. I'm sorry to speak to my superior in this tone, but the pair of you have me fair demented, especially as it was me that sent her to you."

"What, you mean you told her to come?"

"Indeed I did."

"And she agreed?"

"Not exactly. She's as stubborn as you are! That was some time ago, but I understand now. She was waiting for you, Solly, wasn't she?"

"I believe so, Mary Anne. We came up here today with the explanation, since we both agreed."

"Well, if it's all been explained why was she rushing out an nearly knocking me down the stairs in her hurry, Captain?"

"I've no idea why she left. Anyway, why did you send her to me?"

"It doesn't take much working out. You made her madder than a raging bull, Captain."

"No, I mean why you suggested she saw me?"

"It's about your man that's come with the minimum of notes. No name, no file."

"That's because I have none to give you. The man has been sent here by those in the intelligence service who think he may be a spy, and our job is to nurse him back to the point where we can get some information out of him."

"And isn't that just what Mrs Dinwoodie, and Solly here, are after trying to tell you, Captain."

"Impossible! What could she know about him?"

"Only that he looks like her late husband. Indeed isn't he after being the very double of him, in her words."

"Well why on earth didn't the woman say something? Or you come to that, whoever you are?" He turned to Solly, but it was Mary Anne who replied.

"Could it be now that you might just have bitten the head off of her before she had a chance? I'll leave you to think that one over, Captain, and perhaps we can discuss the files and Mrs Dinwoodie later. That's always assuming that she hasn't jumped on that great black beast of hers and galloped off into the sunset, so to speak." With a wink and a smile to Solly, Mary Anne left.

Ewan Brodie looked at Solly, shook his head and said,

"I'll never, no matter how long I live, understand women! Have you the remotest idea what that was all about? I'm Captain Brodie by the way, the hospital doctor." He held out his hand and motioned Solly to sit again, before taking out a cigarette and lighting up. Solly refused the offer, of both chair and cigarette, and began his explanation.

"I was the late Mr McAlister's clerk. He was Cate's first husband. The remainder of his family sailed to America after his death, and the man I came here to meet, at Cate's request, is so facially like Mr McAlister, that it would seem reasonable, especially since Cate tells me he speaks in his sleep in an American accent, that the man is related to the family. At least it's an avenue worth exploring if you've nothing else to go on."

"How does she know he has an American accent? She's never here at nights. She's never said a word about the man."

"She would have done today. She was waiting for me to look at him, tell her if her suspicions were correct, but I've been in Glasgow. Perhaps she thought you wouldn't believe what she said."

"That's a ridiculous suggestion. My patients are my foremost concern."

"Maybe so, Captain, but you gave her little chance to tell you just now. In fact you spoke to her as though she was a lowly chambermaid. This hospital wouldn't be here without Cate. She made it happen. She badgered and begged until she obtained her husband's permission to use this house. Then she met with all the moneyed people in Glasgow and touched both their consciences and their pockets to get the funds to help equip it. She also physically scrubbed the floors with the others, redesigned and dug the grounds with the men, and employed all the non-medical staff. I daresay you'd not be here without all of that." At the shocked look on the other man's face, Solly took his leave.

Chapter 23

With the late July sun forcing its beams through the blue-black curtain that hung over the industrial quarters of Glasgow and beyond, Dinwoodie removed his jacket and forced himself to concentrate on the order manual on his desk, despite being so tired. The knock on the door and Sheena's subsequent entrance provided a welcome relief.

"Dearie me, you look real tired, sir. You've been working that hard these last few weeks. Perhaps it's time you had a break in Kevinishe?"

"I could certainly do with one, but both foundries are struggling to keep up with the orders, and we don't want to let the army down."

"That's true, with all our men out there fighting for us. Anyway, there's a Mr Scot to see you. Personal he said it was. Shall I show him straight in? And will you want tea?"

"Scot? Scot? I seem to know the name, yet I can't place him. I wonder what he wants with me? Right, show him in, wait a bit, then bring in the tea, and if I want to get rid of him, I'll use that as an excuse." As he waited, he put his jacket on and stood by the window.

"Mr Scot to see you, sir," Sheena said as she closed the door behind the man.

"Take a seat." Dinwoodie pointed to the empty chair. "What can I do for you?"

"Well, no a great deal I don't think. You don't remember me, Mr Dinwoodie, do you?"

"I'm afraid to say I don't, but I apologise for that."

"No need sir, it was a while ago. Now then, I'm here, Mr Dinwoodie, for I've just put my only child, my daughter, under the ground."

"You have my greatest sympathy. We lose so many these days in this awful war that the ones we lose at home seem an even heavier than normal burden to bear. You'd think, with the sacrifices that our men are making over there, a kindly God would at least spare us here. To have to bury a child, Mr Scot, never seems right. It confounds the normal expectations."

"Your right there, but my old mother used to say, 'what's for you will ne'er go by you', and how right she was! I know you're too kind not to ask what all that's to do with you, so I'll get on and tell you straight. By meddling in her affairs, you may remember, I once did your wife a great injustice…"

Dinwoodie hit the desk with the palm of his hand — "Of course! The editor — your reporter!"

"Indeed. Now, I know this is complicated. But once before I interfered, and I can tell you, I hesitated long enough before I came today. Thing is, he was like a son to me, and I tried too hard to keep him. I thought only of myself and…"

"Your daughter?"

"Aye. No only that though. As I said, he was the son I never had. Lost the wife in childbirth, lost the daughter to madness and lost the young man I loved like one of my own through interfering in his life, never mind losing a future outstanding editor. He could write, that one!"

Dinwoodie, unsure of himself, mind in a turmoil, stood, opened the door, and called for Sheena. Asked her to bring the decanter along with the tea. He waited till she'd done so, and then poured whisky into the teacups, before offering it to his visitor. They stood, clinked the cups, and drank in silence.

"You can see now why I hesitated, Mr Dinwoodie," He continued. "Once before I ruined a love story and I was loath to do it again. Mind you, it may mean nothing now, but I thought it only fair. We both understand, it was the existence of my daughter that came between them, and how was I to know, in my terrible rage, that your wife was such an honourable woman she wouldn't fight back — just left the field clear for me. That's a sorrow I'll take to my grave with the others. Once I gave her news that broke her heart. Mebbe now it's too late to mend it. You must understand, I mean you no harm, sir, and whether you tell her or not is up to you, but I'll take my leave, knowing that I've tried to square things as I meet my maker."

Dinwoodie was almost unaware the man had not only stopped talking, but had also opened the door and gone. All he could see in front of him was the memory of a Cate wrought with despair, her heart a bleeding wound, and her world destroyed. In those months after she returned to Kevinishe, it had been a soulless round of work that had been the only thing enabling her to cling onto a life she no longer felt worth living.

Somehow, all this time he'd never been a hundred per cent convinced that he'd be able to hold on to Cate. The spectre of the reporter had never been far from his mind. When he'd finally persuaded her to marry him, he'd understood it was on the rebound, and though he had, by then, grown fond of her, it was as the years passed he'd found himself hopelessly in love for the very first time. A ridiculous thing for a fifty- year-old to do, but there it was. True their love had been tested in these trying war years, but right now they were closer to one another than they'd ever been. With these thoughts pounding in his forehead, he rose, left Sheena to clear the tray and man the office, and made his way outside. He walked as if in a daze. He turned into streets that seemed unfamiliar, though he must have walked them many times. The clacketing of men's steel boots on the cobbles and the ringing sound of the urchins playing football with a battered old can seemed to play a tune for the words, 'he'll come home now, he'll come home now', as they danced inside his head.

A full week went by and still Dinwoodie lingered in Glasgow. Several times his hand rested mid-air above the telephone. Indeed he once went as far as unhooking the receiver before dropping it on his desk as though it was a piece of hot iron from the foundry. While shaving in the mornings the looking glass mirrored his confusion and yes, he had to admit, his cowardice. He knew only too well that he must relay the news to Cate, but he also knew that once the facts were out in the open, he would be gambling with his future happiness. Perhaps it was because he understood just how high the stakes would be that he shirked putting these particular cards in front of the croupier.

Back in Kevinishe, it was another man who filled Cate's thoughts. As often as she could, it was to Patient M, as he was now listed, that she hurried, duties done. She read to the listless man as he lay on the coverlet of his bed. She recounted incidents from her Glasgow years, speaking of Ian, the man she felt sure must be his father, of Ian's sister, Caroline Bradley, and of his grandfather, McAlister. But the only response she got was the man holding out his hands for her to stroke. It had been the first thing she'd done for him when he arrived at the hospital and seemed the only connection that he responded to. Cate knew Captain Brodie was

205

equally frustrated during his sessions with the patient, though no doubt taking a great deal of pleasure out of the fact that she too was having no visible effect on their mystery man.

Duncan, on the other hand, seemed to need constant attention, and Cate understood that. Being anxious to unlock M's silent state and yet giving Duncan the necessary reassurance was stretching her. Between the two of them she was becoming unduly tired, and in dire need of some invigorating mountain air. It was the thought of the mountain that made her remember her promise. She found Duncan in the garden and outlined her plan.

"I thought you'd forgotten all about it, Miss Cate."

"Well I had, and then again I hadn't. It's just that bed neighbour of yours needs help. Thing is, I'm hoping he could solve a problem for me."

"Unlikely, the state he's in! Can't I help?"

"No, I'm afraid you can't, Duncan. Go now and ask the Captain's permission for an outing on the mountain. If he's agreeable, I'll bring the mare for you, and we'll take that jaunt. If we go, while we're away, I'll tell you the bones of the problem I'm struggling with."

The following day, with the sun out, the two riders made for Cate's favourite ledge. It was as she was spreading their picnic lunch that she remembered the last time she'd been here with Dinwoodie. How he'd love to be here now instead of cooped up in the Glasgow office! She'd been so taken up with the hospital patients lately that she'd not noticed the passage of time, and it did seem that her husband had been away longer than usual. She knew he was hell-bent on fulfilling the foundries' quota, so as not to let the soldiers down, but he wasn't young anymore and ought not to be working all hours. As the duo ate their lunch in a companionable silence a sudden thought darted across Cate's mind. It stayed there during lunch, while she showed Duncan the golden eagles' nesting site, and all the way back to the hospital as she retold the events that had culminated in losing baby Sarah. Duncan had been sweet and concerned for her, and it was good to know that they had strengthened the existing bond between them.

Once back in the office the thought intruded once more, and stayed there as she rode back to Craigavon with the horses. That evening as she sat on the end of their marital bed, she cast her mind back to May and Dinwoodie's horror and tears at the sight of the scars on her neck. It was only then she'd realised the true depth of his love for her and of course that day fitted her suspicions exactly! Well, if he was too busy to come to the glen, she must go to him! Slipping into his side of the bed she sniffed the faint odour of his tobacco on the pillow and fell asleep with it cuddled against her barely rounded stomach!

Ever one for immediate action, Cate spent the next day making sure that all her commitments were up to date, and, with her excuse of sudden urgent business in Glasgow, arranged to travel with the Post Bus to catch the train to the capital. She then took the tram to the foundry, and found a certain amusement in the motley assortment of women on board, tongues busy rattling out the Glasgow patter. Over the years she'd forgotten the sounds and the speed of the native speech, and she found herself concentrating hard to make sense of the hubbub around her. Listening to the scraps of conversation she understood, Cate was transported back to the tenements and the doughty Mrs Petrie. Collectively these women were her! In the front there was one wrapped in a similar pinny. Another nearby had curlers producing a pattern of bumps in the same sort of knotted headscarf as she used to wear, and at the back she could hear a mother threatening her unruly band of children with a bogeyman! It brought it all back: Mrs Petrie in her familiar outfit, shepherding the little group of children down the tenement stairs, amid a constant stream of chatter. Cate hoped the woman, who'd helped to look after the baby Rhoddy back then, was alive and well somewhere. She'd been a kindly soul, though a mite thriftless!

Cate was almost sorry to leave the tram, and her Glasgow memories stayed with her as she walked along the unfamiliar streets. Despite her earlier delight in the journey, she soon found herself lost and began to wish she'd telephoned Dinwoodie to meet her train. Hesitating at a junction, she saw a cab and hailed it.

Once inside the foundry gates, an inquisitive workman, who insisted on showing her the way, directed her to the office. She was amused as the man was heckled by passing workmen and appeared delighted at the none too polite suggestive remarks thrown at them. The imp of mischief in her longed to see their expressions change should she inform them who she was. It was only then that a shadow of doubt crossed her mind — would Dinwoodie be less than pleased at her arriving like this? Well, she was here now, and she'd soon remove any displeasure he displayed.

Her companion interrupted her thoughts by pointing to a stout wooden door at the end of a corridor, so she thanked him with an amused smile, and watched him whistle away, with a jaunty walk, until

207

he was out of sight. She knocked lightly on the door, opened it, and waited for the woman typing furiously at her desk to look up.

As the door closed, Sheena stared, rose, left her desk, and with a shake of her head, said, "He's gone to Kevinishe, Mrs Dinwoodie!" as she crossed to meet Cate.

"Are you sure, Sheena? He hasn't telephoned to say he was coming home."

"I think it was all unexpected. You'll not have heard? You may not even have known him?"

"Known who? I can assure you I know my husband very well indeed!"

"Of course. No, it's just about a week or so ago Mr Dinwoodie was visited by a Mr Scot. Wait a minute — I've the Gazette here somewhere." Sheena rifled through the desk drawers and extricated the paper. "Here, there's a picture of him. He's only gone and hanged himself!"

Cate took the paper from the secretary and looked at the picture. "Scottie!" Dazed she handed the paper back to Sheena, and whispered, "I did know him, a long time ago. Why would…?"

"Oh they say here," she waved the paper in the air, "that he was a great drinker, so maybe that's got something to do with it. Shame though — it was a good paper."

"You think the paper will close?"

"They think so in this article. Would you like some tea, Mrs Dinwoodie, I see I've fair shaken you. Only I thought maybe that's why Mr Dinwoodie went home, otherwise, I'd never have said to upset you. What'll you do now? Would you like me to book you into a hotel?"

"No thank you. Since my husband isn't here I might as well get a train back today. Should he telephone, please tell him I'm on my way home. Goodbye now." Cate left, her mind in a whirl, and this time made it outside the gates without being noticed.

In a cab once more she was about to tell the driver to take her to the station, when she changed her mind and gave him Gordon Wiseman's office address. When she'd paid the cab, Cate wasn't quite sure why she'd come here, but she climbed the stairs anyway, checked if Gordon was free and went in.

"Why, Cate, this is a surprise!"

"Do you know the editor of the…"

"Hanged himself, yes, I think most people in Glasgow do. And it's fair to assume the funeral tomorrow will be well attended, though I'm

208

not sure where he'll be buried. The Kirk's not keen on those who take their own lives."

"You mean, a pauper's grave? Surely not!"

"Perhaps unhallowed ground then. You seem upset — I remember now! Didn't you know, and then the re…?"

"Yes I knew him and his chief reporter, as you've just remembered."

An embarrassed Gordon coloured and said, "I'm sorry, Cate, I didn't mean…"

"I know. Can Mary fit me up with your landlady for a night or two? You know — the one you use for your clients?"

"You don't need to do that. You can stay with me."

"If you think about that suggestion a little more, you'll understand why I'm not going to take you up on it!" Cate managed a smile, before she turned to go, "but you can dine with me tomorrow when I find out the time of the funeral, if you like."

"You're going?"

"Yes, but I'll see to a couple of things first, if Mary can book a room for me." With that, Cate left, a determined set to her face, ready to begin her search, at almost the exact time that the train she'd told Sheena she was taking, left the station.

A couple of hours later, a footsore Cate opened yet another undertaker's door, and waited for someone to come. When they did she asked her question yet again, not really expecting any success, and was pleasantly surprised when the man announced that they indeed were in charge of preparing Mr Scot for his funeral the next day. It took only a few minutes to find out where the service was to be held, and that where the actual burial was to be was still uncertain.

Cate hailed another cab and, giving the driver the piece of paper the undertaker had written out for her, she slipped off her shoes and sat back. When the cab stopped, she squeezed her feet into her shoes, winced and, ordered the cabby to wait. Then she stepped out to have a good look at the front of the shabby church. A quick visit to the graveyard behind and an enquiring look at the back of the building satisfied her. She returned to the main door and, twisting the heavy wrought-iron handle, entered the church. The cleric was busy at the altar, so she made her way down the aisle and waited by the front pew until he turned round.

"Good afternoon, can I help you?" the cleric asked.

"I believe so. I'm told there's to be a service here tomorrow for Mr Scot.'

"Indeed there is."

"So his burial will be in your graveyard?"

"Not as such, Madam."

"I'm not quite sure I understand." Cate replied, knowing full well what he was about.

"The coffin will be laid elsewhere as is the normal practice for these cases."

"Well in that case," Cate answered, "You can help me. You see I wish Mr Scot to be buried in your churchyard. Before you begin to tell me that you are not prepared to do that, may I say that I see both the graveyard and the rear of the church itself are in dire need of repair, wouldn't you say? Now, should you wish to give me an assurance that Mr Scot would indeed be buried in the graveyard, then I would feel inclined, tomorrow at the end of the burial, to make a decent-sized donation to offset the cost of repairs."

"I'm surprised at you. That's bribery — and to a man of the cloth!"

"I'm a business woman. I want to buy a grave in your churchyard, by doing so I would provide you with funds to begin at least some of the repairs. Now if you're quite content to let this shabby church of yours become even more run down, then I'll go elsewhere to find a burial plot. Good day to you." With that Cate walked slowly down the aisle, wondering just how far he'd let her go before the bribery turned into a benevolent donation in his mind. Though as her hand reached for the door she did wonder whether he …

"Well, of course, with the death of his daughter a few weeks ago….."

"His daughter's dead?"

"Indeed she is, and the wife, a long time ago. Been ill for many years has the daughter. A deal of sadness Mr Scot has had to put up with in this life and, since no new plot would be required, it would seem churlish after the suffering he's endured, if you take my meaning?"

Cate barely heard the answer. Alashdair's poor wife was dead. Did he know, she wondered? Now she fully understood Scottie's reason for seeking death: family all gone, and no hope of the 'son' to follow in his footsteps and save the paper that he'd sacrificed everything for. And that had been because of her!

"You did hear what I thought, did you not?" The now anxious cleric asked.

"What…oh yes, you might just be persuaded to change your mind."

"Just so, considering the circumstances. Yes, indeed."

Cate held out her hand, and the minister shook it with his bony one making Cate remove hers with a moue of distaste. "Until tomorrow then, I'll be here. You have my word on that, and I'll produce my part of the bargain as soon as Mr Scot is interred. Good-day." She couldn't get out of the church soon enough. Although she had succeeded in her quest, the whole thing seemed so underhand. How dare these frocked Christians refuse a good man a proper burial just because life had become untenable for him! Green eyes flashing with temper, she slammed the cab door after her, making the Cabby jump!

The next day, invisible amid the mourners and the sightseers, Cate sealed her bargain and made her way back to Gordon's office. When she was shown in, she wasted no time in preamble. "How much does a paper cost to buy?"

"Well I don't think the tuppence-ha'penny will beggar you," Gordon replied with a smile. Then, with a careful look at Cate's stony expression, he said. "You're serious aren't you? You mean buy a paper, as in to own it, don't you? But …"

"No 'but' about it. What would that cost?"

"I'm sorry, Cate, I don't know offhand. You mean Scot's paper, The Gazette, don't you, but why?"

"It's a long story, and I'm not in the mood."

"Cate, this is madness! As your solicitor, I can't let you…"

"And how much will it cost to make you change your mind?" She almost sobbed the last words.

"My dear Cate, what is it?" Gordon asked as he came round the desk and held her, now that she was crying in earnest.

After a few moments, Cate took a backward step and motioned him to his chair before saying. "I'm so-o-o sorry. Oh Gordon, I've just been to his funeral and had to pay a sleazy little man money to bury him properly in a graveyard, and his daughter's dead too and it's all my fault there's no one to take on the paper he so loved. They both did."

"The daughter too? I'd heard she was mentally ill."

"She was," Cate sniffed before carrying on, "I meant Alashdair, the chief reporter. Now let me dry my eyes and please take me out to lunch so that I can cleanse my mouth of this grubbiness and guilt."

"Of course I'll take you out to lunch, and I'll look into the paper query for you. Perhaps one day you'll tell me the fascinating story behind all this."

Cate dried her eyes, forced a smile, and said, "Perhaps."

Chapter 24

Lunch almost completed, Gordon asked, "Are you staying another night? If so why not dine with me here this evening?" When there was no reply he turned to see what it was she was so interested in.

"Gordon…"

"Ah, you've remembered I'm here!"

"I'm sorry. That was rude of me, but that man over there, at the small table in the far corner…"

"What about him," he asked after pinpointing the one she meant.

"Do you know him?"

"As a matter of fact I do. He's a client. Why?"

"He's been staring at us. For some time, I think. You know when you get a strange feeling someone is looking at you. I ignored it at first, but then I turned to look at him. Funny thing is he just keeps staring at me as though — oh it's too silly, but he reminds me of what I do before I begin drawing something — I'm probably being ridiculous again."

"I must admit you've certainly been doing some fairly unusual things in the last two days. Anyway, forgetting him for now, I was asking you to dine with me this evening."

"Gordon, I must get back, I'd intended to take the train home two days ago!"

As they rose to leave, the man approached them. "Excuse me, Mr Wiseman, may I have a word?"

"I am accompanying this lady to her train. Why don't you…?"

"Go ahead, Gordon, I'll wait for you". With that, Cate made for the powder room, where she took her time before reappearing, surprised to find Gordon and the stranger both still there.

"Cate, Mr Finkelstein thinks he may have something to interest you."

"You must forgive me for staring, dear lady. I am confused. I do not know where you fit into the story." The man said.

213

"Come now, you're confusing both of us, as we have no inkling of any story." Gordon said.

"Forgive me, but we Germans have to be careful, Mr Wiseman. There is much trouble for us now with this hateful war."

"We didn't start it, Mr Fink..."

Cate put a hand on Gordon's arm. "I have a strange feeling that I would like to hear your story, Mr Finkelstein, I feel some sort of — this will seem odd — but I feel a connection here. Come, Gordon, we can order a pot of tea in the foyer surely?"

"If that's what you'd like. Are you agreeable, sir?"

At his nod, they seated themselves, waited for their order to be delivered, and then the man began.

"Some weeks ago a kinsman of mine sought refuge with me. He had, shall we say, some trouble and needed a hiding place, not that he'd done anything wrong, as such, but then refusing to..."

"Take up arms, Mr Finkelstein?"

"But, dear lady, how...?"

"Hansi! He is your kinsman?"

"But, yes and you..."

"A friend. Is he still with you? Is he safe?"

"Cate, what..."

"In a minute, Gordon. Let him finish. Is Hansi with you?"

"No, I sent him and his friend..."

"Charlie?"

"Cate, stop interrupting or we'll never get to the bottom of this, and I have clients to see."

"I'm sorry, Gordon. Do carry on." She said with a smile at the other man.

"I will be brief then. Between these two they had a quest. They gave me this." He pulled out a crumpled piece of paper from his pocket and Cate took it from him, recognising her drawing immediately. She waited for the remainder of the story.

"I looked after them for one week and sent them to several pawnbrokers, even asked around a gallery or two, for the painting that resembled your sketch — it is yours?" When she nodded. He continued. "They had money and were intent on locating the painting. One day they went out and did not come back. For many weeks now I have waited. So as not to lose hope, I took up the search myself. Dear lady, it may be of little comfort to you, but I do now have your painting, but alas we have lost the searchers, and they were so determined to find it for you. I

214

cannot help but think they came to grief! Otherwise why have they not returned?"

Cate rose and patted him on the shoulder. "Not those two. Though I agree they'll be in trouble no doubt, so we must find them."

"But, Cate, your train?"

"This is the second time, Gordon, I have determined to catch it, but that will have to wait. Do you think the restaurant will let me use their telephone?"

"Of course they will. I'll ask them."

Her telephone calls completed, the two men agreed that Mr Finkelstein would deliver the painting to Gordon Wiseman's office, where Cate would collect it, and then they said their goodbyes. She settled into the cab that had been hailed for her and wasn't surprised when the cabby looked shocked at the address she'd given him.

When she entered the police station, Lord Monroe was already there. She held out her hand, and niceties exchanged, he regarded her with a stern look before continuing. "I do hope this is not another of your wild schemes! Dinwoodie would never forgive me if he knew I was meeting you here."

"Lord Monroe, if you knew the trouble I'm in already for playing truant from the Highlands, this can't possibly make it any worse! The fact is the young men I told you about were on an errand for me and I feel responsible for them. I know they were in Glasgow, but they've disappeared. I've tried the hospitals and you were my last chance. I was so glad you were in your office."

"I'm not so sure it wouldn't have been better all round if I hadn't been! Well, I'm here now. Who are we looking for? Names?"

"That might be a problem."

"Don't tell me you don't even know their names?"

"How about Charlie and Hansi? We don't use surnames on the estate, and I don't really know one of them."

"You certainly know how to make a person worried. Are you sure you want to go through with this?"

"Yes please, sir."

"Chtt! Don't come the obedient little woman with me! Remember I'm a crusty old bachelor! And I've seen you charm a roomful of people on occasion. Right, let's get on with this. I'll tackle the sergeant on the desk. You stay here, until you're needed."

Cate sat in the draughty reception area and shivered as she remembered the last time she'd been there. The final horror after her beating by Hardy had taken a long time to fade. At the sound of voices she stood, trying not to be too hopeful, but, as she heard her name, she pushed open the inner door, and there, handcuffed to a policeman, was a shamefaced Charlie, fading bruises a pattern on his face.

"Charlie, what on earth?" She rounded on the sergeant who took a step back. "Are you responsible for…"

"Shoost woman! This good man is on our side." Monroe barked.

"But look at him!"

"He's here and he's upright. That'll do for now." Turning to the sergeant he said, "Thank you, you can return the prisoner to his…"

"But I want…"

Even Cate, being the recipient of the famous Monroe glower, had to shut her mouth and watch in despair as Charlie was led away. Before she had a chance to speak, Lord Monroe took her arm and marched her out to his waiting limousine.

Once they were underway, having given him her landlady's address, she was informed in no uncertain terms to leave everything to him. He did however unbend a little as he deposited her at her lodgings. "Goodnight, my dear. It may take a few days, but your henchman will be released and be able to give you the full story as to why there's only one of them there. Trust me, I can be very persuasive!"

As she watched him depart, Cate couldn't help thinking that it was such a shame that some lucky lady somewhere in the land had not ensnared his heart! He was indeed a great and good man. Now she'd just have to content her soul in patience, but why was Charlie in prison and where, oh where, was Hansi?

A week later, settled in the train, Cate hugged a large parcel, while Charlie attended to their luggage. She noticed people on the platform were staring at him. No wonder. His face was still an awful sight!

"Right, we're all set, Miss Cate. What're you smiling at?" Charlie asked as he sat down beside her

"Your coloured face, and those others out there watching you."

"Aye well, the polis are no so very soft when you start a fight."

"Tell me again what happened, I haven't quite got hold of it all in the rush."

Charlie told her again how he and Hansi were heading for the recruiting station so that Hansi could sign up for a non-combatant's role,

216

when they saw a policeman coming towards them. Scared of being arrested, Hansi pushed him in front but being off balance Charlie had cannoned into the uniformed man, who promptly grabbed him by his collar. To give Hansi time to get away he'd set to with his fists on the officer, who was none too gentle in his response. Events from there were via an overnight stay in a cell, an appearance in front of the bench and back in the cell with a two months prison sentence for assault and battery. Then came his unexpected release two weeks early after she'd come to the prison.

"I knew you'd sort it, Miss Cate. Who was that man with you in the prison?"

"A lawyer."

Cate thought it better to leave it at that and changed the subject by asking another question. "What I can't understand is why Hansi wanted to sign up. He was so against war."

"It was like this, Miss Cate: we thought all ways round it while he was in Kevinishe, and this was the only way…"

"You mean to tell me that you both knew what he was going to do once you left, and you didn't tell me?"

"Aye well, now what would you have done but stop us? It was for the best. This way I'm sure he's in the thick of it, and at least there he's in an honest sort of danger, if you take my meaning. We'll just hope he makes it, but we were gey sorry no to have found the picture for you. Though I was set to carry on, before…"

Cate pointed to the seat and the large flat package resting there. "You have to thank Mr Finkelstein for that." She said smiling at Charlie.

"He's never gone and found it?"

"Indeed he has!"

Charlie turned his face away to hide his emotions and, to give him time, Cate looked out at the rushing world beyond the window, uttering a silent prayer of thanks to the Gods of the countryside for the return of her battered warrior and the painting, plus a plea that they would watch over the young man with the badge of the non-combatant on his arm as he rescued the wounded on the front line.

Back in Kevinishe, Maggie watched through the drawing room window as an army truck pulled up in front of Craigavon, and she saw Lizzie, a twin on either hand, turn towards the vehicle. Work forgotten, she remained at the window and watched as the doctor joined Lizzie and

217

the boys as they continued on their walk. Once they were out of sight, Maggie headed to the kitchen, for an earlier than normal cup of tea, with Cook.

"Now here's a funny thing, Cook. That army truck's just turned up and Cate in Glasgow! Yon doctor's been a bit on the sleekit side, him knowing she'd no be here, and he could have a craic with her."

"Who now? He canna speak to her if she's no here?"

"No, no, it's Lizzie he's come to see, Cook, an Cate'll no be very pleased, I can tell you."

"Maggie, you don't think…"

"I do that. Lizzie's been telling whoever would listen just how 'nice' the new doctor is, an he was more than anxious for Lizzie the morning of the accident."

"But Cate's always on about how horrible he is. One of them's wrong surely? And why would he be worrying about Lizzie? You said nobody was hurt — just a bit shaken."

"Indeed I did, but he was on about her limp, so he must have thought she was hurt, back then in the hedge. I tell you, there'll be sparks flying when Cate gets back! Listen — was that the door? Wheesht now! Don't let on we've been talking about her."

To their surprise, it was Dinwoodie, not Lizzie, who walked into the kitchen, where both women, mouths agape, stared at him.

"You look as though you'd been caught unawares. Don't tell me you've been up to no good?" Dinwoodie joked before continuing, "And I see Cate's found herself a new mode of transport. I didn't think she was on good enough terms for the dreaded Captain to lend her his truck."

Maggie was the first to come to her senses. "No her, she used the Post Bus, as far as I know."

"What on earth did she want with that? Who drove the truck here then?"

Before anyone could answer him the kitchen door swung open, and the twins hurled themselves at Dinwoodie, David shouting first. "Mama gone away."

Lizzie walked into the stunned silence following the child's cry, and then everyone began to talk at once.

"We weren't expecting…"

"She's in…"

"The Captain called to check…"

"Papa, Papa, the man came…"

218

Dinwoodie held up his hand for silence saying, "One at a time, please. I can't make sense of any of this!" Then he bent to hug the children he'd given his name to so willingly. Would that, now their biological father was probably on his way back to Scotland, be altered?

Later, in his study, Dinwoodie mulled over the explanations in the kitchen, as he drank the tea Maggie had laid on the table in front of the giant flower arrangement Cate had put in the empty fireplace. His prime concern was why she'd rushed off to Glasgow. She couldn't have heard Scot's news could she? 'Urgent business', she'd told them here. Had Cate been contacted by Charlie? Had anything happened, either to him or the German? It didn't make sense, any of it. Of course he'd known of Lizzie's interest in the Captain. Had he now taken the place of Solly in her affections? Were women so easily persuaded to change their minds and their affections? The avalanche of queries and emotions, his and others, all seemed to blanket his mind. He sat in his high-backed wing chair, exhausted by everything, and closed his eyes until the sleep, that had been elusive since the editor's visit to his office, finally claimed him.

Dinwoodie heard the constant ring of the telephone. As no one seemed to be around, he rose and answered it. After the conversation he put the phone down and returned to his study. A full week had gone by and now it was Sheena who set his thoughts whirling again. So Cate had gone to Glasgow to see him! Why? They'd no urgent business to discuss. And what had Cate wanted Lord Monroe's office number for?

As he paced up and down he also wanted to know why she could telephone Sheena, and presumably Lord Monroe, but not himself! Damn it all, he was her husband! There were times when he thought Cate carried on in life just as she must have done as a lonely tinker girl, responsible to no one but herself, disregarding the feelings and expectations of others. He sat at the desk and tried to piece together snippets of information he'd gathered from his secretary. Cate needed Monroe's office number. Sheena had apologised but said, 'Mrs Dinwoodie was adamant that she required it', and no, 'Mrs Dinwoodie said nothing about why she'd come to his office, though she did say she was catching the next train home that same day'. Well, Mrs bloody Dinwoodie had not done that, so where the hell was she?

Chapter 25

The Post Bus was en-route to Craigavon with Cate and Charlie aboard. Benjamin chatted away to Charlie, and Cate was glad they were preoccupied with Kevinishe gossip. Ever since she'd left the train she'd felt odd, and she was grateful they'd only a few more miles to go. She closed her eyes so the men might think she was asleep. Indeed she felt so weary that her bed would be very welcome.

A sharp pain in her stomach had her biting her lip and, though she thought she hadn't made a sound, Charlie took one look at her face and, with a note of urgency in his voice, said, "Mebbe we could go a wee bit faster, Benjamin. Miss Cate is real tired." Then he took one of Cate's hands in his and whispered, "Hang on: we're nearly there."

When they arrived at Craigavon, Cate, still carrying the precious painting, was the first through the door, to be met by a less than pleased Dinwoodie with the others crowding behind.

"So, you've finally remembered you live here, I see!" He was too cross to register the expression on her face and it was Charlie, following her in, who took her arm and the painting, saying, "Excuse me, Mr Dinwoodie, sir, but she's no well."

"Please, Dinwoodie, let's go into the drawing room, I think I need to sit down," Cate pleaded. As her husband moved aside the others followed, and with Maggie and Charlie by her side, Cate was about to take a seat when she was gripped by a fierce pain and doubled over. As it eased, she managed a muttered "Maggie!" before another pain had her moaning.

Maggie took control. "Cook, get a warming pan ready for her bed. Now then, Cate, can you manage the stairs?" Maggie guided her towards the door, not waiting for an answer.

"Cate, what is it?" Dinwoodie asked, his irritation forgotten.

"Not now. Let me get to bed firs…" another pain made Cate hang onto Maggie until it eased and then she reached out her free arm to Charlie. "The painting — let me have it."

221

As Charlie moved forward, Dinwoodie tried to wrest the package from him, and, in the tug-of-war, it slipped to the floor. Cate's screams had Maggie turn on the two men. "Have some sense! She's in trouble enough without the pair of you upsetting her at this time. Bring the parcel, Charlie. I'm sorry, Mr Dinwoodie, but we've to get her to bed before — well, before it's too late. An she needs to be calm. You can speak to her once she's settled. C'mon now, lass, we'll do our best, but..." Biting her lip, Maggie shook her head at the others and made her way upstairs, with Charlie following on behind with the painting.

Left alone in the entrance to the drawing room, Dinwoodie hovered, unsure what to do. Cate was rarely ill, and the earlier scenes had mystified him. Charlie's appearance on the stairs galvanized the master of the house.

"Come, Charlie, I think we both need a drink, and you can fill me in about those bruises of yours and anything else that happened in Glasgow." Dinwoodie knew, as he poured their drams, that not a word would Charlie say that would land Cate in trouble.

Charlie recounted his adventures with Hansi and his prison rescue. Then added, "An that's the long an the short of it, Mr Dinwoodie. Whit Miss Cate was in Glasgow for I canna tell you, for she didna let on to me."

"So, the German has gone to war after all."

"That he has, sir. It was just the thought of the shooting of ours, or theirs that had him no willing to fight. This way he's doing his best to help, but no against his conscience."

"And what about you, Charlie? I know Cate stopped you from joining the army. Didn't you want to follow the German?"

"I did that, but I'd an errand for Miss Cate, an she'll always be the first thing I see to. An now as she's in good hands, I'll need to be away to my own family, for they'll have worried, me no being home for a time. So good day to you, sir." With that Charlie put his empty glass on the dresser and left, closing the door quietly behind him.

With Cate settled in bed, the women fussing over her, and the precious painting leaning against the wardrobe where she could see it, Maggie knew they'd done all they could for now. She sent Cook down for some beef tea, asking her to let Lizzie know what happened, and to tell her to keep the twins away from Cate for now. Then she went downstairs to see Mr Dinwoodie.

"Now then, Maggie, thank you for what you've done, but just what is the matter with Cate?"

"Well now, sir, she'll no want someone else doing the telling, so why don't you go up an, if she's still awake, I'm sure the sight of you will make her feel much better." With that Maggie left for the kitchen and a welcome stroupic.

Cate opened her eyes as she heard the door closing, and was about to sit up, when Dinwoodie stopped her, "You lie still now, or I'll have Maggie berating me yet again. How are you now? You gave us all a fright, my dear."

"Oh, Dinwoodie, so much has happened and I did mean to catch the train, but then — oh don't be cross, but Sheena told me about Scottie and…"

"So you know his daughter…"

"Is dead, yes, and that he hung himself…"

"The paper man committed suicide?"

"Yes. It's so sad. And I felt guilty."

"That's nonsense! Why should you feel guilty? You're not making sense.""

"Perhaps, but that's why I was late home. I went to his funeral, bribed a horrid cleric to bury him with his wife and daughter, and then I found out about Charlie."

"I know. He's put me in the picture. Saying that, I apologise for my attitude downstairs, though I believe you put too much faith in the painting to help…"

"Dinwoodie!" She held up her hand to interrupt him and was rewarded with a resigned look.

"Alright, you believe in the old stories, but to me it seems ridiculous to worry about something which happened almost three centuries ago! And I still don't know why you were in Glasgow?"

Cate patted the side of the bed and said, "Come, Dinwoodie sit close to me, I wanted to tell you a secret before anyone else guessed and now my wretched body's let the news out."

'You're speaking in riddles, my love.'

Taking his hand in hers, Cate leaned into him, took his hand and laid it on the bedclothes above her stomach, and said, "You, Mr Iron Baron, are about to become a father, that is…"

"You're pregnant? I'm the father?"

"Dinwoodie! How dare you…?"

"No! No, Cate, that came out all wrong! I — well I'm —but…"

"Yes indeed, now there is a 'but'. Maggie thinks we may save the wee one, but we cannot be certain. I've been rash, but I so wanted to be with you, see your face when I…"

"Shsst now," Dinwoodie comforted her. "Lie still, and do as Maggie says. Let's hope that luck is with us and all will be well. Sleep now and I'll see you before I retire tonight. I've been banned from our bed, you know, and in no uncertain terms, by Maggie!" He waited, holding her hand, until she closed her eyes, and then went to his study, mind racing with this latest piece of news. Would they manage to save this precious child? Would he really have an heir of his own for the foundries, rather than one of the foppish Lord's sons? It had been so long since his own son had died that he'd given up hope. Hope, that's what they must all do now. The saving of their child and the end of this wretched war — surely hope would come to their aid?

Three weeks later, Cate was sitting in her bedroom longing to be up and about, but, with Maggie's constant surveillance and Dinwoodie home once again, she daren't put a foot outside the bedroom door, and the incarceration was making her irritable. She'd like to go to Kevinishe House to hang the painting, but Dinwoodie had forbidden her. They said Charlie was fully recovered, but she'd like to see for herself. She wondered daily how those at the hospital were faring, and uppermost in her mind the thought of Rhoddy and Hansi on the Western Front was always with her.

In his study, Dinwoodie was also thinking of France and the continuous slaughter on the Western Front. He imagined the stretcher-bearers moving mindlessly from day to day as they fetched and carried the wounded to and fro. How would the German cope? Would he scan the German prisoners, as they were herded behind the Allies' lines, looking for his relatives? And what of the hard-pressed Major dealing with the casualties brought to his field hospital? Would he drop exhausted onto his bed at the end of each day of bedlam, and seek refuge in the memory of his Highland sojourn? And would yet another offensive deplete ever more the decreasing numbers of available men for fighting? So many questions unanswered!

Amid these concerns, Dinwoodie had to add the ever-present worries of the continued depredation of British shipping that the U-boats were making from the Belgian ports. Would this proposed Flanders offensive really be able to secure these ports? Although he understood the necessity of launching yet another one, Dinwoodie, like many of the home front, was sceptical of it being successful. The newspapers, radio, the reporter's letters all voiced their doubts. Too often in this hateful war success seemed to give way to stalemate, or German advances. It was not often that he let the state of the war invade his thoughts like this, but as he collected another foreign letter on his way to see Cate, he hoped that it would contain at least a little good news.

He moved onto more pleasing thoughts because of what Maggie had told him earlier that day. With care, Cate should be able to keep the child full term. The problem being that his wife was usually anything but careful! Indeed as he entered the bedroom she leapt out of the armchair, hugged him, and pulled him into an impromptu jig.

"Stop, Cate! What are you thinking of?"

"I'm thinking of the acres of fresh air waiting for me now I'm allowed to be up and about!"

"You, Mrs Dinwoodie have not listened to Maggie's advice — no, don't interrupt. Just listen! You have to be careful, Cate. We've had one scare. We don't want another. So, just you pay attention to me. The list is extensive: no riding, no rushing about, a minimum of work, no gardening — indeed, the more I consider it the less activity I feel you should indulge in. Just sit still and wait! That's what you must do."

The wail of protest when it came was long and loud, but Dinwoodie was unmoved. He pointed to her chair and Cate obediently sat down. He then waved the letter at her, and, taking the other seat, opened it and began to read.

Dearest Girl,

I've just heard the sad news that Scottie is dead. Cate, I'm not sure if the news has reached you, but he took his own life; hung himself. I realise we all three parted on bad terms, but the man was like a father to me. I'll never know for sure, but I believe he intended to make an editor out of me. Cate, you may remember he first met me as a youngster helping my drunken father home from the pub.

He offered to help, but I was so ashamed at the sight we made, that I shrugged my shoulders at him and carried on.

It didn't stop him from going out of his way to walk the route from time to time continuing to offer his assistance, and in the end things were so hard for me I accepted.

From then, especially once my father died, he was always there: pennies given for checking some fact for the newspaper; following someone he believed was worth a story; then a wage for being the tea boy in the Gazette office. Finally he took me on as a cub reporter and eventually I became his chief reporter.

Oh, we had our rows, as you know, and we parted in anger. After that he even refused to print any of the copy I sent him from abroad in the run-up to the war, so that too fuelled my anger and resentment. Writing it now, Cate, brings back the terrible sadness of it all.

I should have gone home when his daughter died, but he never let me know and, even when I found out later, I was too pig-headed to return and comfort him.

I don't flatter myself that he regarded me as irreplaceable, but he invested a lot of kindness and training in me over the years. I feel that with his wife and daughter dead, and then to lose the person he'd groomed as his understudy in the Gazette, my leaving must be partially to blame for his death. I can see now that back then my refusal to reveal the truth about my marriage spun a web that entrapped the three of us, making us all losers, and may well have finally led to his committing suicide. I know that day his outburst about my marriage was meant to hurt you, but he was only trying to protect his daughter, and perhaps he thought he was also trying to save me from ruining my career.

Whatever the reasons, I do hope you at least have been able to forgive him. He meant a great deal to me.
In sorrow and regret,
Alashdair.

"I don't want you to let this upset you, Cate."

"It is upsetting, knowing he's out there blaming himself."

"No doubt he is, just as you did when you found out the man had died. But you did all you could by enabling his body to be buried with the rest of his family. I grant you it is possibly harder for him, for there is nothing he can do now. Come, my dear, the weather has improved and an outing might lift your spirits. What would you like to do?" Dinwoodie watched her rise and go to the painting. "Oh no, Cate! Once you go back to the hospital you'll be involved again."

"Dinwoodie, of course I will, but it's office work, sitting reading to patients, talking to them, nothing strenuous. I can't and won't sit still till for months. Be reasonable. I'll go mad! I can't stand the thought of just existing until then. I want this child as much as you do, and I promise I'll walk Midnight, stay away from Satan, and anything else you want — within reason. Please, let me out, Dinwoodie!"

"Alright! I'll have Morrison drive you there this afternoon, but I don't want you riding again till after the birth."

"I promise I'll be good. And thank you." Cate rose sedately from her chair and arm in arm they made their way downstairs to lunch, though Dinwoodie's thoughts were still with the Scribbler and the nagging suspicion that he might return at any time.

With the painting back on the wall in Kevinishe House, a walk through the wards with Mary Anne, and afternoon tea with Snowy all completed, Morrison brought her back to Craigavon and let her out at the stables to see Charlie and the horses. It was only later when she was preparing for an early bed to please Dinwoodie, that she realised she'd seen too little of Lizzie during the time she'd been laid up. So, tired though she was, she made her way to the nursery. Shona was seated in the rocking chair and the twins were holding her skein of wool, though not very successfully. They didn't improve matters by abandoning their task, leaving a tangled mess on the floor, as they rushed to greet her. Hugs over, Cate picked up the skein, held it, and chatted with the boys while Shona finally managed to complete her wool winding. It was as they were preparing to go down to the kitchen for their supper that Lizzie arrived in the doorway.

"Lizzie, it's so good to see you. I don't know why Maggie forbade you my bedroom. I can understand her not wanting the twins bouncing all over me, but I've missed you sorely." Cate ended her words with a hug, and was slightly surprised at her friend's involuntary stiffening.

"It's good you're up and about now," Lizzie said as she moved to collect her apron. "Shona, I'll take the boys down, if you'll see to their bath, and yes, Cate, I missed you too, but I'll need to get along now. Come on then you two, or Cook'll be cross." With that she shepherded the boys out and left a puzzled Shona and Cate in the nursery.

"I thought you did the supper with the boys, Shona."

"Aye Miss Cate, I do. Mebbe Lizzie just wanted to do them tonight. I'm that made up with my job here, I'll do anything to please Lizzie. I dinna mind the extra."

"Well, that's kind of you, and I'm pleased with the work you do, but we mustn't take advantage." As she shut the door behind her, Cate's mind was wrestling with the change of atmosphere when Lizzie walked into the nursery. Thinking of walking, it suddenly occurred to her that her friend's cheeks had been unusually flushed, almost as if she'd been for a hearty walk on the moors. Of course that was nonsense, as Lizzie did the minimum of walking and then normally with the twins, so why hadn't she taken them with her today?

Part Four

1918 Will it be Victory?

Chapter 26

By the end of September 1917, with Dinwoodie in London, Cate was becoming so irritable with the restrictions laid down by him during her pregnancy that she determined to find some way of leading a half normal life again. Wherever she went and whatever she did there was always someone around to gainsay her. However, on this particular morning, Maggie was busy changing the window drapes over, hanging the thick woollen ones in readiness for winter. On inspection, Cook was deep into the making of bramble jam, and there was little or no sound from the nursery, so the boys would be out for their morning walk with either Lizzie or Shona. With a wicked smile, Cate made for the boot room and, clad in a heavy winter coat and her riding boots, she slunk out the back door to freedom.

The mistress of Laggan House was having her morning coffee in the sunroom when she saw the figure approaching across the lawn that fronted the moors. Puzzled, she rose and studied the intruder. It wasn't until Cate, a finger to her lips, was almost up to the house, that her friend gave a delighted squeal and opened the French windows. Cate slid inside and collapsed on one of the chairs. "I've run away, and it's taken me forever to come across the moor!"

"What in the world are you walking for? A simple phone call would have brought me to you."

"No, no, I didn't want you to come to Craigavon…"

"Now that's a hurtful thing to say, seeing as you're sat in my chair and, I daresay you'll ask for some tea while I finish my coffee. Rude individual that you are! Explain yourself!"

Sometime later, explanations over, coffee and tea drunk, baby news, and Dinwoodie's restrictions outlined for her friend, Cate said, "So I've come to you for help. Any idea as to how I can get round all of them would be very welcome. I know they'll have discovered my absence by now, and I'll have to get back."

"Goodness me, you have got yourself in a pickle, though, after what's happened, your husband is right you know."

"Yes, but I'm not going to be an idiot! It's just that when he's not here I can't get out and about. Truth is I can barely breathe with the lot of them boxing me in."

"For an intelligent individual, you're not seeing that the answer is in your own hands."

"I don't understand."

"Think of your stable."

"I do all the time, but Dinwoodie has forbidden me to ride."

"I'm not suggesting you ride. He's quite right there."

"Then what has the stable…?"

"That weird contraption you brought me home in…?"

"The sulkie, of course! How clever you are and — oh no! He's specifically said I'm not even allowed to use the mare!"

"Don't then!" Her host replied as she rose and rang the service bell.

Cate watched as the maid answered and her friend instructed her to fetch the ghillie. When the man appeared, his owner said, "Donaldson, I need that pony for a time —the one you use to bring home the deer. Is that feasible?"

"But it's yourself that'll be too…"

"I'm not going to sit on the beast, so you needn't worry about my weight."

"Begging your pardon, Ma'am…"

"Will it work between shafts?"

"No, Ma'am, that one is too thrawn, but I know where I can lay my hands on one that would, though I'm thinking it's buying you'll be after having to do."

"Get it for me, then. As soon as possible and don't let them rob you in the process."

"Indeed no, Ma'am. There's no a body around who's got the better of Jock Donaldson!"

"Right then, man, get to it. I want it delivered to Craigavon."

The ghillie turned to Cate before he replied. "It'll be a terrible change after those wild beasts you gallop around on Miss Cate, but considering the circumstances just now, it may very well be wise, if you take my meaning."

"I believe it will, Jock, and I look forward to you and the beast arriving at Craigavon."

Turning to his current boss, the ghillie doffed his deerstalker and took his leave.

"Now then, Cate, since I didn't know of your 'circumstances' how in heaven's name did he? After all he spends his days traipsing over acres of bog and moor!"

"In this wild expanse rumour, gossip, blether, craic, whatever you like to call it, is one of the most efficient ways of spreading news that I know of!"

"Right, when the deed is done you will have your transport, but mind you stick to a lady-like trot, until the New Year, or I'll have the Ghillie bring the pony back! Is that understood?"

"Oh, Cecily, you've managed to banish my vapours! And I will heed your advice. I've no wish to lose this child, but I must be outdoors! I can't breathe unless I can scan the moors, watch the wild life, and be FREE!"

"You've had quite enough freedom this morning already, madam. They'll be sending out search parties for you with all that walking. Talking of which, I take it that you know Ewan is walking out with your nursemaid?"

In the resounding silence, the older woman wished she could retract her words. The shock on her visitor's face made her uneasy, and she tried to undo the damage. "Of course, as you say, gossip is rife here…"

"But she's my best friend, like a sister to me, why…?"

"My dear girl, do be sensible. The world and his wife know you can't stand the man, and I believe the feeling is mutual. Oh, I understand why. Ewan's a tough medicine to take, but perhaps your Lizzie is it?" At Cate's nod, her friend continued. "Well she may find something in him that you and I don't. But whatever it is, I wish them no ill, and so must you, my dear."

"But…"

"No, no buts! You listen to me! If you want to keep a lifelong friendship sweet you must hold your tongue. Don't go charging in, as is your wont. Let the news break freely, and then be the friend that Lizzie thinks you are. No doubt it will be difficult for you, I know, but essential for your friendship. Now, the car is ready to put you back in your gilded cage, so go, my wild friend, and take care. Remember all of us want only the best for you."

Wiping a tear from her eyes, Cate hugged the older woman and left.

At the end of the week, as Morrison drove towards the house, he gestured to his employer in the back before speaking. "Looks like you've visitors, sir."

Scanning the army truck, the Laggan Daimler, and a horse-drawn trailer, with various members of his staff standing around, he answered his chauffeur. "I'm afraid this may not be good news."

"They don't look too worried, Mr Dinwoodie. There'd be long faces if anything had happened to Miss Cate."

Nodding, Dinwoodie said, "I daresay. Let's get parked and find out what's going on then." As soon as the car stopped, he let himself out, and, seeing Maggie, made straight for her.

"Oh, sir, would you look at what Jock Donaldson has brought!" She greeted him, pointing to the trailer.

Following her directional arm, he spied a coffee and cream pony being unloaded. Not the rounded shape the twins were led on, but a much sleeker, slightly taller beast, now handed over to Charlie by Jock Donaldson, the Laggan ghillie, under Cecily Campbell-Broughton-Stuart's eagle eye. Charlie then led the beast towards the stables, with a huge grin on his face as he passed the assembled crowd.

Puzzled, Dinwoodie turned to his neighbour and asked, "My dear Cecily, what is going on? By the looks of you all, there's mischief afoot."

"How right you are, Dinwoodie! I'm here orchestrating a couple of things and we must get a move on or our sedate walker will be back before Charlie's ready."

"Well, whatever it is, why don't we all go indoors first?"

"Oh no, that would never do. You must wait for the others."

"Others? Heavens, there seem plenty here already! Who exactly are we expecting, and when?"

"He'll be here in about five minutes I should think. It's timed you see. The sulkie is all prepared — and, here he comes now!"

Dinwoodie looked in amazement as he turned to watch Charlie trotting along in front of the house driving the new arrival, and looking as though he'd been driving a sulkie all his life.

"Well done young man," she said. "Now then, Maggie, will you fetch the others." At the bemused expression on Dinwoodie's face, his neighbour began to enlighten him. "You can't keep that young hoyden of yours indoors, Dinwoodie. She'll pine, and that's not good for either her or your child, hence the little carriage. Though we do have another, possibly more difficult, situation to orchestrate today, which I hope we can bring out in the open while your wife is transfixed by her freedom carriage."

With immaculate timing, Ewan Brodie and Lizzie came out onto the doorstep as Rory and Cate appeared from the direction of the summerhouse.

"This, could go spectacularly wrong, Cecily," Dinwoodie warned, at the sight of Ewan Brodie, as Cate drew nearer.

"It may very well do, but Charlie has his instructions, and we're to follow them. To a man!" she finished, admonishing both Dinwoodie and her nephew with a threatening look.

Cate, when she saw the sulkie, went straight to the pony's head, spoke quietly to him, stroked his forelock, and blew in his nostrils. She seemed entranced, and it was only Charlie jumping down and taking her elbow that seemed to make her aware of all the others.

Under her breath, Dinwoodie heard Cecily mutter, "Come on, Charlie, get on with it."

Seeing her husband and expecting trouble, Cate shot him a pleading look as she was guided into the seat. Charlie jumped up beside her and, with a flick in the air of the short carriage whip, the sulkie trotted down the drive.

"So far, so good. Now then, Dinwoodie, let's all go inside and prepare for part two. Tea and biscuits all round I think, Maggie." At the housekeeper's nod, the older woman called to her nephew. "Come, Ewan, introduce me to this charming young woman, before we go inside!"

Meanwhile Cate and Charlie had reached the end of the drive before Cate could drag her glance away from the high-stepping little creature that was to be her path to freedom. "Was I mistaken, or did I see the hospital truck in front of the house just now, Charlie?"

"Aye, you did that, an her from Laggan House is there too, an she's to blame for it all. See here, I'm to tell you it's for your own good, Miss Cate. She's ower fond of you that one. Mind we've to play the game she wants, so I'll start. See, she knows, so she tell't me, that yon army man an your Lizzie, weel…"

"Have been walking out?"

"Aye, that they have, an no doubt you'll no be pleased."

"Exactly so. Carry on, tell me what's happening next?"

"We've done 'next' — you're to be so taken with — have you a name for him?" Charlie asked pointing to the pony.

"Spice, I think. It brightens up cooking when used, and he will do the same for my life in the coming weeks. And I suppose, as this is my treat, it's to soften the blow…?"

"Indeed, an was that no the way the great lady was seeing things?"

"You're all a conniving lot, but what about Dinwoodie? I'm surprised he didn't stop me getting into this, never mind trotting away before him."

"I think you'll find, Miss Cate, that that one from Laggan will have the measure of Mr Dinwoodie if I'm no mistaken," Charlie added with a chortle. "Anyways you're no to go driving alone, I'm to be with you, an she says Mr Dinwoodie will agree to that. Mind you, I wouldna like to disagree with her myself!"

Cate shook her head and watched Charlie turn the sulkie with consummate ease. "I see our trip to the Black House with Hansi has given you practice."

"Well now it was a beginning, but see you, in the big car I've been to Laggan House for a few wee lessons before Donaldson fetched the pony here. Mind you, I know her man is an army something or other, but she herself would be a fine organizer in the trenches, would that lady. Mebbe even put fright to a German or two!"

Both in fits of laughter at the very idea they trotted back to the front door, where Charlie helped Cate down before returning Spice and the sulkie to the stables.

Meanwhile she joined the others in the drawing room. As the men stood, Cate went to Dinwoodie and asked, "Well, do I have your approval of my new mode of transport?"

"I suppose so. It's a foolish man who doesn't know when he's beaten, but Cecily assures me that you will not venture out alone. Though she appears to have more faith in that pledge than I do."

"Nonsense, Dinwoodie!" His neighbour rasped. "It's quite simple. No young Charlie, no outing! Believe me, that young man is possibly even more devoted to Cate here than the rest of us, and he'll see she follows orders. So that's an end to it! Now then, Cate, while you were gallivanting with Charlie, I've made the acquaintance of young Lizzie here, re-introduced Dinwoodie to my nephew, and I'm delighted to see him invited here today, so thank you for that." The others looked astounded at this unlikely statement, but no one spoke, till Cate steeled herself to greet the Captain. "I see you've found a walking companion, Captain."

Ewan Brodie, under the steely gaze of his aunt, continued the charade. "In…yes, yes Indeed. I've accompanied Lizzie and the boys on several walks and have enjoyed doing so. It lets me get away from the hospital on occasion, and of course I'm delighted to be here today, Mrs Dinwoodie." With that, feeling he'd done as ordered, he took a deep breath and with a relieved glance at Lizzie, sank as far back in his chair as he could.

Chapter 27

As he walked ever onwards, still without funds, towards Paris, Bruce wondered just how many more times he'd have to thumb lifts and repeat his various sob stories of thieves taking all his cash, his vehicle breaking down, losing his way, or any other excuse he could think up at any given time. He was less than enamoured over the way he had had to doss down in the unlikeliest of abodes during his efforts to get back to the apartment.

Deep in thought, as he trudged along feeling sorry for himself, he was almost unaware of the chauffeured limousine that pulled up in front of him. Straightening his shoulders, wishing his clothes looked a bit smarter, he marched round to the passenger side and opened the front door. Seated in the back was a silent woman draped in black. So Bruce turned his attention to the chauffeur and politely spun his weary tale of abandoning his non-existent vehicle miles back and would they perhaps be heading for the Capital.

They dropped him further along the road to Paris and, as he watched the limousine turn off into a rather stately set of gold-tipped wrought-iron gates, he wished they'd extended an invitation to go with them. As the light dimmed in the early November darkness, he trudged on till he came to the next village. There he staggered into a ruined courtyard and, began looking round for somewhere to sleep. He'd just located a shabby barn when he felt the muzzle of a gun in his back. At the insistent prod he stumbled forward until they'd reached a door. The gun remained at his back, but an arm came round his body and banged on the wooden panel.

As the door was opened a crack, a woman peered out and said, "Mon Dieu! Qui est-il?"

"Boche!" spat a rough voice from behind.

"No, no," stammered Bruce "I'm English! No, I mean — well, I'm Scottish."

"Ecosse?" queried the gruff voice.

"Mais oui. Certainement. Je suis Ecosse."

The gun was lowered, and a hefty thump on the back sent him sprawling onto an earthen floor, where he lay as the man and woman surveyed him. At last the man bent down, grabbed his collar, pulled him upright, and motioned him to sit at an ancient deal table, before putting his gun on two nails drilled into the rough stone wall. He then sat and growled at the woman in French, while never taking his eyes of Bruce.

The three of them had only just begun to eat the bread and boeuf aux carottes that had been put on the table, when the door opened and a young woman entered. She hung her coat up underneath the gun, and, smiling at Bruce, slid onto the bench beside the old woman.

Meal over, he was shown the barn, while the others made ready to retire. As he lay on the straw beside the cow and horse, he couldn't help thinking about the girl. She was passable and, being from a peasant family, he wouldn't mind betting on her being only too willing to 'accommodate' him. A pleasant dalliance with her before he returned to Paris would make the last weeks much more palatable. He'd bide his time. Take advantage of her when the old man and his gun were well clear of the house! He fell asleep with that pleasant thought uppermost in his mind.

The next morning, before Bruce was even awake, the man appeared, gun draped over his arm, with a bucket of water and some bread and cheese. He roused Bruce, gestured to what he'd brought, and watched while he ate, drank, and then washed his face and hands. Using the gun barrel, the old man gesticulated towards the courtyard and, with the gun prodding him on his way, Bruce crossed the yard and out onto the road leading away from the village. He halted and tried to turn back, but as the gun clicked into the firing position, he thought better of it and went on his way, cursing the fact that the old man had got the better of him.

He'd only been walking for a short way when he came across a heavily-laden rickety old lorry with its back wheels halfway into the ditch at the side of the road, with the owners struggling to rescue it. Bruce joined in. Together they heaved and pulled, and at last, with a multilingual spray of curses, the ancient vehicle was freed. Bruce joined the farmer in the cab relegating the lad to squeezing in amongst the household paraphernalia piled up in the open back. What with the taciturn driver and Bruce's not too fluent French, the conversation was limited, but when the lorry turned off the road and stopped, Bruce got out, and was delighted to find he was almost in the Parisian suburbs.

By the end of the day, though weary with the brisk pace he'd set for himself, Bruce knew he was within easy walking of the apartment. It was not long before he began to recognise the various bistros he'd frequented in the past, as he'd moved ever outward in Paris to find new sources for his particular kind of violent sex. It was dark by the time he reached the apartment, but, when he managed to rouse the old concierge, the man refused him entry at first. Not only that, but Bruce was horrified to learn that Rhoddy had apparently been gone almost as long as he had. After much persuasion, the concierge was made to understand that the only way the rent now owing would be paid was if Bruce gained access to the mail that he hoped would be waiting for him.

Once inside he sifted through the letters, the concierge's rheumy eyes fixed firmly on his movements. Although still worried over Rhoddy's absence, Bruce relaxed when he found letters from both Stuffy and McPhail in the mail. Waving the bank drafts they contained at the old man was enough to persuade him to fetch some food and drink, though his muttered gestures when he returned with them made it quite clear that he would be back in the early morning. Bruce knew that he would be shadowed all the way to the bank and relieved of a good portion of his new funds the next day, before he could claim them for himself.

As to what had happened to Rhoddy, the old man said the boy had left with an Englishman weeks ago. Bruce concluded that either McPhail or Stuffy, who'd been directed to send the money to Paris rather than his estate in the south of France, were the only possible people who knew of Rhoddy's whereabouts in Paris. He very much doubted that Stuffy would bother to come to France, but McPhail was much more likely to want to get his hands on the boy, use him as a negotiating tool, to ensure he was paid what he demanded.

His meagre meal consumed, Bruce read the letters and was horrified to learn that Stuffy's father had died. The terse note from his old school friend also assured him that therefore the enclosed draft would be the last, since there was now no one to care what they'd got up to when they were seventeen. The content of McPhail's letter was equally worrying. Not being privy to Bruce's travelling to France with the boy, his cousin's anger at the situation was as obvious as Stuffy's relief. At the mention of sending an investigator to find them, Bruce assumed that he had done so, and that Rhoddy would by now be safely back in the Highlands with McPhail. The spark of relief about the boy was soon

241

superseded as he read on. His cousin's critical opinion about the French episode was followed by a veiled warning as to the likelihood of the continuation of more funds, now that the MacNishe heir could not be found. This puzzled Bruce, but he assumed that either the letter or the concierge had got the timing wrong, for McPhail, or indeed his investigator, must have taken Rhoddy out of France. It was the only possible reason for the boy's absence.

With that thought came the relief that he need no longer worry about hiding his son. Even if in the beginning the Iron Baron had set an investigator on his trail, it had gone cold long ago. The thought of outwitting, not only the bitch of a tinker girl, but also the mighty Iron Baron was certainly a pleasant one. And the idea that without the boy he would be free to follow his own interests was also appealing now that he had funds again.

While he made ready for bed, these thoughts, however, lost some of their attraction when he remembered that his own time in France would have to end soon. There was of course still the lonely wife with a husband at the Front — though by now the details of her whereabouts had dimmed — but she had, at their last debauched meeting relieved him of all his remaining funds and dumped him in that godforsaken old hovel of a barn. No, perhaps he'd give her a miss! And yet physically punishing her for her treachery would be enjoyable and just what she deserved. As he slid beneath the cold damp sheets, however, he considered the uncertainty of raising money in the future, and his last thought before drifting off to an uneasy sleep was that he'd stick close to the apartment and scour the neighbouring streets for his pleasures.

The following morning outside the bank, Bruce watched the concierge stuff the money for the rent arrears, plus an advance payment for the coming month, into his pockets and shuffle away. The rest of the notes in his hand, Bruce felt, should at least last that long, and he'd worry about how to get back to McPhail and Rhoddy in Scotland when the time came. Right now he was about to treat himself to a hearty breakfast, then he'd while away the time in a couple of bistros until dusk.

The thought of what the evening might hold had him wishing the intervening hours away. After all, it had been some time since he'd been able to indulge himself!

Back in the apartment Bruce waited for the last of the Parisian daylight to fade and then made his way to the nearby familiar quarter famed for its 'ladies of the night'. He deliberately took his time in choosing what was on offer. He'd always found this restraint had heightened his excitement. One by one he dismissed the women, until he caught sight of a rather striking red-head making her way into one of the bistros. Bruce followed her and once inside he ordered wine and smiling at her asked the waiter for two glasses. When they'd finished the bottle, and arrangements had been made, he ordered another and followed her outside and down an alleyway with it.

The red hair reminded him of the bloody tinker woman, and the more he thought of her, the more enraged he became. Soon he was immune to the shrieks and cries of the woman he'd now pinned against the wall. Bruce continued to rape and beat her and it was only when he was fully satisfied that he stopped. The woman, now bleeding freely, slipped unconscious to the ground as he released her. Doing himself up as quickly as possible, Bruce knew he had to get out of the area before anyone appeared. But he was too late. Strong arms behind him pulled him away from the woman's body. Despite his frantic pleas the two attacking men slammed him against the wall time and again, continuing to beat him till he too lay senseless on the ground. With a final thorough kicking of his inert body, they ransacked his pockets, lifted the helpless woman between them, and made their way into the night.

Some of those who occupied the alley later, checked the already empty pockets, spat on the spurned body, and removed themselves before they could be associated with it. Near dawn an ancient crone, huddled in a shawl, bent to offer assistance to the mauled heap of human flesh, but, finding it was too late, made her way to an all-night bistro, where, for a small measure of absinthe, she told her tale and left those inside to make of it what they would.

Far from being safe in the Highlands with his uncle, Boy, as he was known, was still on the Western Front, where at this particular moment he was battling against the lice that were causing every part of his body to itch. No matter how often he scratched, it had little effect on the constant irritation all over his skin. Where others used their cigarettes to run down the seams of their clothing to evict the lice that tormented them, he could only access the few in the open. Right now he was supposed to be asleep, but the lice were making it impossible.

That night Grabber and his group were due out as a repair detail to mend the barbed wire defences in front of their section of the trench. So far their part of the line had not been required to go over the top for repairs, though several of those further down had been out the previous night, and two of them had been killed outright. Boy was unsure what was happening. He'd understood little, but it would be safe if he stayed close to Grabber.

While he'd been occupied with the lice, the other men had all fallen asleep. In a panic now, Boy looked around for the man. He was too far away to see him, so he began to crawl along the line. He had to find Grabber, the one who'd made him his companion these last months, and was his safety. Because he still wasn't close enough to reach out and tug the familiar tunic, his usual way of talking with the man, he instinctively mouthed, "Grabber". As a slight sound echoed in his head he was puzzled, but then it became apparent that his tongue, frozen along with his muddled mind, had made the sound.

For the next few minutes Boy moved his tongue around, making weird noises he didn't recognise. Then he tried 'Grabber' again. This time it came out just loud enough to arouse the man.

"Who? What? Shurrup! Silly buggers! Go to sleep — we'll be awake soon enough!" With that Grabber shuffled around to a more comfortable position in the trench and, with a noisy yawn, settled down again.

Boy, confused with the turn of events, got up, picked his way over the remaining bodies till he reached Grabber and shook his tunic. When the angry man sat up he looked at him and said, with more emphasis, "Grabber! Grabber! Grabber!"

"Bloody 'ell! What? You can speak? When? Why? So who are you? 'Ow?"

Frightened by this raft of questions, the shaken lad shrank against the side of the trench in shock.

Wide-awake now, Grabber, understanding the panic, tried to reassure him. He patted him on the shoulder, and motioned him to settle down to sleep again. Then he took out a dog-end, and in the flare of the match he studied his frightened companion now resting beside him. With the stub glowing, he sucked on it, deep in thought. He'd seen enough shell-shocked soldiers to realise that the mind could do strange things. For months now the youngster had hung onto him almost as though there was no one else around, though the place was always heaving with people. In all that time, despite urging from the others, even a grilling from the corporal, he'd not uttered a word. All the questioning had resulted in nothing but fits of the shakes, and no one but himself could pacify the silent youngster.

The two of them understood each other and functioned in this hellhole of war with an efficiency that surprised the others and was the main reason Boy hadn't been shipped out before, though, as his identity and origin were unknown, where were they going to send him anyway? As the glowing end of his butt began to burn his lip, Grabber spat it out with a muttered oath before he too settled down again to sleep. Time enough to decide what to do about the lad once their work party were back safe.

In the wavering light of his lantern the corporal moved along the trench at midnight shaking the group awake, while distributing wire and tools. When they were ready, Grabber let the others move off and motioned Boy, complete with rifle, to stay at the lip of the trench, where he'd be safer and perhaps give them some cover. Then he too climbed out. For the first hour there was silence as the men worked in the dim light from the lantern, but suddenly there came a crack of gunfire and, as the bullet tore into his chest, Lou dropped the light, which sent up a flare as the flame caught his clothes. The enemy line, aroused now, peppered the group, who dodged and weaved on their way back to safety.

Boy tried to fire, but was so terrified he dropped his rifle and, for a long moment stared at the fireworks of German shots beyond. In their fractured light he suddenly caught sight of Grabber going down. Frozen for a moment, as the realisation that the only thing that made sense to him was lying wounded out there, the thought of being without the man dispelled his fear and made him scramble over and lunge towards the spot he thought he'd seen him go down.

It was the unexpected flare of pain in his leg that made him fall towards the body he believed was Grabber. Instinct made him shake the fallen soldier's uniform for attention, in the familiar way of the previous months. The wounded man responded with the usual muttered oaths.

"I told you to bloody stay where you were, you silly bugger! Now we've both copped it." With an effort Grabber moved forward, flinching as his wounded shoulder collided with the hardened mud. And with much muttering against the fates, he slowly began the laborious task of pulling both himself and the injured Boy across what seemed a never-ending space to safety. Before long he was forced to rest as the pain overtook him. Boy, seemingly aware now of what Grabber was doing, took his turn in easing them forward. When, both exhausted, they could

245

move no more, they lay as the firing from the opposing trenches sputtered to a halt. Then they caught the sounds of whispered comforting voices, and before long strong arms eased them upwards, and helped them on their way to safety.

In the confines of the dressing station Grabber said little as they bound his shoulder, and when it was done he watched them bind Boy's leg before saying, "That young 'un doesn't speak. 'E weren't supposed to come out with us, silly beggar! Do us a favour, mate: he's frightened to death out 'ere, so keep us together when we get to the field 'ospital, otherwise no one'll know anything about 'im." Reassured by a friendly nod, Grabber's cunning brain began to sift through the various possibilities ahead of them. They'd be useless until their wounds healed, and if the shot had splintered a bone in Boy's leg that would take time, and God knows what damage had been done to his own shoulder! If he could keep the young 'un from talking, they might send them back together, now that it looked as though they'd both collected 'Blighty Ones'.

It all depended on how much the lad now remembered and if he spoke. Did he have a home somewhere? What about a family? It could be tricky, but if he made sure Boy kept quiet, carried on as they were, then he might be able to swing it. After all he was the only mate he had, and he'd offer to keep an eye on him, whatever happened. First off he must make sure his young companion said nothing. Not a word to any of them when they got to the clearing station. Stands to reason: the pair of them'd made a good job of their thieving while out here, so who's to say they couldn't do a better one in good old Blighty?

Once they'd been assessed, the wounded were sent on to a field hospital. As they were loaded into the ambulance, Grabber let out a cry of pain, before shouting at the handler, "Whose side are you on then? Mind what you're bloody doing will you! The 'un's done enough damage as it is — and you look out for that young 'un! Not right in the 'ead 'e is, poor bugger!"

On arrival, their wounds were checked and, both of them had the bullets removed the following morning. They were then put in a tent with what was known as Blighty labels. This meant that they were to be taken to the next hospital ship leaving for England. So far, without any further effort on his part, Grabber's plans for them both seemed to be working.

Chapter 28

Back in Kevinishe Captain Ewan Brodie, re-read the letter again. A party of army Top Brass were to arrive as part of a tour of all hospitals. It gave no hint as to why, when, or for how long — just the bald statement that they would be coming. The very idea made him uneasy. He knew things had been going too well of late. He was proud of the fact that a number of his cases were making quite drastic improvements. The new ward maid, Bella, a quiet soul, was providing a soothing experience on the wards, and even his relationship with Mrs Dinwoodie was not as fraught as it had been, though it would never be good. But at least the woman had not as yet stifled his blossoming relationship with Lizzie. Indeed he had a plan that might even improve the strained cordiality that existed between them.

He now knew that Lizzie's limp had not been caused by the road accident, but was the result of a badly set broken limb years ago in Glasgow. Without telling anyone, he'd arranged to take her to be seen by an army friend of his in Edinburgh who was involved with the manufacture of restructured boots and shoes for the many soldiers whose lower limbs had been damaged in the war. But now that would have to wait until this inspection visit was over.

The one patient that had not progressed at all was the American. At least they had been able to tell the intelligence people that he was unlikely to be a spy and he had to admit that that had been thanks to Mrs Dinwoodie, even if it had resulted in yet another bust-up between them. Over time his opinion of the woman had changed somewhat. She seemed to have an uncanny knack of relating to his patients. He couldn't quite work out what it was. In fact the ancillary staff all seemed to regard 'Miss Cate' as something special, and Lizzie certainly held her in high regard, saying that, 'Cate had transformed her life'. Whatever it was that the others saw, he didn't, and that made him uneasy.

He put the letter back in its envelope and tried to shrug off the idea that both letter and Mrs Dinwoodie heralded trouble for him. With his ward rounds complete for the day and knowing she was still in her office, he made for the truck and a quick visit to Craigavon for a walk with Lizzie and the boys.

Cate finished the orders list and, as it was teatime, made her way to Snowy in the kitchen. Mary Anne, Morag, and Bella were already there, teacups full and scones on their plates. Cate had just sat down when one of the orderlies came looking for Mary Anne because the American was having a 'turn'.

"Since I haven't started tea I'll go, Mary Anne. You come through when you've finished." At the worried look on her friend's face, Cate reassured her. "I'll call if we can't cope, so go on with your tea." And then she left, following the orderly to the ward where the American was huddled against the windowpane thoroughly agitated. Cate walked towards him, with the orderly behind her, and held out her hand. It took some time, but gradually the shaking lessened and he put his hand in hers. For a time she stroked his palm and then, as he began to relax, she gently coaxed him to the chair beside his bed, waving the orderly away. Once seated, Cate picked up the children's picture book she'd brought for him the other day, sat on his bed and began reading, pointing to the pictures as she read. As usual, it was not long before his head began to droop and his chin settled on his chest. Cate put down the book and watched him as he slept. Since the Captain had furnished the intelligence people with what they assumed his name to be, it probably wouldn't be long before his unit was traced, and then who knew what would happen to him? One thing was for sure; she'd get no meaningful information out of him about Sarah, and the rest of his family, unless they were able to unlock his mind before he left.

When Mary Anne arrived, Cate left her to it and returned to the kitchen, her thoughts still on the man and their inability to make any headway with him. She was surprised to see Robbie chatting to Snowy.

"You cadging a scone and tea then, Robbie?"

"Now then, Miss Cate, he did nothing of the kind. He was waiting to see you, so I thought he might as well join us till you appeared."

"I was teasing, Snowy! What did you want to see me about Robbie?

"A while back, Miss Cate I minded on a puzzle my grandfather carved for me when I was but a toddler, and I thought something like that would do fine for the boys, so I set to, and here it is."

"Robbie, that's wonderful." Cate said, admiring the puzzle. "You're so clever with your hands. Just look at that! The frame is lovely, never mind the pieces of the train. Thank you. It was very thoughtful of you, and the boys do play with all the things you've carved for them — more so than anything Dinwoodie or I buy."

"It pleases me to do them for I fair enjoy the working of them." Robbie gave a sly glance in Morag's direction, before saying, "You never know, I might well be doing them for sons of my own one day."

His words made Morag blush, and the others were somewhat taken by surprise.

"Really!" Cate said with a smile as she bit into her scone.

Embarrassed now, Robbie took his leave and Morag lifted her teacup and drank while her blush faded. The others now showed great interest in the jigsaw, leaving any teasing of Morag for another day.

Tea finished, Cate took the present with her, and went to check the American again. He was still in the chair but awake now. For no real reason she began to explain about the wooden puzzle, and showed it to the man as she spoke. He hesitated, but then stretched out a hand to stroke the wood. Cate smiled at him and as he drew his hand away, she turned it upside down on the bed and watched as all the pieces fell out. She was unprepared for the blows as the man began to mutter and slap at her in anger. She reached for his hands and held them away from her as he bowed his head, and was surprised when a tear splashed on her wrist. She then let his hands go free and turned to the puzzle on the bed.

"Don't fret! I haven't broken it. Look, see — first we turn the board the right way up and now the pieces go back in. I think, let's do the wheels first." She placed them in the frame and, keeping an eye on the man, pretended to hesitate over the next piece to put in. She could see she had his attention now and so deliberately chose a piece that wouldn't fit. She shook her head, frowned, and tried another piece. His hand stretched out over hers, and although he hesitated, he then picked up the piece that fitted above the wheels. Cate clapped her hands and nodded her head in approval. She then tried yet another wrong piece, but he shook his head and reached out for a different one, fitting it correctly. Cate sat back, waited and watched as bit by bit, and with great care, he completed the puzzle. When he looked up at her she smiled and said, "Well done!"

She was slightly taken aback though, when he picked the completed puzzle up, got into his bed, and hid under the blankets. Unsure of her reaction, he flashed her a nervous look, and when she smiled, got up, waved at him, and walked away, he relaxed, lay down, clasping the blankets that hid his newly acquired treasure, and closed his eyes.

Cate went in search of Mary Anne and found her in the linen room, where she was checking the sheets with Bella. Joining them in their task, Cate relayed the story of the puzzle.

"Well now it's a good job the boys didn't know about it, so there'll be no harm done, and I daresay he'll forget about it before long", Bella said.

"I'm not so sure about that." Mary Anne looked thoughtful as she spoke. "Back in the convent, earlier in the war, there were a couple of men who spent all day playing with toy motors. Seems the horrors they'd seen had made them regress to childhood so they had, and any attempt we made to confront them with reality, had them screaming and backing away."

"So, grown men from the army becoming children, while the few young boys in the village here play at being soldiers. 'Bang! Bang! Bang!', with their wooden make-believe rifles. What a strange world the war has made for us!" Cate said. The women continued inspecting the linen in silence, each occupied with their own thoughts, until Cate continued, "Still it's given me an idea about the man."

"Well you make sure you tell the Captain, Cate. It's been quite peaceful here this last while so it has. Don't go upsetting him! And he's worrying over some sort of inspection coming up, so in the name of the Good Lord just you be careful," Mary Anne warned.

"I'll go and speak to him now before I leave. If Charlie is looking for me, tell him I'll only be a minute."

"Cate, you'll not find the Captain in his office. I heard the truck go out just before tea."

"Are you sure, Bella?"

"Yes, I think Duncan said the Captain was going for a walk."

At her mention of Duncan, Cate and Mary Anne exchanged looks. Both knew Bella seemed to spend more time with him than any of the other patients.

"Well, if that's the case, I might as well go down and wait for Charlie, because I know where the good Captain does his walking!"

This time it was Bella and Mary Anne who exchanged looks. They were well aware that Cate didn't approve of the Captain seeing Lizzie, and if she left now she might meet him at Craigavon. They waited till she'd gone before speaking. "Do you think, Mary Anne, that it's serious with the Captain and Lizzie?"

"I do know Lizzie thinks well of him, Bella, and he doesn't traipse all the way over to Craigavon for just a walk. There's plenty walking to be had right here in the grounds of the hospital. Sure and I'm thinking it must be something in the water, I do!"

"What do you mean?"

"Well, with Robbie making sheep's eyes at Morag; yourself favouring Duncan, and Lizzie and the Captain, it's looking like a disease that's spreading!"

"Mary Anne, really!" Bella hid her face as she concentrated on the sheets, while her friend grinned at her bowed head.

As Charlie brought the sulkie to a halt at the front door of Craigavon, the walking party appeared round the side of the house. Cate took her time dismounting and the boys ran ahead of Lizzie and the Captain, anxious to get a ride to the stables in the pony and trap.

"May we, Mama? Just this time!" David cajoled.

"Go on, Charlie, but bring them straight back when you've put Spice away. And you two behave!" Cate admonished the twins.

"Don't you worry, Miss Cate, there'll be no bother from them, or there'll be no more rides," Charlie said, giving the boys a knowing look before they scrambled aboard, into Cate's seat.

"Lizzie, Captain," Cate greeted them as they joined her to watch the boys drive away with Charlie.

"He's very good with them, Cate, isn't he?"

"He is that, Lizzie, and they think the world of him, though they know they can't get away with anything when they're with him. Oh, by the way, Captain, have you a moment? Perhaps we could go indoors?"

"If you wish, Mrs Dinwoodie."

"Really Captain, this is too silly! Please feel free to use Miss Cate — everyone else does."

"Very well, if you insist." He replied. "Er, what did you want me for?"

An exasperated Cate led the way into the drawing room followed by the Captain, who would much have preferred to make his way to the kitchen with Lizzie.

Since they were both uncomfortable, Cate got straight to the point. Told the story of the jigsaw yet again, and then, after a moment's hesitation asked, "I wonder if finding something else that he could work with his hands might be worth trying. What do you think?"

Aware of her hesitation, and the fact that she was actually asking for his opinion in the matter, seemed to confuse Ewan Brodie. A raging

251

flame-haired woman he knew how to handle. "I — I can't see that it would do any harm, Mrs — er — Miss — um, Miss Cate."

"Right, I'll have a word with the engineer from the distillery. He's always fiddling around with things, and I'll let you know if anything comes up. Now you'll be in a hurry to return, so I'll not detain you any longer, Captain." She rose to see him out and almost at the same moment Lizzie appeared and looked warily at Cate, who smiled before she said, "It's alright, Lizzie, he left in one piece!"

Then the twins appeared and Lizzie bore them off for supper and Cate's thoughts turned again to the easy relationship she'd had with the Major in the hospital before he was sent back to the war. There were three of them to worry about now: Rhoddy, Hansi and the Major, all in or around the Western Front. And what about Alashdair? There'd had been no word from him for some time now. Was he still reporting from behind the lines, or had he been injured? And Bruce MacNishe, where was he? Not forgetting the invisible McPhail, another of her bogeymen. She chastised herself for being morbid, and went upstairs to check the blue room that was being redone for the twins, so that the nursery could be made ready for the addition to their family in the New Year.

Chapter 29

It was barely dawn as Maggie and Lizzie returned to Craigavon, but Cate, who'd been anxious about Kirsty, had been up all night and was supping yet another cup of tea when the weary couple entered the kitchen.

Cate was so anxious for her friend that she bombarded them with questions before the others had time to sit down, "How is she? Is she all right? What's she had? Come on you two — say something! Did it all go well?"

"Let us at least get through the door, Cate! All is indeed well. She's had a wee boy, though as a first it was a long old day an night. She's fair tired out with it. Donald Uig is strutting round the village as though this was the only bairn ever born in Kevinishe. Oh, an they're to name him for Murdo, God rest his soul. An now I'll get some porridge on the stove — oh no need, here's Cook." Maggie sat down again while Cook began the porridge and Cate took the kettle off the hob and refilled the teapot.

Breakfast over, Cate walked slowly to the stable to get Charlie to take her to see the latest addition to the glen, before going to the hospital with the news the women there had been waiting for. She had to admit she was envious of Kirsty with the birth over, and would have liked her own pregnancy to be finished, but she'd weeks to go yet and the burden was becoming cumbersome. As for Dinwoodie, he was getting more and more nervous as each week passed, and she knew, when he arrived home in a few days, he'd insist she left the hospital, and no doubt he'd restrict her other movements as well.

After the wetting of young Murdo's head with a drop of whisky, and a silver coin tucked into the little hand, both old established customs, Cate left the bottle of whisky and her back door cake for Donald Uig to welcome the rest of the village when they came to pay their respects. Charlie took her to the hospital; only to find the army inspection was underway. Not wishing to meet them in her present state, Cate had Charlie drive back to Craigavon, and there on the forecourt, unloading the car, was Morrison.

She found Dinwoodie in the kitchen and, as she went to greet him, he held her at arm's length and said, "I'm glad to see you're no longer working, my dear."

"Oh no! I'm still at the hospital, it's only today some of the high-ups from the army have arrived. They're doing some sort of an inspection, but hopefully it'll only be for a day or two. The others can cope with that, and then I'll go back."

"You, Cate Dinwoodie, will be taking more than a few days off, now I'm here. With only weeks left, I'm going to work from home until the big event."

With a resigned sigh, Cate sat at the table with the others, her mind less on the chatter about Kirsty's new baby and more on the hospital inspection. After all, the army had upset her once before by removing the Major. What had they in store for them this time, she wondered? She'd no need to wonder what Dinwoodie had in store for her till the child was born, but she did wonder how she was going to cope with the constant surveillance!

Two days later the argument continued. "I will not have you putting yourself at risk, Cate, to say nothing of our child!" Dinwoodie ordered.

"For goodness sake, Charlie is driving the damn sulkie slower than I could walk! I'm not Kirsty. This isn't a first time for me! We're talking about sitting quietly either in my office doing paperwork or walking sedately around the wards. A friendly nod here, a chat there, perhaps read to one patient, write a letter for another. It's no different than doing those things here at Craigavon, though all this fussing at home is more stressful than being at the hospital, I can tell you!"

"Cate, if you think you're stressed, take a moment to consider how I feel!"

"I know, Dinwoodie. You thought your chances of having a rightful heir had been and gone, but at least give me credit for some sense. Yes, I realise that earlier I was foolish and it was tricky for a while, but we survived that, and now your child is safely snuggled in my womb, frequent kicks and movements mean it's alive, and the chances of anything else going wrong are few and far between."

"That's as may be, but don't defy me in this, Cate. I want you here at Craigavon. Oh, I daresay you'll toe the line for a time if I let you carry on working, but something will happen and, no matter what it is, off you'll go to deal with it, caution forgotten. So no, you stay here, for there'll be no one to prevent you being foolish at the hospital." As Cate was about to take issue with him, Dinwoodie raised his hand to silence her. "Look round the table here — ask any one! If I'm misjudging you, and you know full well what…"

"Damn it! I don't much mind what you all think! Today, I haven't come home because I was weary, ill, or anything else. I felt, in my present condition, it would be unseemly to be around at the inspection with senior figures from the army, so I made the sensible decision not to go to work. I'm not Kirsty, a first time expectant mother. Neither am I some ignorant young girl. Though when I was, both Maggie and Lizzie can bear witness that I was scrubbing stairs when my labour started! And two days after that I was combing the streets for work to feed myself and my child, and both of us, in case you've missed the fact, survived!" Her temper rising at the mere thought of being unfairly chastised by Dinwoodie in front of everyone, she rose and stalked out of the kitchen, before she said anything truly damaging.

After a somewhat silent lunch, Cate went in search of Charlie. She felt she had to get out of the house, but she met Benjamin at the front door with the post and much to her relief, saw the foreign postmark on both the letter and the accompanying parcel. Still annoyed with Dinwoodie, she contemplated taking Alashdair's letter to read on her own. However, exasperated both with herself and Dinwoodie, she closed the door after the postman, went to her study, put the parcel in her safe, and made her way to the drawing room, where she sat toying with the envelope until Dinwoodie appeared for afternoon tea.

When he did, she surprised him with a sweet smile and said, "See, I've sat and twiddled my thumbs since lunch, and I'm quite bored, but at least we do at last have a letter from the front. I was beginning to think something awful had happened to him."

"Would it matter that much if it had, Cate?"

"Dinwoodie! What? How can you even ask that? Of course it matters! I thought myself in love with the man once. How could I not be affected by it? Oh, open the damn letter before we're at odds yet again! Somehow there's no pleasing you these days!"

He realised that the unguarded question, asked out of residual jealousy, had indeed upset her yet again. It looked as though these next weeks were going to prove a trial for them both. He sat and opened the letter.

> The Western Front Autumn, 1917
>
> Dearest Girl,
> The sadness of my last letter is still with me, and is deepened as I sit next to some of our soldiers on respite from the front line during the third battle of Ypres. For the first time since this conflict started these men seem to be, if not defeated, almost losing their spirit for this fight.
> I've written before of the vagaries of weather and its impact on the War. Cate, it's like yet another enemy. In these long months in Flanders our men have gained a little, lost a little, and felt they'd made a breakthrough, but then, just as in the Somme, the rain began again. This time though, it still hasn't stopped.
>
> Alashdair.

"They won't really give up, will they?"

"Who knows? I must say, my dear, he's right though. One wonders how any of the poor devils, be they on either side in this hateful conflict can find the resolve, never mind the physical strength, to continue after years of giving their everything to the fight with little or no real success."

"It makes one ashamed to be sat here, comfortable in our own home. Can you ever see an end to it, Dinwoodie?"

"Oh Cate, we must trust that the politicians can find a solution. Though after the immense loss of life, with very little gained for it, our leaders daren't capitulate. The Germans are probably faced with an even worse dilemma."

"In what way?" Cate asked.

"Think about it. The war began with Germany as a nation completely ready for it. The largest army, the most equipment, the biggest appetite for the struggle all belonged to them. The fact is that those at home quite rightly expected their soldiers to have defeated the allies in the first months of the war, never mind four long years later. Now, neither side dares seek a truce because all the warring nations need to claim victory in order to get the best out of any peace treaty."

"What you're saying is that this next year looks as though it's going to be the same, if not worse, than the last. It's too dispiriting even to think of it. I'll have a sedate walk to the stables and speak to the horses." Cate eased herself out of the chair, wrapped her shawl round her shoulders and left, followed by Dinwoodie, who headed to his office and the dispiriting pile of paperwork Sheena had given him to check.

Chapter 30

Pearson had run out of ideas. He'd spent the last months veering between exhaustive visits as near as he was allowed, and without going to the heart of the fighting, at the front in fruitless searching for any chance mention of the underage Rhoddy. At one point he thought he might have managed to trace him, when he heard that the army had indeed rounded up some of the younger lads and put them in a holding camp. Others, he'd been told had been sent home, but neither of these leads had been successful. His return trips to both the estate, where MacNishe had hidden out in the beginning, and back to the apartment in Paris, had been equally abortive.

In Paris once more he despaired of ever tracing his quarry, and though he'd been hungry when he'd ordered food in the café, now he pushed his half-eaten meal to the side. He'd failed, and he might as well get on the next train for home. London first and, if his employer was not at the foundry there or at his club, he'd have to journey on to Glasgow, but wherever he found him it was not a meeting that he relished. He was so bound up in his own miserable thoughts, it took him a moment to realise that someone was tapping his shoulder. As he assumed they wanted the table since he'd finished, he stood and was about to make for the Gare du Nord when his sleeve was shaken this time, and he turned to find the concierge from the apartment Bruce MacNishe used whenever he was in Paris.

The old man was more animated than normal, and, with a flicker of hope, Pearson motioned him to sit and called the waiter. Coffees drunk, and more ordered he had the old man repeat his story, questioning every detail. The slight hope was soon extinguished however as the old pattern looked to be continuing — once more MacNishe had vanished — but then the old man gestured to the doorway. A puzzled Pearson followed his gaze and was taken aback when an old — 'hag' was the only word he could think of — made for their table. Listening to their rapid conversation it dawned on him that perhaps MacNishe hadn't after all left Paris but was still in the vicinity. He paid closer attention to the remainder of the story and to his horror understood that it looked as though his quarry was indeed in Paris — in the local morgue!

It took only a short walk accompanied by his two informants to reach the Commissariat de Police, inspect the cadaver in the mortuary, identify it, and even less time to reward the gendarme, and the other two, before he made arrangements to hold the body there until he'd sent the news to England and had a reply.

True to his resolve to stay in Craigavon till the birth of his child, on this particular morning Dinwoodie was waiting for Cate to join him for elevenses when he heard the telephone ring. It was Maggie who appeared in the doorway to summon him to the hallway.

He listened to his secretary, and then said. "I think you'd better open it. It could be good news, though I daresay it will be just his normal report, though why he should have done it by telegraph I'm not sure. So, yes, Sheena, open it and read it to me." Dinwoodie said.

As Cate came down the stairs she heard the gasp, and, as her husband was on the telephone, she hoped it wasn't bad news. Although if it was, there was consolation in the thought that it might at least take him away for a bit and relieve her of his constant surveillance!

"So he's waiting for instructions?" Dinwoodie paused before continuing. "I'm not sure what the right thing to do is. Better leave it with me and I'll have a think about it and get back to you, Sheena. In the meantime, if he should ring for instructions, put him through to me here." As he replaced the telephone, Cate arrived at his side. Unsure what to say without alarming her, he settled for, "I think Maggie is about to bring our tray. Shall we go in?"

When they were settled with teacups in hand, and aware that her husband had made no attempt to explain the telephone call, Cate opened the conversation. "Was that a foundry problem then? You seemed taken aback. Is it really bad news? Don't tell me we've gone and lost the war! That I couldn't bear after all the men we've lost."

"No, Cate it had nothing to do with either the foundries or the war. In fact I think it might not even be bad news, though you're right — it did take me by surprise."

As she sipped her tea and waited for him to explain, his silence and obvious reluctance alarmed her. "Come on, Dinwoodie, what is it?"

"Cate this is why I hesitated. You musn't get in a state at this late stage of your pregnancy. It is not…"

"Dinwoodie, I'll tell you what it's not!" She interrupted. "It's not sensible to mention bad news and then leave me to worry about it. So, is it bad news or what? Just tell me, for goodness sake."

"This is what I was afraid of…"

"You ought to be more afraid of me throwing this tea at you! Can't you see you're the one who's overdoing it for once — not me." She slammed her teacup on the tray, where the force made a pool of brown beneath the cup, and waited for Dinwoodie to say something.

Forced now to explain, he began in a heated voice. "Alright! That was Sheena on the telephone to say that she'd received a telegram from Pearson." He waited for her reaction, but, as she said nothing he continued. "It would seem that Bruce MacNishe returned to the apartment in Paris."

"And Rhoddy?"

"I'm afraid not, Cate."

"Still, he must know where Rhoddy is. And Pearson will follow Bruce, wherever he goes, won't he?"

"Well, yes. You know he does."

"And?" This was worse than drawing teeth!

"I'm afraid Bruce MacNishe is lying in a Parisian morgue."

"What?" Cate didn't seem to understand. "Where?"

"I knew this would upset you. Your face is chalk white!"

"But — I thought Pearson couldn't find him — how — did you say dead? Did Pearson say? Come on Dinwoodie! Answer me."

"No, Cate. He said very little. Just that he wants to know what to do about it. After all, it was only a telegram. I didn't speak to him, get exact details or anything."

"Well then you must contact Pearson and get some!"

"Does it matter? I thought you'd be glad that your enemy was no more?"

"True, there was a time when had he been near and I'd had a knife, I would have plunged it into him and taken the consequences. But I had Rhoddy to care for, so I didn't have a choice. Is he really dead?

"Apparently, his body is being held in Paris until they have further instructions."

"It's strange, I've hated him for so long. But revenge, like most emotions, dissipates as time passes. Though his taking Rhoddy from me was unforgivable. Anyway, if he is truly dead, then you must get hold of Pearson, and get him to bring the body back to Kevinishe."

261

"Why on earth would you want to do that?"

"We can't leave him there, Dinwoodie." Cate became silent as she thought of Old MacNishe, Rab, and Lady Sarah, Bruce's parents. In many ways it was better that they'd all died, and didn't have to face this.

"I don't see why not, my dear. After all it doesn't much matter where he's buried, as I imagine there'll be no one to mourn him."

She rose, looked out of the window, visualised the MacNishe vault in the tiny graveyard on the hill outside the village, before she turned to him and spoke. "You don't understand, do you?

"No, I can't say I do."

"Think, Dinwoodie. We can't leave him in a morgue or even some pauper's grave in a foreign land!"

"Why ever not?"

"Because he has to be returned to the place of his birth and buried next to his ancestors, with a proper funeral as befits the Clan Chieftain."

"Good Lord! Anyone who's known or had dealings with Bruce MacNishe has never had a good word to say for him. Cate, he was a wastrel, a drunkard, a bully, and a man with some unsavoury sexual appetites. Why on earth would anyone mourn him, much less make the effort to come to his funeral?"

"I know all about him, but I'm afraid now he's dead none of that matters. He was the current Clan Chieftain. The normal niceties must be followed. Don't look so bewildered, Dinwoodie. It's the Highland custom. Now I must begin the preparations and…"

"NO Cate! NO! You must do nothing of the kind!" Furious, he leapt to his feet.

"Oh yes I will, Dinwoodie! Tradition has to be adhered to and I must do it. If you don't believe me, ask the others — Maggie, Donald Uig, even Lord Monroe, though he's no Highlander. They would all agree that that's what has to be done, and I intend to see that it is, even if I have to disobey you and attend to it all myself!" With that she left the room, leaving her angry husband to ponder over her words of defiance.

Cate wasted no time in bringing the combined opinions of the village represented by a sombre Donald Uig, plus that of her friend and neighbour Cicely from Laggan House, to Dinwoodie. Outflanked, and with the greatest of reluctance, he was persuaded to instruct Pearson to use the age-old method of bribery to obtain an autopsy report stating that the cause of death was a drunken seizure: not difficult for the clothes on the body were, 'soaked with wine when it was discovered', so the gendarme had said. The French coroner was expensive to convince because of the state of the battered corpse, but at last all was taken care of, and the body of the Clan Chieftain was unceremoniously bundled into a makeshift coffin, to be returned to the Highlands, complete with all the necessary papers, by Pearson.

On arrival in Glasgow, Morrison met him and between them they transferred the body to the car and headed for Fort William, where the coffin, hewn from the oaks on the Kevinishe Estate and lined with the clan tartan by the women of the village, had been delivered to the funeral parlour. There, prior to the arrival of the body, it had been decorated with the Clan crest and other brass fittings. Once the exchange had been completed, Morrison saw Pearson off on the Glasgow train, before driving to Kevinishe distillery, and depositing the coffin there for the body to be made ready for the funeral.

On the day of the funeral Cate was not surprised to see the black-armed figure of McPhail assume the lead position in the funeral procession lined up at the distillery, behind the Meenister. He too was merely following tradition, being the nearest senior male member of the clan available. The village men hoisted the coffin aloft and everyone else fell in behind and made their way to the tiny church up on the hill. At the entrance to the graveyard the women stopped at the gate, as custom required, and waited till the service was over and the coffin was led to the vault.

By the time the male mourners were on their way to the wake in the distillery barn, the women were only too pleased to move their frozen feet and follow them. Cate remained at the gate cradling her icy fingers beneath her cloak while stamping her feet to get the blood circulating. As she waited she was overcome by a tremendous feeling of weariness, but knew she'd at least done what was expected of her over the previous weeks. Now she wished Charlie would hurry up with the sulkie to get her home and in the warm.

Later, back at Craigavon enjoying her afternoon tea, Cate toasted her icy feet before the splendid fire that Maggie had built up when she realised how cold Cate was.

"You'll have the worst chilblains ever with your feet that close to the fire," Maggie warned her as she came in to refresh the teapot. "An another thing, you look right weary to me. It's all that running about you've done in the past weeks. You never even had time for Hogmanay, never mind Christmas. An what for? That no-good MacNishe! An him dishonouring you all those years ago, never mind he set yon criminal to burn the Black House with you in it. An afore he died, of the drink no doubt he'd stolen young Rhoddy away. God preserve us from such wickedness."

"Indeed, Maggie, what you say is true, but you know as well as I do we couldn't let the clan down. Fisher would have done the same, and I've always believed he died because of Bruce MacNishe. While I was arranging everything, somehow I felt I was doing it for your brother and old MacNishe. Anyway the niceties have all been observed."

"Aye well, as long as you've no come to any harm — mercy me! Who's come hammering on the door now?" Maggie exclaimed as she went to investigate.

With Maggie in charge, Cate leant back in her chair and, lulled by the warmth of the fire, was about to drift off to sleep when she was roused by Maggie's voice.

"It's The McPhail" she said in a voice colder than the weather outside.

"Thank you, Maggie." Still seated, Cate turned her attention to the visitor, but before she could speak he forestalled her.

"I'm told that but for your insistence my clansman would have rotted in a pauper's grave, and for that you have my thanks."

"Good afternoon, McPhail, I appreciate your words of thanks."

"I also have evidence that you and your husband sent a private investigator to France in search of your son, my nephew. I too have had someone looking for him, though he's had no more success than yours. However I cannot understand, having done all that, as to why previously you were only too happy to blacken the name of my deceased kinsman. I suppose that was to cover your previous actions."

"I can assure you that, although I believe all that has been said about Bruce MacNishe, I personally kept my thoughts to myself, unlike him. He didn't hesitate to inform you of the most monstrous lies about me."

"I feel that he must have believed a portion of what he told me. No one could fabricate that evidence! Therefore you must know why I have no real trust in you, and because of that, I can only demand that you keep me informed with any news that comes your way. You have to understand that though I only lead a distant sept of the MacNishe clan, without your son I would be the new Clan Chieftain, and I will require to take possession of Kevinishe Estate, and…"

"Here we go again! How many times do you have to be told? You are being ridiculous! Neither you nor Rhoddy can do that!"

"Just as I thought. Bruce was right. You intend to defraud your son of his rightful heritage, just as you stole the distillery from my cousin. Well let me tell you, I'll stand for none of it! Bruce always said it was your deceit and lies that caused his misfortune. Should Rhoddy be found I will join him here and guide and protect him from you!"

"He doesn't need protection from me — he's my son for God's sake!"

"He was ready enough to run away from home because you treated him so badly"

"You stupid man, he was taken from me by your dastardly cousin! I don't suppose he told you that?"

"That's nonsense! It would have been a criminal act, and since I never heard of it…"

"Only because you've shut your ears to the truth, you bigot! Open your eyes and look at the evidence — Bruce MacNishe kept the good people of Glasgow and Edinburgh, talking for years about his drunken, devious…"

"I've heard enough. You're a bastard Tinker Girl, whose slept her way to gaining control of the MacNishe distillery, and now you've made such a hash of running it, the place is closed. If that's not theft I don't know what is! I'll make sure you'll regret both your words and your theft!" With that he turned and left.

Furious now, Cate shouted after him, "You'll do no such thing!" She rose and, despite her swollen body, dashed to the door, and followed him to the forecourt, determined to make him understand that Bruce had lied to him. She tried to forestall his driving away, but the car seemed to judder into life and come straight at her. With a strangled scream, she made an effort to jump out of the way, but the side of the vehicle caught her and she fell to the ground.

Not long after The McPhail had roared down the drive, Charlie, who during Cate's pregnancy now walked the yellow Labrador for her, brought the dog to heel and continued round the side of the house, only to find Rory shoot off in front of him again. Puzzled, Charlie strained his eyes in the dusk and was just able to see the dog was nudging at something in front of the house. He couldn't quite make out what it was but, as the dog's whimpered whining increased, he had a terrible suspicion that set his feet pounding forwards.

"Move! Rory move!" He pushed the dog aside and knelt by the inert body. "Miss Cate! Dear God what's happened here?" With trembling fingers he felt for a pulse and at the faint response he ran to the front door, screaming for Maggie. He picked up the hand bell in the alcove and rung it till he heard them coming from below stairs. All he could manage as they reached him was "Miss Cate," and then, leaving the door ajar, he ran back to his beloved Mistress, shrugged off his jacket and laid it on top of her while he waited for Maggie to say if it was safe to move her.

"We need her inside. Can we move her, Maggie?" he asked when she knelt at his side.

"Aye, we'll have to. Run for Stevie, an see if the …" she stopped as the lights from a vehicle lit up the drive. "Thank God — it's Himself an Morrison. Go you and get them to leave the lights on, till we see what's happened here."

In the lights, Maggie could see an ugly bruise rising on Cate's forehead, but to her that didn't seem enough of a reason to…. Her investigation was cut short as Dinwoodie pushed her aside.

"Cate! Oh Cate, what…?"

"Not now sir." Maggie interrupted him. "We must get her inside."

Between the four of them they lifted Cate's body and staggered upstairs to the main bedroom. Maggie began pulling the covers back, and it was then that she saw the great tear in Cate's funeral dress.

"Sir, would you look at this. Down there! Look — the dress has caught on something and been ripped, but there's none of the bushes by the front door that would be doing that. An anyway she's been nowhere but the funeral and the drawing room."

Then she realised that the dress was sodden. It was fierce cold out there but no frost and definitely no rain. "Mercy me! The wet! The Waters! Mr Dinwoodie, the Bairn's coming early!" The realisation galvanised Maggie. Within minutes she had the men, except Charlie, banished downstairs. Him, she used as a runner, fetching hot water, brown paper, a feather, the pig, and other warming pans. Lizzie was called to her side, and between them they'd soon stripped Cate of her wet clothing, and wrapped her in a woollen blanket, just as Charlie returned with the water and things.

"Good lad, now we need sheets, warmed, and fetched up here. Oh, an then get Cook to give you the hart's horn crystals, and a bowl of thin gruel ready on the stove. Quick as you can now!"

While they waited, Maggie and Lizzie set about rubbing Cate's body to try to get the circulation going. At Charlie's arrival, they had him scoop the blanketed Cate in his arms, while they stripped the bed and remade it, complete with brown wrapping paper and old sheets turned ends to middle, that were kept for a birthing. Charlie then laid Cate on it and all three were relieved when she muttered something.

"Praise be! I was afeared she was gone, Maggie."

"Aye well, just you be keeping your praises for a while. We're a long way before we can sort this trouble out. Now then, Charlie, away you an get more hot water and the gruel when it's ready, an give young Shona a shout, for I've a message for her. Oh, and thanks, Charlie. You've turned into a right proper help!"

Before long a puffing Shona appeared and listened as Maggie instructed her to bring some whisky from the drawing room.

"The fancy bottle thing wi' the bonny crest on it?" she asked.

"Dear Lord, girl, we're to be giving sips in gruel, no washing her in it! A dram glass is all we need, an see you an hurry up, now!"

Wrapped in the now warmed linen, and with Lizzie still rubbing the body, Maggie wafted the bottle of crystals back and forth under Cate's nose, and tickled her throat with the feather. She stopped when the gruel and whisky arrived, and with a minute dram in the bowl she rubbed the spoon against Cate's lips, but to no avail. Discarding the bowl and, using one of the clean rags dipped in the whisky glass, she eased it between Cate's lips with one hand and continued passing the salts to and fro with the other. To her great relief she was rewarded for her pains with a feeble snort from Cate.

"Now, Lizzie, raise her head a bit an put yon bolster under her. We'll try some watery gruel — see if we can get that down without choking her. Her, an us, are going to need all our strength before this night's out."

Except for the girl Shona running in breathless demanding a dram, he was on his own. He could hear the running about, but no one seemed to have time to include him. He felt useless and somewhat isolated. Dinwoodie finished the dram he'd poured himself and decided to follow the sounds to the kitchen. He was astonished when he pushed open the door to see so many people there.

"Mr Dinwoodie, is there any news from upstairs?" Cook asked.

"Not that I'm aware of, Cook. I thought I might as well wait in here with you, but I didn't realise you had company. Good evening to you all, and do sit down again, I'd like to join you, Cook. I felt so far away from everything alone through there, and now I'm glad I came. Like the rest of you, both my head and heart are up there with your Miss Cate. By the way is that fresh bread I smell, Cook?"

"It is that. We're waiting for it to come out of the oven. The men here came straight when they heard of the trouble, so they've no had a bite. That's if you don't mind, Mr Dinwoodie?"

"Mind? Indeed not! I'll be only too happy to have some as well, as it appears no one has given a thought to my evening meal."

"Dearie me, you have the right of it there! What with all the hot water, feathers and such for upstairs I clean forgot!"

"That's alright, Cook…" He was interrupted by a loud knocking at the back door, and continued, "It would appear we have another guest for our bread feast. I wonder who it is?"

Lachy the stable boy rose and opened the door for Donald Uig, who entered twirling his flat cap in his hands.

"Come in, come in and join us." Dinwoodie said.

"Evening sir," Donald Uig greeted Dinwoodie, and nodded to the stable hands, gardeners, and Morrison, who made room for him at the table.

"Cook is about to produce new baked bread and I've no doubt all the pots and plates on the table will be filled with a veritable feast to supplement it, and we'll be glad to share it with you."

"I've no come for a bite as such. It's Miss Cate — the village, every last one of them, is waiting on the news."

"Well they're all in good company, Donald Uig, for that's exactly what we're doing. So come on, Cook, dish up that bread! I daresay if I was to bring the decanter through, the assembled company wouldn't mind joining me in a dram," he said as he left the kitchen to fetch the decanter and glasses.

Upstairs, Maggie cursed inwardly as she realised they now had a new problem. Lizzie wiped away the sweat on an exhausted Cate's brow, and tried to understand the signals her mother was sending.

"Lizzie, get Charlie in again, then try to get her to stop pushing. I'm in trouble here." As Maggie stood to shield her patient from sight, Lizzie returned with Charlie.

"Right, lad, downstairs with you and tell Cook I need a bar of carbolic and a bucket of hot water wi' plenty salt in it, and be quick about it. Run lad!"

"Cate, listen lass, the bairn's lying wrong. I'll have to turn it."

"Get on with… AAAGH!" Cate groaned.

"Aye, as soon as Charlie's back. I need to make sure everything is as clean as it can be so — ah, here he is."

"Maggie, Miss Cate, the men…" He got no further

"Damn the men! AAAGH!" Cate shouted through clenched teeth as another wave of pain overcame her.

"She's no exactly in the mood for gentle words, lad, so tell them it's coming along."

With that Charlie set off to deliver the message, then hurried back to his post outside the door.

Maggie, having scrubbed her hands with carbolic and dipped her arms in the salt water up to her elbows, looked at Lizzie and nodded.

"Cate," Lizzie said in a soft voice. "See we need your help now. Try not to push; Mammy's turning the bairn. No, Cate, try harder! You've got to hold back, so's Mammy can work there!" Lizzie held onto her dear friend's hands and continued to whisper words of comfort to her, while keeping an eye out for trouble at the other end, as Cate did her best to control the overwhelming desire to push.

Her screams, while Maggie worked as she'd never done before, brought a rigid fear to all those in the kitchen. Charlie stuck his fingers in his ears when he could bear the sound no longer. Meanwhile, Lizzie used all her strength to hold Cate, crying tears of pity for her friend as she did so.

Maggie's cry of "God be here!" was uttered as she guided the two limbs she'd managed to get a hold of outward. To her great surprise and relief, the rest of the tiny body came shooting after them, the arms pushed upwards with the force of the exit.

Lizzie's shout of joy, "Oh, Cate, the bairn's here! It's here!" was then silenced by a grim look from Maggie.

"We've still work to do, before we start shouting, Lizzie! Leave Cate now and pass me that blue towel from the pig." Then she concentrated on the scrap of flesh that as yet had not uttered a sound. With a thin

269

corner of flannel she cleared the tiny nostrils and, with a freshly sterilised little finger, scoured the rosebud mouth for mucus. She upended the baby then and gave it two flat smacks on the back. The weedy cry of outrage was the most blessed sound to be heard throughout the house.

Then Maggie washed the wrinkled flesh with a soft cloth, dried it, and swaddled it in a beautiful swansdown wrap. "Right then, Lizzie, give the bairn to Charlie to take to Himself. Tell him not to keep it there too long, and then get back up here. C'mon then, lass, now we have to make sure we save Cate. We want no childbirth fever here! Right Lizzie, on that side. Now, Cate, a real good last hard push! C'mon now! It's near to be over, lass."

In utter silence the women worked as one: palpating the now silent Cate's body until the afterbirth was expelled, and then cleansing the area with the carbolic and salt water. Cate was then washed and made presentable.

"Maggie you didn't say. It's a boy, yes?"

Maggie didn't answer Cate's question, but as the door opened, beckoned Lizzie and they tiptoed out of the room, as Dinwoodie walked in.

A smiling Cate sat up and held out her arms for her child. Dinwoodie bent down and tucked the baby into Cate's outstretched arms.

"Here, my darling, Cate, is our beautiful daughter."

"But Dinwoodie! Your heir! The Foundries? It was to be a boy. Damn it all, I've failed you! I'm so sorry."

"Cate, I wouldn't trade this gorgeous little girl for all the boys in the world!"

"I was certain it was a boy. After all the trouble the poor wee thing had put up with, I thought it was bound to be a boy. Are you sure you're not disappointed, Dinwoodie?"

"Disappointed? How could I be? Come, Cate, take a good look at little Miss Dinwoodie. If I'm not mistaken that appears to be a fluff of red hair peeking out above her wrapping, and I wouldn't mind laying a bet on her having green, green eyes, when they open properly. I can't think of anything better than having two versions of the woman I love!"

"Oh, Dinwoodie, I do love you so."

He was so taken aback by this unusual forthright declaration that he was unable to speak. In his darker moments he'd always dwelt on the knowledge that he hadn't been her great love, and because of that he'd resented the Scribbler. Was deeply jealous of him, if he were honest.

"You're very quiet."

"I'm overwhelmed by you both, my dear. My two wonderful female treasures!"

The sudden piercing cries of a baby demanding attention lightened the atmosphere, and both Cate and Dinwoodie laughed at the tiny, squirming red-faced tyrant in her arms.

Chapter 31

The Captain and Mary Anne watched as their erstwhile patients, now in full uniform, marched out the front door of the Hospital and climbed into the army transport. The officer in charge barely acknowledged the two of them as they looked on.

"They could at least have thanked us or something, Captain."

When he didn't reply, Mary Anne laid her hand on his shoulder and said. "It's hard I know, but no one could have done more than you. At one point I thought they might have marched you out and shot you, the way you stood up to them and refused to send those poor souls back to the front."

"And a damn lot of good it did, Sister!"

"True, but the Good Lord knows you did try, and it's hard so it is, when you and I both…"

"Exactly. The first set of shells that come soaring into whatever part of the Western Front they're in, we both know that the work we've done with them will be blasted out of their minds. One almost has to hope that they'll be killed outright, rather than go down the tortuous path of mental torment yet again."

"Thing is, Captain, I would have thought they — the patients I mean — would mebbe have said, 'we're not going' or 'we're not fit', but …"

"Come on, Sister, the Top Brass know exactly how to engineer the return of any soldier, whether he be blind, deaf, crippled or dumb. You heard the questions."

"That I did! 'Now then, soldier, are you a coward?' What man is ever going to answer yes to that?"

"Right, and from there it was two or three more of that ilk, and every silly bloody one of them, squared their shoulders, got into uniform, and agreed to return to the war."

"Now I know full well you won't agree with me, Captain, but we could have done fine with…"

"Mrs Dinwoodie, Sister! I must admit it would have been some sight if she'd set to on the pompous asses. We might even have had some patients left, but don't you dare tell her I admitted that, or I'll sack you for disobeying orders!"

"Well now, Captain, seeing as we're both reduced to tending to just the American, we're more or less sacked anyway. What will you do?"

"What a soldier always does, Sister: do as I'm ordered."

"Let's away and have a cup of tea. With young Bella mooning over Duncan's return to the front, she'll be in need of comfort, and mebbe Snowy will read the tealeaves and tell us our fortunes!"

"Right. You go on, console the quiet Bella. Tell her I did my best, not that that will be any comfort to her — I'll tackle the inevitable paperwork first. Truth to tell I'd rather bury myself in the work than think about those poor devils and what lies ahead for them. Damn and blast the bloody Army! And, Sister, you never heard me say that."

"You're a good man, Captain, and a first class doctor of the minds, and I'm glad to have met you. So be off with you before I come all over feminine and start blubbing." She watched him make for the stairs before the thought struck her. "Oh Captain, will you be going to tell her?"

He turned to face her with the ghost of a smile and said. "Me? Never! Admit to that woman I let the army walk away with her patients? Not bloody likely! You're on your own, Mary Anne, and, as you frequently say: may your God go with you when you do!"

He would never know what instinct made him turn into the empty ward, but when he saw the swinging figure, he had no time to think. He bellowed for Mary Anne, then ran across the room and grasped the man's thighs, shoving them upward to take some of the weight from the leather noose. Then it was long moments before he heard the pounding of feet in the doorway and hands reached above his to lessen further the weight on the noose. A figure pushed a chair by his side, leapt on it, and sawed away at the leather. Once again the time seemed forever, but then the freed body slumped on top of him and they crashed in a heap to the floor.

Mary Anne, Bella, and the orderlies stood for a moment, hypnotised as the open noose swung idly above them. Then the reality of the situation made them turn their attention to the two on the floor. The Captain seemed to have hit his head when he fell, concussed most likely, she thought, so Mary Anne tended to him. The American was still

274

gasping for breath and the welt on his neck was red and angry. The orderlies made sure he stayed still while Bella dealt with the throat.

It was some time before doctor and patient were settled in the other ward. Mary Anne sedated them both, and, leaving the orderlies on guard, the two women headed for a restorative cup of tea to settle their shocked systems.

The stream of visitors at Craigavon over the next week seemed endless, and the nursery had taken on the persona of a baby shop. Dinwoodie was amazed at both the number and the craftsmanship of the goods these loyal villagers had produced. As the doorbell jingled yet again, and voices echoed from the hallway, he rose from his desk and went to greet the latest visitors. He was astonished to see not only the Captain and Mary Anne, but also Cecily Campbell-Broughton-Stewart.

"Good day to you all. This almost looks like a deputation."

"It is just that, Dinwoodie. Of course we women want to see Cate and the new daughter, but there's another matter to be dealt with first."

"Ah, back organising again are we, Cecily?"

"Quite so, Dinwoodie. Now if we may we would like to speak to both you and Maggie — in the drawing room if you don't mind."

"Of course. Come along, and Mary Anne perhaps…"

"Yes, Mr Dinwoodie, I'll find Maggie, and then I'll go and see Cate."

"Sister, um, well I'd like you to — well, you might…" The Captain was unsure how to put it.

"Give you some moral support, Captain? Don't worry! I'll be right back. Come on now, think of the Generals you almost conquered at the hospital, and remember," she pointed a finger upstairs, "Herself is confined to bed!" With an encouraging grin, Mary Anne went to find Maggie.

With everyone assembled, Dinwoodie was intrigued as to what was afoot, but true to form, his neighbour gave him no time to think. She thrust her nephew forward with the well-intentioned command to: "Get on with it, Ewan, before the coffee gets cold."

"Dinwoodie, mmm, Mrs Maggie —well I would — it's about Lizzie. I would like — that is…"

"I know what you'd like, but so far no one else does," his aunt rasped, before shaking her head in despair and speaking for the hapless Captain. "Maggie, what he's mumbling over is the words to say that he wants to marry your daughter." Then, turning to Dinwoodie, she continued, "I'm not sure I can recommend him, but I will say that your Lizzie seems an excellent match for him, and he does have my blessing. Now as head of this household and, Maggie, as her mother, you should both have a say in this matter."

Mary Anne forestalled Maggie, with a quiet rebuke to the imposing figure of his aunt. "Ma'am, I think you do the Captain here a disservice. I've worked with this man for a time now, and you won't find a more diligent worker on behalf of his patients, and sure it's a great attraction that our Lizzie must be, for over the last months he's developed a liking for walking on this particular patch. So if it's worrying you he's no sincere, then let me tell you, you've got it all wrong."

Rather taken by the forthright speech by Mary Anne, his aunt softened her own tone and said. "Right then, Maggie, the opposition has stated their case, so now it's up to you."

Dinwoodie looked at the woman who'd seen his Cate through hard times in her life, and was always there when either of them needed her, and smiled at her as he said. "Go on, Maggie. Apart from Lizzie and the Captain you are the next most important person, and all of us must heed your words and feelings."

"Well, Mr Dinwoodie, it takes some getting used to. I'd no thought of my Lizzie marrying, what with the limp and — well she was just my little Lizzie you know. But if she wants him, an I think she does, though she's no said a word about marrying, I'll no stand in your way, Captain." She looked straight at him then, before continuing, "Mind, I'll be after you if I feel you're no treating her right, an that's telling you straight!"

"Right then, Ewan, it looks as if you'll be set fair to put your proposal, since all concerned seem agreeable." His aunt produced, for her, quite a benevolent smile as she turned to him.

"Not quite all, Cecily!" Cate said as she opened the door.

Taken aback by her sudden appearance, the others waited for the inevitable battle they'd hoped to avoid on this pleasant occasion.

"I believe I might have an opinion on the matter." Cate stated, as she took her time to cross the room to stand opposite the Captain, before she spoke again. "You do know that…"

As he had done for the majority of their disagreements, to the surprise of the others, the Captain waded straight in with forceful words. "I know exactly what you'll say, and it will be no surprise that you don't want this engagement. You've never liked me, but I love Lizzie, and I'll not let you, especially you, come between us and…!"

"So, Captain," Cate, interrupted in a slow deliberate voice. "You know what I'm about to say, do you? Well, I wasn't actually going to give an opinion on the subject. It was a question I was about to ask. You really are too hasty."

At this the others had to stifle their snorts as the proverbial pot called the kettle black!

Though well aware of the others' reaction, Cate continued. "So I suggest you listen carefully, in case you make yet another mistake! With you about to propose to the girl who's as good as my sister, clever man that you are, have you a ring?"

The others in the room were baffled at the unexpected response to the proposed marriage. It wasn't only the Captain who'd anticipated trouble. Cate's question, though in some ways an obvious one, made them wonder why none of them had thought of it, but still they were bemused at it coming from her.

"I take it, Captain, that your lack of response means, you've never given it a thought, and therefore don't have one?"

"Mmm — that is yes — I mean no."

"I thought as much." Cate nodded in satisfaction and, with a slight smirk, held out her right hand and slipped the ring that was there off her finger. She studied it for a moment, took two steps towards her erstwhile foe, and held it out for him.

"A long time ago Lizzie introduced me to a man, a very good man I may add, and that self-same man was the first person to ever give me a gift of jewellery, this engagement ring. Now I would like you to give this to her when you propose, because it was down to Lizzie's goodness that I began to work my way upwards in the world, and I shall never forget that."

As the stunned Captain made neither movement nor sound, Cate leant forward, slipped the ring into his top pocket, and turned to leave the room. Then stopped and, with a wicked smile, looked back at him and added, "Oh, Captain, for heaven's sake, don't tell her you forgot! You really must make more effort to understand us women!" And as she passed the others she winked at the two visiting females before saying, "I thought you'd come to see my latest effort at production?" Then she sailed out of the room with a chuckle.

In the nursery after the women had expressed their admiration, and each one had held the young Miss Dinwoodie, she was put down in her crib and Cecily left for Laggan. It was only then that Cate tackled Mary Anne on something that had been puzzling her.

"I thought either you or the Captain had always to be on duty at the hospital. So why break the rules today. I mean your interest in my offspring I can understand, but why was it so important for the Captain to break his own rules, so that he could propose to Lizzie today. Surely tomorrow would have done?"

"I'm not looking forward to this, Cate," Mary Anne began. "You know the inspection visit?"

"Ye-e-e-s" Cate answered in a guarded voice.

"Well, they came."

Aware that Mary Anne was reluctant to give an answer, Cate prodded her. "What? What's happened? I can tell you're hiding something."

"Cate, I don't want you blaming the Captain."

"Dear God, Mary Anne, will you please spit it out, before I start imagining that the most awful things have happened!"

"They took all the men back to fight." Mary Anne waited for the outburst, but there was an eerie silence. "I'm sorry. I shouldn't have upset you in your present state, Cate, but I promised the Captain I'd tell you, and for the love of God, go easy on him! You should have heard him rage at the Top Brass! I thought they'd take him out and shoot him, so I did, the way he stood up to them!"

"So, there's nothing left?"

"Not exactly, the American was left, but there's more. When the other men had gone, your man put a belt round the rafter…"

"My God! He's not dead?"

"He lives, but only because of the Captain's quick thinking."

"It's all too much to take in, Mary Anne. Why would he do that? And then the hospital! After all the fuss we had getting it up and running it seems — I mean, it's such a waste to now lose it! And those poor men."

"That's what the Captain and I thought as we watched them march out. The devious questions those snooty officers asked them — the patients were tricked. Their pride made them march away like they were fit and healthy, when we all know they'll be shattered shadows of themselves the first time they come under a barrage."

Both women were lost in thought, as they envisaged the men they'd cared for and were in the process of bringing back to a fragile normality, when the baby began screaming for attention.

278

"Lord love, us, Cate, that's some lungs the wee one has." Mary Anne went to lift the querulous child who continued to wail. "Is she always like this?"

"Most of the time, if not even more so!"

"And her that little! She's a feisty soul, so she is! Heavens, I forgot to ask her given name."

"We've not named her yet. Though, I've been thinking about the trials she had early on and then even more of them at the birthing. She arrived all in a rush, the wrong way round, and it minded me of the story of those monks of yours who fought the fierce waves to bring religion to us wayward Scots, and how those same waves spewed them out with tremendous force, on the shingle of Iona."

"Well now, I feel she's kin of mine already!"

"Good. So assuming Dinwoodie has no objection, 'Iona' it is. Mind, when she becomes impossible, I'll send her to you! You always knew how to handle me, and I've a nasty feeling I've spawned another one to match."

By the next day, with the engagement now out in the open, the thoughts of all at Craigavon turned to the wedding date. It was presumed there would be no immediate hurry, though some did wonder why the Captain had been so eager to get engaged. However both unspoken questions were settled the following week, when Captain Ewan Brodie was informed by letter that he was being posted within the month to the Western Front to aid the medical staff there, who weren't equipped to deal with the rising number of patients suffering from shell shock. It would be his task to screen and assess them prior to deciding which of them should be sent straight to Craiglockart, and then to treat the remainder, with a view to returning them to the front as soon as possible.

The letter also stated that the hospital in Kevinishe would now be used for the recovery of amputees, and a doctor would be arriving with the first batch shortly. The news that the hospital would continue in Kevinishe was very welcome as far as the glen was concerned, but it did leave very little time for wedding preparations.

Cate resurrected the white gown she'd worn for that first Distillers' ball, and she and the sewing girls worked all hours to turn it into the wedding dress. Their Laggan neighbour produced not only an antique veil, but also, along with her brother, Lord Monroe, booked a honeymoon for the couple in Edinburgh, where Ewan was to undergo some more training, before being sent to France.

For the wedding, the old barn was decked with whatever they could garnish from garden and moor, and the entire glen cooked and baked to fill it with the wedding feast. On the day, the good folk of the village donned their Sunday best as they went with pride to honour the niece of their much-loved and sadly-missed Fisher.

Dinwoodie gave the bride away, and no lesser person than the Lord Chief Justice, stood as the groomsman. Cate sat well back in the crowd, and she'd dressed with great care, so as not to outshine Lizzie on her day. Truth to tell, with all the work she'd put in to make this day successful, she was not only a trifle weary, but also quite sad. It had never occurred to her that dear Lizzie would marry someone out of the glen, and her going to Edinburgh would leave an unfillable hole for Cate. Indeed she had also begun to wonder if the spiky Captain, with his general antipathy towards women would really be right for the woman she loved so dearly.

When they rose on completion of the ceremony, Cate watched as Lizzie, unbelievably pretty, came back up the aisle on her husband's arm. She was almost undone as Lizzie nudged the Captain's arm, stopped, turned, and blew her a kiss, before moving on. Cate knew then that 'her Lizzie' would always be just that. Yes marriage, and a family of her own, would take her away for a time, but their bond would surmount that and any other obstacles that came their way. With good fortune they would grow old together, and when their individual families were grown, the two of them might very well spend their dotage in Craigavon. With that emotional thought, Cate waited till the last guest had left, then made her way to the sulkie and Charlie, waiting at the lych gate. Once in her seat, Cate, still in an emotional mood, placed her hand on Charlie's holding the reins, and mouthed 'thank you' at this other staunch supporter, friend, and link with days gone by and absent friends, as they made their way back to the red-haired morsel left in Cook's care at Craigavon.

Chapter 32

Cate was in the kitchen cradling a sleeping Iona in her arm and demolishing a plate of stovies with her free hand, when Charlie arrived with a letter. She recognised Alashdair's writing, and put it on the table. So much had happened in Kevinishe since his last one, and with Dinwoodie's absence from the foundries, they'd paid scant attention to either radio or papers. Although she understood that the fighting continued, it would be good to know exactly what had happened in the latter weeks of 1917 and at the beginning of the fifth year of conflict on The Western Front.

When they'd finished their meal, Charlie, who was now sleeping above the stable, went to say goodnight to his brother Lachy, before the latter made his way home to their cottage on the outskirts of the glen. Cate took her letter upstairs, where she put the baby down in her cot, and held her breath until she was sure that Iona was asleep, then sank into her own bed, exhausted after the last few days, and fell fast asleep.

Dinwoodie made straight for the bedroom when he arrived home later that evening, and enjoyed a little time watching both his sleeping females. Iona was the first to awaken, and though he picked her up immediately and tried to quieten her, Cate woke up too. With Iona fed, changed, and put down for at least part of the night, and with Cate sitting up in bed, Dinwoodie sat in the nursing chair and opened Alashdair's letter.

Paschendale, November 1917

Dearest Girl,

I write of a flat French land where drainage ditches have been devastated by shelling, and the resulting plains must be as near an image of Hell as one could imagine. The stories filtering back from the front are of a Paschendale debacle, where men die, disappear or drown in the appalling sloughs of mud that are so deep even the horses, carts, and supply mules are lost without trace. I well remember your passion for your horses, Cate. From what I hear, this cruel loss of these brave animals would break your heart. The men here are every bit as taken up with their animals as you used to be. I can barely look at the sadness in their eyes as they recount their losses.

It seems even those soldiers with slight wounds die. A shell explodes, a duckboard wobbles and down they go into the festering shell holes to drown! As if that was not bad enough, they speak of a new type of poison gas drifting above the mud sponge of Flanders catching the soldiers unaware, making them slide hacking, coughing and screaming into the cesspit that the French terrain around Paschendale has now become!

Here we are, almost at the close of another year of senseless slaughter, and to what end? I cannot see how these dispirited men on both sides can find renewed hope for 1918, after the unspeakable horror that has been Paschendale!

Alashdair.

"That's a bleak picture he paints, Dinwoodie."

"I'm afraid it is. The weather has once more become an enemy for all out there, to add to their existing problems."

"Talking of problems, with these air raids in England, I worry about you having to go back to London. You will take care, won't you?"

"My dear Cate, I can only do as others there are — take heed of the warning sirens and seek shelter, but right now I'm going to my bed, and you must get back to sleep. No doubt Iona will be crying for more food before long. I do worry about these very disturbed nights for you. Let's hope she soon begins to sleep a little longer. Goodnight my dear, I'll see you in the morning."

At the end of the week, breakfast over, and with Dinwoodie on his way to Glasgow, Cate and Maggie sat in the nursery, discussing the wedding.

"There's no doubt about it, Cate. I'm getting too old to be up late at nights! By the time all the dancing and drinking were done it was morning, an we still had all the sorting out of plates, food and drink — not that there was a lot of that left! Then the last bits of clearing took ages. Mind, it was as good a wedding feast as I've ever seen! It was a real shame you werna there. You'd have enjoyed it, though wise enough, as by rights you should still be in bed."

"Maggie, don't you start!" Dinwoodie almost didn't leave today for just that reason. Though, I daresay that little madam there," Cate nodded at the child asleep in her crib, "had something to do with his reluctance to go back to work!"

"Aye, I do believe he's ower fond of her. Now, with Lizzie mebbe stopping on in Edinburgh, Cate, who'll do the nursery once you're back at the hospital?"

"Well, the boys will be five soon, and they don't really need a nursemaid any longer. In fact I've been thinking about getting a tutor for them."

"What, take on some kind of woman teacher like?"

"No, Maggie, I don't think a woman would work with those two, especially David. I've watched the way Charlie handles them, and he's good at it, but then he doesn't have the learning required and, as Stevie's not as young as he used to be, Charlie will be needed for the horses until Lachy has a bit more experience. To tell you the truth, I've come to depend on Charlie, a bit like I used to depend on Fisher, when he was alive. It's difficult to explain. Somehow he fits into the role that both MacNishe and Fisher played in my life. A long time ago, Charlie came to me to ask if he could be some kind of — I don't know — bodyguard of sorts."

"Mercy me, what would you do with one of those? You've a husband, you've a household full of people, never mind the rest of the glen to watch over you."

"I did say it was kind of silly, but I believe, perhaps not now, but in the future perhaps, Charlie will be — Oh never mind. I guess you're right. Anyway we were talking about a tutor for the boys, and though I do think Charlie will be important for them, because they need a male around, as Dinwoodie won't be here all the time till he retires, we need to look elsewhere, for a tutor that is."

"So, someone from the towns then?"

"We've spoken about it, but the situation here is unusual, and I don't believe someone from outside coming in would make a fist of it. So I'm not sure at the moment what we'll decide. Anyway we'll carry on for now, as I have to make quite sure that Iona has as many feeds as she'll take — she's still way underweight. I'll not rest easy till she's a bit more of the 'Bonnie Bouncing Baby', so I won't think of going back to work just yet, but I'll give the nursery situation more thought."

"An we've no idea when the Captain will be sent to the Front, or even if Lizzie will stop in Edinburgh, Cate. She might fine well come back here when he goes."

"I'm trying not to pin my hopes on that, Maggie, for no other reason than somehow it would make life too simple for us both. And with the date for the arrival of the new patients and doctor still not definite, it's very difficult to plan anything for the immediate future."

Their conversation was interrupted by shrill demanding cries from the crib.

"Of all the bairns I've helped to bring into the world, Cate, I've never once heard the likes of that one! She seems to wake up raging every time!"

"You don't think there's anything wrong with her, do you, Maggie?"

"Colic mebbe? We could try vinegar, baking soda and malt mixed in warm water. Mind I'm no so sure how it was made up."

"The thought of swallowing that lot makes me feel ill, never mind giving it to the wee soul!"

"Aye well, I mind the old ones used to boil the rhubarb leaves and give drops of the water left with anything sweet. An, there's a good few other potions like chamomile to line the stomach and ease the gripes. I canna just mind the name of another plant, but the brown seeds of it were used in liquorice, an my mother put the sticks in a jar with water, and shook it till the water turned grey. Then used it as drops."

"That sounds worth trying. She cries way more than any of my others, and she seems so angry all the time. Still I suppose I'd be angry if I'd had all the kerfuffle she's had along the way."

Over the next few weeks both Cate and Maggie tried every colic remedy they could find, until in the end Cate decided to try the vinegar one. One part of her was afraid she'd damage the child, while the other knew that unless she managed to get a good night's sleep she was in danger of doing some damage to the child herself. Even with Maggie sharing the nights when she could, Cate still woke to the shrill cries, and by the first week in March, she'd put her doubts aside.

With no real idea of quantities it made sense to swallow it herself to ensure that what she gave to Iona was palatable. After several nauseous tries, she felt the balance of the ingredients was about right. Then she tried the idea of administering minute drops while the mixture was still fizzing. This seemed less ill-tasting, and worth a try.

It took another month, but with a combination of the drops and her rubbing Iona's stomach, plus what seemed like miles of floor walking singing the old tunes, Cate began to get at least three to four hours sleep a night. Not good, but so much better than before. Then two things happened to improve the situation even more. Firstly Lizzie returned to Craigavon pregnant, and with smart new boots, a wedding present from her husband, that minimised her limp. And then notification of the first quota of patients arrived at the Hospital.

Chapter 33

With Lizzie at least temporarily back in the fold, and with Shona and Maggie covering baby duties during the daytime, Cate went back to the hospital. It felt strange to find the wards empty. She wandered from bed to bed, her mind slipping back to the meeting with Mary Anne in the Willow. The fight to get the hospital established, her joy working with the Major, and her constant battles with the Captain! Now she'd have to face up to yet another Army man, so she'd better go and find him.

Her first sight of Doctor was reassuring.

"Ah, the missing 'Miss Cate', that everyone's been telling me about, I presume," he said on Cate's appearance.

"Captain? Major?" Cate queried.

"Neither, I'm afraid. Does that disappoint you?"

"Not at all, but you have the advantage of me by knowing how to address me, and I would like to afford you the same courtesy, so you are?"

"I'm a retired surgeon, who's been called upon to supplement the Army Medical Corps in their time of need. There are quite a number of us retirees in civilian hospitals that are being filled with casualties from the Front. Fraser Stirling, Miss Cate, and I've been sent to facilitate these poor devils," He pointed in the direction of the wards. "Getting to grips with their disabilities, once they get here."

Cate held out her hand, "I'm glad you're here Doctor Stirling…"

"Plain old 'Doctor' will do fine. Now I must get myself ready for their arrival next week, or Sister Mary Anne'll be after me!"

Cate gave a sigh of relief as she watched the Doctor walk away. This was a medical man more in the fashion of the Major, and though she dwelt on thoughts of the latter at the Western Front for a sad minute or two, she knew that the hospital would be a more peaceful place with the advent of the new man. With the wards re-arranged to accommodate the twenty new amputees, the hall emptied to leave space for their practice sessions and the breakfast room commandeered for a gym, the only remaining problem was if further corrective surgery were required. Cate, Mary Anne, and the Doctor spent the next morning checking out other spare rooms, and at last they decided on the gunroom because it housed the huge slate billiard table. With this as a base, the doctor left again for Glasgow to pick up the remainder of his personal belongings and surgery equipment. Meanwhile the three women and the two orderlies set to and scrubbed the gunroom. Cate and Bella cleared out and sterilised an adjacent washroom, then checked that Snowy didn't need any help in the kitchen, before Cate left for Craigavon. Over the evening meal she gave a glowing report of her first day back, and the rearranging of the wards as the new patients would have such different needs to the old ones. Dinwoodie then produced a letter and an unusually large parcel from the Scribbler that had arrived in her absence, and, when they finished their meal he opened the letter.

Western Front, January 1918

Dear Cate,

Yet another new year of War and everyone is wondering what it will hold. While we wait I've spent some time with our soldiers returning from home leave and waiting for their postings once the weather improves. With cigarettes alight their conversations usually turn to their recent stays with family or friends at home in Britain.

Cate, it is hard to believe but many of them hadn't enjoyed their leave! They couldn't believe how little those at home really knew, or wanted to know, what the War in France was like. Some even found life away from the front almost unbearable! To them the 'real world' now was the trenches and the bonds they'd formed with their soldier companions.

They couldn't get over to people at home what it's like living in squalor under constant fear of death.

The gulf between the two ways of life is too great. Only those sharing it understand it. Their War has removed

them from normality. It's as if they, and indeed the rest of us out here, are on another planet, with its own rules, its own way of life and death. 'Back Home' has now no place in our hearts and minds.
Alashdair.

"It's barely believable! Fancy not being able to communicate with those they love. What's this war doing to us, Dinwoodie?"

"I do believe I can understand. Think about it. When you're here your mind is taken up with Kevinishe and when I'm away my world is the foundries. We're luckier than the poor soldiers because we do at least share some knowledge of our differing worlds. Theirs are just too far apart."

"How will they cope when the war is over? They'll have to go back to their old worlds then?"

"I fear, Cate, the answer to that is they won't"

"Not go back! Surely they will, Dinwoodie?"

"Oh they'll go back, but whether they will be able to cope there, I very much doubt."

"Will it be the same when Rhoddy comes home?"

"There will bound to be adjustment problems, and it will all depend on how he is currently coping. Come, we're upsetting ourselves by worrying about one and all. Bed, Cate, we have quite enough to worry us as it is, without concerning ourselves about the far-distant future."

With the wedding all but forgotten, and the hospital up and running again, the glen settled back into normal life, with barely a ripple when Captain Ewan Brodie returned to bid his wife, Aunt, and good friend, Mary Anne, goodbye before embarking for France and his new posting. Iona gained weight, and though she slept more, she clung onto her habit of screaming in anger whenever she wanted attention, doing little to ease her mother's nerves and concern over her.

The American, his wound healed, though left with tell-tale scar tissue, was now more of a problem case. Immediately after his failed suicide attempt, he'd let no one near him, refused food, and became incontinent. On the new Doctor's advice, he was removed from his single room and installed with those patients whose prosthetics had arrived, in the hope that all the moving about might get him showing at least a modicum of interest. Even Cate, who visited him daily, brought books, photographs, and anything else she could think of to stimulate him, was unable even to stroke his hand or gain his attention, as she'd done before. Indeed he seemed to shrink even more from her than the others, and that was particularly depressing. She was certain he held the key to the missing Sarah and she could think of nothing other than patience to try and regain the ground she'd lost with him.

Cate's days began with seeing to her daughter before she handed her over to Lizzie or Shona and left for the hospital. Once there she saw to the ancillary staff rotas, the ordering of supplies for Cook, and then anything she could do in the way of helping on the wards. It was not long before Doctor Stirling discovered that she was invaluable for the easing of aches and pains, and that her encouragement to those struggling with the newly fitted prosthetics worked wonders. With a full day's work to be done, Cate's delicately balanced hospital and Craigavon daily routine fell apart when the inevitable happened. Both Maggie and Lizzie went down with a chill. They'd been out, a couple of days before, to help with a village birthing. It had been long and arduous, not helped by the soldier husband, newly returned on compassionate leave, who'd spent the entire time accusing them of not knowing what they were doing, while he coughed and spluttered all over them.

With Shona willing to take charge of the baby, Cate couldn't risk leaving the boys with her too. The mare chose to start foaling that morning, meaning that Charlie was fully occupied with the other stable hands. Cook had more than enough to do feeding everybody, so Cate simply bundled the boys into the sulkie and made for the hospital. Her plan was to leave the boys with Robbie, but to her horror she found he was away at a wedding and wouldn't be back for a day or two. There was nothing for it, but to set them down in her office with paper and pencil, and hope it would keep them occupied.

When Mary Anne stuck her head round the office door, the boys made straight for her, pencils and paper forgotten. Between their garbled chatter and, with a few interjections by Cate, their presence was soon explained.

"I've done my rounds and came up to see if you were ready for the morning tea break. Why don't I take these two scalliwags down with me, and that'll give you a break to get some work done without interruption?" she said.

290

"Mary Anne, that'd be great. I can get as much done as possible, and then I'll make time to amuse them. Thanks. And you two," she pointed to the mess they'd made, "get that lot tidied away and see you behave with Mary Anne, understand?" As two heads, one black one blonde, nodded vigorously, she relented. "Oh go on — off with the three of you. It'll be quicker doing it myself!" With a sigh of relief she cleared up and returned to her desk.

When Mary Anne returned alone, Cate looked up puzzled. What have you done with them?" she queried.

"Nothing! Sure and didn't the good Doctor take them off my hands. Says he's going to show them his magic arms, legs and hands."

"I do hope they behave then. Won't that be a bit — you know, gruesome?"

"Never a bit of it. In the Convent when I was young, the boys were all for the gory bits — never far away from the sluice room if they could sneak in there!"

"I do remember the tinker boys always around if someone was injured. They loved it when the boxing was going on, as the two men used to near maul one another — lots of blood and gore! At least I'll get more done before they return, and thanks again, Mary Anne. See you later," she added as her friend left.

It was indeed much later when the Doctor returned with the boys.

"That was very kind of you to take time with them…"she began.

"Nonsense!" he interrupted her. "They remind me of my grandchildren when they were young. Why don't you take them down to the wards when you go? That would cheer the men up I'm sure. They miss their families. Do them good. And it would mean they didn't miss your daily spell with them. Now that would disappoint them!"

"You're very kind, and I enjoy my visits to them. As long as you don't think the boys…"

"Oh I don't, I'm sure a good time will be had by all. However, in view of your domestics problems, I should cut your day short."

"I will, and thank you."

Once in the ward both men and boys chatted to one another, or rather David did the chatting and Cam mostly listened. When she thought all had had enough, Cate began to round up her offspring, only to find Cam was not with David. She retraced her steps to the other ward and to her amazement the American was holding Cam's hand and smiling at him. She went back collected David, returned to the doorway and, finger to her mouth, silenced him, as he was about to shout to his brother, motioning him to wait. As she wondered whether this might be a breakthrough, David, aware that her attention was elsewhere, dashed across to Cam and began pulling him away. Cursing herself, Cate went after him and with a quick shove sent him in the direction of the doorway, but it was too late. Cam had dropped the American's hand and the man was once more cowering against his pillows, as the boy went after his brother.

Chapter 34

In later years, Grabber would still remember the horrors of the repatriation from the Front. The ambulance swung and swerved between the constant traffic on the roads, bouncing them around, avoiding civilians with their baggage piled high, while army transport choked the highway in both directions. Additional stabs of pain came from his wounded shoulder, and he was unable to comfort Boy, who seemed to slip back into the throes of madness that had afflicted him when he was first thrown into their group at the siding as they'd returned from leave. The transfer onto the troop train to take them to the coast was no better, and once on board the hospital ship, it was one long bout of seasickness for both of them.

In the overcrowded civilian hospital, he let it be known that Boy was a distant relative, had got caught up in the war looking for him, and once they were pronounced ready for discharge, he took the demob papers and Boy before anyone was aware that he had done so. Once back in London, they found a bombed-out house, and began to sit out their convalescence.

It took time for their wounds to heal completely. They stayed close to their base to forage for food — in Grabber's vocabulary that meant steal — but bit-by-bit they made their new home at least as comfortable as their erstwhile trenches. And, with his constant companionship and no other distractions, Grabber, in a long slow process, loosened his charge's tongue to a certain extent, but the mind remained fragile. A fragment of that first encounter — something about a chief — was the only thing Grabber could remember. It was at least a beginning. With laborious repetition, he was able to build up a somewhat flimsy background for the youngster. It became clear he'd left his family because he was unhappy but concrete details of their whereabouts and the reasons for the discord took much longer. Then there was both a breakthrough and a setback.

An over-zealous warden, attracted by the light in the derelict building, came upon them one night and, although most of what he said

Grabber couldn't understand, as the man had a broad Scottish accent the boy became animated as they collected what they could carry and went to look for a new hidey-hole. They moved well away from their present area and, once inside the remnants of another derelict building, they found it had a cellar that was at least watertight. It took time to gather the bare necessities, both of food and damaged furniture garnered from tips in the area.

Once that was done, Grabber connected the 'chief bit' to the accent, and spent many more weeks probing this new lead that seemed to lie in far-off Scotland. There were days when he thought he'd best forget the whole identity thing as he made no progress with the lad, and get on with planning a life in what was left of the East End. But something told him that if he could unlock the youngster's mind, there might well be a financial gain for him. However, he'd become fond of Boy and, with no wish to find the remnants of his own family, and probably a prison sentence if he did, he would miss the youngster. Grabber decided to explore the new area, look for chances of committing petty crimes, and continue to use Boy as he'd done in France. Whatever happened, he was sure they'd make a living and, if Boy recovered fully, he'd exploit whatever leads came his way.

After a day out foraging, Grabber and Boy staggered down what was left of the stairs and collapsed in the cellar doorway. After a brief breathing space, they heaved the two mattresses they'd found through the narrow door, and set about making their hideaway into a bedroom and living area. At least Grabber did, while the other watched. Boy left everything to him. This laziness coupled with the youngster's untidiness, annoyed him. It confirmed his suspicions that Boy had never had much to do in the way of domestic duties. Either he'd been a spoilt youngster or he'd come from a home that boasted domestic help.

Grabber divided the stash of blankets they'd collected over the previous weeks, and threw each bundle on a mattress. Then he made up his bed, set about knocking bits of stolen timber together to make a rough set of shelves next to his new sleeping arrangements, while keeping an eye on Boy. He'd learnt in the time in the trenches that the youngster was not unintelligent. He'd obeyed commands, and still did so, but he showed no desire to do anything on his own.

"Right then, let's see what you can do! Get yer bed made first." Grabber rolled a cigarette, and watched Boy's progress. Ever since leaving the hospital they'd simply rolled themselves in whatever bits of bed linen they could lay their hands on, so the youngster just unrolled the contents of the bundle on his bed and sat on it.

Grabber nodded his approval, then pointed to the timber and tools, but nothing happened except Boy shrank further back onto his bed, eyes drooping like a spaniel.

"Come on then! At least make a bloody effort!"

But the lad shook his head at Grabber's harsh words and clasped his hands in front of his body, showing a certain stubbornness.

"Oi! This is no chief's palace! If you can be a tealeaf, you can do some charring. This here's a doss for two. I can't be a doing everyffing. I'm off out…"

At these words the youngster stood, crossed to the remaining slabs of wood and, as Grabber watched the pathetic effort, placed them in a haphazard pile by his bed, then sat down again.

"Well it ain't no masterpiece, but I guess it's the start of making someffing of yer! Come on, we'll go see if the fine ladies are doing their soup kitchen today."

As Boy leapt to his feet and made for the doorway, Grabber halted him with a shout.

"Oi, silly bugger, get some muck on yer face! Bombed out we are, ain't we!" He began to smear his face with filth from the walls, waited for Boy to do the same, and then they set off.

Spring had given way to early summer, and Cate was no nearer making a decision about the twins' tutor. With Maggie and Lizzie recovered after a very nasty bout of cold, daily life at Craigavon had settled into a workable routine again, though Lizzie's pregnancy was advancing and the boys were becoming more of a handful, so a decision would have to be found before long.

When she arrived at the hospital, Cate found Mary Anne dressed for the outdoors and waiting for the arrival of the Post van.

"Goodness, Mary Anne, are you running away, or what?"

"I'm to yet another funeral. Oh Cate, it's Father O'Brien!"

Cate 's mind flashed back to the elderly priest who'd given herself and Rhoddy sanctuary after that helpless homeless period in Glasgow. She remembered the glorious interior of his church that had somehow softened the pain in her soul, and in that time she'd grown fond of the old man. It was as if each year another dear one was lost from her past: people who'd helped to fashion the person she'd become.

"Come now, Cate." Mary Anne was worried about her friend's silence. "It's not as if he hadn't made his allotted time — seventy-four he was!"

"I know, Mary Anne, but I have such fond memories of him and others who've gone. It's as though bits of me keep breaking off."

"Sure and it's fanciful you're becoming! We all have to go sooner or later. And isn't Himself," she pointed to the sky, "making a paradise there for us?"

"Enough, Mary Anne! You know my stand on that. I'd far rather He make some sort of paradise here below first — rescuing the poor, feeding the hungry, and stopping this dreadful war!"

"Sure and isn't He up there now scratching his white head as to how he can make a decent woman like yourself see the truth of things!"

"Mary Anne, you know…"

"Indeed I do, but…"

"No more! Here's Benjamin. Hurry back to us now. You'll be sorely missed." She watched the Post Bus make it's way down the drive till it was lost to sight, then made her way to her office to telephone Sheena to send a wreath to Father O'Brien's funeral for her. For a moment, Cate felt like running after the bus and accompanying Mary Anne, but Iona tethered her to home at present, and there would be extra work to be done while the Sister was away, so she went in search of the Doctor to see how she could help instead.

It was a week later, just as she was ready to go home, that Mary Anne appeared in her office. Cate knew at once by the expression on her face, that she had been troubled by the Glasgow visit. "Mary Anne, what is it? Was there something wrong with the funeral? Did Sheena forget my wreath?"

"No. Sure and it was nothing to do with the funeral at all."

"Well, by the look of you, there's something else gone wrong then."

"Cate it's — well it's — I saw him on the street corner — selling matches he was."

"Who? For God's sake, Mary Anne, who was it?"

Tearful now, Mary Anne sobbed, "The Major — with half his leg gone!"

For a moment Cate was unable to make sense of the words, but then the awful truth became apparent. "Not our Major? The Doctor?" Cate watched, almost unable to believe what she'd heard, as Mary Anne nodded.

Later, as, Snowy put their lunch on the table, the full story came out. It was indeed the Major that Mary Anne had seen from the bus. But by the time she'd alighted and returned to the corner spot he'd disappeared. The three women sat in silence as the tale ended, each with their own thoughts of the kindly Major and his doctoring skills. It was Cate who spoke first. "We must find him! But what are the army doing not looking after one of their own — and one with special skills that are needed! There must be a mistake! Are you sure now, Mary Anne?"

"As sure as I'm sitting here. I would never forget him. It's your man alright, Cate, an him with but a stump for his left leg."

The mention of the stump had Cate jumping to her feet, meal forgotten. "He should be here then! Aren't we doing just that, right here in Kevinishe? The wards are full of soldiers with bits missing — we must find him and bring him here!"

"Well now, Cate, and isn't Glasgow a big place to be looking?"

"Let's start from the beginning. Can you remember the corner he was standing at?"

"Well, I suppose so, but…"

"No 'buts', Mary Anne. He has to be found!"

"Now then, Miss Cate, who've we lost?" The Doctor asked as he joined them for his meal.

With the story told by Cate this time, followed by her scathing comments on the army and its apparent lack of care, the Doctor set about defending the overstretched medical service.

"There are always two sides to every story, Miss Cate. Perhaps the Major declined help."

"But why would he?"

"I can't say for sure, but as a medical man, sometimes one knows too much about injuries. It could be that your Major has assessed his case and believes it's beyond repair. And before you get really angry at my suppositions, I do agree that it's worth trying to find the man. It wouldn't be the first time that a war-weary injured soldier has gone to ground because he's lost all hope."

"So how do we find him then?" Cate looked at the Doctor for suggestions.

"Leave it with me for the moment. I'll try a few contacts in Glasgow. Sister, you must have his personal details on the files. Can you find them for me? Now, I see you've almost finished your meal ladies, so I'll have mine, and see you in the office later, Sister."

While Mary Anne went through the files, Cate's thoughts were on the last time she'd had to find something in Glasgow and so, at the end of her working day, she headed for Craigavon and the one person who knew Glasgow well and would also recognise the Major. With chopped carrots in her hand she went to the long paddock where, as she suspected, she found Charlie, who was besotted by the midnight blue foal, he'd helped to deliver.

"She's a beauty right enough, Charlie."

"Aye, she is that. Have you a name for her?"

"Not yet — how about you?" She had seen the hopeful look in his eyes, and waited for his answer.

"Well now, it's your choice by rights. Though if it was to be mine — see she comes to my call of 'My Beauty'…"

"Right then, 'My Beauty' it is!"

On their way back to the stable, the foal trotting obediently behind Charlie, Cate put her plan to the young man, and for once she could see he wasn't that keen on doing her bidding. "I promise I'll take great care of her," she said with a smile and a nod to the young foal. "But Iona is too young to be left for any time, and I'm sure you're as keen to see the Major taken care of as I am."

"You're right there, Miss Cate, he was a fine man, but the new one'll soon put him right with all the wooden contraptions he has here in the hospital."

"You'll go then, Charlie?"

"Aye, Miss Cate, I will. Yon Major has to be made a man again."

"That's a strange thought to have."

"See, if he canna walk, he'll no be able to do the doctoring. Now in my way of thinking with the loss of both leg and work, no man'll be able to hold his head high with that."

"I think you may have answered the questions those of us at the hospital have been trying to. See me when you're ready to go, and by then I should have as much information as I can gather. Tell Lachy any trouble he has at home to come to me."

"I'll be better able to search knowing you'll see to the bairns at home if there's trouble." With a brief nod to his employer, Charlie stabled his foal and spent the evening in her stall, planning his Glasgow task.

Cate collected the letters and a parcel in the hall, and went straight up to relieve Shona in the nursery. She was sitting in the nursery chair dandling Iona on her knees, and Cate watched for a moment from the doorway. They made a beautiful picture, the young girl at one with her infant charge. When Shona saw her she made to get up.

"No, don't get up, you both look contented. I hope you know, Shona, I'm pleased with the way you take such great care with her while I'm working."

"She's such a bonnie bairn, Miss Cate. I wouldna mind that bright red hair instead of my mousey lot!"

"Let me tell you, Shona, it may look wonderful, but all I ever wanted to have was the usual glossy black hair of the Highlands!" Aware that she was no longer the centre of attention, Iona began pulling at Shona's uniform, mouthing the usual unintelligible baby noises, and Cate laid the letters on the table, scooped her daughter up and sent Shona for her tea.

Later that evening, as she sat a newly bathed and fed Iona on the bed, she went through her mail, giving her daughter a scrumped-up envelope in her hand to occupy her. The paper noises seemed to fascinate the child as she moved it between her tiny hands, dropped it on the coverlet, and stretched to retrieve the new plaything. Only as she tried to eat the ball, did Cate incur her displeasure, by removing it. Dinwoodie recognised the signature bawl, as he climbed the stairs. He followed the sound to their bedroom and saw his daughter, face as red as her hair, in mid tantrum. He kissed his wife and picked up his little crosspatch, who tailed off her protestations and even produced a wobbly smile.

"There you are, Dinwoodie, I keep telling you she's a little minx! Now she's a new audience, the temper's forgotten. Anyway, she's quiet and ready for bed so I'll take her back to…"

"Let me, I'll tell her the story of my day in the foundry. I'm sure she'll be captivated! After all, it'll be hers one day…"

"Dinwoodie, how on earth will a woman ever survive in that business?"

"Just the same way her mother makes a success of everything she does, and I expect no less from you, young lady," His words were almost lost as he muzzled her stomach with his face, and took her hand in his.

Cate went to their bathroom to change and, by the time her husband returned, she was ready to go down for their evening meal. When he'd freshened up, Cate gave him his mail and the one from Alashdair. Later, meal finished, they retired to the Drawing room, where Dinwoodie opened the letter and began to read.

My dear Cate,

This War reminds me of an article I wrote many years ago. No matter how many different twists, however many times I re-wrote it, the end result was always the same: I never succeeded!

So it is with the Allies out here. In these early months of the year they've been returning to trenches in territory they've fought over before, reviving memories of long-gone battles, but the result is still the same — retreat!

Yesterday I found myself struggling along a road that was a panoply of army units, walking wounded, and endless lines of vehicles. Threaded through these were French civilians, once more packing high their flimsy carts, here a child snuffling, there, an old woman wiping tears with her apron, a pregnant woman holding both hands under her bump as if to warn the precious child to stay there in safety. Old peasant men, shoulders bent, their resolve all but ripped from them, trudged along the dusty roads yet again. This motley crowd, swept ever backwards by the advancing Germans, were all wondering if this was the end.

Alashdair.

"Will it, Dinwoodie, be the end?

"I don't know, but we mustn't give up hope. Yes, the men out there are dispirited, but they'll recover. They must!"

"But it looks as though we're done for?"

"It may look that way for now, my darling, but somehow, deep inside, I feel that if only something were to appear in our favour, all may not be lost."

"But what, Dinwoodie? What would change everything?"

"The Germans are numerically still stronger than us I believe. What we need is either a major blow to their morale, or a serious military setback. Our men are like a body that is dying for lack of blood. We need a complete transfusion, and that is the arrival of the Americans. Sheer numbers, and a rekindled appetite for the fight, could see us through."

"Do you think they're going to keep committing our remaining young men to this war?"

"There is nothing else we can do, Cate. Victory is essential after the carnage of the last four years, and the only way to achieve it is to bolster the armies with more men."

"What, until we've none left, Dinwoodie?"

"Only those who are currently held in reserve, I would imagine."

"Why do we need some to be kept back?"

"I would assume Lloyd George is retaining them in case we are invaded."

"The Germans will never get over here, will they?"

"I don't think so, Cate. Deep down, I believe the soldiers on the Western Front will somehow find the strength to carry on and stop the enemy."

"I wonder how those men who've been there from the start, those that survived so far, can bear to continue?"

"They must, Cate, that's why. To give in now would defeat all their initial hopes —make the deaths of all their comrades pointless. All they've left now is sheer dogged cussedness."

"This is one of the few times I've felt close to prayer, only that would be dishonest! So see, I've crossed my fingers and, dear God, I would try to keep them there till a victory happens for us, though I know I can't!"

"Let's hope tomorrow, the next day or sometime soon, our war luck changes. By the way, before I forget, Pearson is heading for McPhail's village so we will have to wait for any information from there as well as from the war. Was there a parcel this time, Cate?"

"Indeed there was. I've put it on your desk."

"Good, I'll get round to some more reading as and when I can.

Now, it's late and we should get some sleep, Cate."

Next day, Cate felt the change as soon as she entered the hospital. Rather than going to her office, she made her way to the kitchen and Snowy. Not much went on here that she didn't know about. As she pushed the door open her eyes became riveted on the army uniform. "Who on earth…?" As the figure turned towards her she saw a smiling Duncan. "But — what — Oh, where have you come from? What are you doing here?"

Duncan rose and clasped her hand. "I've been on officer training in Aldershot, Miss Cate. I've now got a three-day leave pass before I have to return to the Front."

"I'm so glad to see you again, Duncan. Thank you for coming back to us." As she said this, Cate looked at the others round the table. "Just a minute, why — there's something else isn't there? You all look so smug! What else don't I know?"

Snowy couldn't contain herself any longer. "Go on, Bella, tell her! Show her!"

A blushing Bella held up her left hand.

"So, Duncan, that's what's had you rushing back here! An here's me thinking it was the hospital that was the draw!"

"It was, in a manner of speaking, Miss Cate. And I am glad to see you all, though I do have some bad news. I know at least three if not more, of the lads that were here, have been killed and several others have injuries. A couple more seem to have disappeared, but all the units are getting mixed up now, because none of the Brigades are up to proper numbers and some of the biggest gaps are in the junior officers. They lead the men over the top and, stands to reason, they're the first to go down."

"Let's hope the Captain is safe at any rate." Mary Anne murmured, though her thoughts, like Cate's, were also on that other injured man, matches in hand, balancing on an old wooden crutch.

Cate was the first to break the silence. "Well, you be careful, Duncan. If you've passed this training, and are going to be made up to a junior officer, you damn well take great care if you're to go over the top!"

"I will that, Miss Cate, and there's another thing: I'd like…" He hesitated, looked at Bella, who blushed crimson again, but nodded her head. "I'd like to come back to your special mountain, after the war. We'd both like to make the glen our home in the future."

"Now that's some of the best news I've heard for a while. This calls for a fresh pot of tea I think, Snowy, and I'll hear all the craic I've missed." Cate pulled out a chair at the table.

"I'll have to be getting back to the wards." Mary Anne said as she rose to leave. " So my congratulations to the two of you again, sure and haven't you put the heart back into me this day. What with young Lizzie engaged and married even, mebbe it's my turn next! Mind you, if Morag gets that young Robbie to propose, mebbe not!" With that Mary Anne left.

Later, tea and chat over, Cate made arrangements with Morag and Mary Anne for Bella to have the next two days off, and then checked with the Doctor that it would be all right. By the time she reached her office the morning had gone.

Chapter 35

A few days later, Cate had only just settled at her hospital desk when she was interrupted by a knock on the door. To her surprise, when she called to come in, Kirsty appeared. "Now this is a surprise! I haven't seen you for some time."

"I know. What with looking after Murdo, finding out all the things I didn't know being a first-time mother, and then with Donald Uig under my feet…"

"You're surely not expecting me to find more work for him?"

"Well now that would be a fine thing indeed! But no! He's plenty to do keeping the distillery, the old barn and the warehouse under his watchful eyes."

"What can I do for you then, Kirsty? Not that I'm not glad to see you, but by the looks of you, you've something in mind."

"That I have! You see Donald Uig would never stand for me parking his son with someone else, while I return to the hospital."

"Please don't tell me you're wanting us at Craigavon to take on another wee one? We're only just coping as it is!"

"Now that's what I wanted to hear. What would you think about me coming up to help? Of course I'd have to bring Murdo, but I could be useful, all the same. See, Cate, it would get me out a bit. What with Morag, Bella, and you all working I miss the craic. I've done the housework in no time and I need a fresh space. Murdo's a good wee lad. I sometimes think he's been here before, he's that quiet. Does a lot of watching, and I know it's fanciful, but seems to me he's doing his own bit of thinking into the bargain."

"Kirsty, the first thought that comes into my head is I'll swop my red-headed noisy terror for your quiet fellow!"

"I did hear that the newest lassie at Craigavon was a handful! What do you say, Cate, to me coming up when the housework's done? I'd need to be back in time for his bite at the end of the day though. Mebbe, with a bit of a change of scene, I'd be more pleasant when Donald Uig comes home — but don't you let on to anyone I've said that mind."

"I think we could both do one another a great favour here. I do worry about Lizzie having to do too much with the three children now, though Shona is a great help. With you there it would also release Maggie to spend the time she likes on the housekeeping."

"Right then. I'll come up the beginning of the week and start. Mind, Cate, I'm no looking for silver! You already give me some while the sewing's no going ahead."

"I won't have you doing extra work for nothing. The sewing retainer is because I shut the group down for the duration of the war, and it's only a token sum. But, come to think of it, Lizzie would probably be grateful for some help with sewing her baby things, and I could certainly do with your ability to carve out some reasonable wear from those floating garments I had while I was pregnant."

"You're right there, though I was twice the size you were! I'll be off now and let you get on. See you Monday, Cate. That'll give the others time to work out what they want me to do."

As Kirsty left the office, Cate felt a shiver run through her. Things seemed to be working too well. Was this a sign that the truly difficult problems, like Rhoddy lost in the vastness of an army that didn't seem to know where half its units were, never mind who was in them, were never going to be sorted? Her thoughts turned to the Brigadier, who'd tried without any success to locate her son. Though she knew Cecily's husband was at headquarters rather than in the trenches, she hoped he was still safe. Thinking of the army and the Western Front, might Duncan, being in the throes of the battle, be any more successful in searching for Rhoddy? It wouldn't hurt to ask him.

Her mind then slid on to the other missing person. She'd heard nothing from Charlie as yet, and wondered whether the Major thought if Mary Anne was in Glasgow, he'd better go to ground like a hunted animal? She'd liked the man from the very start. She remembered worrying about his limp — was it the same leg he'd had amputated she wondered? She'd been concerned about his ability to climb the stairs, and they'd laughed about her dirty gardening hands. She'd so hoped he'd be safe in his field hospital, but it seemed he hadn't. With her thoughts on war, soldiers, and field hospitals, she also found herself thinking of the Captain. Dear Lord, for Lizzie's sake she hoped he too was safe, and her ingrained honesty made her give a wry smile. He'd been a constant irritation, like a burr under one of her saddles, but she had to admit a lot of their disputes were partly her fault. In truth the man never really had a chance after the way he ignored her at that long-ago meeting in the

306

Willow Tearoom. How angry he'd been! No civilian women indeed! My God, the females he'd had no time for were now employed in work formerly done by men, freeing up more of them to go and fight for the country!

By the end of the day, Cate had caught up with her work and had spent time as usual with those in the wards. One particular patient, Mungo, seemed to be in a great deal of pain. His new leg lay abandoned at the foot of his bed, and Cate sat down to ask why.

"It's gey sore. I dinna want it on, Miss Cate. I'm fine with the crutch."

"Well, it's your leg, but let's see if I can help." While she spoke she flexed her fingers and then laid them on the stump. She was horrified to find it was swollen and full of heat. Very gently she began to massage further up the joint, speaking in a low voice while she did so. It took time, but he closed his eyes at last and Cate went to look for the Doctor. She found him in the kitchen with Snowy, finishing his lunch.

He listened to what she had to say before speaking. "Yes, you're right. There's a new source of infection there. I took a swab earlier today and I'll have to go to Glasgow to get it analysed. My fear is that I'll have to remove some more of the stump to save the top. For now, Sister Mary Anne is to use the solution of lime. It hurts, but it will kill the infection, we hope. By the way, while I'm in Glasgow I'll ask around the hospitals about your Major. There are a number of possibilities: he may have had initial treatment at his field hospital, or he may have been transported straight to the base hospital, where he could conceivably have had the amputation. On the other hand he could have arrived back in Britain and been sent to a hospital for treatment here. Even if he had come back on a hospital ship with the leg amputated, he would still have been sent to a hospital when he disembarked. Anyway I have all his details and I'll do what I can."

Cate was not surprised to see Morrison unloading the car when she arrived home. What with the goings on in the hospital today she was much later than she'd intended. Dinwoodie was in the nursery with Lizzie and Iona by the time she got there.

"I'm sorry, Lizzie, it's been one of those days! Trust you to come home on the one time I'm really late, Dinwoodie," she said before kissing him and peering into the crib. "My, Lizzie, you've got her off to sleep, I see!"

307

"She's been good for most of the day, though she tried it on with Mammy when she put her down after lunch."

"I'm sure Maggie has the measure of her."

"She has that! Just turned her over so she could see no one and left her to it!"

"Lizzie, I've some good news. Kirsty is to come in from next Monday and she'll help both with the nursery and freeing Maggie up a bit more. No doubt you and her will be able to get a bit of sewing done and have a good craic into the bargain."

"What about Donald Uig? He'll no like it, I don't doubt."

"That's up to Kirsty, but she thinks he'll agree as long as she brings young Murdo here."

"Another youngster, Cate? The place'll be like a kindergarten before you're finished!" Dinwoodie shook his head as he spoke.

"The more the merrier, as they say, but it'll do Kirsty good to have some company and she'll be a real help to us here. Right, I need to freshen up and then you can tell me all your news, Dinwoodie."

Later, at the dining table, Dinwoodie listened while she recounted the news about Bella and Duncan, and was sympathetic when he heard about the Major. He was silent for a moment, and then said, "Pearson rang in today. I'm afraid he's had no success. He's combed all the units he could find that've been brought out of the line. He's also visited as many of the casualty stations as he was allowed into, but again a blank. He feels that perhaps he should be checking the hospital ships and trains that bring the wounded and those who get leave. Back to Britain."

"But if Rhoddy was wounded, wouldn't he or the hospital let us know?"

"I'm not sure, Cate. We have no idea if he knows his father is no longer alive, so he may be waiting for some contact from him."

"And then there's The McPhail, Dinwoodie."

"I hadn't forgotten him or his threats, not after what he did to you, my dear. I do think you have a point though. We know someone had a tail on Pearson in France. It may have been MacNishe before he died, but it could have been McPhail, so perhaps we could play tit-for-tat."

"I'm not sure I understand."

"We know McPhail's home whereabouts. Say we bring Pearson back from France, send him up north to McPhail's territory so he can recognise the man, and he should eventually get some form of contact either with McPhail or someone who is working for him. Don't forget he was in an almighty hurry to stake his claim to Rhoddy, and it'll be all the more so now that he knows MacNishe is well and truly dead and buried. I can't explain it but my feeling is he fancies himself as the next MacNishe."

"That's ridiculous! I'm nearer to the title than that horrid man will ever be."

"True, but he's been blinded by envy. The MacNishes had a large estate, a distillery, wealth and kudos. He's persuaded himself that as he's a near relation he ought to be part of it."

"Does he really believe all Bruce's lies? Why hasn't he checked his stories?"

"I should think because he wants to believe them."

Cate rose to pour the evening's dram, and sighed as she brought the glasses to the table. "All this, Rhoddy and the Major: it's truly like looking for the proverbial needles in a haystack. Sometimes I despair of ever seeing Rhoddy again. After all he's been through, even assuming he's not been killed, he'll be a young man by now, with probably no connection to Kevinishe. And what are we going to do to keep him out of the hands of that man McPhail? Then how do we go about finding the Major — a grown man who doesn't want to be found? And how much time have we got before his stump becomes infected and he loses either the lot or his life? Dinwoodie, he was such a good man!"

"Come, drink your dram, my love. We can only do our best. I see no reason, by the way, why we can't set Pearson on the Glasgow trail. The man needs some time with his family there anyway. Would that help?"

Cate rose, stood behind him, and put her arms round him. "Indeed it would. At least I'll feel I've done all I can. By the way, I've sent Charlie down there, to see what he could do."

"Well let's hope it doesn't end up like the last errand you sent him on. Monroe gave me a right wigging for letting you and your henchman run amok in the city!"

"Would you remember the face of him, when I brought him home — black and blue didn't even come close to how he looked!"

With the memory of Charlie's beaten face, they made their way to the nursery, where for once their red-headed bundle lay sleeping peacefully, with almost a smile on her lips.

Chapter 36

By the end of July the domestic situation in Craigavon was working smoothly, and Cate found time to do a little more riding. She spent time with all four children in the long field with the foal, but underneath the surface of hospital and domesticity, Cate worried about those she cared about who were still in France. Above all her heart was sore at the thought of that gentle man, now back in Glasgow, who'd made the decision that it didn't much matter what happened to him. What atrocities had turned him into a defeatist? Why did he no longer value his life?

She felt such an urge to save him from himself, to make him understand that there were those who cared for him, to prove to him that with help he could work again. It was so frustrating knowing that if she could only talk to him, she could perhaps persuade him to embrace life again.

Her thoughts were still on the missing Major when she arrived at work. The Doctor stopped her on the stairs on the way to her office.

"Good morning, Miss Cate. I've just had a note from the Glasgow Infirmary — I'm afraid friend Mungo's stump is in trouble. I had hoped to have an anaesthetist from there come up, but they can't spare one so I'll need both you and Mary Anne in the theatre. I'll have to remove as much as I dare to ensure we get rid of the infection, Think you can take it?"

Cate had no hesitation, "I'll do what you want and try to remember all the things you've told me when we've discussed the possibility of me helping."

"Good! I'll make sure all else is well first, and, if nothing is amiss, we'll operate in the morning. Can you get here around seven?"

"Yes, I'll sort out the domestic routine at Craigavon and get here on time."

"Oh, I forgot to mention — the note also had an update on your Major."

"They've found him?"

311

"Well, yes and no. He was admitted to the Infirmary six months ago. Like Mungo, there were problems, and they had to remove the remainder of the leg to the knee. There should have been no problem getting him rehabilitated, but one morning they found he'd slipped out in the night and no one has seen him since."

"I wondered if something like that had happened. Thank you for trying though."

"Don't be too downcast. I've alerted several of my colleagues in the city, and provided them with a photo of him. That's the other thing. He's left his army pay book and all his documents in the hospital. Goodness knows how he's coping financially!"

Before she could stop herself Cate replied, "Selling bloody matches!"

"We both know that's not going to work. We'll just have to hope the Almighty will take care of him."

Cate's indignant snort startled the Doctor and set him wondering at this woman who had healing in her soul, but apparently not a lot of room for God."

The following morning the hospital was unduly quiet. The other patients knew that it could well be them being wheeled into that room. In the theatre when they were all scrubbed up, Mary Anne took the table at the back with the anaesthesia equipment while Cate spoke quietly to Mungo. When the Doctor was ready he indicated the instruments that were all sterilized and laid out on a tray in order of use. Cate looked at them carefully for a few moments and, when she was confident, nodded to the Doctor, who in turn nodded to Mary Anne.

The Sister took a deep breath and handed the first gauze mask to Cate, who held it, as she'd been shown, about an inch above his face. Mary Anne began to drop the chloroform onto the mask and Cate continued to talk quietly to Mungo, which seemed to relax him. At the command from Mary Anne, Cate gently laid the mask on Mungo's face. When Mary Anne spoke, Cate removed the mask and then Mary Anne passed the next one to her. This time she used drops of ether and continued till the gauze was soaked. All three waited till Mungo gave no answer when Cate spoke to him and, then the Doctor began.

Apart from nods and brusque requests for instruments, the three worked in silence. Cate, for whom this was all new, felt that she'd never forget the rasping sound of saw on bone or the stench from the wound as long as she lived. At last it was done, and the Doctor handed over to Mary Anne who skilfully packed the wound with the lime solution and wadding, and bandaged the stump. It was then Cate's turn to sit with Mungo until the other two cleaned up.

When the others had rid themselves of their outer garments, and scrubbed up again, they sent Cate out to do likewise. The Doctor appeared satisfied and he and the Sister left Cate to watch over Mungo until he came round. She clasped both his hands in hers and gently massaged them while she told him tales of the Highlands, so that when he opened his eyes he thought he was still in the ward, where Cate often helped him defeat his pain in this way. She sponged his forehead and continued to talk quietly to him as he drifted in and out of sleep.

It was only as Mungo, more or less fully awake, was wheeled back into the ward that Cate began to breathe normally. Studying her, the Doctor smiled and said, "Well done, I'm proud of you."

She was so tired she could barely answer him, so she nodded and smiled back.

"Now then, Miss Cate, off home with you. Mary Anne and I will check up on him later, but he's fine now with the orderly, and the other orderly will see to the theatre swabbing, so we've got it all covered. We'll see you in the morning."

As Cate made her way to the stables she felt as though her feet were laden with boulders from the mountain. She leant against Midnight in his stall for ages before she could find the strength to pull herself up in the saddle. Once there she rode as fast as she could out to the moors until her lungs were near to bursting with good clean Highland air. Only then did she feel she could face the world again.

When he arrived home from his latest trip, more than ready for his late supper, Dinwoodie felt the change in her. When he went to freshen up he checked the silver salver in the hall, and it was empty, so it was nothing to do with the Scribbler. Had she perhaps had bad news of the lost Major? Was there a telephone call from either Sheena or Pearson? His next step was to the nursery, but the little minx lay there deep in sleep. For good measure he felt her tiny forehead. All was well. After a brief wash he returned to the dining room, where Cate looked at him and smiled. "You're very late tonight. You must be tired."

"A little, but what about you? There's something not quite…"

"Right about me? I know, my mind's been on — an extraordinary day — I helped, at least I think I helped, at quite a difficult operation in the makeshift theatre today."

313

"No wonder you're…"

"Not quite here? Yes, I — used my healing skills to help quieten the patient, but I had to hold the masks, and then, when the sawing began, it was horrible, Dinwoodie. The stump was infected, quite badly, and to know that you're doing it to save the remainder of the stump is one thing, but to actually watch it being done — I had such a muddle of feelings in my mind! Somehow it wasn't Mungo on the table, but our Major, and then I understood. It was Charlie who suggested the Major had lost not only part of his limb but also part of who he was. In that tense private place today, I became aware of why he ran away from the hospital. He believed he'd lost the essence of himself."

Not wishing to dwell on her feelings, she chivvied Dinwoodie. "Come, we must eat, let me serve the supper, we'll have it on a tray in the drawing room I think — more comfortable there." Cate busied herself with plates, food, a dram, and then led the way next door.

"I knew there was something different about you tonight. I can see what happened at the hospital today has moved you in a way I've never seen. I'm surprised you could handle it, as it was something you'd never done before. I'm proud of you my dear, very proud." Dinwoodie raised his glass in salute and sipped the malt, before continuing, "As to your Major, Pearson has had no success. I told him it couldn't be that difficult to spot a one-legged man selling matches, and was horrified when he told me they weren't all selling matches: some had wicker baskets, others dishcloths, wooden coat hooks, and I forget the rest. What I do remember is the list of injuries: a missing leg, both hands lost forcing them to use their teeth! Unbelievable, Pearson said. An eye missing here, an arm foreshortened there. Cate, he said wherever you looked there was a man with bits of him missing, desperately trying to make a few coppers and fumbling for a new way of living!"

"I know. You hear of these tragedies, but to see them for yourself, rams home the uncomfortable truth that you take your body for granted and your ability to go on living your life as you wish, while for those damaged souls there is no life now as they knew it. It's a colossal double burden, physical and mental: no wonder running from a future like that seems to them to be the obvious solution."

Cate raised her glass, stared into the amber liquid for a time, before saying in a voice full of a deep emotion that she herself could barely understand. "Our salute to all the 'Majors' lost in the aftermath of this hideous war, that promised so much, but lied to them. Took the eore of themselves from them and tossed them on the shores of disability, grief and hopelessness." Cate threw the whisky down her throat and tossed the glass over her shoulder, where it fell on the oak planked floor and rolled towards the sideboard, before it hit a knot in the wood and smashed into the large iron cauldron stuffed with wild flowers. The ensuing quiet seemed to wrap husband and wife in a statuesque silence. Dinwoodie broke it as he leant into the fire to light a spill and put it to his pipe.

"I do want all this to be over, Dinwoodie. I feel we're being pulled in so many directions, and we'll get nowhere till this dreadful war is finished."

"Just like the rest of the world, my dear. We can't do much about it, but as we're in the here and now, I think we both need a good night's sleep, before we meet the problems of another day."

Chapter 37

In his small gallery just off Sauchiehaul Street, Mr Finklestein was preparing supper for himself and Charlie. The latter was downhearted. He'd searched for days for the Major, and though there were many old soldiers with an infinite variety of disabilities, not one of them had been him. Meanwhile, his host tried to cheer him up with stories of his boyhood in Russia and Vienna.

"You see my grandfather was a concert pianist, my grandmother an opera singer, but with the Pogroms, people who were jealous of Jewish success attacked our communities, stole our valuables, drove us from our homes, and so once more members of our race fled to seek new homelands. My Grandfather had to leave his father as he was too old to travel, or too stubborn — we children never knew, but we missed him. A family in its entirety working hard to accrue position, wealth, and security, has little time for the very young, but the old man understood us in his great old age. He was nearer to us children than he was to the adults.

We never knew what became of him. There was nothing of value left in the house. They'd taken all of that, our jealous erstwhile Russian neighbours. I can still see his bent old form, white beard breasting his shrunken stomach, black velvet skull cap slipping to one side, sitting in the doorway of the home we were fleeing, without us understanding the reason for our flight or his abandonment." Pulling his thoughts back to the present, Mr Finklestein served the supper.

As he ate, Charlie was fascinated by the details of a life so different and strange, and yet his own forebears had suffered in much the same way in the Highlands of Scotland. Then it was torches put to the turf roof, rush mattresses thrown onto the wet outside, a chair, a settle, a few pots and pans, perhaps a spare shawl, slung after the bewildered crofters, with a belief that the perpetrators, sent and paid for by the fine landed gentry, were not stealing the worldly goods of the poor. They simply took their way of life, forcing them to find another, with neither the silver

317

to pay for one nor the knowledge of where to find one. Those who squatted for a time in caves or ditches nearby, watched as sheep were brought in, grazed their meagre plots of land and sheltered in the remnants of the good stone walls which centuries ago, according to custom, they and their forebears, had erected in the given time between a dawn and a dusk. Other people they might have understood, but to be cleared for a lower form of life was doubly humiliating. Just as Mr Finklestein's Pogroms gave him history, the Highland Clearances had done the same for himself.

Supper eaten, the two of them donned coats and scarves, for it was wet outside, and made their way to the theatres and playhouses, the night time playground of the rich. As Charlie looked around he could understand Mr Finklestein proposing to search here. There were beggars and prostitutes on every pavement, but no old soldiers that he could see, or at least identify. These beggars were as blatant as the 'ladies of the night'.

The older man patted his shoulder and indicated they should move on. Their next stop was a much more salubrious neighbourhood, with late night outlets for those who could afford the best. Charlie nearly missed him. He'd glanced too briefly, but Mr Finklestein nudged him, bade him look again, and this time Charlie knew it was him. Ready to charge forward, he again felt the older man's hand on his shoulder.

"Slowly, my friend. Remember the story of the nurse. One look, a brief recognition of you and the good man will vanish, as he did with her. No, that isn't the way to snag your quarry. In here," he said, and the pair slipped into a doorway. "Now I will try and persuade him to come with me. Stay hidden and when we've gone out of sight, wait a little longer, then follow us to the gallery, but be careful, he must not know of your presence, Charlie, otherwise we'll lose him."

Frustrated at having no further part in the journey, Charlie moved right out of sight into an alleyway. He pulled his coat tighter round him, shoved his hands deeper into his pockets and slid down to sit on his hunkers till the time passed. The order to wait reminded him of the time that he and Miss Cate had hidden Hansi from Mr Dinwoodie and the others in the Glen. Mr Finklestein's news from the Front was that, as a stretcher-bearer, Hansi'd managed to avoid being injured so far. He'd found the work dangerous, and the soldiers he rescued were not always as grateful as you'd expect, so he hoped the war would soon be over. Not a lot there to upset his uncle in those wisps of news, but neither a lot to give Charlie an insight into what he was missing not being involved in the war.

Meanwhile Mr Finkelstein stopped to study an entertainment poster on the theatre notice board, while listening to the Major's half-hearted enticements to the evening theatre crowd. Sliding behind a noisy group of revellers Mr Finkelstein soon found himself face to face with the man as the group moved on.

"Matches, sir?" The Major held out the tray and Mr Finkelstein scooped several of the boxes into his hand, then took his time rifling in his pocket for the loose change and dropped it in the tray. At that moment, there was a roll of thunder and the night sky grew ever darker as another downpour threatened.

"This is no weather to be out in. Feel — the drops begin. Come, I too have stood in streets. With nothing to sell I had to resort to begging for my food. None of the people, even those who bothered to glance my way, ever suggested I accompany them for a meal. Had they done so, I would have gladly gone. My home is not so far away and there's some stew that has only to be heated. No, no arguments now. Please, the rain is making us wet. Come home with me," he pleaded. "Two old men, a little food and warmth, perhaps some talk to while the time away, and to get the wet out of our coats. Hmmm, is good is it not?" He was aware that injecting a little more foreignness into his speech would make the Major realise he was in no danger of being recognised, and might perhaps make him feel less inferior. At that moment the rain became quite vicious, a heavy summer downpour and, without acknowledgement of the invitation, the two men walked away.

Back in the gallery, Mr Finkelstein showed the Major into the small spare stockroom on the ground floor. It held a sofa of sorts; a table; a couple of chairs; a number of picture frames, and one or two canvasses being stretched. A dim light outlined a basic washroom to the rear of it. While the Major put down his tray of matches and shook out his now sodden coat, his host busied himself upstairs resurrecting the remains of their earlier meal. Before long he was back down to the stockroom and set about laying the table. He could hear the Major in the washroom, so took the opportunity to remove the tray and wet coat.

Meal and conversation, mainly about the weather, the pictures, and the meal, then Mr Finkelstein went to the Gallery door and returned with the report that the rain was showing no sign of easing. "The business is closed for the weekend. If you like you can spend it here. It's humble but may be of use to you. For myself it is lonely at times. When the gallery is open I have my clients, my work, but like now it is good to have someone to while away the lonely hours. I am ready for the bed. Stay or go, but I must double lock the door. What do you say?" He could see the Major wanted nothing more than to stretch out on the sofa and rest. "I think like me you are tired, so goodnight my new friend, sleep well."

After checking the main door, aware that Charlie always used the back entrance, a habit begun when they were hiding Hansi here, Mr Finkelstein made his way upstairs. There he was busy for the next hour, collecting the necessary things. He was relieved when Charlie touched him on his shoulder. Motioning the young man to follow him to the bedroom out of earshot of the stockroom, he patted him on the back. "Now, my young friend it is all up to you. Here I have packed some little food. This pouch," he jingled it in the air, "will be enough for you to get to the good lady, Miss Cate."

"But…"

"No, no buts. Neither you nor I could convince that good man downstairs that he is still both worthy and essential. No, my friend, we need the wondrous Miss Cate, or our mission will fail. Hurry now, the night mail train, leaves in an hour. You must be on it and we need the lady of the glen here, now if not sooner. It is most urgent and a very important task for you to carry out, young Charlie."

Minutes later the back door eased back into the frame and then there was silence. With a deep sigh, the old man lay on top of his bed. This was how they had slept for many years, he and his family. Always clothed, always ready for flight. Though tonight he had no need to fill the hidden pockets in his clothing with the money he'd saved ready to flee into the night from his attackers! But he had to be alert in the morning. How could he keep the good Major prisoner? How soon would the young woman, who'd so impressed him at their earlier meeting, get here?

A bleary-eyed Benjamin looked longingly at the station café. It was his reward for the early start, that hot breakfast. But Charlie had come off the mail train with a demand that they get to Craigavon as fast as possible. So with a sigh he turned towards the Post Bus and waited for Charlie, who'd gone to the washroom, to bundle into the seat beside him.

"Here, Benjamin, I think my friend the old man in Glasgow called these foreign things creepes. They're too sweet for my liking but it'll fill a hole in your stomach till we get to Craigavon."

The Postman accepted the limp role gingerly, but as his stomach rumbled yet again, he wolfed it down. Foreign or not, it would do till he was sat in the Craigavon kitchen, where most likely there'd be a fine hot bowl of porridge, followed by bannocks and sour cream, washed down with tea blacker than the Post Bus tyres. The thought had him turn the engine and start with such a jerk that Charlie nearly found himself in the back.

"I need to get to Miss Cate alive, if it's all the same with you, Benjamin!"

The miles passed, the gossip shared, the war news digested and finally they rolled into the Craigavon drive.

Back there, Cate had been walking the floor since the early hours. As Cook came down to riddle the stove, and make the early morning tea, Cate was more than ready for the large teacup that she handed her. With one hand she sipped the tea while with the other, she shoogled her daughter, whose green eyes remained defiantly open. "You're a green-eyed monster, so you are, Iona Dinwoodie. I'm tired of walking around with you. See — the sun's up, and I've things to be doing." As her daughter gave a sleepy yawn, Cate put her cup down, and lifted the child to her shoulder. "Not now, I don't want you to go to sleep, you little besom! It's time for food and my…" The sound of a vehicle on the drive interrupted her. Puzzled at the early hour, she went to the drawing room window to see who it was. When the Post Bus stopped at the door, she couldn't make sense of it. He normally came in the afternoon. Then she saw Charlie. Her first instinct was to put her daughter down and rush out to meet him. For a moment she considered leaving her on the floor, but knew she'd wake the whole house. So she made for the back door, dropped her daughter into a puzzled Cook's lap in the kitchen, and had the door open before he got there.

"Charlie, have you found him? What is it? Are you in trouble?" She threw the questions at him and he simply waited till she'd run out of breath.

"We have that, Miss Cate, me and old Mr Finklestein. Thing is the Major's at the Gallery and there's no knowing how long he can be made to stay. So, you're to come now with the Post Bus and the next train to Glasgow, or he may run out on us again."

Ever the one for action, Cate raced past Cook's astonished eyes, and up the stairs, tearing her dressing gown off as she went. She pulled out the first clothes she laid hands on and, when dressed, gave a quick lick and polish to face and hair, before speeding along to Maggie's room. Waking her as gently as she could, Cate explained the situation, and begged her to take charge of Iona for what could very well be two days. With Maggie in charge, or would be when dressed, Cate was free to run downstairs and out to the Post Bus. Benjamin meantime, with not even a smell of the much-vaunted porridge in the Craigavon kitchen, was beginning to wonder if the world had gone mad!

As the train puffed down the line, Cate went through the various scenarios that could be played out in front of the Major, but none of them seemed right to her. She tried to see herself through the Major's eyes, and in doing so she realised how difficult the task ahead would be. With both of them suffering from a lack of sleep and nourishment, it was not long before the rhythmic clickety-clack of the wheels lulled them to slumber. Hours later, it was with some surprise that Cate and Charlie awoke and realised they were slowing down and approaching Glasgow.

Cate hailed a cab and made sure that the driver would drop them off in Sauchiehaul Street. They had to approach the Gallery discreetly, as they had no way of knowing where the occupants, if indeed the Major was still there, would be. With great care, they entered the back yard and made for the kitchen. It was empty so Cate left Charlie foraging for food and went down to the shop floor. She could hear the murmur of voices so stood well back when the stockroom door opened, and heaved a sigh of relief as Mr Finklestein came forward.

With his fingers to his lips he motioned her towards the door he'd just come through, and then he went upstairs, where he and Charlie paced around, drank cups of tea, sat down, then got up again, before returning to their seats once more, as though they were two anxious parents waiting for a teenage daughter who'd not returned home overnight!

Downstairs, Cate waited till she'd found the right approach. She knew the men above would think her mad, but she'd made her decision. Squaring her shoulders, she knocked on the door, turned the handle slowly, and entered. "Good morning, Major. I hope you slept all right. The couch, Charlie tells me, isn't all that comfortable, but better than the rain." Two steps took her across the room, and she grasped his hands before he'd got over the shock of seeing her.

He flinched at her touch, while inside the glow that this woman had imparted while he was at Kevinishe, the warmth of her farewell words, he'd held in his heart through the over-heavy work load, the shellings, his own hospitalization, and the slow imperceptible slide to acceptance of himself as a maimed and useless man, caused a flicker of hope. But as the vibrant young woman continued to hold his hands, the very energy he could feel flowing from them, made the divide now between her and his useless self, seem more impossible.

"Oh Major, I can't tell you how good it is to see you again. I was so afraid you'd be killed." She pumped his hands up and down while she spoke and then dropped them, and clasped him in a deep hug, before continuing. "How I've worried over you! And here you are, back with us again!"

At this the Major moved away, killed the hope that there was a way back. "No, no, it can't be. I must go." He tried to push past her but, unbalanced as he was, he was no match for her steady hands now on his shoulders. In a quiet voice she said. "Please, Major, sit for a moment, I have something to say and I would be grateful if you'd hear me out, and then you may do as you wish." It was a huge gamble, but she knew she couldn't kidnap him. If this was to work then only he could make the decision to take part in life again.

She noticed he'd pulled his coat across his shortened leg, the one with the original limp, so she laid her hand on top of it. He tried to shrug it off, but she refused to lift it.

"Strange, here you are, having lost part of your leg," she patted the stump with her other hand, "and but a few days ago I had to assist in an operation to save part of someone else's leg." Knowing she now had his attention and perhaps a spark of interest, she began her persuasion. She lifted the hand holding the coat and it fell to the floor. With the trousered stump obvious between them, she looked at it while she spoke.

"You've no idea how bereft I felt when you were posted back to the Front. Damn it all, you'd already been wounded. It seemed so unfair on you." She shook her head at him as he tried to interrupt. "Yes, yes, I know the wretched army needed you, a soldier's duty, helping wounded men, I understand all of that." She lowered her voice again, lifted his hand to her cheek, before continuing, "I felt you were the perfect match for Kevinishe. Oh, I probably did the Captain an injustice, but he'd poured scorn on Mary Anne and myself in the very beginning, and that seemed to set the pattern." She smiled at him then and said with a chuckle in her voice, "He's only gone and fallen in love with Lizzie! They're married and she's expecting! How's that for a mad old world?"

With no response, she became serious again. Dropped his hand, moved to the stock room door, and opened it. Then she spoke. "The front door to the Gallery is always double-locked out of trading hours, but I've been told how it works. Before you rush through it to disappear again, let me tell you what I think — no, if I'm honest, what I want, as well as need: it's you back with me, where you were such a friend, such a good doctor, and such a perfect fit."

"I was, but no more, I'm neither whole, nor any use as a doctor now, so I'd be obliged if you'll unlock the door and I'll hobble away."

"Fine! If you want to wallow in your self-pity and loathing do so. Go!" It was what she'd expected, and she couldn't keep the touch of exasperation out of her voice. "You don't know the changes there's been in the hospital." She sat down beside him on the sofa again. "You haven't said, but I bet you're puzzling as to why we knew you were no longer overseas…"

"Mary Anne, on the bus I suppose. She must have recognised me, and presumably took the news back to Kevinishe."

"Indeed, that was the start of it. Did you really think we'd leave you to duck and dive, lose yourself, perhaps even let go on life, sink into the underbelly of Glasgow?" She rose again, took a few steps, and then returned to stand in front of him. "Let me tell you I've a hospital that's full of men lacking bits of their body. You're no different. They're there day and night, struggling with wooden arms or legs. One of them has only one good eye. Another has no legs and he's deaf, but they're all trying. I've a carpenter that has no hands, an engineer who can barely see, a lad who's half an arm and who has no relatives — at least none that want him. Whereas you — you've no idea how you're wanted. You've doctoring skills, and there's a whole population there in Kevinishe, who've gone generation after generation with no doctor close by, and they want you. I do my best, but I want — NEED!" She shouted the word at him and, her voice full of emotion, continued. "I think I'd always known that you must be persuaded, whole or not, it makes no matter, to return. You see I also need to save Kevinishe. The villagers, the distillery and all in it, they've lost the old Laird, and his right-hand man, Fisher. Now there's only me. Even the government has taken their livelihood away, by closing the distillery — though I put it to sleep before they got round to it. All of that means it's a huge responsibility on my shoulders. Back then, with our respect and friendship for one another, I hoped that you'd return. I need your help, now and in the future, though perhaps, I should be thinking more about your plans than mine."

She left him then and went to the washroom, had a glass of water and returned. He was sat there, the combination of defeat and stubbornness evident in his drooping shoulders. This intelligent man had surveyed the possibilities and dismissed all of them — in favour of what? Letting his life ebb away? The idea made her angry. She returned to the fray!

"Yes, Major, the hospital has changed, just as you have! The man I was forced to wave goodbye to didn't want to return to the Front but had to. Now he's back! Yes you've been maimed, feel you don't want this life that's been forced on you, but that man back then wouldn't just give up! For God's sake, I've a hospital full of cripples and I love them all, would do and have done anything I can to help them. What makes you think one more stubborn bloody man with a bit of leg missing would make that much difference to me? " She leant towards him and put her hands on his shoulders, shaking them as she spoke. "Do you think I see each and everyone of them in the light of their disabilities? Good God, man, what do you take me for? I don't suppose for one minute you consider I'm not worth saving, never mind I'm an evil tempered, bossy bitch! Now do you?"

They stood across the room from one another. With all the emotion swirling around, because she cared so, so very much, it suddenly seemed farcical to lose her temper, and she began to smile — at herself really — knowing she'd lost. Then she saw his lips quiver, and that made her laugh. Neither of the anxious listeners upstairs could make sense of the mirth. They rushed down and stood staring at the red-haired woman and the one-legged man, and worried for their sanity.

Of course it wasn't easy. The Major wouldn't, said he couldn't, manage the train. Then he didn't want to go anyway, wouldn't go. Thought he might, then threatened to disappear. Never one noted for her patience, Cate swallowed her annoyance, pandered to him, shouted at him, pleaded with him, and finally bullied him into returning to Kevinishe. She borrowed Morrison and Dinwoodie's vehicle, and a week later they at last set out for the hospital.

Cate hoped that as the inside was fundamentally different, it might help the Major to settle better at the hospital. Not a bit of it. He covered his fear with angry protests and refused to co-operate, but Cate realised why and shepherded him into the ward with a bed next to Mungo. "Meet the Major, Mungo." She introduced them to one another, turned smartly and, from the ward entrance, called out, "Be a good fellow, and show the Major how things work around here now." Then she left.

Mary Anne, watching from the hallway, said, "That's a bit tough isn't it?"

"I know! I should really have wheeled him in and explained I'd brought another doctor to help out here. He might only have one and a half legs, but will be a great asset to the hospital, and all the rest. Trouble is the wretched man doesn't want to be here, doesn't want to have anything to do with doctoring, and every step forward I make with him, he just jumps back again."

"Sure, and it's little of the jumping he'll be doing with that bit of leg! Is the Doctor to see to him then, or do I go in and do the usual introductory checks? Or is he still in your charge?"

"Me in charge? Mary Anne, right now all I can think about is that I've removed my husband's means of transport, while Maggie has had sole charge of my permanently indignant daughter for the best part of a week and could well be climbing the walls of Craigavon by now. I've worn the same clothes for God knows how many days. I've slept little and eaten less. I believe dumping him here with others, who have similar problems, will either make or break him, but right now, for a few blissful hours, I don't give a damn! I wish you well with our esteemed Major, and I'll see you in the morning!"

Chapter 38

Grabber was adept at being aware of all that went on around him, wherever he was, so it was no surprise that he realised the same man just happened to be in the area whenever he and Boy were out and about. Without letting the stranger know, he took careful note of him. When he was completely satisfied that he was neither the law, nor a member of the 'family' that ruled this particular manor, his mind turned to other explanations.

If the stranger was to make a move to oust them from their present cellar, he knew enough about their movements to strike fairly soon. If on the other hand he was a crook looking for a partner in crime, Grabber wanted nothing to do with it. He still believed that Boy held the answer to their future and he wanted no lightweight tealeaf sticking his nose in, spoiling the possibilities. If the fella thought he himself was in with the 'family', mebbe this was his pitch. He'd keep an eye on him, just in case.

Later that day, with a few odds and ends that Boy had snaffled from various places while he'd done the chatter, they were on their way home, when he caught sight of a rag-and-bone man having trouble with a heavy load on a rickety cart.

Grabber said, "Get yerself 'ome, Boy, I'll catch yer up." He then crossed the road and gave a hand, before going on. Once out of sight, he checked the couple of notes he'd stolen while pushing beside the man. Not bad, he thought as he put them in his inside pocket, and he'd left enough for the geezer, so he wouldn't go without. This jolly thought disappeared when he saw the stranger talking to Boy.

"Oi, you! What's yer game? Leave 'im alone. We wants none o' you dirty pansies 'ere! So ger off!" He watched as the stranger shrugged his shoulders and moved off. "'Ere, what did 'e want then?" he quizzed Boy.

The lad shook his head, waited a bit, then shook it again, and said "Dunno!"

"He must've said sommat. Saw him jawin, so what was it?"

Boy stopped, seemed to be trying to remember, and then offered, "The trenches and Scotland. S'aall."

"Did 'e now?" Well, well! Didn't fink of that, did I? A bloody Dic! Now then, the war and Scots eh? I fought I was onto someffing wiv that bluebottle. So, what's 'is game? War and Scots! Right then, we'll need to keep an eye on 'im. 'Poacher and gamekeeper' I fink. That ought to do it."

As the weeks passed Grabber was losing patience. With winter ahead of them he'd reckoned he'd have found a more permanent place to stay and have a decent amount of money in the kitty. But they'd wasted too much time on the Dic. In the first place the man was useless at his job. His idea of a trail, now that Grabber was convinced he was trailing them, was to follow the pair on an almost daily basis taking any excuse to catch Boy alone and chat to him. It was time they moved away from this manor and that bloody annoying Dic.

On this particular miserable morning Boy was slouching along in the rain and Grabber knew the expression on his face from old. He was about to get troublesome. In fact the youngster was becoming more of a trial the longer they spent squatting. That was one more thing that convinced Grabber the young 'un had never had to live rough. There was no doubt in the older man's mind that Boy had been used to better things before he lost his mind at that railway siding. 'He's a clan chieftain' had been the last sensible words boy had said then. Grabber knew little about chieftains, Scottish or otherwise, but he'd take a bet not many of them lived as squatters. The title in his mind spoke of money.

With a brief look behind him he could see there were few people around in the filthy weather, and no sign of the Dic, so he thought they might as well take a break and make for Big Mal's Café. They'd eaten at the café a few times, since it was close to their latest squat, and he'd always made room for them in a discreet corner where they'd at least be able to dry out. When they'd had a bit of luck, they'd seen him right, but the big man would soon chuck them out if they didn't drop him another sweetener soon, so once the bloody rain stopped they'd better put their minds to a bit of thieving if they wanted to go on eating there.

Only a matter of a few streets away, the supposed Dic was cowering behind the rickety desk in his shabby 'office', no more than the front half of a ground floor bedroom, under the daunting glare of an angry and dissatisfied customer.

"What do you mean this one's not right? For God sake, you saw him often enough in France and you've the photo I gave you!"

"No, you see…"

"Don't you tell me you've brought me all the way down to the East End of London and he's not even the boy…"

"It's not that he's not! It's that he's not…"

The fist that exploded on the desk made the Dic jerk backwards and fall off his chair. With the man now seeming twice his normal size viewed from the floor, the Dic pulled himself upright and tried to make his tongue say what he meant but, though he mouthed the words, they were soundless.

It was too much for the frustrated man in front of the desk. He leant forward and pulled the hapless Dic towards him till their faces were all but touching. "Is he like the photograph, the same boy who was in France with his father, or are you wasting my time, you snivelling creature?"

Voice choking, the frightened soul struggled again to get the words out. "He's like — the picture — it's, he's — well — older, and by 'not right', I didn't mean the boy wasn't the right one, I meant there's something wrong with him."

"In what way?"

"He — he doesn't speak, seems — well backward."

"Then he's not who we're looking for! You never said anything like that about him when you were trailing him in Paris. He can't suddenly have lost his tongue!"

"There's something else."

Releasing his hold, the other man threw a frosty stare and said, "Well, what is it?"

"The man he's with — never lets him out of his sight. I told you before — he's always there with him. I follow them all the time and he keeps butting in every time I try to get near the lad — try to get him by himself — ask a few questions — get him to come to the office with me — so you can take him home like you said."

"He's never alone?"

"Not once."

"Alright, keep contact then and see if you can earn the money I'm throwing away on you. I want that boy where I can see him and get hold of him. So get on with it! I'm not a man who tolerates failure. Do the job or I'll get someone to deal with you and the job!"

In Kevinishe, Cate took more than a few hours to get over the Major episode. She took charge of Iona, and when the child slept so did she, it was another week before she returned to the hospital, full of apologies. She went straight to her office and dealt with the work that had built up. It was only at a late lunch, that Mary Anne tracked her down.

"You'll be glad to know that the Major has no time for me either!"

"I did hope, Mary Anne, that your working with him here would help."

"Not a bit of it! Though I have to say he and Mungo are chatting."

"That's something! What about the Doctor?"

"There was a right old hullabaloo, over that."

"Go on then, explain."

"As I said, I did some of the usual admittance queries, and not a word! Just refused to answer me, but he let me do the measurements, bits and pieces, then pretended to sleep. A couple of days later Doctor saw to him. I heard the rumpus and went to help. The orderly was holding your man down and Doctor had pulled the trouser up and was inspecting the stump. The Major was having none of it. So Doctor used one of those new-fangled tin tubes with a needle for the sedative, shoved it into him, and that quietened him. Then we had a good look. It might be okay, but there was discharge, so we cleaned him, bandaged him, took his trousers away and burned them."

"Right, I'd better put in an appearance. By the way, how is Mungo?"

"Go and see for yourself." With a smile Mary Anne went back on duty and Cate finished her lunch.

As she entered the ward, Mungo caught sight of her. "Stop there! Give's a minute." He struggled with his new leg, fixed it on and began the long walk, for him, to the ward entrance.

Cate clapped her hands, as she watched his uneasy approach.

"Bet you didn't think I could do it, Miss Cate!" He beamed.

"It's wonderful, Mungo. Good for you. What's happened to your crutch?"

"Lent it to old miserable there, so now he has two." He pointed to the Major hunched down in the bed.

"No joy with him then?"

"He's alright, bit leery when it comes to medical things. Plays a good hand of snap."

Cate went back with Mungo and could see just how difficult walking was for him, but so pleased he was at least making the effort. With that thought, as Mungo managed to remove his leg, she moved to the Major's bedside.

"And how are you today, Major? Hasn't Mungo made good progress with his prosthetic?" As he gave no reply, Cate moved to the other side of his bed, and sat down, whereupon the Major turned the other way.

Mungo leant across and gave him a poke. "Here you, that's rude that is! Miss Cate here's the business. Does the office, looks after us, bullies us, holds our hands when we're fed up, and all sorts. So you liven up. If you're not nice to her, the card games are off. Miserable beggar," the last words said to Cate.

"I've had a thought, Mungo, since you both like playing games, somewhere or other I've a fascinating game. I'll have a search for it, and bring it down. And," she got up and whispered to Mungo, "keep the card games going. It's a way of getting him to settle in."

Work complete, Cate took her keys and opened up the library. After a thorough search she couldn't find the chessboard anywhere, but sat for a moment before climbing the stairs where she studied *the Red-headed Woman's* painting. It seemed a long time since the woman had threatened to drown her. Now she was back in Kevinishe, the curse ought to have lost its menace but, looking at the painting on the wall, Cate felt a longing for that comforting presence of her youth, if only to prove the restoration of the picture meant the age-old curse was at least suspended, even if it could never be removed. God knows she could do with some help now and again, though she knew better than to demand it!

Next she unlocked the study, but apart from a small bureau that was locked, she couldn't find what she was looking for. She fetched another bunch of keys from her desk and, though she tried them all in the bureau, none fitted. That sparked her curiosity and she determined to ask Dinwoodie if he knew anything about it.

Because she'd been away, she rode to the distillery, before going home. With a light burning in Solly's office, she went up to have a chat. As she approached the door she could hear him talking to someone. Curious now, she knocked and opened the door. Solly and the stillman, Monteith, looked taken aback at her unexpected appearance.

"You look as though you're planning mischief, the pair of you. Don't look so surprised, I've been away and thought I'd better have a look round and see Donald Uig, but I saw your light, Solly."

"No mischief, Cate, but Stuart here — well he can tell you straight now."

Cate had wondered how long the empty distillery and the retainer instead of a good salary would convince the stillman to sit it out with the rest of them. "I've a feeling I'm not going to like this, Stuart."

"A body canna be taking silver for nought, Miss Cate, even though it's no a wage. Och, it's no the loss of the wage, it's the idleness. See now I've been approached…"

"So you're to leave us then Stuart."

"September when the harvest is over. I'm that sorry, but a stillman needs a distillery that's making whisky. Look you now I'll leave you and Solly. I'll see you before I go, Miss Cate." Embarrassed, he took his leave.

As the door closed, Cate gave a sigh and sat down opposite Solly. "When we lost our postman you brought your cousin Benjamin up. I don't suppose you've a cousin who's a stillman lurking around in Glasgow looking for a job?"

"I'm sorry, Cate. You look like you could do with a dram. He rose, went to her office to fetch her decanter, and waited till she'd poured her dram. "What will you do now? Close the distillery for good?"

Cate spluttered whisky over the desk as she near choked at the question. "I'm dammed if I will! You know as well as I do, no distillery no village. Anyway, there's nothing I can do till this awful war is over."

"I think I might be able to make a case for compensation for us. Let me look into it. I'm sorry we're losing Stuart. He's a good man."

"I'm not disputing that, and yes it's worth a try to see if we're eligible. Just don't tell me that you're going to go too!"

It was Solly's turn to look indignant. "As if I would! This is my home. I love my work. You and I go back too far to go our separate ways now."

She looked at him and smiled. "You do know how much I depend on you? I couldn't run the distillery without you. Oh, Solly, I probably take you for granted. I don't mean to — it's — there always seems to be too much to do to stop and give you the thanks that you're due. But I want you to know that I look forward to our little nucleus of a 'family' growing old and grey together. Now to the practical: is the excise man happy with the bond in the warehouse?

"I think he's amused by the fact that 'the angel's share' seems to be less now the men are no longer here!" Solly said with cheeks still blushing from her compliment.

"Well, you and I both know we'd have to strip the majority of them stark naked before we could say there was no leakage. So I suppose when we reopen — we will do, Solly, make no mistake about that — the 'share' will soon rise, but we've never had trouble with the Excise and I'd like to keep it that way. Anyway, if anything comes up, I'm at the hospital most days and then I'm at Craigavon. Who has Donald Uig made night watchman, now that Angus works at the hospital?

"Johnnie, Charlie's uncle, the one who cuts our hair. Wullie comes in for a craic most evenings. I suppose that's alright?"

"Yes, indeed. They can keep one another company. They both need it, since Madge and Murdo have gone. Will he stay a widower — Johnnie, I mean?"

"He's not much choice, the village isn't overflowing with women looking for husbands."

"No, I suppose not. Right, I must away. I'll be around, Solly. Thank you."

As she was later than she meant to be, she left the visit to Donald Uig, and made for home. There was no car in the drive so she would have time to see to Iona and change before Dinwoodie arrived. In the nursery Shona was busy sewing with Lizzie, but the crib was empty. "Well you two look cosy. Where's Iona?"

"Himself has taken her somewhere," Shona said.

"Really, Lizzie? Any idea where?"

"I think he said he was going to the garage and Morrison."

"Strange! I thought they hadn't arrived back. Right, since he's not here, I'll go and change."

"Mammy says to tell you she's put all the mail on your desk. She said you'd sort it."

"That's fine. If he comes back before I'm ready, give him Iona's bottle," Cate said with a giggle.

"Oh, Miss Cate, the Master would never be feeding her. It's no right, so it's no." Shona looked quite offended.

"Nonsense, we're a thoroughly modern family." Cate made for her bedroom, wondering whether Shona would indeed hand the bottle over. She very much doubted it, but what if she did? What would 'Himself' think of that? Thoroughly amused, she washed and changed.

When ready she went through the mail in her study, collected Dinwoodie's and the one from Alashdair, though no parcel this time, and took them to his study. Then she went back to the nursery to the

333

sounds of the twins racketing round. When she opened the door, the boys rushed at her, and David squealed as Lizzie tried to catch him. "Mama, we've given the brat her drink!"

It was only then she saw Dinwoodie in the nursery chair. "Right, you rascals what's going on here?"

"It was Papa! He did it, then we did, but I don't think the brat liked it."

"David Dinwoodie, your sister has a given name."

"Iona,' Cameron said quietly.

"Exactly, Cam, and you, sir," pointing at Dinwoodie, "I'm sure you've orchestrated this wild performance."

"Guilty, Madam! But we've all had fun, except I think I've upset Shona. What do you think, Lizzie?"

"Right enough, Mr Dinwoodie. She never would have asked you, but Cate, you're just as much to blame. It was you suggested it."

"True enough. Right, you two bath, and Lizzie will check on you. Dinwoodie, I've put the letters on your desk, and there's one from Alashdair. Oh, and Stuart Monteith has had a better offer, so he's off in September. Ah, here's Shona. Don't be cross with us, Shona — it was only a bit of fun. Now Mr Dinwoodie has letters to see to, so we'll leave you to wind and change Iona. Lizzie, you okay?"

"I'm fine, so stop worrying about me. I'd a letter from Ewan an he's fine too, so that's good."

"I'm glad. Come, Dinwoodie. Maggie'll be waiting. Goodnight all."

The evening meal and gossip with Maggie over, they went to the drawing room to read the letter.

Dearest Girl,

Well the news over here that has shocked everyone is that the Germans are bombarding Paris and them still about seventy-five miles away! They must have a new and much larger type of gun. The French soldiers I've spoken to on leave here say they could well do without the Germans having that kind of advantage! All they want is no more guns of any kind, though they tell me there seems to be no hope of their wishes being granted at present.

The big question for the tired Allied soldiers is: when will the Americans come? The men on the Western Front, Cate, are bone weary, mentally and physically spent. They need peace!

The reason I'm in Paris again is I'm catching up on my writing during a period of convalescence. I was unlucky enough to come into contact with that awful new gas the Germans were using. I suppose careless would be a better description. The truth is I was after a story I'd heard and in pursuit of it I got too close to the fighting area and did not make allowances for the drift of the latest poison gas attack from the Germans. However, I was very lucky to be included with other victims taken to the field hospitals, as if they weren't overcrowded already without careless idiots like me to make matters worse! I recovered readily enough but took myself off to Paris to recuperate. I have been warned that my lungs will now always be suspect, so I'll have to take more care, like you after your bout of pneumonia.

Alashdair.

"But gassed?"

"Come, Cate, he has made light of it, and so must you. As he says you both have to take care in future."

"He could have been killed, and what a death that would have been!"

"He could have been, but he's alive, Cate, so don't make such a drama out of it. Now I must get some work done."

Cate watched him go and wondered idly if he would ever truly believe that he had no reason to be jealous of Alashdair. With a sigh she picked up her sewing and tried to concentrate on that, while her mind still whirled around the war and its poisonous gas.

Chapter 39

As it was such a beautiful August morning, Cate rode to the hospital the long way round. She stopped for a moment or two on the moors to watch the old crones gathering the fresh heather to perk up their sack mattresses, sewn and filled with straw, for the coming winter. Although the younger women derided the old ways, sending off to the catalogues or going to the towns for modern bedding, there were still plenty homes in the village where the tradition continued.

She veered off the moors and rode along the shoreline, letting Midnight splash in the shallows, followed by a wild gallop where there was a bit of sand exposed. Her guilt finally overcame the truant desire, and she hurried off to the hospital. Stabling Midnight, slinging fresh hay into the manger, and filling his water butt all took time, so Cate was very apologetic when she cannoned into Mary Anne in the hall. About to extend her apologies, she saw Mary Anne was really upset.

"What is it? Am I that late?"

"Praise the Lord, you've come! I'm at my wit's end! The Doctor has a fever, Bella has the toothache, and Snowy's seeing strange lights and vomiting with her megrims, as she calls it!"

"And here's me meandering in at nearly halftime. I'm so sorry, Mary Anne."

"Sure and you're here now, so that's a mercy so it is!"

"Right, how far did Snowy get with the breakfast?"

"Tea, toast, and crowdie, that's all."

"Okay, bacon and egg for nineteen as fast as I can. Get me Morag…"

"She's started the water and the simple dressings."

"Then it'll have to be young Neil to do the running, even if it's only with his one hand."

"Cate, he's had one of those letters, so he has!"

"Then he's out! I'll have to get on. See if you can take over from Morag in about fifteen minutes, and tell her to put plates out by every bed. I'll just bring the food in on the skillets." With that Cate ran to the kitchen, threw some dry kindling on the stove, crashed the skillets down on top, walloped a healthy dollop of lard on them, and went foraging in the scullery.

The next half hour was a Celtic version of bedlam. The three remaining women, cooked, served breakfast, filled mugs of tea with one hand, completed the dressings, bedpans, and medicine with the other, while they persuaded, pestered, and pressured their patients to co-operate, until the morning routine, in one fashion or another, was complete.

"Sure and didn't that just go arseways on us now!" Mary Anne said as she collapsed at the kitchen table.

Morag took one look at the plate of bacon and eggs that Cate laid in front of her, pushed the plate away, said, "I'm done in! I've no idea whether I dressed wounds with bandage or fried egg, so you can take it away, Cate! I might manage a cup of tea, mebbe, before my knees buckle."

"I don't blame you, but pour one for me while I soak these skillets. That sink will need an army to get it all washed — and lunch just round the corner!"

"I'll wash up, Cate, if I can sit by the sink," Morag offered.

"Now I've had my breath, I'll away and set the orderlies on the scrubbing, Cate," Mary Anne said. "Here, that's the third egg and bacon sandwich you've eaten! How in the name of the good God are you still stick thin? Anyways, if you're finished, can you go round and do a bit of patting and chatting. They can wait for more food, and I'll see if Snowy's fit for lunch, or at least find what she was going to give them — that's if the feet will carry me up those stairs!" Mary Anne levered herself up from the table.

Lunch, when it came, was a cauldron of stovies, served with a mug of tea, and some fried clootie dumpling. It wasn't pretty, it wasn't on time, and it wasn't well received. However, no one quite had the heart, or perhaps the courage, to take the matter up with Cate, who'd given a straight choice: the lunch provided or nothing!

It was well into the afternoon, when, with the kitchen clear, and safe in the knowledge that Snowy, being brave, felt she could manage the evening meal, Cate remembered young Neil. He wasn't in the ward. None of the others remembered seeing him after lunch so she set off to find him.

She combed the hospital from top to bottom, but there was no sign of the lad. What she did find, crumpled by his bed, was the ghastly letter Mary Anne had spoken about, from the old prune of an aunt! Paraphrased it said, 'He'd never been much help before, and with one hand he'd be useless to her now. Since he'd run off to the army, they couldn't expect her to take on their leavings, and he needn't bother her any more, for her door would be shut as far as he was concerned'. There was much more of the same and by the time Cate had read it all she was incandescent with rage. The evil old bitch! The lad had been a slave to her after his mother died. No wonder he'd run off to the army — anything must have been better than that. But she was all he had! Cate went to look for Mary Anne.

"Sure and the woman's no heart, so she hasn't," Mary Anne replied when Cate gave her the bones of the letter.

"Exactly, and now he's simply not here. Oh, Mary Anne, what next?"

"Will you go out and look for him? Morag, the orderlies, Snowy, and I'll cope with the supper. It'll have to be you, Cate, as you know the estate better than any of us."

"Can you ring Rachel then at the exchange and get her to tell Craigavon what's happened, for it's likely I'll be late. I could do with Rory here, but it'd take more time to go and get the dog, and perhaps Neil hasn't gone far, so I'll get on with it."

She walked the garden area first, in case he was hiding in the outhouses, but with no luck. She collected Midnight, and rode out, though he jerked his head in surprise when she turned off the road home and headed towards Laggan. With no sign of him in that direction, and with a feeling of foreboding, she made for the loch. There was no obvious sign there either. She leant forward and fondled the horse's ears, while she wondered if Neil could possibly have turned towards the mountain, or even gone to the foreshore. She let Midnight drink for a moment or two, while she thought over the various options before carrying on. As far as she could remember, Neil came from Perth or thereabouts, so she gambled on him heading for the high land, rather than the shore. Wheeling Midnight round she began to climb. It was not long before she spotted something out of the ordinary. Pushing the horse on, she found the lad, lying between two boulders, and it didn't take her long to discover he'd broken his leg.

Neil was beside himself, and Cate cursed her stupidity in not remembering at least a drink for the poor soul. It simply hadn't occurred to her that he would have gone so far. "Shsst now, Neil, she said as she cradled him. I'll get you back as best I can."

"Don't want to go back! I'm running away."

"Mebbe so laddie, but where did you think you were going? There's nothing but mountain up here. Anyway, we don't want you to go."

"Who wants the likes of me? I'm no use. She said so."

His cries pierced her heart. A lad of seventeen, eighteen mebbe, with no home to go to! Was that how Rhoddy, wherever he was, felt now? Did he too think he was no longer wanted? Was he perhaps lying injured in a foreign land, without hope? These thoughts hurt, but she'd no time to spare for them now. She couldn't help Rhoddy, wherever he was, so she set about rescuing Neil.

"Come now, we'll worry about where you go, or who looks after you later, but first I must get you back to the hospital. It's going to hurt, a lot, but I promise you, when it's mended and your new hand comes, we'll find someone who wants you. Your Aunt is wrong, so wrong! Of course you can be useful, but not right now. Or then again, mebbe you can. Neil, try pushing yourself up with your right leg, then hold onto the top of the boulder with your hand. It's lucky it's the left leg that's gone." Cate put her hands under his shoulders and, trying to blot out his screams, managed to get him upright. "Now, I need you to hold on there. Just lean on the boulder and try not to move the left leg."

The only answer was his renewed sobbing. Cate concentrated on the problem of easing him out, and, as she looked around, her eyes fell on a broken hazel, where a stag had been rubbing his antlers. "Neil, I'm going…"

"Don't leave me!" He begged, making a grab for her hands, but then began screaming in agony as the abrupt movement had jerked the broken leg.

"I'm not leaving you. Be still now! Look, over there! See that damaged hazel? I'm going there to get a couple of sticks so I can bind your bad leg and get you back to the hospital. Just keep looking at me. You can see all the way over there, can't you?"

At his tearful nod, she unclenched his hand, and slowly backed away from him. "Now when I get to the bush I'll have to turn round. In fact you can help, Neil. I'll keep backing, but when I'm near the bush, give me a shout."

Ever so slowly, keeping her eyes firmly on him, Cate walked until she heard his shout. She took her time turning round, but then, as fast as she could, she broke off several of the strongest bits and retraced her steps. She'd nothing to bind the wood, so she unclipped Midnight's reins, squeezed between the boulders, and on her hands and knees, did the best she could with the binding. Neil's cries were frightening but she had to shut her ears to them. The leg had to be splinted so she could get him back.

The next step was even more difficult. The best method would have been to get Neil to put his arms round her neck and lean on her till she reached Midnight but, with one arm bandaged and no hand, that way simply wouldn't work. She went round the back of the boulders and found they were wider apart there. It wouldn't be easy, but if he could stand on his good leg she might just be able to pull him clear through the space. With the leg now firmly bound, it could work.

"Neil, listen to me. I'm behind you now. I want you to take your weight on your good leg when I put my arms under yours. Then I need you to lie back against me, so I can take your weight. Okay?" At his nod, she continued, "I'll step backwards and if you can use your good leg to push without putting the injured one down, we should be able to get you through this space." It was long and painful for them both, but at last they were clear.

"Now, rest here, I'm going to bring the horse over. Midnight! Here, Midnight! Good boy." Midnight cocked his head, snorted, and trotted over to Cate. Hoping that the lad still had some reserves of strength left, she guided the horse so he was as close as possible, leapt on his back and, with her heels prodding him, said, "Down Midnight, down! Good boy, good boy." With the horse kneeling on his forelegs, she knew she had to get the boy on board quickly, because Midnight only stayed down for the short time it took her whenever she wanted to open a gate. She dismounted and said, "Right, Neil, this is the last problem. Lean across the saddle and use your good arm to pull, and I'll try and lift the rest of your body up. On three…" She counted slowly and, then with both arms round his thighs, gave a mighty heave, ignoring his screams, before Midnight stood. They were both exhausted, but at least with Neil now lying across the saddle, they were ready for the long walk home.

Back in Craigavon, Maggie was sick with worrying. It was all very good and grand, Herself running off looking for lost people, but it was getting on, and still no word from the hospital as to whether she was back or not. Well she wasn't going to sit here worrying the way she'd done last time this'd happened. Couldn't they keep those people where they belonged? Anyways, they were all supposed to be legless or wooden-legged, or no arms and such like. How could they go romping over the moors in that state? Had they no sense? Knowing Cate, she was most probably giving whoever it was a piggy back all the way home! She'd soon see about that!

Once at the stable, Maggie got hold of Charlie and told him what she wanted him to do.

"Thing is, Maggie, where is she?"

"Well now how would I be knowing?"

"See, if the missing man was to be found anywhere near the road, I'd take the sulkie, but I think he's most probably way up on the moors, so I'll take Satan, and hope I can control him!"

"Fine then, lad. Off you go! I think you've got the right of it. The moors it'll be. I hope it's no at the top of her mountain, or it'll be tomorrow before we sight any of you!"

Cate's legs were feeling the strain, after the day she'd just had, and they still had a way to go yet. Neil had gone very quiet and she halted Midnight for a moment while she checked the boy. He looked okay, but she was worried about him. With no reins, and little room on the saddle, she couldn't get up beside him. Anyway, if they moved any faster, the leg could come to more harm. At least they were now on the moor proper and the going was better. It was to be thanked that this had happened in the summer, and she needn't worry about the light going.

It was just as well because it was quite late when Charlie came upon them, with Satan throwing his head about and generally playing up, as he did with anyone but Cate.

"You're a sight for sore eyes, Charlie!"

"I can see you've found him, but why aren't you riding home with him?"

"His leg's broken, and it looks bad. Any movement other than walking slowly might damage it more. If you've the legs for it, you could walk the rest of the way back with him? I'd be the better for riding — mine are fair spent. And I could get the Doctor and Mary Anne prepared to set the leg."

342

"Aye, that would be the best. I'm fine to walk the horse back to the hospital. More comfortable than riding yon beggar of a beast!" He pointed at Satan.

Cate patted Midnight and whispered thanks in his ear. Then she went to Satan who, now Cate was in the vicinity, was standing quietly. After she'd spoken to him, he whinnied and rubbed his head against her shoulder. At Charlie's expletive at this behaviour, Cate laughed, mounted the stallion and before long was out of sight.

Once back at the hospital, Cate explained what had happened to Mary Anne, and asked her to get the Doctor, while she cleaned up.

"Cate, remember he's no fit! He's real bad with the fever."

"Oh my God, I forgot! Can you do it?"

"With the best will in the world, I'd be loath to set that young lad's leg. It might have more than one break. Even if it didn't, the one break might be splintered. I'm sorry, Cate, but we'll have to get him to Fort William, or Glasgow."

Cate screamed her frustration, "We damn well can't do either of those things. We'll just have to try by…."

"By what, Cate? Where're you going, lass?"

"To get a doctor, whether I have to pull him to the theatre by his hair. Get the orderly there and start scrubbing up, Mary Anne."

"Good evening, Major, Mungo." Cate said as she entered the ward.

At her tone, Mungo looked at her as she walked towards them, "You alright, Miss Cate?"

"I hope I will be Mungo, but I may need your help."

"Any time, you know that."

"Good. And what about you, Major? Can I count on you?"

"S'pose so."

"That's not a very enthusiastic response."

"What do you want then? I should get up and dance at your appearance?"

"Major, don't! I've had a long and trying day, and I'm just about at the end of my patience. I'll tell you what I want, and you'll do it even if I have to bodily drag you to the operating theatre."

"Don't be stupid. How could I? Whatever it is, what's wrong with the doctor you've got?"

"Do you think I would be wasting my time here with you if Doctor Stirling was available? Of course I wouldn't! He's ill, has a fever, and in no condition to work. But he at least has remained true to his Hippocratic Oath, which is more than I can say for you!" It was all too much for Cate, and tears began to stream down her face.

"Miss Cate!" Mungo stood as fast as he could and hopped to her. "What is it?"

"It's — Neil has run away and he's broken his leg. He's — I found him on the moor and walked him most of the way home on my horse but, I don't know if he'll survive — and his rotten aunt has told him he's not wanted — and I'm afraid —we must get him to Glasgow…"

"Don't be ridiculous! How could you get him there anyway?" The Major suddenly turned on her."

This was too much for Cate. Tears forgotten, she rounded on the man she'd had such high hopes of. "Don't! Just don't you sit there telling me I'm ridiculous! Bloody man, you doctor you — who won't save a lad's leg, and him with only one hand. He's been lying with the broken leg for God knows how many hours and then he's hung on —been bumped on the back of a horse all the way here! And you — all you can do — is — sit — I could —" She leant forward and in her temper yanked the Major upright.

"Miss Cate, look, take care…" Mungo began before she cut him off.

"Care! Care! He doesn't care! There he is — a damn doctor, used to be a good one at that but, now he's so sorry he's lost that bit of his leg, he won't — Oh!" With that she shook the Major's shoulders, and kept on screaming and sobbing at the same time. Mungo tried to calm her, and before long the entire staff had arrived at the scene.

"Cate, Cate, you'll damage the man!" Mary Anne cried out.

Cate dropped her hands and rounded on her friend. "The man? This being is a man? A doctor? I doubt all of that!" she spat. "Come on Sister, we'll set Neil's bloody leg by ourselves! I will not let that boy be neglected anymore."

"Stop, right now!"

Mary Anne used the silence, after the Major's shout, to intervene.

"Cate, Cate, we can't! He'll have to go…"

"No, Sister, he won't. Mungo, your shoulder and your crutch! Then get your leg on! It would appear we've a job to do!"

As everyone else stood around, mouths agape, the two men hobbled out of the ward.

344

"Would you look at that! Jesus, Mary and Joseph, he's going to do it! Cate, lass, c'mon! Charlie's here! We've to scrub up! C'mon."

With the four of them scrubbed and gowned, Mary Anne provided the chloroform and Cate stood close to the boy, talking until he was out.

The Major worked his hands over the leg, before speaking. "It's broken in two places on the lower leg. That's easier than if it'd been his thigh. With the injury, the surrounding muscles contract, and our job is to manipulate them by stretching so that the bone parts can be reset. While Mungo steadies me, I need you, Cate, to help with the stretching and, Sister, you keep an eye on the patient's vital signs. Give him more of the chloroform if he screams."

The Major had to have a number of rests during the manipulation, and Mungo looked weary with the effort of holding him steady. Cate's arms trembled as they repeatedly stretched the muscles, till the Major was satisfied. "Now comes the tricky bit. I have to set the bone pieces in exact alignment to those of the other leg. Get it wrong and you saddle the lad with a lifetime limp."

"Like Lizzie"

"Yes, Cate, like Lizzie. Now hand me that cane from the trolley. Can you make sure his good leg is straight, and then put the cane by his heel." As Cate did so, the Major set the pieces of bone and, to every one's relief, the stretching had worked and both legs were equal.

As the wooden splints were attached to the leg, he looked at Cate. "You did a good job with the hazel and rein binding. In earlier times that'd be all they did, but it often resulted in crooked legs once they'd healed, but, you never know, Cate, you could have been lucky."

With that, the Major slumped against Mungo, and Mary Anne had to steady them both.

"Come on, you two! You've done a grand job, so you have, but let's get you back to the ward."

With the help of the orderlies, the two men were escorted back to bed, and Mary Anne broke out the emergency brandy bottle in their honour. Neil was also put back in the ward, and because he'd suffered such a lot of pain, Cate stayed by him to reassure and comfort him as he woke. While she waited, she stole a glance or two at the Major when he wasn't looking. What would happen now she wondered? She didn't have to wait long. Mary Anne offered her some brandy but she made a face and pushed it away. The movement caught the Major's eye and he called out to her.

"I'll take that since it's not wanted, and when the good Doctor Stirling is recovered, would you be kind enough, Sister, to get him to consider preparing my stump for a prosthetic?"

Chapter 40

Dinwoodie crumpled the London paper, and tossed it aside.

"Not bad news is it, sir?" Morrison asked.

"There's talk of battles being won, but the paper's version never seems to stand up to the truth, once it surfaces. They say the war will be over in days, but I wonder?"

Dinwoodie was weary. These last months, with the focus on maximum production, he'd worked all hours. With Iona at Craigavon, he had to admit to snatching several unnecessary trips home, but to have a child this late in life was something he'd never dreamt would happen. His mind turned again to the war and its possible conclusion. Would the Scribbler come back — come to Kevinishe? What about the twins? Would Cate admit they were his? Since the birth of his daughter he'd felt more secure in his marriage, more certain that Cate did love him, but were they right to deny the man knowledge of his children?" He ought to have a talk with her. Might be best to do it soon, in case the papers were right for once. Better to be prepared.

Maggie met him at the door of Craigavon, as she usually did when she mothered him on arrival, and he gave silent thanks for this homely woman who kept 'the home fires burning' with such loving efficiency.

"Maggie, there's no better tonic for a man to come home to than the welcome sight of you."

"Aye well that's as mebbe, but the high jinks that's gone on round here of late have fair flummoxed me."

"Really? Nothing too awful I hope?"

"It could've been right awful, save for Cate, out rummaging for one-armed folks who'd have done better to stay abed!"

"No one's been badly hurt, I trust, because…"

"Not a one of them, save Charlie."

"Heavens, what's happened to him? Cate will be upset…"

"Not at all! Laughed long and hard, she did. Mind, Charlie has the right of it! That Satan'll be the death of abody yet! Now here's me rattling on and you desperate for a stroupic like as not. I'll bring it to the study as she's not back from the hospital." With that, Maggie sped off to do her duty.

Dinwoodie took his case from Morrison, and went to his study. As far as he was concerned, the hospital absorbed too much of his wife's time, but he knew she'd never agree. And he'd little to carp about since she'd acceded to his demands while she'd been pregnant — on the surface at least. Cate was strong-minded and devious enough to follow her own instincts, and he was well aware of it. That she'd been born wild was a fact, and it was one of her many traits that he both admired and at times found difficult to live with. Maggie's knock interrupted his thoughts.

"Ah, tea. And what a selection you've brought!"

"You know fine well that me and Cook think they don't feed you proper in those clubs and things you eat at. More's the pity Cate stole that Snowy from you, as she's a fine hand at the baking!"

"She'll be more appreciated at the hospital. I've never had a great interest in food."

"Seems strange like — I've said it before — them's as has silver to load the table with all sorts are the ones who're no bothered, and the poor and starving never have the silver to be greedy! Ah, that's her at the door now. You'd think them's as built this house long ago knew the big door had to be that stout just so's she canna splinter it! Anyways you'd be the better of getting stuck into that tray, or she'll be up here and eating half of it. Now there's one who'd eat the plate if she could!"

Cate tracked Iona and the others to the kitchen, where there was an air of excitement about them all. It was Shona who couldn't keep quiet.

"Miss Cate, the bairn's walked! Look! Here we are, Iona. C'mon then lass. There's a good bairn — come to Shona, come on!" she cajoled the child, who after a little hesitation stood, then lurched towards the nursemaid.

"See, Miss Cate!"

"Well done, Shona! And you!" she lifted the child in her arms and swung her round. "Right, we'd better go and show her father. He's in the study. Off you go with her Shona. Show him your good work."

The girl coloured with the praise, "Would it be right though, me being…"

"You being Shona — it's perfect. Off you go." They watched as the nursemaid scooped Iona up, and head held high, began her walk to the study.

"That was kind of you, Cate. She'll be that made up."

"She does a good job for a young one, Lizzie, and praise where praise is due. What's for tea, Cook, or has it all gone upstairs to Himself? You and Maggie spoil him you know."

"And isn't he the one that deserves it," Maggie said, "but there's plenty left for you, Cate!"

The women chatted as Cate ate, until they heard the sound of steps.

"Ah, here he is." Cate announced as her husband came to the table with his daughter in his arms and Shona behind him. "And what did he think of his daughter then, Shona?"

"He was that pleased, Miss Cate." She had a shy look at him and, plucking up courage said. You were sir, weren't you?"

"Indeed I was, Shona, I think you're both clever girls."

With cheeks red from her forwardness and his praise, she held out her arms for the baby and dandled her on her knee while the grown-ups talked.

Tea finished, husband and wife were about to go upstairs, when Maggie remembered the letter. "Cate, I forgot there's a foreign letter for you. I canna just mind what I did with it. Oh, here — it's in my pocket."

After they'd gone, Cook said, "I've often wondered who writes all these foreign letters."

Maggie muttered about pitchers and ears, and Cook had to be satisfied with that.

Upstairs, Cate and Dinwoodie settled in his study to read the letter.

Dearest Girl,

Good news: the roads to the Front are awash with young American soldiers, fresh-faced, bright eyed, and enthusiastic to be 'over here'. And what a tonic they are! After four long years of war the Allies are a faded, dejected shadow of their former selves, with sunken eyes, bereft of hope, and with a certain stubborn belief that this war would appear to be going on forever! And they don't even have the choice of not fighting any more.

But with the transfusion that was the Americans, when yet another attack came, the old Allied warriors, with a few of the new, held them off! Just the thought that there are many more, even if not yet battle-ready, Americans actually in France, has made all the difference.

My pen is flying over the paper here. Somehow, I do believe, as more of the Americans become ready, that we will match the Germans in numbers. Now that could be a turning point. For months now the allies have been outnumbered and have suffered the consequences. I daren't put pen to paper with my hopes, but all is good for now.

Alashdair.

"We'll have to keep the wireless on all the time, or we might miss the news that it's all over!"

"Cate, the Scribbler said 'a turning point'."

"Yes, but…"

"No buts! Even if the German troops want a cessation, their leaders still have to persuade the politicians at home, never mind the Kaiser.

We've been through all this before: 'Three weeks we'll be in Germany' and all the rest of it, on the few occasions we gained ground."

"So you don't think the war will end, despite what he says in the letter?"

"Ending it is not just a simple, right we'll stop shooting now. Organizing the suspension of a monster the size of this 'war to end all wars,' as they're calling it, won't happen overnight. I've a fair idea how politicians work, and believe me it's not fast."

"They started it fast enough!"

"True, but you must remember the allies on the Western Front were only a part of the whole. Troops have been battling it out in countries galore, never mind on the sea and in the air as well. All of these spheres of war have to be considered, including, and especially now, America. I would hazard a guess it'll be months before it can all be co-ordinated, if indeed there is to be peace, but until then the fighting will continue. And don't forget his letters and our newspapers and radio are not synchronised, he talks of August, and here September is underway. We've no idea what the current situation is, allowing for the passage of time. Now I've work to do and nursery time is near, so off you go, and content your soul in patience — that way you won't be disappointed."

Chapter 41

By the middle of September Pearson had found out as much as he needed about McPhail. The estate was small: the big house, a few ragged cottages, a post office and, several crofts scattered amid the barren moor. Here it seemed McPhail was regarded as a poor substitute for his Grandfather, Red Rhoddy, who, though generally regarded as a villain, had been popular. The old man's son had been a weakling and died young. The grandson, the current McPhail, as far as Pearson could gather, was mean in every sense of the word: wages paid were miserly, he was well known to hold a grudge, he was unpopular with his tenants, and he seemed to spend a lot of time away from home. Absentee landlords were not viewed with any great loyalty up there. One evening at a ceilidh in the village hall, among the notices he saw an advert, complete with photograph of McPhail, for a piping competition, when the prizes were to be presented by him. Pearson felt this was the final piece of information he would need for his search. So he returned to the deserted cottage on the moor and stayed out of sight, till the piping competition was over and McPhail headed out again.

After a busier day than normal in Glasgow, Mr Finklestein, was more than glad to double lock the Gallery door. Eating his meagre supper, he listened to the news and all the speculation about the American President Wilson proposing a charter for a possible peace and stepping in at a future date to get all sides agreed that the war should be stopped. Frankly he was tired of hearing the endless tales and numbers of people killed. He wondered if, in what was left of his life, the world would ever be at true peace.

He switched the wireless off, and wished his nephew Hansi was home. Not that the boy had a home of his own worth going to, since his flat had been stoned by protesters and looters who'd wrecked it. He was glad his sister, whom he missed terribly, and her husband had died before all this race hatred had spilled over into Glasgow.

Thoughts of family brought him to the thorny question of the young Hansi and the scholar he'd turned out to be. The office job in the foundry, doing basic design work, was well beneath him, for he spoke three languages — four if you counted Yiddish. But Hansi wasn't a practicing Jew. He'd heard too many tales of the race's misfortunes and persecutions to want to be an active one. Not that his uncle minded. His plan for Hansi was to take over the Gallery, which was a good business, and live with him when he came home.

The boy could do well with his intellect. He should immerse himself in the art world — perhaps branch out. Other Galleries were doing well with sculptures. Or expand his rare objects line, and let his old uncle retire. With that comforting thought in mind he made preparation for an early night.

Much later someone hammering on the Gallery door woke him. For a moment he thought he must be dreaming, or reliving those dreadful incidents in the past when noise like that meant the end of a way of life, a struggle to make a new one, after a journey fraught with terror. Quite awake now, he realised it was still the middle of the night. Who would be out there at this time? Then the noise from the front stopped and he let out a sigh of relief. Disturbed now, he decided to get up and make himself some hot milk. He'd barely raked up the dampened down flame, when something hit the kitchen window. Then he heard a voice shouting his name. Still wary, he put some kindling on the fire and poured the milk into the pan, settled it atop the flames.

The banging began again but he refused to take any notice of it. Someone was playing tricks on him. If only Hansi had been here instead of a world away in France. But when a voice called, "Mori Finklestein", he was about to go down, when the milk boiled over. In his confusion he burnt his hand on the panhandle and spilled the remainder of the milk. By the time he'd seen to his hand and cleaned up the milk the calling had stopped. There, it had been nothing other than a bad dream! Then another stone hit the window. That was real enough. He went slowly down to the back door and, summoning up all his courage, opened it.

"What kept you uncle? I thought you'd never come down."

"Hansi? It is you?"

Hugging the old man, Hansi chided him. "It is indeed! Your only close relative, your missing nephew Hansi, home from the war!"

His uncle hugged him and pulled him inside. What miracle had transformed his thoughts into the reality of Hansi?

Once upstairs, the old man made a dish of tea and they sat round the table, Hansi waiting, while his uncle murmured his Jewish prayers of thanks, before he began his story.

"I've been lucky, what with a dose of trench fever, and some gas damage, the doctor in the base hospital, wrote me a 'Blighty' ticket."

"AY-YAY-YAY! The foot trouble perhaps, but gas…"

"My eyes still hurt a little, but my chest more so, but with care…"

"Oy Gevalt! My little Hansi! One must breathe!"

"I know, but they said, back there, that with care, nothing too strenuous, the damage would be limited, but they said I should now go home."

"But that can't be so. On the wireless they say the war is crying out for yet more men! They are much needed, so why…?"

"With the foot fever, it would recur if I went back. As a stretcher-bearer you need two good feet and a chest that works well, for the terrain is difficult, and injured or dead men are hard to lift over a distance. Remember, I was not a soldier, just a non-combatant, so I would never have a rifle. That's why they discharged me."

"But in the middle of the night?"

"No, Uncle, no! I've been in hospital down south. I came by the mail train, but then I could find no cabs, and anyway, I have little Gelt, to pay the fare."

"Ah! You must be told! The mail train has been in my life, with your young friend from the Highlands. The one of the painting search."

"Charlie has been here, but why? Don't tell me he's gone to the war!"

"Ah, no, he will not leave the Miss Cate, that one. He is her shadow I think."

"So, why…"

"My boy, we were to kidnap the good Major."

"Major?"

"From the hospital in the Highlands and then the war. He was become a beggar, and the caring Miss Cate, she wished to save him from that."

"That's Miss Cate for sure. You know I must work…"

"Yes, yes, but, my Hansi, I thought you were a Gonif, come to rob this poor man."

355

"Well, now I've disturbed you we must Gay Shlafen, for there are but few hours, Uncle, before the Gallery must be open, and I need to look for work, for I wish to repay Miss Cate, and perhaps I have a fancy to stay there for a while."

Mr Finklestein saw his dream fading, but he determined to persuade, fight even, for his future happiness, and for the companionship of his only relative. The boy would see the sense of it.

"As you say, a good Jew must always pay his debts. We are the ones who guarantee others' debts. We lend the money, Hansi. Come, we will talk of all this again, but for now, as you said, we must sleep, goodnight, my boy, and Shalom.

Chapter 42

September 1918 seemed strange in Kevinishe, the harvest was in, the school was open, but the spectre of the sleeping distillery affected everyone in the glen. The Highlanders were great ones for tradition. Their lives were ruled by habit. Yes, the war, that might or might not be ending in this fifth year of fighting, had distorted their timetables. That they could, or had to, thole, but the missing throb of a working building, the smell, the smoke, and indeed their illicit drams, from their (for they felt it belonged to all of them) distillery, left the villagers like the live herring emptied from their nets, floundering in this unknown situation.

At about the same time in Craigavon, Cate was becoming concerned about Lizzie, who was within weeks of giving birth. She simply had to get her to stop working, lighten her load, no matter how much she protested. Cate went in search of Maggie, who she found in the blue room, standing over the twins. All three turned with rebellious expressions, as she entered the room.

"By the looks of you, there's been trouble. David, I suggest you begin to tell me what's happened."

The boy looked at her and shook his head.

"Cameron?" There was silence, and in that silence Cate's mind fled to what seemed so long ago, when Rhoddy had refused to own up when he'd been troublesome. Where was he now, her eldest child? Wounded, alive, or dead? If only she knew. She forced her thoughts to return to the present. In a sober voice, she asked, "Maggie?"

"Had Lizzie in tears, too many high jinks, toys everywhere, rude backchat…"

"Right! Both of you, go to my study and…"

"But Mama it's lunchtime," David, full of charm as usual, gave her his most appealing smile.

"There will be no lunch! Go!"

The two women watched, as Cam made straight for the door, while David scuffed his feet and tried again. "We'll say sorry to Lizzie. She won't mind really." For a moment he let his true feelings show as he glowered at Maggie. "It was her…"

"David Dinwoodie, you are an abominable child, I…"

"Mama, you love me! I'm not."

"Oh we all love you…"

"So I may go to…"

"I hadn't finished. Listen very carefully. As I said the children in this house will always be loved, but right now I do not like you! Not one little bit." She opened the door, at which Cam had stood, waiting.

"Maggie, I'm so sorry. Only this morning I was thinking of Lizzie, and trying to find a way to lighten her load."

"You've tried before, Cate. I'm no blaming you. I know she's refused your offers. Now though, it's time. She needs to take it easy. She's no you, nor yet even me. We can work through anything, and have, but she's no strong like us. Mind, with her man at the war, it doesn't help. We mebbe think little of him, but Lizzie's ower fond of him. It was a surprise, mind you, her choosing him! I aye thought it would have been Solly, but there you are, there's no knowing other folks' fancies! Now I'll tell Cook there'll be two less for lunch, and leave you to deal with them, and mebbe have another thought of a man teacher. It's what they need. Failing that, what'll we do?"

"Until then it'll be the village school. I'll march them down tomorrow, Maggie!"

The next day, Cate was as good as her word. The long walk to the village school was a shock to the boys, as was this cold Mama. She introduced them to old Mr McQuewen, and left before she faltered. He was a good man but getting beyond it. She could envisage the time that young David would have the schoolroom in chaos, and his lively mind, often held in check by the more sober Cameron, would dance round the old man and befuddle him. It wouldn't do. In the meantime, Charlie would monitor their leisure periods at home. It was time Lizzie's health came first.

She'd not walked any distance since bringing Neil home. He was making good progress with the leg and both Doctor Stirling and the Major were pleased with his recuperation, although the thorny problem of what do with him had not been resolved. She walked along the shore road, stopping to speak to those out in the autumn sun. The herring catch, the hay, the children, whether the hens were laying well: all queries and answers easily fielded till she came to the two recurrent questions. When would the war end, and when would the distillery be awakened?

358

Striding out for Craigavon, she dwelt on other thoughts. The tutor problem was the most pressing, so she might have to go to Glasgow. The war prevented her dealing with other problems. If it were to end soon, then that would signify the distillery starting up again and the closing of the hospital. Or would it? As yet she'd not spoken of her incipient plan to Dinwoodie, and, with no revenue from the distillery, it would mean delving into her capital, and that wasn't a limitless source of investment funds. Here was another reason to go to Glasgow: Gordon would advise her and might even know of a good tutor. She was so deep in thought she didn't hear the car until the sound of the horn brought her back to the present.

As Cecily-Broughton-Stuart wound down the window, Cate's smile of welcome disappeared. It was obvious that the figure dressed in black, with a veil over her face, was in mourning. "Cecily, what…"

"It's the Brigadier…"

"Oh no, not the dear man, but I thought…"

"Yes, we all did, but he was travelling to headquarters and…" Her voce broke.

Cate waited, while the grieving woman searched for a handkerchief, wiped her tears, and indicated that she should climb aboard.

Once seated next to her friend, Cate could only hug her. This was one death that had never even occurred to her. What next!

"Thank you, my dear, I'm on my way to Cuthbert. We must stand together for this. You see, that's not all: Ewan's father, my brother-in - law is, or at least was, in Mesopotamia, and he too has died. So we must let Ewan know, and, dear God, I hope he, at least, is safe, for we're down to three now."

"What a terrible shock for you! Will they bring their bodies' home?"

"I doubt it. There almost as many graves, marked and unmarked, out there as we have remaining troops, I would have thought."

"Cecily, I know it's little comfort to you now, but your three family members will soon be four — and five if you've taken Lizzie to your heart."

"I look forward to that, but first I must do my grieving."

"Are you en route to Glasgow now then?"

"Tomorrow I hope. I've just telegrammed my brother, and he'll come straight from London. We need to be together. Ewan, I think, will get leave, and he'll want to go to Glasgow to be with us, though if he

359

gets enough leave, tell Lizzie there's a chance he'll come here before returning to service."

"Would it be possible for me to travel with you?"

"It would be a great comfort to me if you would. And later I count on you to help with clearing out our things from Laggan House."

"You'll leave the glen?"

"When the war's over. Now, can we drop you off?"

Next day, in her solicitor's office, Cate put her ideas of revamping the hospital to Gordon Wiseman.

"Cate, I don't think you can go on subsidising these businesses of yours in this way. You must get some return from somewhere, or your capital will start to disappear. Of course, I imagine your husband's wealth must have increased considerably with all the work demand…"

"That should have no bearing on my plans."

"Cate, listen to me. Money makes money grow. You've capital, but you're not increasing it. Should you want a large investment, you might have to borrow, and that's not a good field to be in. Now the Iron Baron…"

"Iron Baron, nothing…"

"But, Cate…"

"No. Between us, Gordon, we must keep Kevinishe safe. As soon as this wretched war is over, I hope to get the distillery productive again. The sewing group and the retail catalogues will also be revitalized. I know for a fact women have been struggling to clothe themselves, with little or no new materials available, especially up there where we've never had a plentiful supply of clothes to practise make-do-and-mend. So that should also start replenishing my income. Don't forget the money put aside to buy the Glasgow Gazette was never used, because you were so against it."

"Let me think this over, Cate, and when you've a firm plan, and the necessary costings, come back to me. I know how you feel about the glen, but you cannot — must not, beggar yourself for it! Now, are you going to lunch with me?"

"Sorry, I've a dear old gentleman I must go and see. I left him in a bit of a hurry last time, and I owe him a very large thank-you. Next time perhaps, and thank you, Gordon." She leant across the desk and gave him a light kiss on his cheek.

The Gallery was quiet, so Cate, went round to the back door, opened it, and called up the stairs. "Mr Finkelstein, hello!" To her surprise it was not the gallery owner who appeared at the top of the stairs, but Hansi.

"What? How? You're here?"

"Miss Cate, what a pleasant surprise! Come up. My uncle has gone to take some papers to his solicitor."

"Goodness, that's where I've just been! But tell me, how did you get here?"

Over several cups of tea, Hansi told his story, was brought up to date with the goings-on in Kevinishe and the reasons why Cate was in Glasgow. The old man returned and Cate thanked him for all his help, not only in finding the Major, but also helping her to return him to Kevinishe. She produced a twelve-year-old bottle of Craeg Dhu, and gave him a hug as she presented it. Then she felt it was time to leave as she still had one more business deal to settle.

"Now, I must go to the University, for I need advice to find a tutor for the twins. They're at the village school for now, but I need to find someone soon."

"Miss Cate, I need to repay you for your care of me and…"

"Nonsense, Hansi, you owe me nothing."

"But you see I gave you my word I would. You see, I've only just returned and have not yet found work."

"My boy," Mr Finklestein said, "there is work here for you. See, I will give Miss Cate what you think you owe and then you work for me, yes?"

The atmosphere grew heavy round the table when Hansi did not reply. The old man had put in his bid, but was aware it had not been accepted. Hansi could see a golden opportunity in the air, but was dogged by sympathy for his uncle. Cate sensed the strain, and made ready to leave, but Hansi stood forestalling her.

"Wait, please wait, Miss Cate. I think I have a solution." He turned to his uncle. "You did not expect me back till the war ended. Let me take this brief period from you. If I accompany Miss Cate and tutor the boys, then I would feel my debt was clear. A little time will pass, and then we'll talk again of careers and permanency, huh Uncle?"

Back once more in Kevinishe with Hansi, Cate took the boys to school, and apologised for the twins' short stay. Thanked the headmaster

361

for their brief period of tuition, and left a donation towards more books for the school. It appeared that both Cam and Mr McQuewen were delighted to have David removed from the premises. He'd been a trial to both, she was told. That titbit of news confirmed that the elder of the twins needed restraining, if not retraining. As she drove them home in the sulkie, she informed them that, Hansi, the man she'd brought back from Glasgow, would now tutor them. Give them proper lessons that would take place in the old schoolroom. They'd have their meals there as well, and the ajoining room would be their new bedroom. If and when they reformed their behaviour, David in particular, they might be allowed occasionally to join their parents for the evening meal.

Out-of-school-hours would be spent with Charlie in some outdoor pursuits, weather permitting, and in stable and craft projects when it didn't. In other words there would be no more opportunity to disrupt the household, or to wheedle food or indeed anything else from the women. The nursery would now be under Shona's supervision, and out of bounds for the immediate future for them. Kirsty would continue to bring young Murdo in, and would join Shona in the nursery. Lizzie was not to be disturbed. The remainder of the journey home was silent.

Craigavon was a hive of activity for the next few days, and everyone, as instructed, paid little attention to the twins. Cate knew it was hard on Cam, so whenever she could she included him in the preparation, hoping to make the point to David that it was his behaviour she was really cross about.

With Dinwoodie away for a week or two, Cate decided to let Hansi share with Charlie in the stable for the moment, but her idea was to give them one of the spare bedrooms in the house, and move Lachy into the stable bothy, always assuming Charlie was happy for Jeannie to be alone in the cottage with the twins. That still worried her, but she'd try to find a better solution. When he came home she would ask Dinwoodie if Hansi could be accommodated indoors. She wanted no recurrence of the earlier feud.

Once the new system was underway, Craigavon was a deal quieter, and the women complained she was being too harsh. Cate was unrepentant! The memory of Bruce MacNishe's, and to a certain degree Rhoddy's, behaviour made her adamant the twins would not go the same way. Now she could get back to work in the hospital, plan the restoration of her key businesses, spend time with Cecily, watch over Lizzie, chivvy the Major and get him to agree to stay in the glen, and find a solution for Neil.

Her impatience to read the news in the letter that was waiting for her on her return could be contained no longer, but she'd let Dinwoodie know she'd read this one, not out of spite, but a raging curiosity!

Western Front Autumn 1918

Dearest Girl

The war goes on. From August into September, our troops returned to the old battle sites, like Bapaume and Arras, but this time they came out on top! This was despite earlier in the year being pushed further back than ever before when the Germans launched two massive attacks.

Soldiers out of the line now have wide smiles and squared shoulders for the first time in years. Staff officers tell me that the Allies instigated so many attacks from different points, that the Germans had to retreat to their Hindenberg line. Great news from the Western Front!

Alashdair.

Cate folded the letter with a sigh, put the accompanying parcel in her safe, and left the opened letter on his desk. As usual, Dinwoodie had been right — the war had not ended! She'd so hoped that the letter would signal peace, but it was not to be. Now she must continue, wondering and waiting for Rhoddy to return. Oh God, what if he didn't? The pictures in the papers showed heaps of bodies, dead or injured, Allied or German, who knew? As Cecily had said they could not see to burying all those. Even identifying the maimed would be difficult. In her quiet house, that she'd so hoped would be a symbol of a lasting security and a happy family, Cate finally faced up to the fact that her eldest son, like many other mothers' sons, could by now, be already dead.

In bed later, sleep would not come. She tossed and turned, got up, tiptoed downstairs to the kitchen, where she refreshed the fire in the stove and when the kettle on the hob boiled made herself a stroupic, adding a dram of Craeg Dhu in the hope that it might hasten sleep. She cradled the cup as she sipped and stared into the renewed flames.

She shivered as a mist appeared and blocked the fire from sight. Then the fire reappeared and, her eyes seemed to bore deeper and ever deeper into the red-hot heart of the fire. Now she could make out men fighting, falling. The scene faded, but then she saw the outline of a barn, with a peasant woman, a child, and another insubstantial figure she couldn't make out, in the depth of the fire. Then they too disappeared, and the mist cleared.

She was cold and shaking. Her hot tea, that she'd no memory of spilling, was splattered on her dressing gown, and only now began to scald. Still she could not rise.

The Sight held her again, as out of the flames appeared the Red-Headed Woman, wringing her hands, as she came towards Cate, and passed through her, taking the fire with her.

Cook found her in the early morning, hunched in front of the last of the cinders. "Mercy me, Miss Cate," she shook her mistress hard, but it took some time to wake her. "Come, lass, you should still be abed!" She then set to with a will, put kindling in the stove, filled the pot belly kettle, hung it on its hook over the renewed flames, and finally emptied the oatmeal she'd soaked the night before into the porridge pot and put it on the hob. "Hot tea and porridge inside of you and back to bed, I would say."

Maggie was next down, and she all but fed Cate. Then she not only ordered her to bed, but also followed her upstairs. When she'd pulled the coverlets over her, she could see Cate was still shivering and had no real sense of where she was. Maggie understood then what had happened, but no one else must know. What strange new trouble for them had *The Sight* brought?

Cate returned to the hospital the following day. She still felt shaken by the fire episode, though a tiny part of her was grateful for the appearance of the *Red-Headed Woman* not threatening her this time. She never again wanted to experience the fear she'd felt by the pool on the mountain. The things she'd witnessed were easily explained by the reading of the war letter and her late night insomnia, but the barn and the other figures were a puzzle. As she rode to work, she tried to forget it all and concentrate on her remaining problems.

Mary Anne was the first to see Cate at the hospital. "You're a welcome sight! How was Glasgow?"

"Instrumental in solving one of my problems."

"And? Or is it a secret?"

"Not at all. With Lizzie near to giving birth, the twins were getting too much for her, but she wouldn't give up. Now she has. I've brought back, at least for a time, a young scholar, called Hansi, to tutor the boys. It was a surprise, but I could do with more surprises like that, should they solve my other problems."

"I've a surprise for you then, Cate."

"Really? A nice one I hope!"

"Come with me." Mary Anne led the way to the ward. The Major, Mungo, and Neil were playing cards. "Neil, turn round for me. Now what do you see, Cate?"

"Your hand — has come, Neil!"

"And I can put my weight on the leg, Miss Cate. But the two doctors say I mustn't do too much."

"I can see, now we've recruited a second one, that life here in the hospital could get muddled!" Cate sent a playful glance in the Major's direction. "I think we'd better stick to 'the Major' and 'the Doctor'. What do you say, Major?"

"Will thank you do?"

"Splendidly!"

Later, Cate had another surprise when she was delivering the mail. In the other ward, with Bella for an audience, Hamish McLeod, the distillery engineer, was fiddling around with some bits of metal, and patient M, Ian McAlister, as she continued to think of him, was engrossed as well. Cate slipped away and went to find Doctor Stirling in the office. She was amazed when he told her he'd simply followed up on her earlier advice, had Robbie make some more puzzles, and then Hamish had appeared with other things. He was quite certain that this part of the patient's brain was now working well, and he felt that perhaps they should refer him back to Craiglockart for further treatment. Cate was only too ready to agree. Anything that would unlock the knowledge that he had, if her belief that he was indeed a McAlister was correct, would be a great boon to her, and would perhaps enable her to at last find her older daughter.

Part Six

1919 Beleaguered

Chapter 43

When Dinwoodie arrived home at the end of the fortnight, he was met as usual by the housekeeper. "How good it is to be home again, Maggie."

"Aye well, you'll need to be 'awfu' carefull' as Angus would say. She's cracking yon whip of hers with a vengeance!"

"Cate? Not actually I hope?"

"If the new rules are no kept, a slap here and there could well be in the offing!"

"Now then, Maggie, I'm intrigued. Let me guess — David has overstepped the mark!"

"That he has…"

Cate's arrival from the stables interrupted the dialogue, and Maggie bustled off to prepare their afternoon tea.

"I've been told you're on the warpath, my dear. Is it safe to demand a kiss for the weary husband home from the concerns of war?"

"Maggie's been over dramatic again! After all that's happened since you were last home, I can think of nothing more enticing than to cuddle up in your warm embrace, so come here!"

With Maggie's reappearance they separated, made themselves comfortable in the armchairs and consumed their tea in a pleasant silence. Cate was the first to finish and, eager to settle the question of Hansi's return, opened the conversation.

"Maggie's right in a way. I've had to discipline the twins because they were so rude to Lizzie, and Maggie took issue with them as well. Anyway, I marched them down to the village school…"

"You never made them walk there?"

"That I did, Dinwoodie. Lizzie was upset, while Master David showed no remorse whatsoever."

"So they're now at school?"

"No, I knew the Dominee wouldn't be able to cope for any length of time with them, so I had to find another answer. I would've waited

369

till you came home, but I met Cecily — poor thing: the Brigadier's been killed and so has her brother-in-law, Ewan Brodie's father."

"That's dreadful. What about the funeral? I've come straight from London, so I've heard nothing."

"I went to Glasgow with her and it seems that there's little or no hope of their bodies being found, never mind returned, so there'll be a memorial service, once the Captain gets leave."

"That was thoughtful of you, Cate."

"Well it actually suited me to go, as I wanted to thank Mr Finklestein for tracing the Major, and I intended to enquire at the University about a tutor for the twins. However, the most amazing thing happened." Cate studied her husband as she tried to find the right words to explain what she'd done.

"And?"

"Dinwoodie, you must believe me that — well at the art gallery, staying with his uncle, I found Hansi, wounded, repatriated and looking for work."

"As I said before, and?"

"He's a scholar and a linguist so I've employed him to tutor the boys till either he's had enough or they reach the age for Fettes. The thing is — I think both he and Charlie should live in, but I won't insist on that if you object. I know it's all very sudden, but with Lizzie's confinement almost upon us, and the fact that Hansi was looking for work to repay my help, as well as being friendly with Charlie, it just all seemed to fit."

"So where does he sleep at the moment?"

"He's doubling up with Charlie in the stables."

"Mmmm. Let me meet the man first and I'll think about it. Though I appreciate your waiting for my opinion, Cate. Now I've one or two things to clear from my desk before supper."

"And I need to see what Charlie and the twins have been doing this afternoon. I'm determined that, with your approval, my plan for the boys will work. For once I'm in charge of the situation, and this time I simply will not allow myself to make a mess of rearing these three younger children."

Dinwoodie shook his head at her steely words. "My darling wife, as usual you've caned yourself for the past and are setting the most demanding standards for the future. There's no black or white, my dear. Most of us struggle through a world of grey. Perfection, I would think, occurs rarely, and by hankering after it you'll inevitably be disheartened."

"But Dinwoodie…"

"No 'buts'! Just do your best. Try not to let your work ambitions, your social conscience with regard to the village and, your weird construction of a 'family' all demand more than you can give. Now, with that bit of homily, I must tackle the letters I picked up before I left today"

"Of course, the letter!"

"The Scribbler?"

"I couldn't wait. I thought it would be the end."

"Of him or the war?"

"The war, Dinwoodie!"

"Fetch it for me and I'll read it in my study. We've spent too long over our tea as it is."

"It's already on your desk."

Later that windy night, Cate cradled in his arms, Dinwoodie found sleep elusive. With the shaft of moonlight flickering over her face, he stroked the outline with a fingertip and then curled a strand of the hair he adored, but which she'd give anything to be rid of, round the fingers of his right hand. Rarely did he see such a placid Cate. Her waking hours played host to a myriad of expressions, from the whimsical, the humorous, the happy, the sad, to the angry, all transforming that sleeping face into a kaleidoscope of Cates!

The unwelcome cramping of his left arm broke into his musings and he was forced to take possession of it again. Cate murmured at the movement and snuggled closer, while he continued to extricate himself from her warm body.

With no hope of sleep now, he rose quietly and slipped out of the room, tying up his dressing gown as he made his way downstairs. When he pushed the kitchen door open he was surprised to see a figure, head submerged beneath a towel over a bowl. On closer inspection he realised that, with the pregnant bump, it could only be Lizzie. So as not to startle her, he coughed a little, but as she was doing the same over the basin, she didn't hear. He pulled a chair from under the table and waited till the towel was pushed back when she came up for breath.

"Mr Dinwoodie?" a surprised Lizzie queried.

"Sorry to disturb you, but I couldn't sleep. You, on the other hand, I think are having breathing difficulty."

With a belated sniff, Lizzie took the towel off, rose and emptied the bowl in the sink, before answering. "Ever since that soldier came home with his rotten cough, my nose has been bunged up, and I've had a cough. No sooner do I clear it than back it comes. I'm cross, because the man would get in me an Mammy's way when we were helping to birth his child. I wish he'd stayed over in the war, so I do!"

"You poor thing! Would a good hot cup of tea help?"

"It would that, Mr Dinwoodie! I'll get on and make one."

"You, Mrs Brodie, will do nothing of the kind. I will make the tea!"

"I'm still no quite used to the name you know. Marriage to an army Captain, and a doctor to boot, was never how I saw myself, Mr Dinwoodie."

"But you're content Lizzie?"

"I am that, though…"

"Now then, what about this 'though'?"

"You'll no say about it to Cate or my Mammy?"

"Come now, did I ever divulge your crush on Solly? I'll make the tea and you keep talking."

"It's daft really when you count up the number of birthings I've been to, but — I'm that feart."

Dinwoodie brought the tea to the table and took Lizzie's hand in his before speaking. "It's not a subject I'm well versed in, and yet I can understand your apprehension. You've no idea how afraid I was before and during Iona's birth."

"Aye well, there's an example! Cate was great — angry wi' it all but no scared."

"Oh Lizzie, we'll never know exactly how my dear wife felt. She is adept at masking her feelings if she wants to. But you, my dear, are not Cate! Now then, have you written to the Captain about it?"

"Well no. With both his father and uncle newly dead, seems he's enough to worry about."

"In that case I believe you should confront your fears by letting those here who love you help." He held up his hand as a frightened Lizzie tried to interrupt.

"A fear faced with love from others will not go away, but you'll feel stronger if you let their love cushion you at this difficult time. You're very dear to us all, Lizzie. Never forget that fact. Anyway the Captain may well get back in time for your confinement. I believe there's to be a memorial service for the family in Glasgow as soon as he can get leave. In the meantime, I'm certain late nights and worry won't be good for the young Brodie, so off to bed with you, and remember, we're all here to help."

Breakfast over the following morning, Dinwoodie, on his way to his study, stood outside the old schoolroom eavesdropping. He could hear the man talking quietly, but no sound from the twins, so he headed off to deal with his mail. Engrossed in his work, it was almost lunchtime when he heard the knock on the door. He realised that it couldn't be one of the family, as they all entered after knocking, so he rose and opened the door. Although taken aback by the sight of the stranger, he did recognise him as one of the men from his Glasgow design office.

"Come in. It's Hansi, is it not?"

"Yes, sir."

"Has my wife asked you to come and see me?"

"No, sir. Now that you are here, I felt I should come and apologise for using your vehicle to escape my tormentors. I had no intention of being there by the morning, but I have little memory of my actions after my beating. Once discovered, I intended to return to Glasgow but…"

"My wife insisted you stay."

"That is so, and I will always be grateful for her care of me. I would also like to say that being here to tutor the boys means a great deal to me. When I was younger my father insisted a trade was the best I could hope for, being both a Jew and foreigner. I would have liked to go to the university rather than an office, but one obeys one's parents."

"So now you would like to live in my house?"

"Why no sir! I stay in the stables with Charlie."

"Do you now?" So the move indoors was, as she said, her idea. "I believe it might be more convenient for you to live in the house."

"Ah, but Charlie he does not do so, and I would feel uncomfortable then."

"Well, I'll discuss it with my wife. Ah, there's the lunch bell, and if I know my sons they'll be rushing down the stairs ahead of us."

"I believe they will wait for me as instructed, so I now will go to them."

As the German left, Dinwoodie had to admit that anyone who could make young David obey an instruction could be a useful addition to the house!

Chapter 44

A sudden burst of organ music drifted out of the Glasgow church alerting, Morrison that the memorial service was drawing to a close. He put his chauffeur's hat back on and stood by the side of the Daimler, his sharp eyes recognising some of the more famous faces that filed out of the open door and lined either side of the path. Before long the deceased's family, led by Cecily Campbell-Broughton-Stewart and the Captain, made their way down the lines. As Morrison caught sight of Mr Dinwoodie and Miss Cate, walking beside Lord Monroe, he opened the car doors ready for them. His orders were to drive them to the cousin's house on the outskirts of Glasgow and, after lunch, take Miss Cate back to Craigavon.

Lunch finished, the party stood conversing on the steps, and then Dinwoodie led Cate and the Captain to the car. Morrison was not only surprised but also a little wary at the thought of the Captain sharing the long journey. It was no secret that those two were less than friendly.

"You take the front seat, Captain. You'll enjoy the performance of Dinwoodie's new car after driving those army trucks," Cate said, climbing into the back and waving to Dinwoodie as he closed the door. The twins were now firmly under the control of Hansi and Charlie and, both Maggie and Kirsty were there should young Shona have a problem. Cate had originally planned to stay in Glasgow. She knew Dinwoodie wanted her to, but today she just had a feeling that she ought to be at Craigavon and, since the Captain had only three days of his compassionate leave left, it made sense for him to come too. With the men chatting about fuel consumption and sundry other vehicle features she drifted into a light sleep.

They still had some way to go when she awoke, and now she was anxious. She had no idea why, but the feeling of something amiss was so strong that she leant forward and urged Morrison to hurry. Both men looked perplexed, but Morrison had been party to the glen gossip often enough to know that she had powers that others hadn't, and he did his best to increase his speed. In the meantime Cate tried hard to concentrate on her unease, but she simply couldn't identify the cause. As they pulled up at the doorway she hurried inside, leaving the men to deal with the luggage. The house seemed unusually still and this increased her worry. Calling for Maggie, she made for the kitchen. It was empty! That sent her scurrying to the nursery, but when she found no one there, she stood perplexed. That was when the shrill cries echoing in the empty house sent her racing to Lizzie's bedroom.

Maggie looked up as the door opened and relief flooded her face as Cate entered. "She's real bad, Cate. Yon cold and sniffles have turned to the pneumonia and then this morning her labour started. See, she's in no state to give birth. Whit's the use of saying 'big breaths now', when any kind of breathing is difficult?"

"What have you tried so far? Poultices?"

"Cate, her chest is red raw wi all the mustard and bread poultices I've put on in the days before her labour started! Now you're here, whit about your leaves an such?"

"In a minute, Maggie. First let me see if I can quieten her a little. Oh, Maggie, the Captain's downstairs, better get him up here too." Cate then pulled a chair close to the gasping figure that was Lizzie, talked to her and massaged her shoulders. "Lizzie, it's me, Cate. We'll try and make you more comfortable and then I'll mix something to make your breathing easier."

"Cate", Lizzie wheezed and held her hand out to her friend.

At the next cry Cate gently ran her hands over the pregnant bump as Lizzie rode the wave of pain. A touch on her shoulder made Cate ease away from the bed and relinquish her chair to the Captain. "I'll go and mix something to see if we can ease the congestion. Maggie fears it might be pneumonia and the labour started earlier today." At the Captain's curt nod, Cate left and made her way to the kitchen, where Maggie was boiling water and Cook was airing blankets.

"Maggie, you go up and do what you do best — bring that child into the world. Forget it's Lizzie! Just think about the child."

"Surely the Captain, an him a doctor an all..."

"Fine if he offers, but I'll wager you know more about birthing than he does. What we want from him is any up-to-date remedies for the congestion in her chest. Tell him that, and I'll get what I can from the larder." Cate made her way to the kitchen, mind focused on what to prepare.

"Cook, make some brose, plenty butter and honey in it, and make sure the water is boiling before you mix it. Then put the rest of the water in that wee pan there in the sink and shove it on the stove. Take the brose up and see if Lizzie'll take any. I doubt it, but it's worth a try till I'm ready." Placing a square of muslin in the boiling water on the stove, she went to the larder and collected her tray with her oil preparations. Cate then poured some of the boiling water into a bowl, added a teaspoon of her Craeg Dhu marmalade, plus a few drops of pine and eucalyptus oils, stirring the water as she did until the marmalade had diffused. She heated a cup with the remainder of the boiling water, fished out the muslin, draped it over the cup, and strained her mixture through it.

Initially neither the brose nor the balsam appeared effective, so Cate concentrated on calming Lizzie. At the Captain's suggestion, he got Morrison to take him to the hospital to see if either of the doctors had more knowledge of childbirth than he did. Cate nodded in agreement as she and Maggie prepared for what was going to be a tough fight. Uppermost in both minds was the knowledge that Lizzie was ill, and giving birth with that handicap was fraught with danger.

A little over an hour later the Captain returned with Dr Stirling, and after an initial check, the doctor conferred with them. Although he'd both ether and chloroform, he advised against the use of either, as they could harm the unborn child now that labour was well underway. As the discussion continued, Cate slipped out and collected some cloves and cinnamon from her pantry jars and made a diffusion of them in boiling water. This she added to a good dram of whisky and returned to the room, where she found Maggie alone, the men having retired to the drawing room.

By the early hours of the morning, and helped by several of Cate's concoctions, Lizzie's breathing was less harsh, but her labour was making slow progress, and Cate could see that her friend was nearly at the end of what little strength she had. Although the foetus had dropped, Maggie could see no further advance. As the late September dawn swathed the tip of Beinn Nishe with a milky mist, the men, after a short sleep, reappeared. Soaking his hands once more in the carbolic solution after his examination, Dr Stirling, with a worried expression, addressed the others.

"I'm afraid the problem is her pelvic bones — seem to have a slight deformation in them. Has she had rickets in her childhood?"

Maggie shook her head

"Did she have a period of malnutrition then?"

377

"If you mean did we go hungry? Indeed we did, many's a time. Would that have done it — made the bones wrong?" As she studied the doctor, Maggie knew the answer. "God damn the Gorbals then!" she swore before returning to the job of somehow delivering this child, knowing that her wee Lizzie was in great danger.

"Maggie, Captain, I think we'll leave it a little longer. You never know. Sometimes labours like this do resolve themselves."

"And if this one doesn't, Doctor?"

"Then, Captain, we will have to intervene. Now come, we'll wait downstairs. The ladies will know when to call if we're needed."

The labour dragged on and, as the hours passed, Cate knew something would have to be done. "Maggie, go and get the doctors. They must help you get the child out, anyway they can. Lizzie's fading!"

At Cate's words, Maggie flew down the stairs, cramped legs forgotten in the urge to save Lizzie and her baby. She all but dragged the sleepy men upstairs again and all three looked to Cate.

"Somehow we need to get that child out, forceps or whatever. Even if you have to break the bone to ease the child through, do so."

"Mrs Dinwoodie, my wife she…"

"Captain, I know! But we have two problems here. Lizzie was never strong. Now the pneumonia has complicated matters, and what strength she has is all but used up. Second problem, as doctor Stirling has just explained, it's becoming damn difficult to get your child into this world. I understand the love you have for Lizzie and the fear you have for your child. I know all this is hard to bear. Maggie and the good doctor will do their best for the child, but my focus must be on helping Lizzie to survive. I also know you're sceptical of my healing skills, and you probably doubt my ability to save Lizzie, but please remember she's always been more than dear to me. I've loved her these many years. Your wife is in danger. We have to try what we can. Your child I would be sorry to lose, but I cannot, repeat cannot, lose Lizzie. Captain, whatever happens, trust me. I know what I must do. Maggie?"

"But, Cate, the danger…"

"I know, but Lizzie is a part of me — I am what I am because of her. I must, Maggie. Understand I have no choice! I must!"

As tears rolled down Maggie's face, both men stood perplexed until Cate shouted at them. "Well get on with it, we've no time for thinking. GET THAT CHILD OUT SOMEHOW!"

378

Cate rolled her sleeves up, flexed her hands, steadied herself, and then leant over Lizzie. With no thought as to what was happening at the other end, she brought hands and mind to the task ahead. She knew her superior strength and energy must override the forces that were draining her friend. The warmth began to seep through her hands and upwards to her arms. Her eyes sought Lizzie's face as her hands travelled over the now weak body, and so her battle began.

Lizzie's feeble cry came as a fierce burst of pain almost overwhelmed Cate, making her hands jump, but she forced them back in contact with the surface of Lizzie's body and then she became embroiled in a field of negativity. She fought her way through it, but the deeper she went the stronger she felt the waves of pain herself. There was no going back now.

At the other end of the bed Dr Stirling fought just as hard, manipulating the pelvic bones this way and that, sweat running into his eyes. Maggie wiped his brow, as she stood ready to help, while Lizzie's cries grew fainter. But at long last the Doctor managed to ease the head and then the shoulders through, and the baby slid into the world. After that, Maggie did what was necessary and handed the scrap of life to the Captain.

"Your son, Captain."

"What about Lizzie — my wife —will she live?"

"Captain, I know you an Cate dinna see eye-to-eye, but trust me, she'll save her if she can," Maggie comforted him.

"But she's doing nothing! Look at her — what good are her precious hands we hear so much about? Just how effective do you think they're going to be? Dr Stirling surely there is something you can do? Proper medical aid instead of all this weird witchcraft stuff!"

At this Dr Stirling suggested, "Captain, why don't you carry your son downstairs and I'll follow with the crib. Our medical aid will be required anon, but for now, your wife's best chance is with the woman who believes she can arrest the fading life source of her beloved friend, and Maggie here must attend to cleansing the uterus."

A reluctant Captain left followed by the doctor. As she worked, Maggie glanced at the silent figures almost entwined at the top of the bed. With one life saved, she knew that two more were in danger. Her Lizzie lay there as if she was dead already. And what of the other one she'd come to love over the years, the pregnant tinker girl she'd watched

379

take on the world? Later, as a defiant young woman, she'd stood in her Gorbals flat and vowed never to forget them, swore that wherever she went they'd come with her. Maggie had never believed her, though she'd hoped it might happen. Throughout all the misunderstanding that followed, Cate and Lizzie had held true to one another. Only she had doubted. Well, they'd indeed come with her, and now would she be the one to be left behind? Maggie couldn't stop the tears. How could she ever have doubted Cate's love for Lizzie? But would that love now cost Cate her life?

As the morning wore on the missing members of the family, sent away by Maggie the previous day, returned in straggling groups. Charlie and Hansi, along with the twins, had spent the time in Charlie's home way beyond the village. The boys had enjoyed the strangeness of the little cottage, the experience of playing with nothing more than their imagination, and tucking into the large bed to sleep under the eaves of the turf roof, head to toe with the other children. The two men slept in the fireside chairs and had porridge with bread and dripping ready for the children as they woke. Then they made their leisurely way to the stable block at Craigavon, where the twins helped Charlie groom the foal and put her in the field.

The men, with no idea how things were in the house, thought it best to take the boys on a ramble. Charlie left the twins and Hansi with the foal, and went to get some picnic food from the kitchen. He was upset when he heard of Lizzie's problems. He'd always had a connection to her as they'd both suffered broken legs when young. He had been luckier than her as his had set well, so he hoped she'd be the one to be lucky now. But he was also worried when he heard that Cate was somehow trying to save her friend. He'd heard enough rumours about his Mistress to know that there were things she could do in healing that involved danger to herself. He well remembered how, almost nine months pregnant, she'd gone scrambling down the rock fall to save Wullie, digging him out almost single-handedly, with no thought of danger to herself, never mind the unborn babe —or babies, as it turned out!

Later on Kirsty, along with young Murdo, brought Shona and Iona back from the village, where they'd stayed the night with her. The younger children played with the little enamel bowls that Cook gave them until their lunch was ready. Once fed, the toddlers were put down to sleep. Although food was offered to the men in the drawing room, neither could face it. Kirsty ventured upstairs with a tray Cook had prepared, but not wishing to disturb them, gave a faint knock and left it at the door.

It was enough to wake Maggie, who'd been overcome by sleep. She took a moment to focus before she made for the door. Then, at the weak cry of 'Mammy', she turned and stumbled over to the bed. Through her tears, she mouthed, 'thank God' as she bent to stroke her daughter's forehead. Both were overwhelmed by the moment, and in their emotion the silent form still laid across Lizzie's body was forgotten. It was only as the new mother tried to sit up that the full horror of the situation struck.

"Oh my God, Lizzie — Cate!" Maggie dropped her daughter's hands and felt for Cate's pulse. She could find none. Next she felt her forehead: it was cold!

"What's she doing there, Mammy? Is she asleep?" Lizzie then remembered her labour. "The bairn! Is it here? Did it live? Where's my man? I need to see him!"

"Oh Lizzie! Wheesht for a minute! We man see to Cate first."

"What's the matter with her? What's going on here?" Lizzie stared at her mother, unable to understand why she was behaving in such a strange way. Then, jumping to her own conclusions, she looked round the room and, seeing no crib, spoke between sobs. "The bairn's deid! So it is? What was it, Mammy? What are we going to tell Ewan?"

"Stop! Leave the questions for later! There's something the matter with Cate an we need to help her. She saved you, an now…" Maggie broke off! It was as if the whisper of a light breeze had caught her attention, so faint she thought she'd imagined it. She leant closer and all she heard was the sound of silence. Now both women watched and waited. The movement, when it came, was as insubstantial as the sound.

Maggie, with her prior knowledge of what Cate had done with Gregor, expected Cate to wake up now, but there was no sign of that. The ripples of movement in the body were so indistinct that neither watcher realised what was happening. Little by little it seemed that Cate's body was transformed from a corpse–like state to a living one. The women slowly let out the breath that they'd inadvertently been holding, and were about to embrace Cate when it became obvious that all was not well. It took many long minutes before the situation became clear. Cate did not wake up! She tossed and turned, wheezed and fretted. Unable to believe what she was seeing, Maggie felt the forehead that she feared would now be burning, and it was!

Chapter 45

As September gave way to October, the guns of war continued to fire, bringing yet more devastation to the battlefields, In Kevinishe, the village watched, prayed and waited to see if Miss Cate would win her battle against the pneumonia that raged now as pleurisy. Only those few at Craigavon knew the full truth of the situation. The rest of the village warned one another that trips to Glasgow were more dangerous than they'd ever imagined. Those who'd seen the party depart to the big city for the memorial service reminded everybody that Miss Cate had been her usual bouncing self as she left. She'd been away a mere forty-eight hours. How could she be felled with such a serious illness in that time?

There were some who talked of the hospital that she'd set up once the war had claimed Murdo. The village pondered on this and the journey she'd made to rescue the Major. She'd not only brought him back, but also, rumour had it, bullied the man an him with half his leg missing, into operating on a patient while she helped. They all knew she had *The Second Sight* and wondered at these coincidences.

It seemed to those in Kevinishe: that the woman who'd forced the men to let her work in the distillery, saved the old ones from being evicted, almost died when the young laird had had the old Black House burned down, and fallen foul of the Meenister for burying Fisher in the distillery grounds, was once again on the verge of being taken from them. Over the years they'd come to understand that their Miss Cate, the little tinker girl they'd once shunned, had become their unlikely saviour. Without her, the distillery, the village, and they, would face an uncertain future. Ill though she was, at least she was still in Kevinishe, and perhaps that would make a difference. In case it might help, the majority sent their pleas heavenward with a fervour the Meenister would have applauded.

Meanwhile the Captain, with the ordeal of his son's birth over and his wife slowly returning to good health, was at the end of his compassionate leave and had to return to his duties. Dinwoodie, summoned from the Glasgow foundry, unaware of the true facts about events in Craigavon, was dismayed on his arrival to find Cate was in the hospital. After a rushed meal, and worried about his wife, he had Morrison drive him there to see Cate. On the ground floor he ran into the Major, who told him he believed that Cate's infection had begun as pneumonia and developed into pleurisy. There was, though, a slight chance that her illness could be part of the terrible flu epidemic that'd first struck in the spring of that year. Although it'd faded over the summer months, it was back now in these autumn days, with a changed form from the original that was much more deadly.

Dinwoodie listened carefully as he was made to understand that the pandemic was spreading fast. The Major told him it was hardly surprising, what with all the moving and intermingling of the soldiers on the battle fronts, plus the coming and going of troops home on leave. This particular version was knocking out swathes of people in most countries. Though it was originally called 'The Spanish Flu' because it had so devastated that country, the general opinion now was that perhaps it had originated in Asia. Wherever it had come from, the trouble was that in most people this strain began with just a cough, chill, or cold, and victims didn't realise that these familiar symptoms were also the signs of the deadly disease, by which time it was too late.

"My God! What are you saying? Cate can't die!"

"Mr Dinwoodie, I was talking in general medical terms to give you a clear picture of the battle we're fighting. Your wife was brought here and put in isolation as soon as her symptoms were obvious, just in case it is the flu. We're watching her very carefully, dosing her to relieve the pain and reduce her fever. As soon as I can say it is a straightforward case of pleurisy, bad though that is, and she shows signs of recovery, you will be welcome to visit her. I'm sure she should pull through."

"Thank you for all of that. Now where can I find my wife, Major?"

"You've not been listening, Mr Dinwoodie. I've already explained — she's been isolated, and it would be a considerable risk for you to see her there."

"Major, it's my wife we're talking about. A fine husband I would be if I left her to fight this battle alone."

"She is not alone. She's under constant surveillance and the minute I can be sure that she is not carrying the flu germs you will be informed."

"Major, let me speak plainly — although the army is currently renting the house, it is mine and I will not be banned from it. I intend to see my wife and, if she has this influenza, then I'll take my chances. I would rather die with Cate than be left without her. It may not be very manly, but I need to see her as much for myself as for her. Now, either you tell me how to get there, or I'll go into every nook and cranny, and bother everyone, till I find her."

Under the pressure the Major relented. Dinwoodie sat by Cate's bed watching this fevered version of the woman he loved. His mind fled back to the time he'd once before been to her hospital bed, and it was there he'd finally admitted to himself he was falling in love. Now he held her hot hand as images of the past years floated through his mind: the unwelcome memories of their bad moments, the delight of their making up, the joy that this wonderful, exasperating, stubborn woman, who at times was a steely opponent and at others almost a frolicsome child, had given him on becoming his wife. He fondled the red hair that was lying lank on the pillow and, with no response but the restless delirium, he was forced to admit, however unwillingly, that this time she might not make it.

As the hours dragged on, the torment, as he watched her bedevilled by pain and struggling with rasping breaths, had him on his feet easing her upwards in forlorn attempts to help her, hold her. It was useless. They were in two separate worlds. Hers spun in that grey mass, inhabited by pills and potions, fevers and pains that was the interval between the colours of the world and death's midnight darkness.

By nightfall, the Major and Mary Anne agreed he had to leave. Because she knew the man, she agreed to approach him, but asked the Major to contact Craigavon first and get Morrison to come and fetch him, and warn Cook to have food ready for him. It was not a task she relished but, as she approached the bed, Mary Anne could not contain her anxiety any longer.

"Mr Dinwoodie, you're of little use here for now."

"Dammit, Mary Anne, she's my wife! I must be with her."

"Mary, Jesus and Joseph, do you think I don't understand your love for the woman? The way you feel her pain? Sure and aren't the rest of us here, those at Craigavon, indeed the entire village, not down on our knees appealing to any saint we can remember who just might be the saving of her?"

She watched him lift the twitching hands with such care to his lips, bury his face there and wash them with his silent tears. With a lump in her throat, medical instincts were forgotten for the moment, as she witnessed the great love this man had for her friend, but common sense had to prevail and she continued to badger him, as she knew she must. She laid her hand on his shoulders and with a stern voice said, "You're not only putting yourself in danger here, as long as we can't be certain it isn't the flu, but what about the young ones at home, to say nothing of Maggie, Cook, and Lizzie only just out of her birthing bed. You've no right to endanger them or yourself. That poor woman, laying there struggling to cope, will need a healthy husband when she recovers."

"She'll recover, Mary Anne?"

"And isn't that the daftest of questions, and you married to her? If anyone can fight this, it's our Cate. So come on, you. Morrison is down below waiting, but a word of caution as you go. You were at the memorial in Glasgow with those other ones from the war, same as Cate. If you feel at all unwell, see you and be sure to get yourself back here. I trust the Good God will see you safe, but watch yourself now."

Back at Craigavon, Dinwoodie sat at the kitchen table toying with the late supper Cook had prepared, almost unaware of the deafening silence as the two woman watched him. Maggie could bear it no longer.

"She's no better then?" She asked. Daft really — she knew the answer before the sad shake of his head. She'd spoken because she needed to know if he was at all suspicious about Cate's sudden illness. Ever since the 'episode' as she called it, her mind had suffered an anguished torment of guilt for withholding the true reason for Cate's illness. But she knew that Cate would want it this way, and if, God forbid, her friend died, she'd just have to bear the burden of silence till the graveyard beckoned her.

"The Major has explained about the illness, Maggie. He believes there is a chance that Cate picked up the flu germs on our visit to Glasgow. It was a typically risky situation, a large community in one space mixing with those returned from the front who might be carrying the germs. I just can't believe it's all happened so quickly"

"But, Mr Dinwoodie, what about yourself? You were there too."

"You're right there, Cook." Maggie answered for him. "An whit about my Lizzie's man for one, an them from Laggan House. You'll all need to be watched, so you will."

"Indeed we will, Maggie. Mary Anne told me off in the hospital about just that. My shock at Cate's sudden illness made me forget that she's an entire community in love with her, all as desperate as I am to see her recover."

"It's sleep you'll be needing now. All the rest are long gone to bed. Oh, I forgot to tell you: Lizzie's had a wee boy and they've called him Ewan James after the Captain and the Brigadier. Two important men for the scrap of a bairn that he is to live up to, I'm thinking. An another thing, yon Hansi's made such a difference to those boys of yours. Quiet he is, but somehow he's made them understand all these new rules Cate's laid down. Between him and Charlie it's as if they've magicked them somehow, and by the time outside antics are done, the pair are fair wabbit by the evening! Now whit else did I have to remember? That's it! There's one of they foreign letters on your desk."

With a forced smile to her, Dinwoodie made his way to his study. He couldn't face the empty bedroom or even his daughter's nursery. However, he did feel glad that Lizzie had managed to give birth despite her fears. He wondered if Cate knew how Lizzie had been dreading it. To distract his tired mind he opened the latest letter from the Scribbler.

The Hindenberg Line, 1918

Dearest Girl,

It's late September now and the Allies have broken through the Hindenberg line and are advancing rapidly over open country. Will this be the point where the retreating Germans sue for peace? I know I must sound pessimistic, but will they? I believe they'd like nothing better, but when you consider that for the greater part of this war they have been dominant, they won't want to walk away with nothing.

They may struggle on as the Allies head for the German border, but the military here think October must see them ask for a ceasefire.

Let's hope it will be sooner rather than later. I doubt there's anyone fighting who could stand another winter

Dinwoodie put the letter in a drawer, rose to the window, and stared into the blackness of the night. Here they were, the three of them prisoners of the eternal triangle. The Scribbler, his love torn from him because of a living lie, marooned in the war that he felt could deliver him success as a writer, but fighting illness too, and himself, more successful and richer because of the unbelievable killing, but now beset by the horror of perhaps losing his wife, not as he'd feared to the Scribbler but to some filthy illness that was taking her very breath away. At last he turned but, reluctant to go to the empty bedroom, he collapsed in his wing-backed chair and hoped for sleep to overcome him.

The roaring of an October storm sweeping down from Beinn Nishe awoke him. For a moment he fantasised that the mountain too knew of her illness and was lashing the glen below in fury, and the thought cheered him. Somehow the howling gale mirrored the screaming protests in his mind that he was unable to utter. Weary and unwashed he made his way to the empty bedroom, to clean up and change.

In the kitchen, as the day got underway, children and adults took turns to peer out at the storm. The boys ran around indoors waving their arms, echoing the blowing sounds from outside, until Hansi thought it was time to calm then down. He settled them down at the table, much to Cook's relief, as she'd no desire to scald them with a coating of hot porridge or boiling tea. Hadn't she had scunner enough already this morning with the draughts from the chimney sending loose soot onto the stove surface? She'd begun to ladle out the porridge when the door opened and Dinwoodie appeared. The excited boys rushed to greet their lone parent with cries of, 'Where's Mama'? Aware of their unease with Cate missing, he gave them each a huge hug and settled them down again either side of him.

Shona and Iona, were next to appear and as everyone shuffled chairs to make room, all eyes were on Dinwoodie. He realised they were seeking reassurance from him, so he did the best he could.

"She was still fevered when I saw her yesterday, but the Major assured me she will pull through." As the combined sighs of relief swept over him like a shooshing wave hitting the seashore, he reverted to the childhood trick of crossing his fingers under the table in the hope that his disregard for the truth might be forgiven.

"Are you fine squashed up there, Mr Dinwoodie? I can serve you in the dining room." Maggie suggested.

"I'd rather be here with the family. We all miss her and together we'll have to help one another in our sorrow till she returns." He was rewarded with a boy squeezing each arm and Iona babbling away in her toddler language, arms outstretched to him.

Down in London the weather was equally foul. Pearson could feel the rain trickling beneath his collar as he pretended to look into a somewhat grubby newsagent's window. His eyes were all the time fixed on the reflection of the rundown building opposite. After leaving the Highlands he'd at last picked up McPhail's trail in Glasgow. Because his employer felt that Rhoddy might have been repatriated down south, it meant that by following his quarry when he entrained for London, he was in the right place to ferret out any information on the man and perhaps get lucky and discover Rhoddy as well. He moved away up the street a little and then, since the man had still not appeared, retraced his footsteps. This time he went into the shop, bought a paper, and began to read it in the shelter of the doorway.

It was some time before McPhail appeared on the pavement, and Pearson had barely memorised the words the Highlander threw over his shoulder to someone in the building before he set off at a sharp pace, splashing through the gutter to overtake those in front of him. The man was obviously intent on going somewhere and, as he followed at a discreet distance, Pearson ran through the words he'd caught, 'mistakes' — 'time' — 'café' The tone had been threatening, so could the unseen person inside have been working in some way for McPhail? Had he failed him? He continued to ponder over the words while keeping both his distance and his eye on his quarry.

The rusted sign hung crookedly on the wall, sending rivulets of gathered rain on those below. 'Big Mal's' wasn't exactly a fount of information, but was all that was decipherable on the waving piece of rusty metal as it creaked and groaned with every whiff of wind. McPhail had no hesitation in entering and, as Pearson passed the doorway he glimpsed the inside of a shoddy café and smelt the rancid smell of fat that should have been changed weeks ago. Now this was interesting.

Why was a man who could afford the sleeper from Glasgow to London, eating here? Consumed by curiosity Pearson trudged on until he found a spot that gave him a view of the place. He did not have long to wait before McPhail reappeared.

Pearson followed him as he retraced his steps and vanished into the shabby building once more. Sometime later he re-emerged and Pearson heard him hail a cab and direct it to an hotel. Confident now that any business of the day had been concluded, Pearson made his way to find a cheaper bed for the night and puzzle over the man's movements.

Chapter 46

As October faded into November in the French countryside, Alashdair, recovering from yet another bronchial attack, struggled outside. With this latest lung infection he'd been unable to leave the small farm, which had been his infrequent wartime home, for days. Today his breathing was a little better, so he sat outside in the weak sunlight dandling his daughter on his knees, while he watched Marthe lift the remnants of their potato patch. In these last bewildering days, as everyone waited for the ceasefire to become reality, the booming of the heavy guns in the far distance confirmed that it was still war, hateful war. When would it end? What then?

Alashdair's thought's returned to the day he'd breathed the dreaded German gas. He'd been well looked after then, better than he'd deserved really, as he shouldn't have been so near the Front in the first place, so in a way it was his own fault he'd been plagued ever since by recurrent chest problems. This one had been the worst yet. The war years had exacted a heavy toll for him, both physically and emotionally. Writing consecutive episodes of his intended war novel, while reporting on the action from the Western Front, had been the method he'd chosen to forget his great love for Cate McAlister, but it had come at a price.

He'd come across Marthe, a French war widow with an out-of-the-way farmhouse, when he'd discovered her being beaten by a drunken man. All his pent-up fury about the damned senseless killing he saw around him erupted at this treatment of a woman. He pulled the man off and squared up to him but he got the worst of it until Marthe managed to hand him a stick she'd found by the roadside and he'd brought it down on his opponent's head. They'd dragged the limp body to some nearby scrub and rolled it over the slight incline out of sight. Marthe then offered to see to his damaged face, and he'd followed her home, only too glad to be well away from the stunned man.

After that first night, when they'd used each other to forget their current horrors, he'd returned as often as he could to help out on the farm, while using it as a base to get his writing up-to-date. When she discovered she was pregnant, he'd left the writing drafts and spent more time on his war reporting for the American newspaper, to provide money and labour for the farm. In a perfect world the baby girl he'd helped Marthe deliver would have been Cate's, but that was neither Marthe's nor little Elize's fault. He wasn't sure whether it was because a ceasefire was now only a question of time, or if it was a result of the increasing trouble with his chest, but his thoughts turned to a future for both his daughter and Marthe. Her sons, whom he'd only met occasionally, would be home again, this time for good, when the fighting ceased.

He'd seen more than once what family members did to women who'd slept with foreigners, in many cases so they could feed their children. It was not pleasant and he wished Marthe no harm. She'd already warned him that without the presence of their father, she had no desire to remain as her sons' domestic slave. Indeed she felt too tired to even look after his daughter, the child she'd never intended to have. At the start of their sporadic affair, they'd both agreed they would go their separate ways at the end of the war. With no family to his name, now that Scottie and his daughter were dead, who would care for Elize if he perished?

As he began to feel the heat drain from the day, the coughing returned, and he took his anxious thoughts and his precious daughter and sought the warmth indoors. He let Elize play on the floor while he poured her some milk from the pitcher. He was always amused at the way she drank. She put the cup to her lips and glugged and glugged till she'd swallowed the lot, then gave a great sigh to signify she'd finished. He took the cup and tousled her mop of black curls just as Marthe came in, and then went to fetch water from the well and wood from the barn, before the day darkened. While finishing his other tasks he decided he'd talk over his thoughts about their future with Marthe later. He'd no fresh news for a letter to Kevinishe, so perhaps he would try to get back to his writing tonight, when Marthe had gone to bed.

Back in the Kevinishe hospital the Major and Doctor Stirling were also considering an uncertain future for those patients who'd almost completed their rehabilitation. They both knew that, with the ending of hostilities, the workplace would be flooded with demobbed men looking to take up the jobs they'd left, sometimes willingly, to become soldiers and join the great adventure. As Mary Anne joined the discussion, she reminded them that a fair number of the jobs formerly done by those men had been farmed out to women for the duration of the war. "I can't see they'll be over-ready to give up the wages they've had to themselves for months on end. If it were my decision I'd get as many of those men in the wards to the nearest demob centre and home to claim their old jobs, as soon as possible, assuming they're capable of doing them of course."

At this point Morag came rushing in, spilling her words out in all the wrong order.

"Mercy me!" Mary Anne silenced her. "What in the name of heaven's come over you, lass?"

"Oh Mary Anne, it's — while I — there was speaking — from the room..."

"Who, Morag? You're making no sense." It was then that Mary Anne saw the duster in her hand and, realised she'd been doing the corridors. She shot to her feet, grabbed Morag by the shoulders and demanded, "Cate! Is it Cate who's after talking?" At Morag's relieved nod, Mary Anne was up and running.

She halted at the doorway, but hearing no sound from within, wondered if the ward maid had been mistaken. Just in case she had heard something, Mary Anne opened the door and walked softly to Cate's bed. The covers were fankled, so typical hospital nurse she began to set them right. It was as she folded back the topmost cover ready to tuck it in that her eyes met Cate's. Afraid to believe that the crisis was past, Mary Anne watched and silently renewed her pleas to St. Juliana, the saint for the critically ill. It was then that Cate tried with little success to lift her head. Mary Anne was there in a flash. Sturdy arms round the almost fleshless bones, she gently eased Cate into the sitting position and packed pillows behind to prevent her sliding down again. Next she poured water from the jug into the glass and held it while Cate sipped.

"Oh Cate, you poor thing! Haven't you just had the frightening of us all!. The praying that's gone on here while you've been sick must have delighted the Holy Father!"

Cate tried to mumble something, but the effort was too much. Despite Mary Anne's pillows, she slid down the bed and closed her eyes. Mary Anne waited for a moment. When she was sure Cate was still breathing and had gone to sleep, she hurried off to tell the others that the crisis might have passed. The Major received the news with a frown.

"Well now, Major, I wasn't expecting you to jump up and down, what with the woodwork on you an all, but sure an wouldn't a smile help?"

"Sorry, Mary Anne. Of course I'm delighted. It's just that Doctor Stirling has been alerted by Donald Uig that there's sickness in the village, and he's gone to investigate."

"Sure an wouldn't you think we'd enough troubles about our ears? Tis the influenza he's afraid of, isn't it?"

"We'll know for certain when he returns, but in the meantime I think we'll at least make plans to follow up on your suggestion to alert the army that most of the men can be allowed home. Since they're of little use on the battlefield, it will be demob and civilian life anyway. And at this rate we may have to admit sick villagers next! We can't leave them in their homes."

"Speaking of homes, what about Neil?"

"I'm afraid Cate was dealing with that, though I've no idea if she'd anything planned. In the meantime I'll relieve the orderly, sit up with her for a bit and give the situation some more thought."

When Donald Uig knocked on the door of the little lime-washed but-an-ben, Doctor Stirling entered, but motioned him to stay outside. Blinking blearily in the peat-smoked atmosphere, the Doctor stared at the throng in the room, most of them elderly. His eyes were inextricably pulled, not to the body of the sick man in the wall bed that Donald Uig had brought him to see, but to the shrunken person at the centre of the proceedings. In his sixties now he himself felt old, but the sight of parchment skin barely containing the projecting bones, claws fumbling the edges of a black shawl that seemed to cover her tiny frame in its entirety, spoke of another dimension of age. A series of questions asked, and then an examination of the man's body, confirmed his diagnosis.

How could he tell this centenarian, who'd lived way beyond the normal span, that the male relative she was staring at, generations younger than her, was dead? Indeed, with the bulk of the black-clothed guests, at what had been intended as a party for the old woman, wreathed in hazy fumes of peat, still and silent as they crowded the walls of the room like some macabre wallpaper, in this small space Doctor Stirling couldn't find his voice, so he shook his head in sorrow. But that was enough.

The pageant of black transformed itself into an overpowering wave of language that flowed around the room, and for a moment the doctor felt as though he'd drown in it.

He cleared his throat and held up his hand for silence. "I'm afraid I do not have the Gaelic. Does anyone speak English?"

"Why did he die? It was but a bad cold he had." A middle-aged man stepped forward as he asked his question.

"I'm afraid it was much more than that. I know this is a sad end to what should have been a celebration. But I need some information. Did the young man live in the village?"

"That he did not. Came all the way from the south he did, and now he'll have wasted the return fare. But you can be sure we'll no waste the food. It'll do just fine for the funeral, and any bits of mould can go the hens."

"How long has he been here?"

"He brought the cold with him, but then what else could he do? The old woman there has forgotten more than he's ever known. It was a great thing this party. From the many glens they've come, and hasn't everyone been boarded out nights for sleeping. Even Hamish over there was in the henhouse." This was followed by a guffaw of laughter, aimed the nodding Hamish.

"I'm very sorry for your loss, but it's my duty to warn you that I believe he died of the flu."

"Well now, an him a sturdy young man to be felled by the flu! Haven't we all had the same, and still did the tending of the croft, the fishing an the making of the whisky." This was accompanied by vigorous nodding. The Doctor wondered if he'd crossed some invisible barrier into a mystic world. The panoply of emotions and language the crowd of Gaels went through before him was beyond his understanding. The laughter, the unused return ticket, the decision to keep the birthday food for the funeral, all washed around him while he tried to make sure that they understood the possible danger they were in. Because the cause of death had undoubtedly been Influenza, it meant he'd have to isolate them. At these words they all turned to Hamish and suggested that he start laying eggs since an extended stay would put the hens off their laying!

Unable to cope, the Doctor made for the door and was delighted to see the sane and sensible Donald Uig awaiting him. The fresh air, the normality of the coast road, the gentle waving of the machair above the sand and the soothing sound of the waves splashing on the shingle restored his equilibrium. He confirmed to the malt man from the distillery that it was almost certainly the dangerous strain of influenza, and explained the restrictions that needed to be put in place. Then they discussed the difficulty of segregating the party group from the rest of the village, and the possible spread throughout the community.

"All of this must be explained to them, and see what you can do to keep any who had no contact with the party members well away for the immediate future."

"I'll see to it, Doctor. And about Miss Cate, is there any change?"

"I wish I could say there was, but I do believe it is pleurisy, not influenza. Now I must get back to the hospital. By the way I appreciate your contacting me. Immediacy is an important tool in the fight against the epidemic."

With a nod, Donald Uig waited till the vehicle was out of sight and then set about carrying out he Doctor's instructions.

Chapter 47

McPhail had had a sleepless night. Ever since Bruce MacNishe's funeral, he'd felt so close to the MacNishe wealth that he could see himself in Kevinishe House with Rhoddy. No wonder that woman had lied! She was another one who wanted the MacNishe wealth. Well he was dammed if he was going to be denied his claim to the family's inheritance, which must now become Rhoddy's. If the Dic he'd hired was right, and there was something amiss with the boy, he would need a guardian, and who better then than his only male relative? The woman would make a fuss, continue to claim it was all hers, but who would believe it with her background? The boy had run away from home after all!

It was not so much that his conscience was bothering him. It was the intricacies of the plan he'd hammered out with that oaf of a café owner. He was the outsider here. The Dic had said that the man with Rhoddy was over-friendly with Big Mal. Would he double-cross him? The money he'd paid with the bonus if it all worked out, should be enough, shouldn't it? He hoped so. Spreading money around was not his style. He'd no stomach for breakfast this morning, so he finished his coffee, scooped up the morning papers intended for the dining room guests, tucked them under his arm, and made for his room, enjoying the fact that he'd saved himself a few pence, even though he'd left the paper tray blank for the latecomers to the dining room.

Pacing in his room he confronted the one fact that had worried him from the beginning. He would be a fool to underestimate Dinwoodie. The man moved in high circles. He'd been astonished to read in the paper that the Lord Chief Justice had been in Kevinishe for a wedding. Neither of those two would he wish to cross. He flicked through the pages of the Times, but couldn't concentrate. He'd an urgent need for action. Dare he make for the café area? His worries multiplied as he went over the timing again. Four hours at least to wait before he went to the hire company. He'd be the better of getting some sleep. He'd try, but if that didn't work, he'd get out. Walk about. Do some sightseeing.

Pearson on the other hand had been well fed in the guest house by his London landlady, and with a sprightly air, thankful for dry weather, made for the vicinity of McPhail's hotel. This morning a flower stall had been erected on the other side of the road and he stood and chatted to the owner while keeping an eye across the street. A number of hotel guests crossed the road and, as a bunch of them crowded around the stall, he nearly missed his quarry.

When he left the hotel, McPhail not only didn't call a cab but also started to walk in the wrong direction. Pearson's early morning buzz deserted him and a feeling of anxiety took its place. He knew of old that once villains altered their habits, they'd either spotted him and were throwing a false trail, or they'd abandoned the original plan. Indecision rattled him for a moment, but his investigative hunch had him trail the man anyway. Provided he kept a sharp eye on him, McPhail wouldn't get the better of him, whatever he was about.

Hours of pointless walking had Pearson confused. What was the man up to? Whenever he'd trailed him before, each move had been made with a purpose in mind. Now he was behaving like a tourist! Not only that but a maniacal one to boot. He'd aim for somewhere, look at it, turn back on himself, and then go and look at something he'd seen earlier! He was taking no interest in anything but the time. Was he due to meet someone? Pearson thought about it for a moment then dismissed the idea. Not in this area he wasn't. Too public, and then his gait was wrong too: his steps were erratic, body twitchy. It was as though — OF COURSE — he was all charged up! This messing about, back and forth, was to fill in time. The man was about to make some type of move, and by God, this time Mr Dinwoodie would get the information he wanted!

The walking pattern continued under a weak midday sun, and Pearson was beginning to suffer from boredom. It reminded him of that first long-gone day when he'd at last achieved a client. For the next three weeks he'd trampled round the city following a moneyman who seemed to be cheating on his wife. When he'd reported back that the man was doing nothing more dishonest than working all hours in search of promotion, the woman refused to pay him, because he'd not proved the husband was having an affair! It was a hard lesson and from then on he'd demanded the money up front, before he agreed to take the job. And some of the jobs he'd had were terrible.

His investigative life took a turn for the better when a younger Mr Dinwoodie came to his Glasgow office asking him to find his relatives.

He'd liked the man on sight. There was a straight-forwardness about him, all the information out in the open. That job had lasted but a few weeks and the news he'd had to give the man had not been good — all relatives dead in a house fire.

Pearson realised he'd been distracted by thoughts of the past, and jerked his concentration back to his quarry. For a moment he thought he'd lost him, but caught the tail end of him as he dodged out of sight down a narrow lane. Cursing himself, Pearson hurried forward, taking care not to dash down the lane in case McPhail was trying to catch him out. However the man was not interested in what was behind him: he was making straight for a car hire firm sign. Within minutes he reappeared from the office dangling car keys and a piece of paper in his hands. Pearson waited till the lane was clear and then raced down just in time to see McPhail turn into a nearby parking lot and let himself into what looked like a red cab.

As he roared away Pearson showed his anger by kicking the nearby wall bruising his toe! With McPhail gone he walked in the direction the car had taken, unsure as yet what to do. After much thought he could see he'd no real alternative, so he'd have to return to the known area of interest, Big Mal's Café.

As it happened Grabber and Rhoddy were almost finished their meal in the empty Café. Big Mal watched them go the washroom and then he locked the café door. He wasn't about to enjoy the next few minutes. Extra notes couldn't be ignored, but then neither could loyalty. But his plan wouldn't quite run along the same lines as the Highlander's. He fetched the old wooden mallet some geezer had left behind, and made for the backroom, then the washroom. Grabber was using the facilities to have a good wash, but Rhoddy stood, sullen expression on his face, making no move to clean up.

It took no more than a moment for the mallet to connect with the back of Grabber's head, for Big Mal to catch him, lift him, and dump him in the nearby broom cupboard, where he locked the door and put the key in his pocket. The boy, eyes wide, mouth open, said not a word as the owner walked past, through the door of the backroom, lock it, bring the brown stained blinds on the window down, and turn the 'open' sign to 'closed'. Then he sat and waited.

It didn't take long before the red cab pulled up and McPhail got out and hammered on the door. Big Mal didn't hurry to unlock the door and let the man in, then he locked it again.

"What kept you? This has got to be done swiftly. That's what I paid you for."

"True enough, Gov'ner, and now, before I hands him over, I'll have the payment for the rest of the deal." Big Mal straightened up, eyeballed McPhail. "I knows what you're thinking: big old stupid me can be double-crossed."

"As if I..."

"Let's not mess about, Gov'ner. 'and over the notes, I'll count them and then I'll give you the boy, otherwise —." he bunched his massive paw, waved it in front of McPhail's face, and held the other one out for the money. With that silent threat McPhail slipped his hand inside his jacket and pulled out a wad of paper money. The Café owner spat on his fingers and leafed expertly through them before stuffing the lot into his crumpled apron pocket. For a big man he moved quickly, first to unlock the main door, then the backroom, and into the washroom. He scooped up the terrified boy and flung him over his shoulder. With McPhail opening both main and car doors, it took but a minute for the boy to be flung on the backseat, and for McPhail to jump in the driver's seat and vanish down the street.

As he drove, the stale smell of urine revolted him, but there was no sound from the boy. With a satisfied smile, he accelerated and made his way to the opposite side of London, passing through the very streets he'd pounded earlier in the day. He was soon out of the city centre, headed towards a poorer area of North London, where he'd hired a room. With difficulty, he managed to get Rhoddy inside and was grateful that the boy did in fact appear to be dumb, for he made not a sound — just stared at him with a terrified look on his face. For a second, the reality of what he'd done almost overwhelmed McPhail, but there was no going back now. He needed to return the hire car, and get back here as quickly as possible. So he drove back across London to the parking lot, locked the car and took the keys to the office.

"How was the old lady then, sir?"

"As I told you earlier today, very poorly. They say in the nursing home she could go any day. So it was good to have this last visit and say goodbye — more for me than her, you understand. She only just recognised me for a few minutes at a time, mind wandering back and forth. The last of my family, I'm afraid, so, as there's no one much to mourn, I'll leave all that to the nursing home. Sad old day!" He finished with a weary sigh.

The hire owner watched the big man walk away with a jaunty step. He'd had a history of iffy stories told him in the old hire business. There was nothing sad about that customer now. The whole story didn't seem to hang together somehow. He'd better check the cab was still there. Motors had been stolen without keys before. He was relieved to see all was well, but wasn't so pleased about the whiff of urine on the back seat. Perhaps the Scotsman had taken the old woman for a drive and was telling the truth after all.

McPhail walked on to get as far away from the hire office as possible before he hailed a cab to take him to the station. He paid the Cabby, said he'd be glad to get back to Edinburgh, and went inside, only to walk straight through and head for the bus station, where he took a bus and, returned to Rhoddy

By the end of that evening, Pearson discovered the owner of the unseen voice in the house that McPhail had visited the day before had gone. The landlady thought he'd been some kind of traveller, as he was always out, though she'd never seen him with a case apart from when he'd rented the room and when he left. He almost knew that, when he reached the café, it too would be shut up. At least it only said 'closed', so perhaps he'd have better luck in the morning.

After a restless night he even failed to be buoyed up by the landlady's good breakfast and cheerful chatter. However, when he arrived at the café and found it open, his mood lifted. He ordered a bacon sandwich he didn't want and a mug of tea. He took as long as he possibly could over them as he watched the clientele come and go, but no McPhail. He left and made his way to the hotel where the Highlander was staying. A lengthy wait around there also proved unfruitful. He crossed to the newsagent's, bought a paper, then walked some distance away and came back on the other side of the road. A young lad was polishing the brass on the hotel entrance as he drew near and, taking a chance, he let the paper slip onto the steps, and the youngster bent down and returned it.

"Thank you. Sorry about that. Got a good shine going there. My friend'll appreciate that when he comes out." Pearson looked at his watch. "Bit late this morning. Wonder why?"

"I'll go and check. Name?"

"Good of you. McPhail."

A few moments later the boy returned, looking very downcast. "I'm ever so sorry, but he's gone."

"That's a shame. I'll have to catch up with him later."

"No, I mean he's checked out. Not coming back — gone home, you see."

"Well I'll be damned! He could have warned me. Not your fault. Here, have this for your help."

"Thank you, sir."

Pearson walked on a little, changed his mind and, avoiding the hotel front, made his way back to the café. He waved the newspaper at the counter, ordered his tea and settled down for the duration. He would come back time and time again, newspaper in front of his face, till he became part of the scene.

This trail went back years: McPhail's early threats to Mrs Dinwoodie, the presence of either him or an employee following Rhoddy in France, his attendance at MacNishe's funeral, and finally threatening Mrs Dinwoodie. So the connection to, and interest in, Rhoddy was beyond any doubt. The answers might not all be here, but some of them, his instincts told him, were, and when he found them he'd have McPhail.

Chapter 48

Beneath the overflowing tide of joy that welcomed the November 11th ceasefire, there were many whose joy was tempered by an undercurrent of grief at their losses sustained in the years of conflict: broken hearts, broken men who would never mend and, for a few, the dreadful injustice of the war ending a week, a day, an hour too late to save their loved ones. Cate rose from her chair, still unsteady on her feet, and switched the wireless celebrations off.

Weary now, she slid back into bed and silently raged at her weakness. She knew she should be grateful to be alive. It helped to know that both Lizzie and little Ewan James were not only alive but also thriving because of her. But the sickness in the village persisted, and she was desperate to help. Word also filtered back from the outside world that some of the disabled men from the hospital were finding it difficult to get work and, even worse, one of them had found their home abandoned, wife and family absconded with a new partner. She'd understood the horror of the war from Alashdair's letters and now Cate felt a new dread because of the influenza in the village, and who knew how far and, how quickly that would spread.

A knock on her bedroom door put a welcome stop to her maudlin thoughts as she called to come in, eager to see who it was.

"Sure and would you look at the long face on you!"

"I'm sorry, Mary Anne. You know the village..."

"I do indeed and yourself would be up and about taking charge, finding answers to all the problems."

"They're my responsibility."

"And isn't it nothing of the kind! You, Cate Dinwoodie, have been seriously ill. And while we're after talking about it, I've an uneasy feeling about the whole episode."

"Well I can't help you there, Mary Anne. I missed it all, till I woke up."

"That's as may be. Anyway I'm here to check your chest, pulse, and temperature, and to see that you're obeying the Major's orders."

"He's over bossy these days. A part of me wishes I'd left him with his damn matches!"

"Oh Cate, I can't tell you how good it is to hear that spark firing again. Sure and aren't you just the cat o' nine lives!"

"Mary Anne, you're talking nonsense."

"That I'm not! The first time you came into my life sure and weren't you unconscious? The second, you appeared battered and bruised, from prison no less. The third, you were near burned alive, and now, at the fourth time of asking, you appear in the hospital with pleurisy!"

"True enough, Mary Anne. Mind you, looking at it like that, I've still got five more goes!" The pair giggled as much from the release of underlying tension as from the humour of the reminiscences.

"Shoost now, and let me see to your breathing."

"Not that damn cold thing on my skin again, Mary Anne."

"Well now, that's exactly what'll happen. Be good now and let me get this done. For once you could practise doing what you're told."

"It'll never happen, Mary Anne," Dinwoodie said as he came into the room. "But I for one won't complain because, if she's objecting, that's better than all your tests, for it tells me she's on the mend. It also reassures me I can get back to work now she's out of danger, but you will keep an eye on her, Mary Anne?"

"Between the Major and myself we'll see she keeps to the convalescent rules."

"Good. By the way, Maggie's bringing a tray any moment, so behave, Cate, and let Mary Anne do her checks."

Lunch and gossip finished Mary Anne left for the hospital and Dinwoodie lay down next to Cate, on top of the covers.

"Do you have to go back so soon?"

"My dear Cate, it is ages since I returned to find you in hospital. I simply must get back to Glasgow. There's a limit to what I can do from home. I'm sorry, I know you'd like me to stay longer, but soon you'll be up and doing, and we'll be back to normal after this most dreadful scare."

"What about the flu?"

"Cate, we've established you didn't have the flu and, thank God you're not dead! So the memorial service, the army officers, including the Captain — none of that has any importance now."

"But we still have flu in the village."

"I know and I do not want you going near there until this episode has run its course. Now I've been short of sleep lately, so I'll slip under the covers and we can both doze."

404

Back at the hospital, Mary Anne and Morag were scrubbing down yet another empty bed. That brought the loss to the flu into double figures, although the dead were mostly those visitors who'd come for the old woman's birthday party. Meanwhile Doctor Stirling was conducting his daily visit at the old barn where they'd moved those of the villagers who'd had no contact with the suspected flu cases. As before, he was able to confirm that none of them were showing any symptoms, but he was adamant they would have to stay for a few more days. He was more cheerful as he left for his meeting with Donald Uig. Together they made their house-to-house check and were delighted to find all was well there too.

On his return to the hospital he scrubbed with the carbolic and changed into his whites. Then he did his rounds and, though they'd lost the one earlier that morning, the remaining patients were improving. Most of his disability patients had already been released, and the remainder he'd restricted to the one ward while they were admitting the locals. It was here he found Mungo and Neil in a dejected mood.

"You look miserable, the pair of you. What's the matter?"

"Me an him are angry, worried, bored and fed-up!" Mungo answered for them.

"Oh, nothing much then!"

"Come on, Doctor. There's him with no home to go to. Then there's me been given the old heave-ho from the wife."

"I see. I'm sorry Mungo, I didn't know."

"Been going on ever since she found I was a cripple. Good job we'd no kids!"

"Well, we'll have to find some answers. I've been notified the hospital will begin a staged shut-down and handed back to the owners."

"How long we got then, Doctor?"

"The army agreed to me using the hospital for the villagers as it was a crisis, but once I'm satisfied, and the remaining few patients are released, I have to inform them. At an educated guess, in time for Christmas perhaps."

"Bloody Christmas!" Neil shouted and left the room.

"Don't mind him, Doctor. No one wants him. I'm lucky see. I'd a good life till now. You know how it is: the older you are the better you handle the rough stuff. Poor bastard, he's had no life since he was young. He needs help he does. I'll go find him. Good talking to you, Doctor."

The old man felt his shoulders drop again, as he made his way to his office, his earlier pleasure lost in the worry over the other two.

Marthe sat at the table and looked at her 'boys' who'd run away to fight for France. Demobbed now, they sat sullen and silent. The only noise was the coughing from upstairs. Elize was too quiet. Marthe understood the child knew these strangers didn't like her, was afraid of their size, and sad that her Papa was sick again. She cleared the table, washed the mugs and dried them.

"Allons dehors! Ma petite."

"English Maman. Always the English!"

"Yes, I forget. Papa is right. Let's go outside, my little one."

Upstairs Alashdair heard the exchange and smiled between his wretched coughing. Marthe was doing her best, but the atmosphere was strained. It was as if she'd lost her sons at the beginning of the war and these two surly men, strangers now, had returned. When they'd spoken of the end of the war, they'd thought this might happen, but the reality was worse than they'd supposed. He'd at least hoped they'd set to and help their mother with outside work, but nothing. They ate the food, spent the days sitting around, talking among themselves, but never a word to the other three human beings living alongside them. It was time to take action.

Beinn Nishe was in one of its ugly moods. The mountain caught the wind and snow and flung it downwards into Kevinishe village. The old Black House on the moor was white, the river, now a roaring boil of foaming muddy water secreted the trout and salmon in the darkness below, coughed and spluttered towards its duel with the angry sea.

Cate, marooned in her study, was entranced by the weather's wild coat and wished only to be out there to feel the anger of the storm, be invigorated by it, and gain the freedom of the moors. However even she knew that one and all would gainsay her, so she turned her mind to the loose ends that needed to be sorted after the upheaval of the war. 'Ian McAlister', as she continued to think of him, the American, was now settled in Craiglockart and she'd check on him there from time to time. The lovely Doctor Stirling had handed over the hospital in Kevinishe to the Major and returned to Edinburgh. He'd been so good for them all in Kevinishe and would be missed. The army were in the process of withdrawing and returning Kevinishe House to Dinwoodie. It was empty for all but the Major, Mary Anne and the two lost souls, Neil and

Mungo. With a hand and a leg missing between them, it was going to be difficult to find occupations for them. Dinwoodie was still absorbed with getting the foundries back onto some sort of normal footing, now their armaments work was winding down. She'd been reluctant to bring up the idea of a cottage hospital for the village. Yet she was equally reluctant to let Mary Anne go, because a cottage hospital needed a good matron if it was to be a success.

Once again the bones of an idea began to flesh out in the back of her mind. She made for the telephone and dialled Rebecca at the Post office. After a lengthy conversation, Cate returned to her study with a smile. Next she looked for the drawing sheet she'd used to sketch the village and work out which ones, thanks to the war, influenza, and relocation, were now empty. She made cardboard copies of the buildings and for the next hour or so moved them around on her drawing sheet until she found some more answers.

Mungo was next on her list, so it was to the telephone again, this time to the hospital. And the Major's answers to her queries also seemed encouraging. Next she took out another sheet of paper and began more sketching. She barely heard the door opening, until Maggie touched her arm. Cate looked up, and was distressed to see that Maggie was in tears.

"What? Oh Maggie, my dear Maggie, what is it?"

"Lizzie..."Maggie sniffed. " She's an army letter. He's gone, Cate! Her man's gone, an we're no even at war anymore! How can that be?"

Cate drew her old friend into her arms and let her sob until she'd gained control again.

"I'll go to her, Maggie. Can you look after Ewan James for a little? At her nod Cate linked arms with her and they made their way to Lizzie's room. Her sobbing could be heard on the landing. Cate opened the door and went straight to the distraught figure on the bed while Maggie lifted the child from his crib and left.

"Lizzie, I'm so sorry. We thought all this had finished."

"No", replied a tearful Lizzie. "See here, it say's he'd been transferred from the field, 'cause the fighting had stopped an he was working in some big hospital in France, sorting those whose minds were sick and arranging where they were to go over here." As her tears flowed, Cate held her tight and rocked her as she did the children. It took a long time, but in the end she quietened and held the crumpled letter out to Cate, while she attempted to dry her tears and compose herself.

"Oh my God!" Cate whispered as the cause of death became clear.

"That's right. Attacked by one of his mental patients. Died on the operating table, so he did."

"Oh Lizzie, and we thought the killing was over. This is awful for you, but remember this is yours and young Ewan James' home, and I'll always be here for you."

"Aye, that's whit you promised all that long time ago."

"I've lost a husband, then a lover. I know how awful it is. I'll go down and get you something to sleep. Now slip under the bedclothes, never mind undressing, and you stay up here till you're ready to face the others."

With Lizzie settled, Cate had now to make the difficult call to Laggan House. As expected her friend was devastated. Within a short space of time she'd lost her husband, brother-in-law, and now her nephew, all victims of the war. Cate asked her to come over and join them. Sharing their grief would surely help. Cecily readily agreed, and arrived later to join Cate, Maggie and Lizzie in the drawing room. The children, with Shona, Charlie and Hansi, passed the remainder of the day in the kitchen and all three of their minders shared the bath and story chores. Once sleep overtook their charges, Shona got on with her mending and the men returned to the stable. Though they begged her to stay the night, Ewan's aunt insisted on going back to Laggan House.

On the following morning she arrived in time for breakfast and announced that she intended to take Lizzie and little Ewan James back with her after the meal, as her brother and Dinwoodie would be arriving that day. Whether it was grief, lack of sleep, or an unwillingness to take the formidable figure on, everyone agreed that it would be an excellent idea. And so they all gathered at the door to wave goodbye to the nucleus of Lizzie's new family.

Cate was grateful to hear the news of Dinwoodie's arrival, because she'd one or two decisions to make and needed to talk them over with him.

He arrived mid-afternoon after he'd been to Laggan House. He was besieged in the kitchen with everyone wanting to know how their wee Lizzie was managing with them over there.

"Am I the only one of you who's actually allowed Lizzie to grow up. People, we're talking about a young woman who's taken on most of you when she felt you were being unfair. She'd the tenacity to pursue a relationship though she knew you all disapproved. She's a wife, a mother, and now a war widow. Drop the 'wee'!"

408

"You've said all that before, Dinwoodie, but this time we'll try to remember it. Now how is Lord Monroe and what does he think of becoming a great uncle?"

"I think he'll surprise you all. He's determined that he'll play a part in young Ewan James' future and, never having children of her own, Cecily is now in her element. I've a feeling with her brother by her side she'll be a great support for Lizzie. And before you wonder, Cate, I'm sure this will always be her preferred home, but you and Maggie will have to get used to sharing her."

Tea over, Cate collared Dinwoodie in his study and, though apprehensive, rolled out her plans for the future of the village. He gave her his full attention and, when she'd finished, went over them again, scribbling details at his desk.

"So by moving people around, if they're willing, you should be left with the three least desirable homes, which you would demolish and turn into a cottage hospital."

"Yes. I can use the extra ground to erect a larger building that the Major and Mary Anne would run. I also want to employ Mungo, one of the last disabled soldiers, on the clerical side there. He could cope with that despite the wooden leg."

"What about experience?"

"Before the war he was in the office of one of the shipyards doing clerical work, so I think he'd soon adapt. I've also arranged for Neil to help out in the Post Office and, with a salary, he could afford to pay for his board and lodging with Jeannie and the twins. I've always worried about her and the twins way out there on the moor. It would also ease Charlie's mind if they had a man in the house, and Neil would get the satisfaction of paying his way and having a job."

"And? I can see there's more coming."

"Well, you'll have Kevinishe House back when the army remove the trappings of the hospital. So, when the new one is up and running, we can start thinking of that hotel!"

"Dear God, woman, you tire me out just listening to you!"

"Just say 'yes', Dinwoodie, please, please."

"Wait till I get rid of this desk between us and Ill show you what I think."

Both Dinwoodie and Cate were back in their respective studies when Maggie answered the doorbell. As she didn't recognise the man standing there, she hoped it was not another stranger about to bring grief to the house. In the silence he moved closer to the door. " You must be Maggie. I've heard such a lot about you."

Still trying to place him, she opened the door wide to welcome him, and it was then she saw the child.

"We've had a long three days travelling from France and Elize here needs the bathroom."

At the mention of 'France', Maggie suddenly understood — the foreign letters! Gathering her wits, she showed them into the downstairs washroom and, like a madwoman, galloped up the stairs and hammered on both study doors in succession. Cate was the first to answer the summons.

"He's here! God help us, he's here!" was all she could say.

"Maggie, what on earth is all the commotion? It sounded like a herd of deer stamping up the stairs. Who's here?"

"The wee paper mannie! An a bairn!"

Cate had always known he would reappear sometime. She took a moment to collect herself, told Maggie to tell Dinwoodie and then went downstairs.

"Is the house on fire, Maggie?" Dinwoodie joked as he came out of his study.

"It's worse than that! He's come back! Him an all those letters."

He understood immediately. This was what he'd always feared, the return of the twins' biological father, and perhaps the collapse of his marriage.

"Thank you, Maggie." He went back to his study and shut the door firmly.

Below, Cate stopped on the stairs for a moment and studied her erstwhile lover. He was so much older, thinner. Had he come for his parcels? Who was the child? Why was he here? She went down to meet him.

"Hello Cate," he came forward, hand outstretched.

"It's been a long time, Alashdair," she said, as she took his hand, and then knelt in front of the little girl. "And who's this?"

"Je suis — Elize. Mais non — English, always English!"

"Is that what he says?" Cate laughed. "Are you hungry?"

"Yes please, thank you."

"Maggie," Cate called. "Oh, there you are. I forgot you were upstairs. This little lady is Elize and she's hungry. Would you see what you can find in the kitchen for her and, when you've a moment, bring us a tray to the drawing room please."

Once seated, knowing Maggie would appear shortly, they spoke of inconsequential things, the weather, his travel problems, and both were relieved when Maggie came in with the tray.

"Thank you, Maggie. Is little Elize okay?"

"She is that. Starving she is. Folks should think twice before dragging a bairn like that from country to country." She sent a baleful look in Alashdair's direction and marched out.

"Oh dear," Cate said with a smile.

"Well, I never expected the fatted calf treatment."

"Come, let's have tea, and then you must tell me why you're here. Is it to collect your manuscripts?"

"That, and to ask you a question."

"A question? It's a long way to come for an answer, Alashdair, or are you living in Scotland now? Here let me pour the tea. I'm sure you must be ready for it." As she handed the plate of shortbread to him, and passed his tea, she said, "Your Question?"

"Well, not only one but two questions."

"Let's not be ambitious. What's the first one?" She sipped her tea and studied this man who'd once been the centre of her world, and listened intently as he began speaking.

"Cate, if you can find even a small corner of your heart that still remembers the love we had, I need to know. I can't, and won't, ask you the second question if you don't."

She shook her head at him and said, "Oh Alashdair, we're chasing moonbeams here. It was such a long time ago. Much has happened to us both in the intervening years. And yet, in a strange sort of way, I suppose I do still love you. How could I not? But the reality is it's only a beautiful memory. There will always be a place in my heart for you. Indeed my heart's a bit crowded. Love in many of its forms has been tucked away there as the years and the people have come and gone. Little David MacNishe who died far too young. McAlister, who taught me not to be afraid of grown-up love, and then you, who showed me the rapture a love could bring, and the pain. Now Dinwoodie has won my love, and so the building blocks of my life are complete. There's your answer. So ask your second question."

"Elize is my daughter."

"I thought so. She has a look of you, the coal black hair."

411

"Cate, you know I will always love you, but..."

"Don't say any more — we've said enough. Ask your question."

"Cate, I'm dying." His voice broke.

Aghast, she let the word sink in, then rose, sat next to him on the chaise longue, and pulled him into her arms. She held him while he wept and, when he stopped, fumbled with his handkerchief, took it from him and wiped his tears. She waited for him to continue.

"It's the war: the gas, the hanging around in all weathers, bouts of pneumonia. Now my lungs have gone."

"How long?"

"Weeks — who knows? But soon I'm told."

"Tell me about it." She listened as he spoke of the missing years, the war, the farm, his fears for Elize, even his concern for Marthe with her soldier sons now home from the front.

"What is it you want of me, Alashdair?"

"When I heard the news, back there at the hospital, it was so much more than a death sentence for me. I have only ever truly loved two people in my life. I lost you and now I must lose Elize. I delivered her myself, you know. From that moment on she helped dull the pain that'd consumed me since leaving you. Outside the hospital, after they told me, I stood with the broken pieces of my life around me, my death-sentence a door slamming on her young life. How could I leave her alone in this ugly world? And then I remembered that other door: the one you found the strength to close and shut me out of your life. That's when I realised I'd found the answer."

"Which was?"

"There was only ever one person I knew, who could look at my fatherless daughter, feel what she felt, understand her need for love, because she too had been left alone. Will you love her for me, Cate?"

"I have two questions before I give you an answer."

"Go on, ask them."

"Does she know, Alashdair?"

"About my being sick and having to leave her? Yes."

"Elize is Marthe's daughter too. She must have a say in this. No mother will willingly part with her child."

"We spoke when I first became ill. You see we were two people, Marthe and I, in an accidental, transient relationship that suited us both: Marthe: waiting for the end of the war, me with my writing moving on and searching for some kind of life. But the unexpected pregnancy changed all that. I have a letter here, because she knew you would ask this question." He opened his knapsack and gave her the letter.

After she'd read it, Cate laid it by the tray, looked at him and nodded.

"Your second question, Cate?" He asked.

"You? What happens now, Alashdair?"

"I'll die."

"I mean in the meantime."

"If your answer was to be yes, I planned to collect my scripts, find somewhere to live..."

"You won't return to the farm, to France?"

"No. Marthe will go to her niece in Paris. They've always been close."

A silence hung between them for some moments, before Cate spoke. "Listen, Alashdair, I believe I know what I'm going to do, but in all fairness I must consult Dinwoodie about this."

"I understand. But I cannot put off..."

"Trust me, I won't keep you waiting for my answer. Rest here for a while. You must be exhausted after all that travelling."

As she climbed the stairs, Cate knew this unexpected interruption in their lives would upset Dinwoodie, fire up all his unwarranted fears that he believed she was unaware of, but now he would have to face them. She knocked and went in. He was not behind the study desk as usual, but sat staring into the fire. She crossed the room, pulled the footstool in front of him and sat.

"So, the Scribbler has returned!" He said in a cold voice.

"Dinwoodie, you're hurtling down the wrong track."

"He's come back, hasn't he?"

"I'm only going to say this once, although I'm already repeating myself, because I've just said it to him downstairs. Indeed I've said it to you in various versions over the years of our marriage."

"I've no idea what you're talking about — and there's someone at the door."

Glad of the interruption, she opened the door.

"That wee lass is asleep. Just what does that no-good fella down there intend to do with her?"

"Maggie, not you too! What's come over you? She's just a child."

"Fine well you know. Him back, you running off with him..."

"STOP! Right there. You and Dinwoodie both! I'd be obliged if the pair of you would at least do me the courtesy of hearing me out. Since you're both so addle-headed, listen carefully. I came upstairs to ask you, get your approval, Dinwoodie, before I spoke of any decisions downstairs. Now I'm not going to bother, you've made me so angry! I was going to ask you to accompany me to the drawing room, but your minds are set before you even hear what I'm going to say." Overcome with anger, she stormed out of the room and down the stairs.

When she went into the drawing room, Alashdair had fallen asleep. Her rage evaporated, and she pulled the blanket from the back of the chaise longue and spread it gently over him. Kissed him lightly on the forehead and opened and closed the door as quietly as she could. Dinwoodie and Maggie were coming down the stairs, so she waited until they were in the hallway.

"Alashdair's come here today to ask me to consider something, and no, it's not to run away with him. And for your information I wouldn't go if he had. It might have been nice if you'd given me the benefit of the doubt you pair of daft — oh, what's the use! Yes, he's come here because of our past love, and he's been a lot more aware of the real me than you two have sometimes. Maggie, once before you doubted my word, and you, my dear husband, have been worrying yourself into an early grave..." The word spoken out loud hung in the air and silenced her, the enormity of its meaning, the picture it flashed through her mind so stark, she almost ran back into the room to give her answer. But in fairness to the others she continued in a subdued voice.

"Alashdair is dying. His time is short. He brought his daughter here seeking succour for her. He's no idea where he'll spend his remaining time, and no, he has no idea whether I will help or not."

"What are you suggesting, Cate?" Dinwoodie asked.

"It may seem strange to you, but I feel I can't let that wee thing be alone as I once was. Dinwoodie, I'm sorry, so sorry, but I also don't think I can stand aside and let him die in some strange room with no daughter, and no one else to be with him at the end. He doesn't deserve that. Please, Dinwoodie let me do this. I broke his heart once, took his life away from him. Let me give it back for this short time, please, both of you. Allow me to enable him to die content in the knowledge that our past love has ensured his daughter's future." Then, at the enormity of what had happened, she couldn't stem the tears, and they couldn't bear to see her so distraught.

414

Her husband pulled her close, and Maggie patted her back to comfort her.

"We'd be the better of figuring out where a' body's going to put them, hadn't we, Mr Dinwoodie?" Maggie said in a broken voice.

"Oh, Maggie, straight to the heart of the problem, as ever. I can take one of you ladies on at a time, but not two! Yes, you'd better see to their accommodation, and Cate, once more we've underestimated the size of both your heart and your conscience. Shall we go in together and tell him, or do you want to be alone with him?"

"Dinwoodie, Maggie, thank you," she managed as she dried her eyes. "No, we're all in this together, it's a family matter, I want you both there."

Downstairs Alashdair awoke to find the three watching him and knew he'd failed. Cate, he had always believed would listen to him, but he could guess who'd dissuaded her. "Forgive me, Mr Dinwoodie, for just turning up. It's okay, Cate. It was always a long shot." He slipped the throw off and stood. "I see it's getting dark. Would it be possible for us to stay till it's light, and then perhaps a little food to help us on our way. May we wait somewhere till morning?"

"Alashdair, you may wait here, with your daughter by your side, until your time comes. Elize will become a member of our extended 'family', so you may leave us with the knowledge that she will be both safe and loved."

"But, Mr Dinwoodie, I thought you'd..."

"Well, newspaper man, you're wrong. Though Maggie and I have to confess we believed you might have, shall we say, other notions for returning."

"Ah well, then you underestimate your wife — when she says 'no' she really means it!" His voiced cracked as the full meaning of the answer swept over him.

To prevent them all dissolving in tears again, Cate took a deep breath and, in a firm voice said, "Indeed I do! We've had tea, Dinwoodie, so break out the drams, I must go and talk to a little lady."

Chapter 49

Pearson had spent the last two weeks visiting the café each day and he was almost beginning to lose faith in his instincts. If nothing happened soon he'd have to return to Glasgow. He gazed at the fat that had oozed out of the day's bacon sandwich and felt he never wanted to see one again, never mind eat one. With a desultory sweep of his eyes round the room, he shrugged his shoulders, opened his paper and began to read.

The morning wore on as all the others had, and his last vestige of optimism deserted him. He'd had enough. There was nothing for him here. Place was empty anyway. He threw the paper on the remnants of the offending sandwich, scraped his chair back, and left, or he would have done if he hadn't been knocked to the floor by the door being flung open in his face. Next thing he knew someone walked over him and made for Big Mal.

"You fucking bastard! Where is 'e then? Where's Boy? If you've 'armed him, I'll 'ave yer!"

"Grabber, you're making a scene. Calm down."

"Calm down eh! Mates we were. And you done the dirty on me! 'Course I'm making a scene. Still got a lump on me 'ead size of a football. It'd got to be you. Took me back 'ome to sleep it off an all. Why, for Christ sake?"

Big Mal came round the counter, got hold of Grabber's coat and pushed him towards the back room, shutting the door behind him. A dazed Pearson could feel his face swelling and his right eye closing, but he'd heard the magic word 'boy' so, as the place was empty, he staggered to the door at the back and listened. When chairs were scraped within he managed to get back to a seat and had the presence of mind to lay his head on the table. He heard the ring of the till, and squinted with his good eye. An envelope was pushed towards the other man and then he blacked out.

The next thing he knew he was drowning, at least that's what it felt like. He tried to shake the water off his head, but groaned as soon as he

417

moved. Then his head was wrenched upwards and it was as if four faces were peering at him. Without realising what he was saying, he mumbled. "Got to find the boy — he's lost — must..." His face was slammed down on the table and he knew nothing more.

"Who is 'e Mal?" Grabber asked.

"Dunno. New face, been in an out, week or so. Reads the paper, pays and goes. Don't pay over much attention to punters once they've paid."

"You 'eard him though. Said 'the boy'."

"S'right. What'll we do with him? Sling 'im out?"

"No! Wait a bit. Back there in the room you said you'd 'elp find him. Bloody right too, after thumping me."

"You've had your share."

"Yeah, but I've lost Boy."

"Grabber, you've gone soft you 'ave. What's he to you anyway?"

"Money, Mal. Money. We'll wait and soften this geezer up. Find out what 'e knows."

Pearson couldn't make out whether it was dark or he was blind. He rubbed his hand over his face, found his nose seemed to have doubled in size and his hand came away sticky with — he held it close and, when he saw the red, his mind fumbled with the two facts. He could see, so it was dark. Someone or something had added to the swollen eyes in the interim. His nose was bust. He pushed hard on the table with his hands. Slowly, very slowly, he got himself upright. After a bit he staggered to the door and tried to get out.

"Oi! Where yer going then?"

"Landlady's if I can."

"Not a good idea. Get back 'ere. 'Ave a rest."

As Pearson didn't move, Grabber gave him a shove.

"Go on then — sit bleedin' down!" Grabber shoved a chair under him, but Pearson missed it and toppled to the ground.

The next time he woke, he was laid out on a bench. Everything hurt like hell, but in an odd sort of way he felt better — not right, but at least in charge of his senses this time. The first thing he heard was the toilet being flushed and the sound filled him with an urgent desire to get there. He levered himself upright and headed in the direction of the sound, but knocked against the wall and the area was suddenly flooded with light.

"Woken up 'ave you?"

"Scuse — piss — desperate!"

418

"Go on, Grabber, get him there. Don't want piss all over my floor. It's a café God dammit!'"

As he relieved himself, despite his pain, those words made him snigger. The floor would be improved if he'd wet it. Wash some of the ingrained grime off it! When he'd done, he made his way back, and as they indicated a table with a mug and plate on it, he felt it was the safest thing to accept. With hot tea inside him and the inevitable bacon sandwich, cut up to squeeze through his swollen lips, Pearson began to feel half human again. The others arranged themselves around his table and the real business began. Grabber's opening gambit was to describe just what the two of them would do to him if he didn't give the right answers. He let them do the questioning, mainly because of his swollen lips. When his answers about Boy (Rhoddy) and McPhail seemed to satisfy them, he began to play his hand.

"Now it's my turn to get some answers."

They were obvious poker players, for they sat and tried to stare him out, so he laid his head on the table as if he didn't care one way or the other. Now, his head could go no further at least!

After a strained silence, Grabber, always with an eye to the main chance, gave minimal details as to how Boy had landed up with them, and it was not long before both accounts blended to make a much clearer picture all round.

Pearson was more alert by the end of the discussion, so he stayed silent while they worked out what to do next.

"Okay, what you got, Mal?" Grabber asked

"Red Cab. Same bloke as made me the deal to thump you. Said 'e was Boy's nearest relation. Seemed right. I just made sure 'e paid enough for us to share. That's it. No one else, that's except 'im." He pointed at Pearson.

"Okay, Mister, now you? Who the 'ell are you?"

"Friend of the boy's family. His name is Rhoddy."

"Is it now?" Grabber said, "And where's 'e from?"

"Doesn't matter. We're wasting time. The Man, McPhail has left London, gone home, the hotel said. I followed him to a car hire firm."

"Did you now? Good one! Right get the motor round, Mal"

Since Pearson was a sight that no one would talk to, he and Big Mal waited with the windows down, while Grabber went to the office. He came back with a length of string, roughly the distance the hired cab could have gone with the petrol used, a grubby map, and nursing home information that might or might not be true. They spread the map out on their knees and Grabber pinned the end of the string on the map where the parking lot was and swivelled it round to give them an idea of their search area. It was obvious they'd never find the nursing home — always supposing the story was true.

Pearson, who felt much better now he'd had some fresh air, took a gamble.

"I know someone who could help," he said pointing to the expanse of map.

"Look Mister, in our line of work we trust nobody." Grabber said. "Anyways all I've ever done is look after a kid who was lying in the middle of bloody France watching me piss. 'Is mind was gone. Nuffink there! I got him through the war, got him back to Blighty, got him out of 'ospital, and I've bloody well wet-nursed him ever since. 'Course we was both shot in no-man's-land. Saved 'im I did. Means I'm in no mood just to 'and 'im over, even if I 'ad him!"

"That's what I mean. I know his family would be grateful for all of that. They'll see you were doing what you thought best. Did you say his mind was gone? In what way?"

"Shell shock. Loads 'ad it out there."

"Apart from that he wasn't actually ill, had a disease of any kind, anything requiring nursing?"

"Nuffink like that, Mister. First off 'e was dumb. Not a bleedin word. Spoke bits later. Always jumpy, frightened 'e was."

"S'right, Grabber. When I 'its you on the 'ead. He stands, mouth open, pissing 'imself. Poor sod," Mal added.

"In that case, gentlemen, I don't think the nursing home story's true."

"What then?" They asked in unison.

"If anything, it would have to be a mental home for a young adult who isn't right in the mind."

"Poor little bleeder. A bloody asylum! They'd never let 'im out again!"

"Mal's right! But look 'ere. I 'ain't gonna let that 'appen. Likes 'im, you know. Could tell a story or two 'bout me an'im in the old trenches. Look 'ere, Mister, it's different now. You get some 'elp. I'll tell 'em everyfink. Fair deal, we'll split the notes. Come on then, let's do it."

"Wait a minute!" Pearson said. "Let me get my thinking straight. He'd have to prove the boy was mentally ill. We're talking maybe certification by doctors, form filling, and other things. He'd have none of that. I've followed him everywhere just lately and he was never near a solicitor, judge or anything. I've a hunch the hire man was right to be suspicious. Suppose the story wasn't true. Made up just to shake us off his tail. We know he took the night train north. What if he's taken him back to Scotland? Now that could be better for us. We can't find them here anyway, so we might as well look elsewhere. Where's the nearest telephone?"

"We'll show you." They said in unison.

In his Glasgow office Dinwoodie was deep in thought as he put the sheaf of papers his manager had provided back on the desk. The personal files told too many disheartening stories. The euphoria of November had given way to a bitter realisation that peacetime had its own problems. Politicians fought now for territorial acquisitions, like youngsters at a children's party, all intent on grabbing the goodies on the table before someone else did, almost unheeding of how those decisions would affect the people there. At home there was not enough work for the influx of returning men, people were still hungry, and a generation of women would be denied marriage and motherhood now that so many young men had been lost or maimed.

Less easy to understand for those on the home front was the emotional wall that was erected by the returning soldiers. The world was now divided into those who'd been there and those who hadn't. The fighting men could never make the civilian population understand that for them the war had been bloody, but they'd also found a deep companionship, loyalty and purpose that peacetime could never replace, and it sometimes made return to their old lives, unsatisfying and unsettling.

The sorrow Dinwoodie felt for the stories unfolded in the files lay heavily on his shoulders. The fund he'd set up for the needy could only cushion, but not erase, the suffering of the people affected. These morbid thoughts were interrupted as Sheena came in to his office.

"Morrison's downstairs, and here are the notes typed up that you wanted for your meetings."

"Thank you, Sheena, I'd better get a move on then."

"Would you mind if I slipped home early today? Mother's not well."

"Heart again?"

"I'm afraid so. How long will you be gone?"

"Difficult to say. Depends on the suitability of the machinery, and the various manufacturers' ability to deliver it on time. I've told Craigavon that it'll be about a week or so. Look here, Sheena, get young — what's her name?"

"Lallie"

"Right. Get her to man the phone in the mornings. She can fob calls off with the truth. I'm away and she's no idea when I'll be back. Take what time you need."

"I won't take long, but a few days would help to get her over the worst. Thank you."

Chapter 50

Cate put the glass down, wiped Alashdair's mouth, and turned as she heard the door open. Elize came in and stood close to the bed.

"Is he going away now, Mama Cate?"

"I think it won't be long. Alashdair," she leant close to him, "Here's Elize, come to say goodbye. Come on little one, up beside him." She helped them both to sit up close together and, when they were comfortable, made to leave the room, but Alashdair caught her hand. He was racked by yet another bout of coughing and had difficulty speaking. When it was over he held out his arms to Elize and she leant against him.

"Papa, where you're going there'll be no more — no English — toux and you will be better?"

"Coughing, English." The other two joined in. "Only English." Their laughter at the joke enfolded them in a web of familiarity, bound together within the circle of shared love, but the effort was too much for him. He took time to catch his breath.

"Listen, girls," he whispered. "I feel it's time. I'm ready now." He paused to find the strength. It was important he mustn't leave anything unsaid. "The rest of the writing, Cate, my knapsack." He struggled to point to where it lay on the floor. "For you and Elize, I leave..." His eyes shut. They watched and wondered. There was a rasping sound to his breath again, but he fought it. "Dearest Cate, you've made it possible..." he needed a lengthy pause before he could continue. "What you've done for us, no one else could or would. Ma petite Elize, I leave you with your new Mama. This is your family now." And still he fought for air, as he whispered, "I'll go on alone, but no more toux, so don't worry." The child hugged him. Laid her head on his chest.

"I've been away before — this time I can't come..." He ran out of breath and as she watched him struggle, Cate could bear the fight no longer. She put her arms round both of them and began to hum a soft lilting tune from bygone days. The child snuggled down beside her father with a faint smile as the melody rocked her to sleep and sent him on his way. Cate slid her arms from beneath them, and then while her tears splashed on his face, she closed his staring eyes, kissed him and sat till the child would wake.

When the little girl did stir, Cate was silent, let her take the lead.

"Mama Cate," she held out her arms as the tears began.

Cate cradled her until the sobs stopped. "Elize, to go away he has to be put in a box."

"A pretty box?"

"Definitely a pretty box, and then he must have a service."

"A what?"

"It's where everyone comes to say goodbye. It's what happens when people have to go away like this. They are taken to a special place."

"But I want him here with me." She looked up at Cate. "Can't he stay too?"

Cate paused for a moment and then thought, 'why not!' "I think that's a splendid idea. We'll give him a special place here at Craigavon where we can visit. Will that do?"

"Yes please, thank you."

As soon as those at Craigavon and the rest of Kevinishe heard about the wee paper mannie dying, from gas they said, and the little French girl's wish, old scores were forgotten and they rallied to the cause. The coopers made the box, the sewing girls lined it, Maggie and Cate dressed the body, the Major was given the French medical statements that had been in Alashdair's knapsack, and signed the death certificate. The men dug the grave. The children gathered heather, grasses, holly and ivy, and the women helped them make the wreaths. Cate, with a lump in her throat, gave the eulogy, and so Alashdair had his funeral, Elize was pleased, and even Cate could consider it was a fitting end. The old barn was decked out and, much to the children's delight; she threw a wake that turned into a party. Yes, there were many queries about death in the following weeks but like all children when they'd been part of the situation they accepted it.

She'd chosen the spot for the grave near her old summerhouse and took Elize there often. They sat and talked of Alashdair, France, Craigavon, and all the rest of Elize's new family. She'd no winter clothes, so Cate let her choose pictures, sketched them and had the sewing women make them up. On days when Elize couldn't cope, and there were many, they went visiting to Laggan. She was entranced with baby Ewan James, and when Lizzie brought him home to Craigavon, she spent long hours with him, more peaceful than with the imp of energy that was Iona. That young madam much preferred to play boisterous games with the twins. And so the family settled in to see the winter months of 1919 pass. The only curiosity was the mysterious big brother, missed especially by the twins, who always seemed to be coming home, but never did. The younger children lost interest, but the adults waited, never quite sure what the future would bring.

Cate busied her mind with the problem of finding a new stillman, in order to get the distillery out of mothballs. She studied the replies to her advertisements and made arrangements to meet the most suitable candidates. She set Donald Uig to preparing everything. Solly was given instructions to find new barley suppliers if he could, while she left a weepy Elize in Lizzie's care and went to Glasgow to interview two applicants. As it turned out she found neither of them suitable, believing they wouldn't fit into the Kevinishe way of life, and returned empty-handed.

Thwarted by the setback, she turned her attention to Kevinishe House and spent some thoughtful hours with the Major and Mary Anne, planning the new layout for the temporary cottage hospital, until the building of the new one could begin. She gave drawing lessons to the twins when the winter weather kept them in, and on suitable days she joined Charlie, Hansi, and the older boys at the stables and gave turns to the two little girls and Murdo on yet another quiet old pony that Jock Donaldson found for her. However busy she kept herself, she couldn't evade the facts. The war was well and truly over. The juggernaut that was the army sent it's returning soldiers home to their demob centres en route to civilian life. But just like Kipling's Jack, no one had seen Rhoddy. He had to be dead.

With hindsight she began to look at Rhoddy's life as he must have seen it: the mother who seemed to have no time for him, the homes he had to leave just as he was settling in, the irksome restrictions she'd subjected him to because she'd not wanted him to grow up to be another Bruce MacNishe. She could put the case that a lot of the time she'd done what she had to do to survive, but, if his short life had ended, it would have been so much easier to accept the fact if she'd tried harder, if he'd been happier.

Her melancholy musings were interrupted by the telephone. She knew the others were out and, as it would most probably be Dinwoodie, she hurried to answer it. She missed him so, and just hearing his voice would do much to lift her spirits.

"Dinwoodie? Your call is..." Her hand began to shake as she listened to a voice that wasn't her husband's at the other end. Tried desperately to make sense of the words. Scrabbled for the pen that should have been there. Found one and scribbled the number. Listened to the repeated threat, and then the phone went dead. She left it hanging there as she sank to the bottom step of the stairs. Was it a hoax? Could he really be alive? That voice? Think, Cate, think! Surely she knew it? What did it matter? Rhoddy was alive! All she had to do was go and get him!

When the others returned later, Maggie left Charlie and Hansi with the children in the kitchen with Cook, and went to tell Cate they were back. When she found the study empty, as were the other rooms, she was puzzled. She knew Cate was due to go to Glasgow again, as she'd not managed to get a stillman, but surely she'd not rushed off while they'd been out? She'd have left a note somewhere. So she went to the hall table, but there was no note, though the telephone had not been replaced. Now wasn't that just typical of Cate! A phone call, and no doubt she'd rushed off, giving no thought to them at home. She'd ring that Rebecca at the Post Office. Like as not, she'd had Benjamin take her to Fort William for the train to Glasgow. When she got through, Maggie said they'd been out and wondered had Cate got away safely. Reassured that Benjamin had indeed taken her in the Post Bus, she thanked Rebecca and replaced the receiver. Sometimes she lost patience with Cate, and she'd tell her so when she got back! Good job Himself wasn't home or he'd have had words as well. And that little Elize would be none too happy when she found that 'Mama Cate' was gone!

Once in London a weary Cate, fingers trembling, dialled the number she'd written down, listened to the instructions, and followed them to the letter. As she did so, her common sense told her that she ought to contact home, but her instinct warned against it. Nothing must stop her being reunited with Rhoddy. She got off the bus and, after a couple of mistakes, found the house and rang the bell marked Laidlaw, according to the instructions. When she saw it was McPhail she was not really surprised. She said nothing, just stared at him, while wondering what sort of fool he was. How could anybody in their right mind, believe the lying

426

drunken sot that had been Bruce MacNishe? And yet he had. Perhaps he wasn't quite right in the head, in which case she'd have to be doubly careful. Nothing must be said or done that would put Rhoddy in danger. She moved inside and he banged the door behind him, locking it in the process. The sound of the turning key made her falter, but she followed him up the stairs. There was no turning back now.

Pearson was exasperated. In all the years he'd been working for Mr Dinwoodie his phone calls had always been answered. He'd no idea who was on the other end of the line, but it wasn't Sheena. With Mr Dinwoodie away and no Sheena, it looked as though he'd have to tell the others he could go no further at the moment. What bad luck when, for the first time, he'd some real information for him about Rhoddy! He shook his head at the other two, banged the receiver down and joined them outside. "He's not there, and they've no idea when he'll be back."

"Fat lot of 'elp that is. Now what?" Grabber demanded.

"We just keep trying. And I need to go back to my room and get my things."

He wasn't surprised when Grabber elected to come with him, though Big Mal had had enough hanging around and went back to the café.

The unlikely trio then settled down in the café, making regular trips out to make phone calls, until Pearson at last managed to speak to Sheena. As soon as she heard about Rhoddy, she knew she had to get in touch with Mr Dinwoodie, and told Pearson to ring later. When she'd rung off, on an impulse she contacted Craigavon, and was disappointed when she heard Mrs Dinwoodie was also away on business.

By the end of the day she'd made contact with her boss and, when Pearson rang back, she was able to give him instructions about meeting Mr Dinwoodie. When she'd done that, she phoned the hospital and was somewhat reassured when she heard her mother was making progress. Well, she'd have plenty to tell her when she visited in the evening. Fancy him being alive after all this time. They'd be so pleased to get him back home again. The worry had gone on for far too long. And wasn't it such awful luck that both of them had been away, and her mother's turn had been bad enough for her to be taken into hospital!

427

Dinwoodie arrived at the station, hoping that Pearson was waiting for him, as they'd have little time before the train left. When he caught sight of him, he wasn't alone, he had another man with him and, as they approached, he wondered what on earth had happened to Pearson's face?

"I got caught on the wrong side of a door opening, and this is Grabber, Mr Dinwoodie," Pearson answered the unspoken questions.

"Grabber," Dinwoodie acknowledged him with a nod of the head and turned again to Pearson. "Sheena's information was sketchy, but Rhoddy is really alive and was here in London?"

"Course he is, Mister. I 'elped 'im get all the way back from France."

"Then I'm indebted to you," he said to the man. Glancing at his watch, he made a snap decision. "Look here, the train leaves before long. It would appear that there is much to be discussed. You're quite sure, Pearson, that McPhail has Rhoddy?"

"That we are sure about."

"Right, we're out of time here. We'll take the overnight train, hoping there's room for all three of us, and then you can fill in all the missing details and we'll search till we find my stepson."

Once aboard the train he began the intensive questioning. He listened intently as he followed Grabber's story and, though the man was an obvious small-time crook, Dinwoodie could see that, while Grabber was in this for the reward, the way he spoke about Rhoddy indicated a sense of warmth for the boy. Yes, he'd used him to steal but he'd looked out for him in the trenches, engineered his return to Britain, and had continued to take care of him. There was a distinct possibility that Grabber needed Rhoddy for more than just the reward. Whatever else, with Pearson, Grabber and the other man he would have three witnesses to put McPhail where he belonged, behind bars, as long as Cate was willing to go through with it. That could be a major stumbling block though. He knew she'd been against the idea of going to law from the very beginning.

As the three men were travelling towards Glasgow, in London, McPhail let Cate into the empty flat. Only then did she become afraid and cursed her stupidity in acting so rashly. But then she heard a sound, searched for it, and there in the far corner she saw him. An older, wretched version of her son huddled against the wall, shaking with fear. With great care she went towards him, holding out her hands. At her approach he tried to back further into the wall, so she knelt until her face was level with his. "Hello Rhoddy. It's been such a long time, and we need you home." She could sense how fragile his hold on normality was, and as McPhail moved closer, the terror in her son's eyes removed any misgivings she had about coming here. She stood up, took care to avoid any sudden movement, and faced McPhail, taking him out of Rhoddy's line of vision.

He spoke before she could. "You can see for yourself the state he's in. Imagine what he'd be like if I'd not whisked him away from the villains holding him captive."

"Why did you? What is it you want, McPhail?"

"I've told you, time and again, I want the boy and his rightful inheritance. It was his father's wish, and I intend to see it's fulfilled."

"And just what do you expect his 'rightful inheritance' to be?"

"Come now, we both know that. With MacNishe dead and the boy in his current state, he needs a guardian. As the only other male relative in the clan, it has to be me. He now inherits from his father and I will be there, making the decisions, running the estate and the distillery."

"You're almost as stupid as your cousin was. I tried to tell you years ago that you couldn't move into Kevinishe House, but you wouldn't listen. Did it never occur to you to check his facts? Did you really take everything he said as gospel? It never crossed your mind to take a look at the land registry, check whose name was on the deeds of the estate? My God, Rhoddy's not the only one in this room who's lost his mind!"

Angry now, McPhail became threatening. "You haven't been so bright yourself, coming here alone! I've been told you usually use your feminine ways to trick men into giving you what you want. Bruce had you all worked out, you lying bitch!"

Aware that raised voices would distress Rhoddy, she moved closer to him and sat on the floor, but not so close that she frightened him. "Very well, McPhail. Let's go to Kevinishe. You can try to regain Bruce's land, but you'll find there's none left. Nothing! No Estate, no money, no distillery. Bruce MacNishe wasted every penny he could get his hands on and anybody else's he could beg, borrow or steal." She saw his eyes narrow. "Ah. I see he made a fool of you as well. Instead of sitting in your Highland home, eaten with envy of your richer relations, you should have worked out that Bruce MacNishe was never a person to be envious of. He was a drunken sot who ended up penniless. I paid for his funeral. The whisky you downed there was mine, not MacNishe's."

429

"As if I would fall for that! Did you really think I would be so stupid as to hand his son over to you? I've waited years to be acknowledged by the MacNishes, and now they're all dead except him, and he's half mad. But now I hold another card. I wonder how much the Iron Baron would pay to know where his wife is? Didn't think of that, did you now? We'll soon see how long you last on your own!" With that he left the room, locking the door behind him.

Cate put her fears to the back of her mind and concentrated on Rhoddy. Slowly she began to stretch her hand nearer to his. Ran her fingertips over the back of his wrist, smiled at him, and in a soft voice began to talk of Kevinishe, Lizzie, Maggie, Dinwoodie — anything and everything that might just reassure him she meant no harm and could even perhaps make a connection. At least he didn't shrink any further into the wall, and as she watched him, it dawned on her, with all that had happened to him, he no longer had any vestige of Bruce MacNishe in his appearance. He'd aged, discarded the youthful face he'd had. She'd never looked at him, even as a baby, without seeing the hated face that had leered into hers as he raped her. All these years she'd been fighting a face, not her son! She studied this new Rhoddy, as he seemed to slide into sleep. He'd been lost for years. She'd found him again! Perhaps there was still time for her to make amends! She'd been handed a second chance, and by God she was going to take it.

Meanwhile, in Scotland, after the long drive from the station to the McPhail home, the men found he wasn't there. A disappointed Dinwoodie then had Morrison drive them to Craigavon. There was just a possibility that the man had contacted Cate. After all, his previous visits had all been to see her. And what else had they to go on? At least he could tell her that Rhoddy was alive, if not very well. The thought of delivering the news she'd given up hope of ever hearing cheered him. He left Morrison to settle the men in the spare room in his flat and take them to the kitchen for a meal, while he strode indoors calling for his wife.

"You can shout for all your worth, but she's no here." Maggie said as she appeared in the hall.

"Are you sure? She'd made no plans to go away — not yet anyway. Not before I got home."

"Mebbe so, Mr Dinwoodie, but that's just what she did. Up and away while we were out with the bairns! Said she'd work to do, fixing up malt men and such, so we left her in her study in peace. Seems she made

430

a phone call, dropped everything and went. A body needs to know where she is. Wife and employer though she is, she can be a right scunner sometimes, an that's telling you straight!" Maggie strode off to the kitchen, her displeasure mirrored in every step.

Dinwoodie remained in the hall eyeing the telephone. Rebecca would have a record of the number Cate had phoned. He hesitated, wary of interfering. Then lifted his hand to towards the receiver but dropped it again as Pearson came in with his briefcase.

"Everything all right here, Mr Dinwoodie?"

His employer looked at him, hesitated and then told him what Maggie had said. The thought seemed to come to them simultaneously. "McPhail!" Dinwoodie picked up the receiver, dialled the Post Office, spoke to Rebecca, asked her to check, thanked her and replaced the receiver. "Cate didn't telephone anyone. A man called her. Rebecca's going to check, but she thinks it's an English number, long distance."

"He's made fools of us, Mr Dinwoodie. He's got your wife as well as your stepson. How in God's name do we find him if he's still in London?"

"There's a chance Rebecca could give us the area code, but it'd still be impossible to search an area that size, wouldn't you say?"

Pearson nodded his head in agreement. "We'd better stay here, keep in touch with Sheena. Your wife or McPhail will be in touch. If he has both of them, they're only of use to him as bargaining tools. He has to make contact — take my word for it. And I don't see him harming them either. Damaged goods never fetch the maximum price. I'm sorry, Mr Dinwoodie — but we can do nothing more but wait."

In London, Cate let Rhoddy sleep as she paced round the room. The windows were locked and she'd nothing to force them with. The room was bare except for a couple of chairs and a bed. She hesitated, weighed up her options. Either she attracted attention, and perhaps drove Rhoddy further over the edge with the shock of the noise, or she did nothing, and God knows what the man would do when he came back. Mind made up, she tried the chairs for size, chose the bigger one and threw it with all her might against the glass. The noise was even worse than she'd anticipated but she'd no time to see to Rhoddy. It had been a long time since she'd had to bawl over the hurdy-gurdies at the fairs, to draw attention to the tinkers' wares, but you never forgot a skill learned, and she needed it now. The street below was soon packed with

431

people as her powerful voice called to them, urging those below to seek help for her sick child.

The wait seemed eternal, the people below more curious than helpful. Then she saw the policeman. She shouted down to him and soon everything happened at once. Whistles blew, then men were kicking the door, a police wagon arrived, and, for an instant she saw McPhail before he melted into the crowd. Now she had time to go to Rhoddy and, as she tried to comfort him, she knew that whatever happened in the future, she would never again let harm come to him, and she'd see McPhail behind bars. Despite her fears of going to court, she owed Rhoddy that and much more.

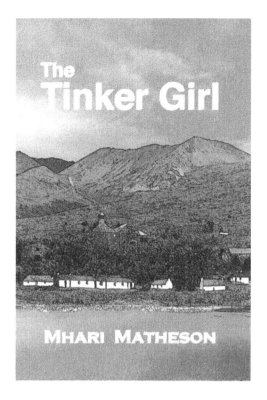

The Tinker Girl is the first novel in the Highland Trilogy.
Available in print and eBook from Cambria Books
ISBN: 978-0-9574894-7-9

Lightning Source UK Ltd.
Milton Keynes UK
UKOW06f0225221215

265155UK00001B/8/P